Prisoner Of Yakutsk

What exactly happened to India's greatest freedom fighter, Netaji Subhash Chandra Bose?
Some say that on 18 August 1945, his plane crashed in Taiwan, killing him.
Some say he survived the crash and lived on in Bengal, as the godman, Gumnami Baba.
Some say he was killed by the machinations of his rivals back home; that the plane's engine was tampered with, causing the fatal mishap.
Some say he still lives in the Himalayas, and will return.
Threads and theories continue to flutter in the wind.
What is true?
In these pages lie the answers.

PRISONER OF YAKUTSK

THE SUBHASH CHANDRA BOSE MYSTERY
FINAL CHAPTER

SHREYAS BHAVE

PLATINUM PRESS

ISBN: 978-93-52011-42-1

Cover Design: Riyaz Merchant, Kitsune
Layouts: Hitanshi Shah
Printing: Nutech Print Services, India

Published in India 2019

PLATINUM PRESS

An imprint of
LEADSTART PUBLISHING PVT LTD
Unit 25/26, Building A/1, Wadala (East),
Mumbai 400 037, Maharashtra, INDIA
T + 91 96 99933000 **E** info@leadstartcorp.com
W www.leadstartcorp.com

TO RENUKA ABROL

About The Author

SHREYAS BHAVE is an Electrical Engineer from VNIT Nagpur, and is one of India's youngest experts on Railway Electrification PSI work. He also runs an entrepreneurial community at www.ourfirstmillion.org.

Shreyas' first three books, the *Asoka Trilogy*, was published to wide acclaim and acquired for screen adaptation. *Prisoner Of Yakutsk* is written as a mystery thriller with the disappearance of Subhash Chandra Bose at its core.

Apart from writing, Shreyas enjoys songwriting, composing music, sketching and watercolours. He plays the guitar and is fond of the blues and southern rock music. He also loves to hike up to the hill forts of Maharashtra.

Other Books by Shreyas Bhave

The Asoka Trilogy, comprising:
Prince Of Patliputra
Storm From Taxila
Nemesis Of Kalinga

Shreyas can be reached at:
shre14uses@gmail.com
www.authorshreyas.wordpress.com

Contents

AUTHOR'S NOTE

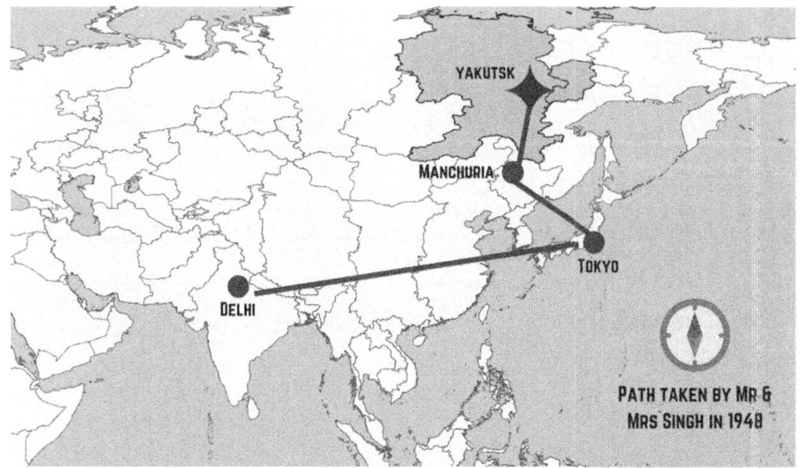

When he was alive, Netaji Subhash Chandra Bose was something of an enigma to most. It is thus perhaps poetic justice that his death in an alleged plane crash on 18 August 1945, in Taiwan, has remained wrapped in deep mystery for over 70 years after the event.

In those seven decades numerous books have been written on the subject, giving rise to countless conspiracy theories about his death, from *India's Biggest Cover-up* by famed journalist, Anuj Dhar, *Bose: The Indian Samurai* by Retd Major General GD Bakshi, the recent *Laid to Rest: The Controversy over Subhash Chandra Bose's Death* by author Ashis Ray, to Alt Balaji's recent web series 'Bose: Dead or Alive'. Most of these accounts have emphasized the controversial point that Netaji did not die in the plane crash as is generally supposed. While the authors have dug deep into their own research, the primary source remains the reports of the four committees constituted since 1945, to investigate the case of Netaji's supposed death.

The first such investigation was carried out before independence, by the British Government. Confronted with rumours about Bose, which began to spread within days of his declared death, Lord Mountbatten, then Vice-

Hindusthan Standard

MR. SUBHAS CHANDRA BOSE DEAD

SUCCUMBS TO INJURY FROM AIR CRASH

ANNOUNCEMENT BY JAP NEWS AGENCY

NEHRU CAUTIONS BRITAIN

CONCERN OVER INDIAN NATIONAL ARMY

roy of India, tasked one Colonel John Figgess, an intelligence officer, with investigating Bose's death. Figgess's report, however, submitted on 25 July 1946, was confidential, and was only made available for public viewing as late as 1997. The Figgess report confirmed four facts based on oral testimonies by witnesses, including that of Habibur Rahman.

- Subhas Chandra Bose was a passenger on the plane that crashed near Taihoku airport on 18 August 1945.
- Bose died in the nearby military hospital on the same day.
- Bose's cremation took place at Taihoku.
- Bose's ashes were transferred to Tokyo.

Post-independence, the work of investigating Bose's mysterious death was taken up by the newly formed Indian Government, which set up three committees to investigate the matter. The first of them, led by politician Shah Nawaz Khan (ex-INA), began work in 1956, and interviewed more than 67 witnesses to the case in India, Japan, Thailand and Vietnam. It came to the conclusion that Bose had indeed perished in the plane crash of 18 August 1945. However, an important member of this committee, Suresh Chandra Bose, who was none other than Netaji's elder brother, refused to sign the final report, claiming that the other members of the group had withheld certain crucial evidence from him, and that the committee had been directed by the then Prime Minister, Jawaharlal Nehru, to infer death by plane crash. In a 188 page minority report released by him, he claimed he had been bribed with the position of 'Governor of West Bengal' to agree to sign the final report confirming that Netaji had died in the plane crash. Historian Joyce Chapman Lebra, later wrote about Suresh Chandra Bose's dissenting note thus: 'Whatever Mr Bose's motives in issuing his minority report, he has helped to perpetuate until the present the faith that Subhas Chandra Bose did not die in the plane crash. In fact, during the early 1960s, the rumours about Subhas Bose's extant forms only increased.'

As the Shah Nawaz Committee had failed to provide a final conclusion to the death of Netaji Subhash Chandra Bose, the Government of India, in 1970, appointed a new commission to enquire into the 'disappearance' of Bose. With a view to heading off more minority reports, this time it was a one-man commission. The single investigator was GD Khosla, a retired Chief Justice of the Punjab High Court. As Justice Khosla was a presiding judge with other calls on his time, he submitted his report in 1974, four years later. Bringing his legal background to bear on the issue, Justice Khosla, in a methodical fashion, concurred with the main facts of Bose's death reported earlier by the Shah Nawaz Committee.

While GD Khosla's authorative judgment should have dispelled any conspiracy theories, in fact the reverse happened as public groups, believing Khosla's report to be flawed, began filing numerous PILs in the Supreme Court demanding the Government investigate the matter yet again.

In 1999, following a court order following one such PIL, the Indian Government appointed retired Supreme Court judge, Manoj Kumar Mukherjee, to probe Bose's death. Had the Mukherjee Commission reaffirmed the findings of the Khosla Commission, the Bose mystery would have been laid to rest once and for all. But what occurred during the Mukherjee Commission investigation turned the story on its head.

The Commission perused hundreds of files on Bose's death, drawn from several countries, and visited Japan, Russia and Taiwan. In 2001, the Commission was informed that a file from the so-called Netaji files, File No Jan/XVII/14, reportedly on the investigations into Bose's death, had been destroyed in 'routine course' by the Indian government in 1972. The contents of this file were supposedly summarized in the Cabinet Secretariat but the Deputy Secretary reported there was no entry of such a file. Though oral accounts reconfirmed the plane crash, the Commission concluded that such accounts could not be entirely relied on and that there was a secret plan to ensure Bose's safe passage to the USSR with the knowledge of the Japanese authorities.

The Mukherjee Commission submitted its report on 8 November 2005. The report was tabled in the Indian Parliament on 17 May 2006. The Indian Government rejected the findings of the Commission with the words:

THE BIG STORY

'An Indian ambassador met Netaji in Moscow'

Bose was in Russia

Find the money

'The Government have examined the report in detail and have regretfully accepted the conclusion that Netaji may not be with us anymore and it is now not possible to comprehensively establish the circumstances of his death; but are not inclined to accept the findings of the Commission that Netaji Subhas Chandra Bose did not die in the plane crash because absence of documents does not conclusively disprove the overwhelming oral evidence of those who survived the crash, as testified before the Netaji Inquiry Committee (Shah Nawaz Committee), 1956 and Khosla Commission, 1972 - 74.'

After the Mukherjee Commission's public conclusion refuting Bose's death in the plane crash, a series of books were written on the subject, as mentioned earlier. All the books took a non-fictional approach. When I decided to tackle the subject for my fourth book, following *The Asoka Trilogy*, I used the literary genre known as 'fiction presented as fact', considering it best suited to the story. This approach has been popularized internationally by Dan Brown, and in India by Ashwin Sanghi. However, no one to date had essayed Bose's mysterious death in this format. I decided to do so, desiring to bring something unique to the table.

The first step was to finalize a conspiracy theory about Bose's end. There have been many of these; some claim he lived in disguise in Bengal after the supposed fake-crash, disguised as the godman called Gumnami Baba. There are other theories that place him in various parts of the world. Some even go so far as to claim that he was sighted and photographed. I chose the theory that is closest to the conclusions of the Mukherjee Commission, and which was also presented by then Member of Parliament, Satyanarayan Sinha, in his testimony to the Shah Nawaz Commission in the 1950s. In the transcript, Sinha claims that a Russian agent called Kozlov told him that Bose had survived the plane crash and was then captured by the Soviets and imprisoned in Cell no 45 of the Yakutsk prison. Kozlov knew this because he himself was imprisoned in Cell no 46 in the same prison, and later released. This is the most believable amongst the plethora of theories about Bose and hence this was the one I used in my book.

Based on my research of materials available on this topic in the public domain, I derived three conclusions regarding Netaji's disappearance:

1. Much of the evidence supporting the plane crash theory comes from oral testimonies of persons who are no longer alive.
2. If we assume, as Justice Mukherjee did, that the persons giving the oral testimonies had valid reason to lie under oath (protecting Bose's actual location), we can question the value of such testimonies.
3. If such testimonies are dismissed, conclusive evidence proves only the following:
    i. That there was indeed a plane crash in Tahioku on the said date.
    ii. That someone's burnt body was taken to a nearby hospital and declared dead.
    iii. That someone's ashes were taken to Tokyo and kept in the Renkoji Temple following this crash.

If the oral testimonies are disregarded, there is no evidence to prove anything else. It is at this point that we realize there could indeed have existed a plan to tell the world that Bose had died in a fake plane crash in order to stop the worldwide search for him (the British, for instance, considered him a WW II war criminal); hiding Bose in a location from where he could continue his efforts towards the freedom struggle.

So what we have are bits of information about his last days, coupled with some oral testimonies that make for an excellent, edge-of-the seat thriller. So I zeroed in on three threads I found common to all the theories:

1. Bose left Singapore immediately after learning the news of the nuclear detonations in Hiroshima and Nagasaki.
2. He was carrying considerable wealth in the form of gold on his last flight. This gold was never found.
3. An inmate of the Yakutsk Gulags claimed that Bose was imprisoned in a cell there.

Using these three points, I have attempted to craft a story a-la-Vikram Chandra's *Nuclear Bomb* climax style, that answers the burning question, 'What exactly happened to Netaji Subhash Chandra Bose?' My book has two parallel storylines - one of the modern day, in which the protagonist Jay Rasbihari sets off on the trail of his long lost grandparents. The other is the flashback story of his grandparents being sent on a secret mission by the Indian Government to discover what happened to Bose. Both stories move to historic locations like the Renkoji Temple, the Yakutsk Gulag, and the charming county of Oxfordshire in England.

The theory of Netaji's supposed ashes in Tokyo being actually those of a Japanese soldier called Ichiro Okura, first cropped up in the Mukherjee Commission report. I have shown the same to be true in my story.

The story of Netaji's gold tooth being discovered in the ashes, thereby confirming the ashes as belonging to him, was covered by many newspapers in 2016. In my story, I have shown the protagonist Jay Rasbihari placing the tooth in his ashes.

All the characters in my story, owing to the sensitive and conspiracy-laden narrative, may be considered fictional, though some have indeed been inspired by real world people. The characters of the modern day storyline, like Jay, Tanya and others, are of course imaginary and serve as plot elements to dig into the past and act as links to the Netaji mystery. But the actions of Julian Assange and the Wilikleaks history are historical. The journalist Anu Dhar is inspired by the real life Anuj Dhar, whose non-fiction book, *India's Biggest Cover-up*, was a great reference point and I felt compelled to use her character in the book as tribute to a great journalist. The KGB team consisting of Alexsis, Sergei and Charkov, is fictional.

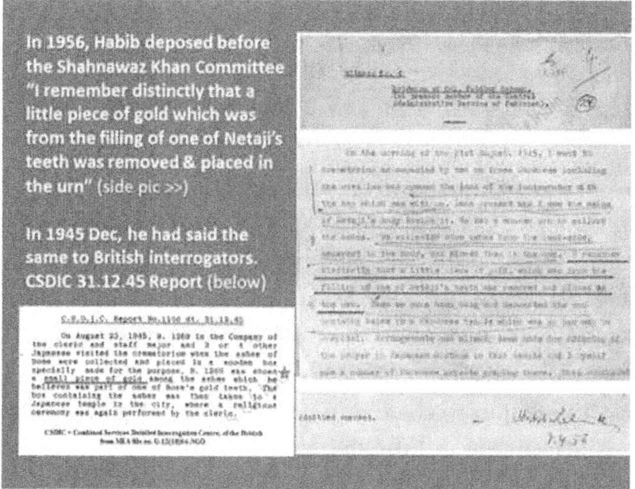

All the characters of the 1940-50 storyline are also imaginary, though the characters of Major and Dr. (Mrs.) Singh are inspired by legendary members of the INA – Prem Kumar Sehgal and Laxmi Sehgal. The character of Martin Bormann is historical too, but his presence in the time period of the book is imaginary. The episodes involving our founding fathers (Gandhi, Nehru and Patel) are fictional; presented for dramatic purposes. However, Sardar Patel's plane crash in 1949 is historical fact, and is mentioned in all Government and public records.

SARDAR REACHES JAIPUR SAFE AFTER PLANE MISHAP

Had A Hearty Laugh Over Incident

BOMBAY, Mar. 29.

SARDAR VALLABHBHAI PATEL, India's Deputy Prime Minister, was completely unhurt when his plane made a forced landing on a public road, 40 miles north of Jaipur near Shahpura, according to a message received by his son Mr. Dayabhai Patel from his sister who was travelling with the Sardar.

The Sardar is to inaugurate the Greater Rajasthan Union tomorrow.

After his forced landing experience, the Deputy Prime Minister telephoned the Prime Minister Pandit Nehru at Delhi late tonight.

Despite his nerve-shaking experience, the Sardar "had a hearty laugh over the whole incident" when he talked to the Prime Minister, the Home Secretary told the A.P.I.

INTER-DOMINION TALKS ON APR. 2

Goodwill Mission To Pakistan

U. S. Protest To Prague

PRAGUE, Mar. 29.

Prime Minister Nehru with the Norwegian Minister in India Mr. Jens Schive.

WELFARE CENTRES CRYING NEED

Envoy From Norway Presents Credentials

SLUMP IN U. S.

NEW YORK, Mar. 29.

Finally, for those who cannot wait to read the complete story to find the answers, here is a short summary of questions and answers:

1. Is Netaji dead?
2. If he is dead, did he die in the plane crash as alleged?
3. Are the ashes in the Japanese temple those of Netaji?
4. Did he, in fact, die in some other manner, at another place? If so, when and how?

The answer to the first question is yes, Bose is indeed dead. However, he did not die in the plane crash as alleged. The ashes in the Japanese temple do not belong to him and he died in another manner in an entirely different place. To know the exact details, you will have to read the complete book, but these are the questions my book manages to answer.

Finally, as I wrote this book, I realized that the challenge before me was not to give a new spin to the controversy of Bose's death, but providing a satisfying conclusion to it. I did not wish to leave the reader agitated at the end of the book by the thought, 'Bose did not die in the plane crash, and all my life I accepted the lie'. The intention was to finally place a full stop to Bose's mysterious death in the reader's head. Whether I managed to do this can only be judged by my readers. Finally, I have honestly and respectfully tried to bring Netaji Subhash Chandra Bose's story to its most satisfying and acceptable conclusion, thereby attempting to accomplish what the three Commissions of Shah Nawaz, GD Khosla and Mukherjee, failed to do.

1
The End

EASTERN SIBERIA, RUSSIA, 2015

At minus 5 degrees celsius, the cold is refreshing and a light hat and scarf are all that are required to keep you warm. At minus 20, the moisture in your nostrils freezes and it is difficult not to cough. At minus 35, the air is cold enough to numb exposed skin, making frostbite a constant hazard. And at minus 45 degrees, metal sticks to your cheeks and tears off chunks of flesh when you take off your sun goggles.

Jay Rasbihari was not wearing any metal, just his fur coat, but the cold was such that even the plastic earphones in his ears felt painful as he tugged at them to listen to his contact from HQ. He waited for the connection to be established. The thermometer attached to his clothes showed minus 40. His ears had begun to sting. Next would be his legs. Nevertheless he stood still and waited.

"HQ to Jay."

His contact's voice filled Jay's ears. He opened his mouth to acknowledge the call but realized the cold had caused his throat to freeze. "Jay here." He willed the words to escape his mouth.

"Start the GPS on your phone so I can track you," the voice from HQ instructed.

For a moment Jay felt envious, thinking about his contact sitting somewhere in warm comfort. Such thoughts were dangerous, he knew. They sapped one's will. He struggled to find his phone and struggled to enter the codes with his numb fingers.

"I see you," the voice from HQ confirmed. "Move forward."

Jay cursed as he lifted his leg and brought it forward. His foot sunk into the snow but he pulled it out and continued. Walking up the slope was a breathless challenge as he was climbing at a snail's pace.

"Okay, stop!" The voice from HQ said once he was on the top of the small hill. Jay halted, struggling to catch his breath.

"Should be at your feet," the voice said.

The mist made it hard to see anything. Jay sank to his knees and groped. He could feel nothing but snow, all around him. "I don't see it."

"Of course you don't." Jay thought he heard amusement in the voice. "Mr. Jay, you're going to have to dig."

###

Fog, rain and snow...all three are insipient enemies of a flying helicopter. Yet, in the thick of a foggy snowfall, the two Russians were flying their rig expertly.

"I don't have visibility," Charkov complained as he piloted the chopper cautiously.

"Just keep an eye on the radar," Sergei advised, lighting a cigarette.

"How can you smoke in this?" Charkov asked. "I can barely breathe."

"I *have* to smoke because of the cold," Sergei muttered.

The chopper hovered over the ground for some time and then moved slowly on through the mist.

"How are we going to find the bastard?" Charkov growled.

"Two words: thermal vision," Sergei replied. He switched on a screen with everything in green. "Anything red is our target."

"Oh come on!" Charkov protested, maneuvering the helicopter away from a steep hill. "The animals will show up as red too."

A sly smile crept over Sergei's face. "Then we'll shoot the animals too."

The helicopter moved on. It was hard to hold it steady in those conditions.

"Whatever you want to do, do it fast," Charkov said, glancing in irritation at Sergei, who was still sucking on his cigarette.

Tossing the butt away, Sergei cursed, turning to the green screen. "The scan has begun," he muttered.

The screen started buzzing and various red dots appeared on it. "One of these is our target," Sergei said.

"And how are we going to know which one?" Charkov asked, struggling with the stick to keep the helicopter in control.

"Like this." Sergei pressed a button and zoomed in on a red dot. "No, that is an animal." He kept repeating the process.

"How much longer will it take?"

"It's process of elimination, partner! Can't force it to speed up." Sergei suddenly leaned over the screen and blew an excited whistle.

"You found him?" asked Charkov, relieved rather than excited.

"Let's zoom in, shall we?" Sergei moved in on the red dot on the hill half a mile ahead. "It's a man," he confirmed. "But what is he doing?"

Charkov stole a glance at the screen. "It has to be him. Nobody else will come out here in such a snowstorm! Let's go." He moved the stick and the helicopter moved forward.

"But what in God's name is he doing, Char?" Sergei asked, eyes glued to the screen.

Charkov laughed as he flew on. "What do you think he's doing, Serg?" he said. "He's digging!"

###

The mist was so thick there was no way he could have seen the helicopter before it suddenly came upon him. But to Jay's surprise, he had not heard it either. *It must be the wind and all these layers over my ears,* he thought, crouching; hoping his white jacket blended with the snow. *Had they seen him?*

The helicopter hovered gently over him. Jay lay unmoving, his hands on the ground, the shovel to his side, by the small pit, eyes on the helicopter.

Slowly, the copter began to rotate on its own axis. Jay's heart skipped a beat. He could see what was attached to its side - a menacing MG42.

Don't move! Jay told himself, clutching the ends of his jacket. M*aybe they will not notice me.*

But soon he could see the heavyset Russian manning the MG42, hold a loudspeaker to his mouth.

"Stand up with your hands above your head!"

Jay stood up, but not to raise his hands. Instead, he ran.

The helicopter soon disappeared in the mist as he ran down the slope. His boots kept sinking into the loose fresh snow. He ran on. One of his boots got stuck in a snow pit. Jay discarded it and then pulled off the other one before running on.

He stopped at the bottom to catch his breath. Behind, he could hear the chopper rise up for a wider lookout.

Jay cursed. There was only one way the Russians could have found him in all this mist. Thermal scanners! A quick smile flashed across his face. *I know how to deceive thermal scanners.*

Detaching his backpack, he placed it in the snow and ruffled through its contents. He hurried as fast as his frozen fingers would allow. He could sense the helicopter turning towards him.

Soon, he found it. The *Mylar foil* was folded in a cylindrical bundle in the bag. He took it out and detached it from its cardboard packing. It was normal silver foil, used to keep food warm. The principle was simple. Thermal scanners sucked in IR rays, which were basically heat. All you had to do was cover your body with something insulating. And he had the best insulating material for the moment in his hands.

Frantically, Jay began to unwrap the foil. He could feel his hands shaking as he covered his body with the foil.

###

"Where in the Lord's name did he go?" Charkov muttered, staring at the thermal screen as he controlled the helicopter with his hands.

Sergei was at the machine gun, looking out of the chopper into the mist. "Look for his heat signature," he called.

"I don't see anything!" Charkov shouted back.

"That slithery bastard!" Sergei cursed as he slowly moved back to his seat in front of the screen, "He has disappeared, hasn't he?"

"He ran that way." Charkov pointed to the left of the screen. "And then he just disappeared."

Sergei laughed as he sat down. "He's hiding," he chuckled. "Or rather, he thinks that he is hiding."

"Can you hide from thermal scanners?" Charkov asked, placing both hands on the controls.

"No. He's probably covering himself with a blanket and lying down." He spit out of the open window. "If that is the case, we just have to wait a while and the heat buildup in the blanket will leak from the sides and show up on the screen like an aura."

Charkov cursed. "Staying in one place in this snow is hard enough."

"Or, if he might be using some kind of insulating cover." He pressed some buttons and zoomed into the screen as he spoke. "Then we have to quit looking for red spots and look for dark green ones. Because then, his insulating cover will block the heat from his surroundings too." He stared at the screen. "He'll become a black hole."

"Well, whatever you are looking for, you better be quick." Charkov was in no mood to hang around in this foul weather.

"Will you just relax and hold on?" Sergei said. "It is already blurry." He was scanning every bit of the area at the base of the hill carefully.

"If we wait long enough, the cold will kill him for sure," Charkov said sarcastically.

"Patience Char, patience." Sergei put his face close to the screen. Then a sly smile crept across his face. "I think I've got what we need."

###

Jay felt his heartbeat double as the helicopter hovered above him. He could feel its vibration though he could not see it. He felt the air pressing onto him as he lay on the snow, entirely covered by the Mylar foil. The snow began to drift into the openings of his clothing. His uncovered socks had become wet and he could not feel his toes at all. They were as stiff as rocks.

"Stand up! We've found you," the voice boomed overhead. The words were immediately swallowed by the falling snow.

Even in that intense cold, Jay felt sweat bead his forehead. *Maybe they're bluffing,* he thought. *If I just lie still...*

"You foil-covered idiot!" the man on the loudspeaker yelled. "Get up! Or do I have to shoot?"

Jay felt drops of sweat trickle down his cheeks as he stood up. Then he realized it was not sweat but tears. *No, it can't end like this!* he thought. *I've come so far!* He pushed the foil off him as he stood up and raised his hands over his head. The helicopter hovered over him like the sword of Damocles.

"Good!' said the man on the loudspeaker. "Now get on your knees."

Jay looked back over his shoulder. *If only he could make a dash for the pine trees. The chopper couldn't follow him there.* But the trees were too far away. And the mist was too dense.

'It's over, Jay."

Was it really over? He was so close!

A cold shiver ran down his spine as Jay watched the helicopter slowly descend. It was indeed over.

###

Ten miles away, the voice from HQ, the woman called Tanya, broke away from her laptop screen. Her knees dug into the soft king-sized bed in her hotel room. She shut the laptop with a snap and sprang up from her position. She reached for the window pane to her right and pushed it open.

Yes, her ears had not deceived her. Three black SUVs had pulled up to the entrance of her hotel. She had heard tires screeching to a halt not ten seconds ago. She caught a glimpse of several men dressed in black descending from the vehicles. Quickly, she shut the window and retreated.

They are here! she thought fearfully as she scrambled back to her laptop on the bed. Propping it up on her knees, she began clicking away frantically.

Upload ready. The message showed on her screen. Picking up the laptop with both hands she ran to the door and rushed into the empty corridor. From the other end she could hear the taps of shoes coming up the wooden stairs.

They were coming!

She ran to the closed door with FIRE EXIT written over its lintel in bold letters. Clutching the laptop against her chest, she unbolted it with one hand and opened it softly. Slipping through, she closed it again, careful not to make any noise.

The screen now read: *Uploading 10%...*

She ran up the stairs to the terrace. The door to the terrace was fortunately unlocked. She kicked it open with one leg. Outside, the air was chilly, but she hardly noticed as she placed her laptop on the ground and bolted the door to the terrace behind her.

Phew! The terrace was empty except for her. She turned back to the laptop. *Uploading 30%...* Now all that was left to do was wait. She crawled to the side of the terrace above her room. She could hear sounds below.

"The bitch is not here," a man said in Russian.

She heard some more muffled voices before the same Russian voice finally stated, "Let's check the terrace then."

A chill ran down her spine as she retreated from the wall and went back to the door. She checked the bolt again. The door was shut tight.

She looked at the laptop. *Uploading 50%...*

There were footsteps running up the stairs, coming closer. Soon, she saw the doorknob turn.

"Senor! The bitch has blocked the terrace door," a man shouted from the other side.

Tanya watched, heart thumping, as the man struggled with the bolted door from the other side. She looked down at the laptop again. The bar showing the upload progress was almost three quarters along. *Uploading 75%...*

Tanya could hear more footsteps climbing. And then a voice shouted "Open the damn door!"

Tanya froze. Instinctively, her hand crawled to her laptop and she clutched it protectively.

"It's over, Tanya Williams!" the voice said. "Open the door!"

Tanya got to her feet. The upload was almost done. Now, if they didn't have a network jammer which could jam her connection to the internet, then it was almost...

"We've got a jammer, Tanya, watch it!"

Tanya looked at the laptop again. To her horror, she realized the upload had stopped. *Uploading 75%...*it still said. She looked back at the door.

"It's over!" the same voice said.

She clutched the laptop, her teeth clenched in fury. *It was indeed over.*

2

The Axiom

File 1/14/Jan/XVII:Top Secret

NEW DELHI, 2016

The history of modern India is rich in records of missing persons, if one is to go by the available documentation since the hundred-and-fifty years of British rule ended. Under foreign rule, missing persons and unexplained disappearances were commonplace as the rulers tended to dispose of unruly subjects and hush up the matter. In most cases, such missing persons were killed and their bodies disposed of. And the police, with the resources to search for such persons, remained firmly under the control and direction of the ruling Government.

The method worked very well unless the victim was a well-known personality. The disappearance of such a person caused an uproar in society at large and caused problems. Furthermore, people tended to actively search for famous missing persons.

The earliest incident of this type related to Nana Sahib, the missing Peshwa and face of the once overbearing Maratha Empire. He was one of the pillars of the 1857 revolt against the rule of the British East India Company. Nana Sahib was never heard from again after the British conquered his final base in Kanpur, in 1857. Legends grew up around the last Peshwa, or the *Lost* Peshwa, as people wildly conjectured about his whereabouts. Some declared him to be the victim of an unknown illness, while others said he had been seen in Nepal.

The British themselves have not escaped such mysterious disappearances. For example, take the case of the once famous mountaineers, George Mallory and Andrew Irvine. Both were poster boys of the English mountaineering spirit as they set off to tackle the most difficult challenge that existed in the world, Mt. Everest! Both disappeared on the last leg of the climb. Almost eight years later, in 1999, Mallory's body was found by climbers. Andrew Irvine's body was never found and he still remains on the list of missing British mountaineers.

A similar case is that of the Australian aviator, Charles Kingsford, a pioneer in the field of aviation. In 1972, Charles flew in his Lockheed aircraft from Allahabad to Singapore, attempting to create a record for the swiftest flight from India to Australia. Needless to say, he never reached his destination, or indeed, anywhere. His plane was never found.

It is not that such incidents occured only in the long gone past and have ceased to occur in modern times because of the availability of modern communication devices. One such incident in recent times is the case of the famous Indian cricketer, Cotah Ramaswamy, who left his house one fine morning and disappeared into thin air. Ramaswamy had famously played the first test match in 1925. He left his home in Adyar on the morning of 15 October 1985, and never returned. He was never seen again.

When all such incidents are taken together and investigated in detail, one clearly notices that there are many common features in these cases.

The first is *the missing body*. The body of the missing person is never found, even after decades.

The second common thread is *the accompanying treasure*. All these disappearances are tied together with the disappearance of a missing treasure, either in the form of valuable physical objects, or some superior knowledge.

In the case of Nana Sahib, there was the missing treasure of the Peshwas that he took with him when he disappeared. In the case of Mallory and Irvine, the great unanswered question was whether the two mountaineers had reached the summit of Mt. Everest. If they had, were they then the first men to do so?

From time immemorial, men have always loved to search for something that manifested in the form of missing treasure or knowledge. From the legendary search for the Holy Grail itself, any kind of missing treasure has symbolized a road of adventures leading to the Promised Land. Men have always been drawn to the search for treasure, be it Columbus, who sailed to find the New World, or Robert Perry, who went north to find the Pole.

The third common factor is *suppressed information*. In the case of each of these disappearances, the concerned Authorities hid or buried some evidence, which only strengthened conjectures about the involvement of those authorities in the disappearances. This last point often fed conspiracy theories, while the first two indicated why conspiracy theories arose in the first place.

The mysterious case of the disappearance of Netaji Subhash Chandra Bose, one of the leaders of the Indian freedom movement, fits this mould perfectly.

In 1945, just after the nuclear bombs had been dropped on Hiroshima and Nagasaki, Netaji took a series of flights; the last one crashing at Formosa in Taiwan, and culminating in his supposed death. Six decades later, conspiracy theories still abound, from the hauntingly possible to the outright bizarre, due to the following reasons.

Firstly, Netaji was internationally famous. He had rubbed shoulders with Mahatma Gandhi and Jawaharlal Nehru. He was renowned as a man of action and the leader of the INA (Indian National Army). His popularity was soaring when his plane crashed.

Secondly, Bose's body was never found. The plane crash happened in a foreign country, where the officials who dealt with his body, did not know or revere him as a national hero. The photographs taken of his body are strangely vague, explained away by the burns he is said to have suffered in the crash. The photographs could have been of any severely burnt man. There are disturbing questions regarding his death certificate, with at least five individuals claiming to have signed it. The actual certificate has never been found.

Thirdly, the treasure in this case was the hundred pounds of gold he took with him on his final journey. This gold was part of the Indian National Army's war chest, which Bose had raised from various South-Eastern-Asian businessmen, to fund the freedom struggle. The gold was never found.

Fourthly, documents relating to Bose's life and death have been classified for over six decades in India, as well as by the Governments of five other countries, including Britain and Japan.

Many people have sought to solve this horrendously confusing mystery since 1945. The Indian Government set up four Commissions in this regard; all of them were perceived as public relations gimmicks. The latest findings reveal the ashes of Netaji, kept at the Renkoji Temple in Japan, are in fact, the ashes of a Japanese soldier named Ichiro Okura. This has served to rekindle conspiracy theories and ignited fresh interest in the mystery of his disappearance.

The approach to solving such tangled mysteries cannot be straightforward. Such an approach is bound to fail, owing to the inaccessibility of important documents pertaining to the case, leading to a lack of evidence. We cannot search for a needle in the haystack with our hands. We must use a magnet.

The magnet in this case is the investigation into a set of allied disappearances, to deduce what actually happened.

Famous persons do not disappear alone. There are others who travel or work with them, and the disappearances of these other people can be used to uncover the main truth. These allied disappearances are not widely known, hence there is a greater chance that clues pertaining to the disappearances are not lying in classified files.

This was exactly the principle Jay Rasbihari followed, though he wasn't aware of it till the very end. He had not thought of the principle at all when he set out to discover what had actually happened to his ancestors, Major and Mrs. Singh, veterans of the Indian National Army. Major Anish Singh had been leader of X regiment, and his wife, Rupali Singh, had been one of the all-women Rani Jhansi Regiment of the INA.

There are records to show this couple lived in Dehra Doon after independence, until the birth of their first child. After that, they disappeared, adding to the list of missing persons in the country. As they were not celebrities, Jay found no trouble in obtaining documents about them. Surprisingly, he uncovered more documents than he expected, thus coming upon a paper trail.

Anish and Rupali Singh had survived the fight for independence and had lived to be citizens of a free India. Most probably, they had been part of the teeming crowds at the Red Fort where Pandit Nehru gave his famous independence speech. It was the duty of an independent nation to find out what happened to this illustrious couple.

This was exactly the riddle Jay was trying to solve when he stumbled upon the lost trail of Netaji. He had no idea this was where he would end up when he began a simple search for his missing great-grandparents. It was only when he had dug sufficiently deep into their mystery that unforeseen connections began to emerge and the search for Anish and Rupali Singh converted into a search for India's lost Netaji.

3
The Characters

HONG KONG, 2015

It was a soft summer's evening. Jay was sitting in the hotel café, sipping a dark decaf and reading The Sun, when he first saw a slender pair of legs strut lazily towards him. The fair and smooth skin of the calves drew his attention away from the article he was reading. The legs sashayed forward, the feet hidden in black high heeled shoes. When the legs stood beside him, Jay put the paper aside.

"Hi, I'm Tanya Williams." The woman held out an ID card but Jay's eyes lingered on her slender frame instead of focusing on her credentials. "I'm with Time magazine."

"Nice to meet you. I'm Jay," he said, still taking in the vision before him.

Tanya Williams seemed beautiful at first sight. She was wearing a low-cut blue sweater that revealed enough, yet left the rest to the imagination. Her jeans were tight enough to suggest her curves yet plain enough to pass off as businesslike. Her hair was done up in a tight ponytail that swung from side to side as she walked, and her skin was flawless.

"Of course, I know you are Jay Rasbihari," she said, smiling sweetly. Her light pink lip gloss shimmered in the warm lighting of the lobby. "It's my job to know. You are CEO and Founder of Oranax Systems."

"Former CEO," Jay corrected, shaking her hand. Her palm was silky smooth. "How did you find me?"

"Find you!" she pouted. "I have been looking for you for a very long time, Mr. Rasbihari."

"Please call me Jay." Recovering from his sudden infatuation, he passed the menu over to her. "Please have a seat, Mrs. Williams."

"Ms. Williams..." Sitting down, she crossed her legs. "I was divorced a year ago. Damn guys at IT haven't got it changed!"

"Would you like some coffee?" Jai asked politely.

"Only if it comes with information," she replied, her right eyelid drooping in a slow wink.

"You journalists ever dig for anything other than information?" Jay joked as he signalled the barista for two lattes.

"Yes, for the person the information is about." She eyed him playfully as she reached for her bag and held up her cell phone.

Jay felt a lump form in his throat as he watched those teal eyes stare at him. "Why were you looking for me?" he asked, swallowing.

"For an article obviously." She tapped her phone with a gleaming fingernail. "I've done Zuckerberg, Adam DE Angelo, Hank Williams. You're next on my list, or rather, you were."

To avoid her gaze, Jay looked towards the service counter and watched the barista bring them the lattes. "You want to know why I quit?" he asked.

"Mm-hmm." She leaned forward and smelled the coffee with closed eyes. "This smells nice."

There was something very seductive about her voice, Jay thought as he lifted his cup to his lips. "Is this off the record or on?"

"Just call it a reporter trying to satisfy her curiosity." Her lips were white with frothy foam. She licked them luxuriously.

Jay smiled. *Two can play at this game*, he thought. "Why? Don't find me interesting anymore?"

"Actually, I find you irresistibly interesting." She uncrossed her legs and leaned forward. "But my editor no longer does."

"So basically you want to know why I quit Oranax." Jay leaned back, trying not to look at her beautiful legs. "And you want to know that just because you are interested, not because you want to do a story on me."

"Precisely."

"So is this like a date?"

"More like an interview."

Jay smiled again. *Playing hard to get?* "An interview, huh. I thought you wanted to know just one thing."

"But it would be impolite to ask you just that without knowing your full story." Once again her finger tapped her phone.

"It's a long story," Jay warned, hoping to put her off.

"Then let us begin at once, at the start," Tanya said.

1989

Jay Rasbihari had always been intelligent, even as a baby. He spoke his first words at seven months, started walking at eleven. On his first birthday, he was walking and talking like a two-year-old, and had learned to say 'Thank you' when anyone greeted him, and to ask 'Where is my gift?' when someone left. The talking did not continue, though.

Soon, he realized that listening to the people around him was much more interesting than just talking to them. As Jay listened, he began to know the house around him, the people, his parents, the relatives who came to visit. By the age of two, he could greet regular visitors by name and identify their relationship to him.

By the age of three he realized there was rough politics between his mother and his paternal grandmother, and he learned to use the miscommunication between them to get prohibited items such as extra chocolates and sweets from the kitchen. His standard method was to ask for cookies first from his mother in the morning, before she left for her job. Since he was allowed only a limited number of cookies per day, he would get that lot from his mother. When his mother left, he'd use the same stratagem with his grandmother. Both women wondered why the jar of cookies had to be refilled so frequently and blamed each other for the secret consumption.

By the time Jay was four, however, a deep sense of mystique had begun to grow in him. He realized that conversations were often carried out in front of him as if he didn't exist. His parents, his aunts, would whisper to each other. It was as if the whole house was full of secrets.

But bit by bit, by carefully listening to those whispered exchanges, Jay slowly began to put together a picture of what was going on, and to his horror, realized the whispers actually had a lot to do with him.

It all fell open one day when he heard his mother ask his father, "When should we tell him the truth about his mother?"

In that moment the truth dawned on him that when his uncle jokingly called him a little bastard for his naughtiness, he was telling the truth.

Instead of feeling sorrow, Jay became interested in uncovering this matter further. His mother was horrified when he asked her casually one day, "Who are my real mom and dad, Mommy?"

His parents resorted to lies, but soon realized that Jay knew much more about this hidden fact than their relatives did. Finally, they told him he would know about it when he grew up to be a big boy.

That was enough for Jay as he became busy with school. He was an intelligent student as well. His favorite subjects were mathematics and science; however, he had a deep love for history and geography.

Once, in history class, they were discussing the life of revolutionaries in the Indian freedom struggle. The chapter did not carry much weight for the exams, but everyone was listening intently to Mr. Dalvi, the history teacher, as he read from the text book in his deep and serene voice.

"Netaji Subhash Chandra Bose was born in Cuttack, Orissa, on the twenty-third day of the month of January, 1897."

Immediately, a hand shot up from the first bench. Mr. Dalvi looked up from the book he was holding, to see who it was, and a smile crept across his face.

"What is it, Jay?" he asked, placing a finger in it as bookmark while closing the book.

"You said Netaji was born in Orissa," Jay said, standing up. "But I always thought that he was Bengali."

Mr. Dalvi smiled. "Netaji was Bengali, son. He was born in Cuttack, in present-day Orissa, but at the time it was part of the Province of Bengal."

Jay nodded and sat down, satisfied with the explanation. Mr. Dalvi continued, "Netaji studied for the Indian Civil Services examination in England, but resigned from the job because he did not want to serve under a foreign government."

The students listened with interest as Mr. Dalvi read on, "Returning to India in 1921, the twenty-four-year old Netaji started the newspaper *Swaraj* and took charge of publicity for the Bengal Provincial Congress Committee. His mentor was Chittaranjan Das, a spokesman for aggressive nationalism in Bengal. In the year 1923, Bose was elected President of the All India Youth Congress, and also Secretary of the Bengal State Congress. He was also Editor of the newspaper, *Forward*, founded by Chittaranjan Das. Bose worked as CEO of the Calcutta Municipal Corporation for Das when the latter was elected Mayor of Calcutta in 1924. In a round-up of nationalists in 1925, Bose was arrested and sent to prison in Mandalay, Burma, where he contracted tuberculosis."

Jay's hand was up in the air again. "Netaji's early life is strikingly similar to that of Lokmanya Tilak," he noted. "Both were part of the administrative system until sent to jail."

Mr. Dalvin nodded, pleased. They had read about Bal Gangadhar Tilak a few days ago and the boy had remembered and put together the parts correctly. He cleared his throat and read on: "In 1927, after being released from prison, Bose became General Secretary of the Congress party and worked with Jawaharlal Nehru for a free India. He became Mayor of Calcutta in 1930. He stood for unqualified *swaraj* (self-governance), including the use of force against the British."

"This showed his experience in administration, just like Sardar Patel and Pandit Nehru," Jay said.

His classmates looked at him in irritation for speaking out of turn. But Mr. Dalvi merely smiled and continued.

"Bose's arrest and subsequent release set the scene for his escape to Germany, via Afghanistan and the Soviet Union. He was kept under British surveillance. A few days before his escape, on the pretext of wanting to be alone, he avoided meeting his British guards and grew a beard as a disguise. On the night of his escape, he dressed as a Pathan to avoid being identified. Bose escaped from his house in Calcutta, on 19 January 1941, accompanied by his nephew, Sisir K. Bose, in a car."

"Escaped from under the noses of the British!" Jay said excitedly. "Just like VD Savarkar, Sir."

Mr. Dalvi nodded. They had studied how Savarkar had escaped from a ship right under the noses of the British, in their last lesson. He read on.

"Bose escaped via Afghanistan and Turkey to Moscow, in Russia. From there, he went to Germany, where he met with Adolf Hitler himself. From there, he went to Japan. With Japanese support, Bose revamped the Indian National Army (INA), then composed of Indian soldiers of the British Indian Army, who had been captured in the Battle of Singapore. To these forces were added enlisting Indian civilians in Malaya and Singapore. The Japanese then supported a number of puppet and provisional governments in captured countries and regions such as Burma, Philippines, and Manchukuo. Before long, the Provisional Government of Free India, presided over by Bose, was formed in the Japanese-occupied Andaman and Nicobar Islands. Bose possessed great drive and charisma and creating popular Indian slogans such as *Jai Hind*!

The INA under Bose was a model of diversity, of region, ethnicity, religion, and even gender."

Mr. Dalvi looked up and his eyes rested on Jay. "You don't have any name to compare with him now, huh Jay?"

The class laughed but Jay stood up. "This part of Bose's life has him doing something very different," he said, "so I can't compare him to anybody else. Here he is carving out a unique identity for himself."

"Well said," Mr. Dalvi murmured before continuing to read. "Unfortunately, the INA and the Japanese failed in their attempts to liberate India. The tide had turned, and Japan was on the losing side. Bose was in Singapore when he heard of the atom bombs falling on Hiroshima and Nagasaki. He left soon after, on a series of flights, but was killed in an unfortunate plane crash in Taiwan. India lost one of her most heroic freedom fighters and one of her greatest sons."

Jay's hand was in the air again. "I have a question this time, instead of a comment," he said.

"And what would it be?" his teacher asked, closing the book and placing it on the table, indicating the lesson was over.

"Why did Netaji take that last series of flights?"

Mr. Dalvi opened his mouth to answer, but the bell rang loudly, signalling end of the class. The somnolent boys in the last row suddenly awoke and erupted into frenzy as recess was next. Mr. Dalvi's words were left unspoken. As he left the class, Jay was left standing, his question unanswered. Little did he know that it would take another twenty-seven years to get an answer.

###

Jay's progress through school was brisk, giving all the signs that he was a child prodigy. When he entered high school, studies began to bore him as he realized he could do them on his own any night instead of paying attention for long hours in class. Instead, he began to dabble in sports and music, soon realizing those were areas the girls took interest in.

And yes, girls flocked to him. Jay's friends were surprised at how many he could attract when they themselves could not even muster the courage to walk up to one. Soon, Jay began to bunk classes, wandering the city streets with new girlfriends every week. He visited pool clubs and snooker houses.

Jay's parents looked at this new development with caution. His mother even said that Jay had become a spoilt child. But his father saw the reality behind the 'bad' behaviour and said, "He's just bored."

And so they introduced him to the engineering exams for the prestigious IIT-JEE, the engineering dream of so many student hopefuls in the country. Soon, Jay was once again buried in his books, solving complex numerical puzzles in physics, mathematics and chemistry. His newfound obsession with the sciences was all consuming and he achieved an All India rank of 3 in the exams. His parents were very happy, but Jay dismissed it with a shrug, saying, "It's just the beginning."

It was indeed just the beginning. He went away to study at IIT Bombay, the best engineering institute in the whole country. Jay went from one semester to another like a Matador, scoring perfect tens in all his computer science subjects. One of his teachers was later quoted as having said that he felt Jay was the next Bill Gates, in India.

The analogy was perfect. Like Bill Gates, Jay too, dropped out of college in his final year. But that would come later. In his later semesters, his professors noticed that though they never saw his face in class, his name inevitably topped the marks list.

It must have been during those low attendance semesters that the seed of the company, Oranax Ltd, must have been sowed. In later interviews, Jay stated that Oranax began in his college dorm, but did not mention that the initial operations involved him and his friends hacking into the college network systems and using their data centers to fund their internet requirements. When the college authorities discovered the breach, they reacted by taking disciplinary action against Jay and his friends. At the hearing, when he was threatened with rustication, Jay reacted by accepting the decision.

Jay and his two co-founders dropped out of IIT in 2008, and immediately started Oranax Datalytics, in the nearby Hiranandani Complex. In their fundraising pitches, they explained that the first software they were developing was a tool for large organizations to systematically catalog vast amounts of data using fewer servers. The algorithms Jay was developing with his co-founders optimized server utilization, thereby facilitating the handling of large storage spaces at comparatively low cost.

Finding Angel investors wasn't much of a problem for Jay and his mates. They were from the most prestigious institute in the country and their dramatic drop-out merely added a glamour quotient to their personalities. Oranax would never want for funds or brain power, and would ride forward like a soaring unicorn.

The problem was when Jay's parents realized he was old enough and called him home to reveal the secret they had promised to tell him in due time. Jay had all but forgotten about it, but apparently his parents had not. So, in the summer of 2014, they summoned him home to tell him the one thing that would change his life forever – the truth about his birth.

QUEENSLAND, AUSTRALIA, 1972

Tanya Williams was born in the town of Townsville, in the vast expanse of rural Australia, to Christine Ann Jones, a journalist, and John Williams, an anti-war activist and builder. The couple separated before Tanya was born, and she was brought up by Christine Ann as a single parent. Unfortunately, Christine Ann was addicted to heroin, and so bringing up Tanya in rural Australia was as rough as it could get.

When Tanya was six years old, her mother married Richard Harrow, her sixth marriage and his third. Richard was an actor, with whom Christine Ann ran a small eccentric theatre company. Tanya had a miserable life at school, often having to answer the other children about why it was that her father's surname was Harrow, and her own was Williams.

Tanya had a nomadic childhood. She had lived in thirty different towns by the time she was in her early teens, for her parents travelled the country with their theatre company, and took her along. Every time, she went through the same ordeal of having to answer the same questions and having no friends.

So she was secretly glad when one day her mom took her to eat ice-cream in a nearby store and broke the news that she was pregnant, and they had decided to send Tanya to boarding school. That was the end of family life for Tanya, and the end of being with loved ones – a feeling she would not experience again for almost thirty years.

###

Detached from her parents at the age of twelve, Tanya was sent to Silver Oaks School, a boarding facility in the idyllic environs of Victoria. She would spend the next six years there. It was the longest Tanya had ever spent in one place.

During those six years, Tanya eagerly awaited the monthly arrival of Alberto Valerio, a jovial and rotund journalist from Melbourne. He would always bring her funny photographs he had clicked at the many places he had been. For Tanya, he was like the elder brother she had never had. But, to her horror, Tanya came to realize that Alberto did not look upon her as his little sister. In those years, money was scarce and her parents hardly wrote, let alone sent her much to spend. So she had to look for a part time job to meet her basic needs. Alberto was the one she naturally turned to. He needed an assistant in his journalistic escapades and she desperately needed a job.

She was happy when Alberto agreed to take her on as an assistant for the weekdays. What she could not have known was that the job would come at a price. But she soon learned. Alberto had a fondness for little girls; a fondness that verged on perverseness. That was why he visited the school.

Alberto did train her to be a good assistant to a journalist. But he also raped her, for the first few times at least. Soon, Tanya learned to just give in. It was much less painful that way. She never wrote to her mother because she never got letters from her, nor did she tell any of her friends, because she didn't have any. The teachers were too strict to talk to. Her only friend had been Alberto, and now he was something very very different.

Tanya's abuse stopped when her mother decided it was time for her to go to college. She studied programming, mathematics and physics at Melbourne University, staying in the college dorms – a weird teenager without friends. In her boredom, she took to playing with computers, which soon turned into a full-time obsession. Tanya began to do something every abused, lonely and computer-obsessed child did those days: hacking.

In 1987, she began hacking under 'Trax', the name of her university dorm. She and her two other partners, known as 'Mendax' and 'Prime Suspect', hackers she had met online, formed an ethical hacking group they called the International Subversives. During this time, they hacked into the Pentagon and other U.S. Department of Defense facilities, MILNET, the U.S. Navy, NASA, the Australian Overseas Telecommunications Commission; Citibank, Lockheed Martin, Motorola, Panasonic, Xerox; the Australian National University, La Trobe University, and Stanford University's SRI International.

In September 1998, they were discovered hacking into the Melbourne master terminal of Nortel, a Canada-based multinational telecommunications corporation. The Australian Police tapped her phone, raided her dorm at the end of October, and eventually charged her in 1994 with thirty-one counts of hacking and related crimes. The same year, she pleaded guilty to twenty-five of the charges (the other six were dropped), and was ordered to pay reparations of A$2,100. She was released on a good behavior bond, avoiding a heavier penalty due to the perceived absence of malicious or mercenary intent, and taking into consideration her disrupted childhood. She was just eighteen at the time.

It was at that trial that she finally met her fellow hacker 'Mendax' face to face. And it was there that she learned that his real name was Julian Assange.

4
The Couple
File 2/14/Jan/XVII: Top Secret

NEW DELHI, 1945

In his autobiography, Colonel Thomas Hardy of the 7th Newcastle Hussar's Division, also known as 'The Chindits', recalls Major Anish Singh and his wife, Rupali, vividly. In his book, he recounts the days of their court martial in December 1945, which he had been deputed to supervise.

The Second World War had ended six months before and the army camps of Delhi were bustling with INA POWs. Hardy writes that it was a misty day, with an occasional burst of rain. The cold had prompted him to wear a khaki blazer over his full uniform as he walked into the Post Office in Victory Square, less than a hundred paces from the famous Red Fort of Delhi, over which the Union Jack fluttered proudly. He went through the heap of files on his table as he waited for his colleagues to arrive. When he grew tired of the files, he looked up and observed the six foot tall Punjabi who stood in the dock. The man was smiling. No one would have guessed he was about to be court marshalled for high treason.

British policy classified all INA men into three categories – black, grey and white. Whites were to be treated the most leniently; blacks were considered the most dangerous.

"So Major Anish Singh!" Colonel Hardy said, going back to the files on which 'Grey' was clearly mentioned. "It says here that you are charged with waging war on the armies of His Majesty."

The tall Punjabi folded his arms, "I certainly did, and I am proud of it."

Colonel Hardy was impressed by the young man's demeanor but he did not let it show on his face. "I'll take that as off the record."

"You can take it however you like, Sir."

"Haven't lost your military bearings, have you?" Colonel Hardy remarked.

"I served in another army after I had left His Majesty's forces."

Colonel Hardy looked at his wristwatch. It was almost time for the Court Marshall to begin. But then there were so many trials squeezed into one day that it was natural for his colleagues to be late for this one. He decided to start without them.

"So, born in Lahore, eh?" he asked, eyes still on the files.

"Born and brought up there, Sir," Major Singh replied. "I graduated from Government College, Lahore, and then sat for the Military Entrance Exam, passing which, I went to the Indian Military Academy at Dehra Doon." Major Singh's English was impeccable.

"Which year batch was it?" Hardy asked, impressed by the Punjabi's resume. He himself was an alumnus of the same institute, though a few years junior to this man.

"1936."

"Good." Colonel Hardy gnawed his lower lip. So the Punjabi Major was his senior by almost half a decade.

"I was commissioned as Second Lieutenant on the Special List in early 1939," Singh said, standing straight in the dock. "2nd Battalion. The Highlanders!"

"Secunderabad, right?"

"Indeed. A boring year until we were sent to the Far East to hold a garrison in a quaint little British port."

Colonel Hardy read further. "Singapore, huh."

"The war was soon to come."

Hardy smiled as he went through the war records in the files. "I see one promotion after another. In less than six months, you were Acting Captain."

"I served with distinction. Your army promotes on talent alone; I'll give you that." Singh bowed.

Colonel Hardy closed the files and looked up. "Japanese prisoner-of-war in Malaya, 1941 - what happened?"

"I was captured in Malaya." Singh twisted his thick mustache. "I had taken my regiment on a midnight raid on the Japanese docking station on the island of Java."

"How many KIA?"

"Almost every man. The Japs were expecting us."

"So how did you end up not dead, huh?"

Singh stopped curling his mustache and clenched his teeth in anger. "If you doubt my valour or my loyalty to my comrades, there are over a thousand dead English soldiers in Burma who would have told you otherwise."

"That's not what I was implying." Colonel Hardy retorted calmly, maintaining his composure. "But I don't see you as a man who would surrender. So what exactly did happen?"

"We walked into an ambush," Singh sighed wearily. "The Japs were ready for us. We faced machine gun fire and landmines. I was carrying one of my injured men away from the firing when two Japs pointed their bayonets at me."

"And then?"

"The Jap officers were unwilling to kill me. It appeared that they had clear orders to spare as many Indian soldiers as they could."

Colonel Hardy nodded with interest. There was a theory doing the rounds which had considerable support, that the Japanese army had planned on recruiting the INA since quite some time before the war.

"So where were you held?"

"Manchuria." Singh coughed harshly. "May I have some water please?"

Hardy gestured with two fingers and the Private standing at the door ran for a glass of water. "Unpleasant memories, huh?"

"Many..." Singh sighed. "The Japanese sure know how to keep a prisoner from escaping."

"How many times?"

"I lost count." Major Singh said, drinking from the glass the Private handed him.

"Still they let you go?"

"They let all of us go. Netaji convinced them. That was why we respected him so much."

The talk now moved to Netaji Subhash Chandra Bose, a war criminal who had supposedly died in a plane crash. Colonel Hardy opened his small notebook to take notes. This topic was important.

"Burma campaign, huh. X regiment." Hardy was back to the files, ruffling pages with one hand while writing in the notebook with the other.

"We preferred to call ourselves Jungle Cats." Major Singh closed his eyes, remembering.

"And Jungle Cats you were!" Colonel Hardy closed the last file on the table. "Your regiment was the deadliest of the Japanese army during the Burma campaign."

"Deadliest of the INA," Major Singh corrected quietly.

Colonel Hardy smiled in amusement. "It's sad really that you guys didn't get what you wanted."

"Our freedom?" Major Singh laughed. "We *still* want *that,* Colonel."

"All you were able to hold were two small border towns – Kohima and Imphal," Colonel Hardy reminded him. "That too, not even for a fortnight."

Major Singh opened his eyes. "It was an impossible offensive. We had such few resources. I'd say we did far more than what anyone else could have done with what we had."

"Nobody's blaming you," Colonel Hardy said.

"We blame ourselves! It is what Netaji taught us to do."

Colonel Hardy smiled, impressed by this young Punjabi. He would have liked to talk more but the door opened just then and his two fellow officers walked in.

"Sorry, we're late," one of them said.

Colonel Hardy smiled in greeting as they took their seats beside him. "No, it was I who was early," he chuckled.

###

Three months later, Hardy found himself in another part time court room of the same building, overseeing another trial, with two different colleagues beside him and a different defendant standing in the dock. This time it was a woman. It was his seventh trial of the day and Hardy wasn't really paying much attention, allowing the men beside him do the talking. Then he heard the woman say her name and his startled attention returned to her.

"It was Rupali Swaminathan. It is now Rupali Singh," she said.

Colonel Hardy sat up straight in his seat and moved a hand over his eyes to dispel the sleep that had been insidiously creeping up on him.

"Why did you change your name, Ms. Swaminathan?" the Colonel beside Hardy asked. "There are no records of your new name with us."

"I would prefer if you addressed me as Mrs. Rupali Singh. I believe it is standard practice to change one's name after marriage, even in your own country across the seas."

That caused a flurry as the officers began frantically flipping through the files. Colonel Hardy kept his eyes on the woman. She was short yet athletically built, her hair was cut short to her neck.

"It says nowhere that you are married," one of the officers said.

"Perhaps because I was married in Burma," she said. "No British records will show that."

"Mrs. Singh." Colonel Hardy addressed her and she looked at him. "What would be the name of your husband?"

"Major Anish Singh."

Colonel Hardy banged the table with the flat of his palm, smiling. "I was at his courtmarshal." Turning to his fellow officers, he whispered something quickly. They nodded.

"It seems rather peculiar for a South Indian woman to have married a North Indian man," one of the officers suggested.

"Love has no boundaries," she said.

"Did you know him from before?" Colonel Hardy enquired.

"No, we met in Singapore."

"Why did a professionally trained doctor like you go to Singapore, Mrs. Singh?" Hardy asked. "Surely our British army must have tried to recruit you before the war."

Rupali raised her head and stared at the men before her. "I did not wish to serve in your war effort. It was not our war. Our war is with you!"

"Did you have family in Singapore?"

"I had close relatives there. I started a private medical practice there. I had quite a good practice. There were a large number of South Indians in Singapore. This was 1940."

"And then the Japs attacked?"

"The Japanese forces attacked Singapore in December 1941. Rashbehari Bose, a veteran freedom fighter, came with them. He started the India Independence League. I, like all the other Indians, joined it. Our property was not considered enemy property by the Japanese. They treated us well."

"Did you want to don uniform, Mrs. Singh?"

"I never dreamed it was possible! There were no women regiments then. But it all changed when Netaji came. He said in his second speech that he would form a women's infantry regiment, named after the Rani of Jhansi, who fought heroically against the British in 1857."

"How many women joined?"

"The response was overwhelming! My doctor colleague, Ms Laxmi Swaminathan, was appointed Head, and she did the recruiting. I, along with almost a thousand other women, joined up."

"Were you trained?"

"We were trained by officers who had served in the British army but were now Japanese POWs," she said. "Our regiment was trained by Major Anish Singh. That is how I met him."

"Would you describe the time?"

"It was a great time! The whole atmosphere was patriotic and revolutionary. The INA was a true force, representing all us Indians. It had men from different parts of the subcontinent, and it also had women. We were all made to learn one language - Hindi."

"What was your regiment's role in the Burma campaign?"

"We moved from Singapore to Burma in May 1944. We supported the X Regiment in its guerrilla activities. My training as a doctor meant I saw more of the wounded and less action."

"So what was it, a hospital love story?"

"I treated him when he was injured in a landmine blast. He was in the hospital for quite a while. We fell in love. He had to go back in the final push towards Imphal and Kohima, and none of us knew what the future would bring, so we decided to get married then and there."

"And after the retreat?"

“We were together in the retreat,” she said, “So was Netaji. A thousand men and women accompanied Netaji back to Singapore.”

“What happened after the surrender?”

“Then you people landed and imprisoned us all,” she said shortly. “I was separated from my husband. He was sent to Delhi immediately. I was held in Singapore for quite some while before I was brought here.”

“So did you see him after coming here?” Colonel Hardy asked.

“No,” she said, her face set.

“Let’s take a break, Gentlemen,” Colonel Hardy said to his colleagues, and walked out of the room.

###

Colonel Hardy managed to get Major Anish Singh to attend his wife’s courtmarshal, as a witness. It was a heartbreaking scene as husband and wife saw each other after so many months. The couple hugged, but did not allow themselves to shed even a tear in front of the *firangis*.

After the trial, both thanked the Colonel for going out of his way so they could see each other. Colonel Hardy laughed and said, that he felt it was his duty to make sure that two brave souls were not pained in this way.

The INA trials attracted massive public attention as the nationalist leader Jawaharlal Nehru himself donned his lawyer’s robes to defend the accused in the trial.

During the trials, mutiny broke out in the Royal Indian Navy. It was followed by an army mutiny at Jabalpur. The British Chief of Staff relayed orders from Britain that the INA defendants were to be judged lightly, to prevent the massive public outcry that harsh sentences would cause.

Dr. Rupali Singh was released due to lack of evidence, in 1946. She settled in Delhi to await the verdict of her husband’s trial. Major Anish Singh was released in early 1947, for the same reason, though he was formally discharged from the British army.

The couple married again in Delhi, in January 1947. They finally had time for something they had never had before – love.

When the Singhs attended the historic Independence Day speech at the Red Fort on 15 August 1947, she was forty-two weeks pregnant. They named their daughter Aazadi, a child of independent India. Their dreams had been realized. Their country was free and life was normal again. They had nothing but a bright future in front of them.

Three months later, Major and Dr. (Mrs.) Singh disappeared, never to be heard of again.

5
The Orphans

HONG KONG, 2016

The bartender poured another large peg of scotch into his glass. Jay watched the liquid splash around the transparent crystal. "That was how we completed our Round C of funding," he said.

"Interesting." Tanya sipped on her cranberry juice.

Jay played with his whiskey glass. *She's getting me drunk,* he thought. *It should be the other way round!* But he savoured the scotch nevertheless.

"How did you guys convince the government officials to play ball?" she asked, taking another dainty sip of her coral coloured drink.

"We did not convince them!" Jay put the glass down on the counter. "We forced them."

"And how did you manage to do that?"

Jay laughed. The question brought back fond memories. "Let's just say we are good at convincing people to do things against their better judgement."

"Your company's growth was phenomenal. Why did you never go public?" It was something that she had long wondered.

"We didn't need to." Jay signalled the bartender for a refill. "Our pockets were always flush."

She smiled wryly. "That or you didn't like being controlled."

"Theoretically, our investors controlled us," Jay pointed out.

"The New Delhi Pensioners Fund, The Hyderabad Insurance Company Ltd.," she read from her phone.

"None of our investors were venture capitalists."

"Nor were any of them techies."

Jay chuckled into his glass. This woman was smart. Smart and sexy. His eyes were drawn to the V cut of her sweater more and more often with each passing drink. He wondered how much more he could take.

"You mean to suggest we fooled our investors?" he asked dryly, not wanting to give her the upper hand.

"I'm merely saying that your investors knew nothing of the technology you were creating," she said, smiling sweetly.

"We didn't need the investors for technical inputs. The technology was our job. We needed the investors for funding."

"That's not how most tech entrepreneurs think," she said, biting the cap of her pen.

Jay realized he found her extremely seductive. "Well, I'm not like most tech entrepreneurs," he replied, smiling.

"No, you're not. A billion dollar valuation and that too, within three years! I believe you are something of a cash cow, Mr. Jay."

"Rather, I was." Jay finished his drink and put his glass down. It was time for action.

But Tanya was not done. "My original question stands," she said. "Why did you leave?"

"I'm too drunk to answer that," Jay responded.

"Then I daresay it's time to get you sober, Mr. Jay."

###

As they kissed frantically in the elevator, her lips tasted of gooseberry and her dress smelt of lilac. They kissed passionately, groping each other, but paused awkwardly as the elavator stopped on the 3rd floor to let a man in. They started again when he exited on the 6th. By the time they were at the 12th, her hair was tangled and Jay had a few buttons of his shirt open. They ran to his room and then waited impatiently as he fumbled with the magnetic card. After three unsuccessful attempts, she took the card from him and opened the door and led him in.

The world seemed to spin around him in a haze as she flicked on the lights and pulled him in by his shirt. Jay felt her rip his shirt buttons open and tug at his sleeves. He tugged at her sweater, pulling it over her head. She complied by raising her arms.

Jay pushed her to the bed and they fell into its soft depths, she pulled him atop her. Jay almost toppled over but held on. "Gosh, you're wild!" he said.

In answer, she tugged at his open collar. Jay captured her hands and bent down to kiss her lips. She gently sucked at his in response. Freeing her hands she tugged at his trousers. Her hand searched for his erection and began to rub. Immediately, Jay felt waves of pleasure travel through his body as adrenaline rushed to his brain. She kept kissing him, sliding her tongue into his mouth. Jay gave into the floodtide, relinquishing control.

###

The mystery about his birth had lingered in his head for quite some time like a forgotten T-shirt in the back of his closet. Jay knew it was there but never felt the need to clear the whole cupboard to find it – until that fateful day in 2014, when his parents did.

"What do you mean you don't know where my birth mother went?" Jay asked angrily, hitting his fist on the table. He was sitting in the drawing room of his parents' house in Mumbai. The hot and humid wind from the sea blew in from the lone window in the room, but it was not what caused the droplets of sweat to trickle down his father's face.

"I'm sorry, Jay." His father was visibly sad.

His mother placed a hand on his shoulder. "It was a long time ago, son," she said. "I don't understand why it even matters to you now."

"If she'd died, it would have been different," Jay said thoughtfully. "But here you are, telling me she may well be alive!"

Jay was angry. The bolt had hit him out of the blue. When his parents had called him to come over on that Sunday afternoon, he had expected a relaxed, laidback family lunch. But what he received was the harsh truth about his parentage; that his mother, the one he remembered as caring for him since childhood, *was not actually his mother.*

"Wouldn't she have returned if she had been alive?" his father retorted. The look on his face was not one of defiance or anger, but sadness. "Look, Jay," he said, "she's dead. I loved her, but she went away in a hurry and never came back."

"And we have loved each other too," his mother said, holding his father's hand. "We both love you. Did you ever want for anything?"

Jay bit his lip, regretting his outburst. It was unfair to blame his father without having heard the full story. "I'm sorry," he said. "I shouldn't have raised my voice. But that information wasn't what I expected."

"What had you expected, son?" his father asked, looking at him.

"That maybe my biological parents had died in an accident or something. And then you took care of me; that I was adopted. That's what I hoped it'd be."

"Well, I *am* your real father. But your biological mother left me years ago and never came back."

Who was she? Jay wondered, closing his eyes. When he was little, his relatives had always commented that he had his mother's eyes. He had always wondered why they looked so sad when they said it.

"She was fair," his father remarked. "She had eyes like your's. She was actually older than me by quite a few years. We met when I was doing my Masters at Bombay University. She was a Ph.D. student."

"What was her name?" Jay asked, opening his eyes to look at his father. "What of her family?"

"She didn't have anyone, she was an orphan; raised in an orphanage in Uttar Pradesh. Her name was registered there as Azaadi Singh. So that was the name she took."

"Did you get married?" Jay asked, his chin on his clasped hands.

"No," his father sighed. "I wanted to, but she said we did not need to put a tag on our love. I insisted when I found out she was pregnant with you, but she refused."

"Why did she leave?" Jay asked.

"I don't know." His father looked down at his hands. "One fine day, she just left, leaving me with you."

"Why didn't you stop her?"

"I would have if I'd known what she was going to do, but I was away on a research trip. When I came back, she was gone, having left you with one of her friends."

"Did you ever try to look for her?" Jay felt anger bubble within him. It all seemed so unfair. Which mother abandoned her baby?

"It was not so easy, was it? I had to take care of my parents, see to my sister's marriage. And I had you too, a baby. I was just a research scholar then, a few months out of university. How many things could I do at once? I didn't have money, like you do now."

Jay took a deep breath, letting the remark about money slide. "Didn't she ever write to you? To tell you where she had gone?"

"Never. It saddened me. I felt betrayed. But life goes on you know."

"I guess I should search for her then," Jay said.

"You surely have the resources," his mother said.

"But are you prepared to hear she is dead?" his father asked. "Or that she has settled down with another man? What if she has another child?"

"I've lived without her my entire life," Jay said. "I can take whatever comes up."

"So are you going to look for her?" his father asked, a long forgotten chord stirring in his heart.

"Maybe I will!" Jay said, letting out a deep sigh.

###

Jay did not look for her. The things that came up at work made him too busy to care. Sure, his real mother was somewhere out there, but his investors had been pressuring him to generate some real money.

By that time Oranax was managing data for a large number of small companies, but a quantum jump in growth had eluded them. As the years had passed, investor patience had withered, increasing the pressure to perform. Oranax needed a marquee client. The problem was that none of the private companies they were pitching to were big enough.

By 2013, Jay realized the obvious choice was to go after the government. No other entity in the country was as big as the government! It was then that they started going after public limited companies. India had some of the world's biggest and busiest organizations. Oranax began pitching to them, showing them how to store their vast amounts of data online, thereby making them smarter. The Railways were his first pitch. Though it failed, it caught the attention of another government giant – India Post!

India's GPO was one of the largest in the world, delivering numerous shipments every day, to the most remote corners of the country. Everything was managed offline. India Post approached Oranax for a more modern solution. It tossed Jay and his team into a crazy work schedule.

Soon, they came up with a plan to store the vast amounts of data in the cloud, thereby saving millions in paper cost. India Post readily agreed and a large contract came Oranax's way. Jay did some really terrific around-the-world hiring to meet the talent requirements of the job. They bought a new office on the 39th floor of the Trident building and began hiring servers.

They started cataloging data from India Post into their secured databases. Life became too busy to care about anything other than business. Jay felt the GPO contract was a sign from God that he should stop thinking about his birth mother. But as fate would have it, as Jay would soon learn, the contract was what would make him look for her.

ENGLAND, 2014

There is strong reason to believe that the association between Tanya Williams and Julian Assange continued after their supposed hacking of the Nortel systems, which got them into legal trouble, and ended with them meeting. From that point onward, while Julian's fame increased to worldwide levels, Tanya Williams' tracks totally disappeared.

After studying at the University of Melbourne, Assange founded WikiLeaks in 2006. What was not known was that exactly two years before, he had mentored Tanya in founding the X Group. WikiLeaks would go on to publish hundreds of exposes over the coming years and it was believed that the X Group, led by Tanya, was its anonymous source.

LIMA, PERU 2008

On 4 November 2008, Tanya was in Lima, staying at the Ritz, which was just blocks away from the office of Hernando Gomez, a key figure in Peru's internal security department and a known government loyalist. He had survived the recent change in the power status quo caused by an oil scandal.

Two months later, in January 2009, WikiLeaks released 86 telephone intercept recordings of Peruvian politicians and businessmen involved in the 2008 Peru oil scandal.

LONDON, 2007

On 31 August 2007, *The Guardian* featured on its front page a story about corruption by the family of the former Kenyan leader, Daniel Arap Moi. The newspaper stated the source of the information as WikiLeaks. If anyone had investigated further, they would have found a young woman named Tanya Williams living at the Ritz, London, just blocks away from the offices of Kroll Associates UK Limited, the company hired by the next President of the United States, to investigate the WikiLeaks matter.

In March 2008, WikiLeaks published what they referred to as 'the collected secret bibles of Scientology', and three days later received letters threatening to sue them for breach of copyright. These leaks happened months after the annual meeting of the Scientology Church in Los Angeles. If anyone had investigated further, they would have found that Tanya Williams, newly initiated as a member of this church, was disbarred soon after the leaks.

In September 2008, during the United States Presidential election campaign, the contents of a Yahoo account belonging to Sarah Palin (running mate to Republican Presidential nominee John McCain), were posted on WikiLeaks, after being hacked by X Group. By now, newspaper readers were aware that Tanya Williams was the Founder-Operator of this hacking entity.

6
The Beginning
File 3/14/JAN /XVII: Top Secret

DELHI, OCTOBER 1947

The British left India in 1947, but they also left many things behind – colossal government buildings built in characteristic colonial style; a massive railway network, which would go on to become the largest in the world; the English language, which would make India the largest English speaking nation six decades later, and an impeccable system of document keeping.

The first Government of India, with Pandit Nehru as its Prime Minister, as well as all subsequent governments, have been most particular about this final legacy. All Government meetings were recorded on paper. All official letters were copied and stored. All records were maintained perfectly.

So when Jay found the piece of evidence in the Russian's file, he found it typed on paper of the best quality, with no tatters, even so many years later.

The date, typed by some office clerk, sat exactly at the top right hand corner: 14 October 1947. The letterhead was bold and clear: Office of the Deputy Prime Minister of India.

The reader may be confused by the title of Deputy Prime Minister, for such a title no longer exists in India. Actually, the title existed for just three years and was held by just one man.

Before the Constituent Assembly of India accepted the Constitution on 26th January 1950, making India a federal Government, it was governed centrally by the Prime Minister's Office, with a Deputy Prime Minister. The Prime Minister from 1947-1950, was Pandit Jawaharlal Nehru. The Deputy Prime Minister was Sardar Vallabbhai Patel.

This paper details a meeting that took place in the PMO between three individuals of the Government and a guest, referred to as one Mr. A. Singh. The conversation that followed and the data Mr. Singh spoke of in the meeting, constitute enough evidence to believe he was the same Major Anish Singh on whose trail we have been.

The other three members of this meeting were most illustrious, the Deputy Prime Minister, Sardar Patel (his name appears clearly as Dy P.M.), Mr. P.M. and Mr. M.K. (the Prime Minister, and Mohandas Karamchand Gandhi, known lovingly as Bapuji). It was standard practice to use initials in shorthand, as the typist had to type at the speed of the conversations, generally quite quickly.

It seems very odd to us today that the three most important men in the country at that time were in a room with Major Anish Singh, who was by then a nonentity. It seemed odd to Jay too, and made him wonder what exactly the agenda of the meeting was.

###

The meeting began in the late afternoon. Major Anish Singh paced the corridors outside uneasily. The enormous height of the ceiling unnerved him. The Secretariat Building in New Delhi was enormous.

"Why don't you take a seat, Sir? The Prime Minister will see you in a few moments," the receptionist at the desk said.

"No thank you, I prefer to be standing," Singh replied, wondering yet again why the Prime Minister wanted to see him.

Less than a week ago, he had received a letter by post, sealed with the new seal of the now independent Government of India. The note had been clear – the Prime Minister wished to confer medals upon veterans of the INA. There was even mention of a pension scheme.

Life had been hard for the Singhs after the birth of their daughter. He had no immediate family to turn to. His distant relatives now lived in the newly formed and hostile Pakistan. Her parents had long been gone, and her maternal relatives lived in Chennai. The pregnancy had been hard on her and she had not been able to continue her medical practice. He had hoped to join the Indian Army, but the Prime Minister had declared that one of the leaving conditions of the British were that no one who had served in INA be recruited into the Indian Army.

Singh had supported the family doing odd jobs but he wasn't sure how long that would continue. He hoped to meet some of his old comrades-in-arms at this medal-conferring event, hoping he might hear of a job opportunity through one of them.

So he was disappointed to find no one at all in the waiting room of the Prime Minister's Office. The Secretary had smiled and told him the Prime Minister was expecting him but he would have to wait for some time.

He had spent half an hour pacing up and down the corridor. Was it all a mistake? Had the letter been wrongly delivered to him? The journey to the Secretariat had taken a fair chunk of what little money he had and he prayed something would come of the visit.

"The Prime Minister will see you now." The receptionist pointed to the ornately carved doors on one side.

Major Singh straightened up to his full height, took a deep breath and walked in. Though he was astonished to see who awaited him in that vast room, he did not let it show on his face. The Prime Minister, or Panditji as he was affectionately known, stood gazing out of the tall windows of his office, the afternoon sun shining on his face and turning his thinning hair to silver. Leaning back in chair, a file in hand, was the Deputy Prime Minister, whose name every Indian from Sindh to Assam knew. And beside him, an enigmatic smile on his face, sat the Father of the Nation.

It is at this point that the transcript document Jay found begins, and runs till the end of the conversation.

Time 12:30 p.m.

Mr. A Singh: Prime Minister Sir! Deputy Prime Minister, Sir! I am honoured to be in your presence.

M.K.: Please take a seat.

Dy. P.M.: Yes, do sit down.

P.M.: So why do you think you are here?

Singh: I thought that I was attending a felicitation ceremony for those who had served in the INA.

Dy P.M.: But instead, you find yourself alone in this room with us.

Singh: I expected a lot of people, Mr. Deputy Prime Minister. That is why I came in the first place; to meet my old comrades.

P.M.: Are you still in touch with these old comrades you speak of?

Singh: None from the INA. However, I am still in touch with some of ex-servicemen who served in the British Army, and live in Dehra Doon.

Dy P.M.: Can you tell us how you come to be here so that Bapuji here understands?

Singh: Three weeks ago, I received a letter by the Ministry of Rewards and Recognition.

Dy. P.M.: No such ministry exists.

P.M.: Pray continue, Major.

Singh: The letter said there was to be a felicitation ceremony, today, at this time and place.

P.M.: And?

Singh: It also said that ex-servicemen of the INA, of officer grade and above, were invited.

Dy P.M.: Did you mention this letter to any of your ex-colleagues?

Singh: As I said before, I am not in touch with any of them. That is why I decided to come in the first place.

M.K.: A small town, isn't it, Dehra Doon?

Singh: Small and without opportunity.

M.K.: Are you contented there?

Singh: No. Being in the army is all I have ever known.

M.K.: And now you can no longer be in the army.

Singh: It seems so.

P.M.: It saddened me to do that but it was one of the conditions Lord Mountbatten laid down before he left India – no ex-servicemen of the INA would be part of our new Indian Army.

Singh: I am not complaining, Sir. Life moves on.

Dy. P.M.: Nevertheless, I suppose we owe you an explanation.

P.M.: And an apology too, for summoning you here under false pretences.

Singh: False pretences?

Dy P.M.: Let us call it a covert summons.

P.M.: And we must also apologize for making you wait.

Dy P.M.: But let it be known that the delay was caused because we could not decide who amongst us should be the one to tell you the truth.

M.K.: And like all hard tasks at hand, these two have left it to me.

Dy P.M.: The Ministry of Rewards and Recognition is housed two floors above, in this very building

P.M.: It is the same place the British Viceroy conducted secret meetings with his generals.

Dy P.M.: The Ministry of Rewards and Recognition consists of five men, each of whom have spent every day since 15th August, doing one thing and one thing only.

Singh: And that is?

Dy P.M.: Going through the files of all ex-INA special ops troops. Congratulations are in order, Major Singh. You have emerged on top of a list of almost a thousand men under review.

Singh: A review for what?

M.K.: For a mission.

Singh: What kind of mission?

M.K.: A mission that will take every ounce of experience you have obtained in your guerrilla operations in Burma. It will put you to test with even greater challenges.

Singh: You mean a covert operation?

M.K.: As I have said before, and I will say it again...I don't believe Subhash is dead. I think he is still alive."

Singh: What!

P.M.: I have seen the papers of the British investigation on this matter. I have read them quite a few times and I can say I have reasonable doubts about his death.

Dy P. M.: Furthermore, even if he's dead, there is the unsolved question of the missing INA war chest he was carrying. Almost 100 pounds of gold, I believe.

P.M.: We want you to go to Taiwan and find out what exactly happened at Formosa. We want you to find him because we believe he is still alive.

Dy P.M.: This will be a covert operation. You will have Government funding, but you will operate on your own.

Singh: Why me?

Dy P.M.: Because you have a wife.

###

As the transcript of the meeting clearly showed, Singh had been chosen for the mission because of his special ops background in the INA, and furthermore, he had a wife. The authorities considered that a man travelling with his wife and a couple of friends would draw no suspicious attention from foreign authorities.

But Singh could not have accepted the mission without consulting his wife first. So he hurried home after his meeting at the PMO. In those days, getting from the capital to Dehra Doon did not take very long. A railway station had been operational in Doon since 1899.

Railway reservation charts from that year clearly show that Singh took an evening train back, just as he had taken a train when travelling to the capital the same morning.

It was close to midnight when he got off the train at Dehra Doon. The Singh house in those days was not more than a hundred metres from the picturesque little station. Rupali, his wife, was not expecting him at that hour. He had told her he had been summoned to an INA felicitation ceremony and expected to be away for at least a day. Lacking means of quick communication in those days meant that a change of plans carried an element of surprise.

So Rupali was somewhat taken aback to see him at their door in less than 24 hours. The noise woke their baby daughter who began crying. Rupali picked her up and fed her while giving her husband a questioning look.

He waited until Azaadi was asleep again. Then he told her all, each and every word that had been spoken at the meeting.

She was as shocked as he had been and took some time to comprehend what was being said. But she recovered her calm quicker than he.

"We have to do this," she said. "We have no choice. It is our duty."

He smiled wryly. "Duty?" He had expected her to throw a fit, to tell him to turn the mission down...but the reverse had happened. Singh was not really surprised. He knew the brave and determined woman his wife was.

'What will we do with Azaadi?" he asked, pointing to their daughter sleeping peacefully in her cradle, sucking her thumb.

Rupali gazed at the baby lovingly. Singh wondered if she would have second thoughts. But her face did not change. Only her glistening eyes gave away the depth of her pain

"Without *Netaji* we couldn't have had Azaadi in the first place," she said quietly, looking at the sleeping child. "If there is any chance he is alive, then it is our duty to go and find him."

Singh turned away, seething with frustration. "*I'll go alone,*" he had pleaded with them in New Delhi. "*Leave my wife out of this.*"

"The whole point of choosing you is because you have a wife who served in the INA," they had told him.

Singh had argued in vain, trying to find another way. There was none.

"You will pose as an Indian businessman and his wife on a business visit," the Deputy P.M. had said. "That will be your cover. If she doesn't go, we won't send you either."

"I have a daughter, you know!" Singh had finally said. "She's just two months old."

"She'll be taken care of," the Prime Minister assured him.

Singh had left the meeting with mixed feelings. The old INA officer in him wanted to jump at the mission; it was his duty to go. But the father in him wanted to take his babe in his arms and run as far from this as he could. So he had decided to let Rupali take the decision. And she had.

"We can't leave Azaadi with our relatives," he warned her. "She'll be placed in some Government orphanage until we come back."

"We *will* come back!" she said, putting her arms around him.

In her arms, Singh felt a sudden sense of comfort. He ran his hands through her hair. She drew him slowly towards the bed.

###

Afterwards, he sat on the edge of the bed, thinking. Rupali lay at his side, not asleep, but spent from their frantic love making. He got up and went for his coat, hanging it on a hook in the corner. He put a hand into a pocket and drew out the cigarette packet lying there. Another habit from the wars, he thought as he struck a match and lit his cigarette slowly. He opened the window to let out the smoke. A gust of cool air came in. He watched the burning tip of the tobacco silently.

Finally, he said, "Do you really want to do this Rupali?"

"Yes," she replied. "I have already told you, it is our duty."

Singh shook his head. Women were far stronger than men, he thought wryly. In that moment he felt overwhelmed by intense love. He finished the cigarette and tossed the butt out of the window. "Then we must leave as soon as possible."

"Where are we going?" she asked simply.

"Taiwan."

"Then its best we go before the winter starts."

"Exactly." Singh rummaged for the old dusty trunk he had pushed under the bed. He pulled it out and blew hard to blow away the dust.

"We'll need a team, won't we?" she asked, slipping into her nightgown again and pulling it down around her.

"The Prime Minister said five persons." Singh opened the latches on each side of the trunk. They snapped open without resistance.

"Have you thought who they should be?"

"I have." The trunk was now open. Singh reached in, his hand touching the coolness of metal.

"They are going to be the old guys, aren't they?" she said.

Singh nodded in silence. He picked up the two Colt pistols lying inside the trunk, feeling the familiar weight in his hands, a smile on his face.

"Well, you already have a doctor." Rupali said, bowing low.

Singh smiled at her. She looked beautiful as she playfully bowed to him, her hair undone, an impish look on her face. Putting the pistols back in the trunk, he got to his feet.

She gasped as his hands moved under the loose gown and rested on her back. “You’re cold,” she said.

“And you’re hot!” he said as he took her to bed again.

7
The Revelations

HONG KONG, 2015

When Jay opened his eyes, morning sunlight filled his room. His head hurt as if it was being bludgeoned by a hammer from within. A bad hangover! He yawned, stretching his arms, planning to turn over and go back to sleep to escape the hammer in his head. But the sight of the empty rumpled sheets beside him brought him instantly awake. Where was his journalist friend from last night?

Jay rose reluctantly, wincing as he walked to the bathroom. The door was ajar and he pushed it open. There was no one there, only the sound of trickling water in the shower. *Was it a dream?* His hand went to his back; he could still feel her scratches on him. Where had she gone? Disappeared into thin air? Jay ran over to the bedside table, looking for his phone. It was not where he remembered leaving it last night. What time was it?

Finally, he found it in front of the mirror, lying there innocently like a TV remote. Jay picked it up and flicked it open, but it would not turn on. The battery was dead. Jay found his charger in a drawer and plugged it into a wall socket. There was nothing he could do but wait.

He noticed his wallet lying on the floor, amongst the pile of his clothes. Instinctively he picked it up and opened the flaps. The cash was still there. Jay was about to flip it away when he noticed something amiss. The wallet felt much lighter. He checked the contents of each fold slowly and cursed. His Platinum cards were missing.

Putting the wallet down on the bed, he reached for his phone. The screen had lit up now, showing the pass code dialogue. Jay entered the code while looking around to see if his cards had fallen out of the wallet. Ding! Jay looked at his phone and entered the code carefully. It made that same noise again. Jay tossed the phone onto the bed, cursing. *He had been robbed!*

Jay looked around for his laptop and found it in front of the mirror. It was still warm! He propped open the screen, which was already lit and showing the password screen. He didn't even try. He knew the password had been changed. Reaching for the landline beside the bed, he dialled reception.

As the phone rang downstairs, Jay felt enormously stupid. How could he have knowingly let that girl seduce and rob him? It was just like in the movies. The operator picked up and mumbled in Mandarin.

"English please," Jay said. "I think I have been robbed."

After several failed attempts to covey his situation, Jay decided to go down to the lobby himself. He dressed and picked up his passport. He was about to walk out of the room when his phone blipped. Jay picked it up and realized a text message had arrived on the locked screen: *Your code is 6996*. Jay pressed the code and the phone unlocked. Immediately, another message arrived: *Meet me in the café. I'll explain everything.*

###

Jay walked into the café to find Tanya dressed in a white skirt with brown stripes, looking gorgeous as she sipped her coffee, a newspaper in her hand. Jay gazed at her for some time and then sat down on the chair beside her.

"Seems like a role reversal," he said when she moved the paper away.

"True!" she laughed. "You were reading a paper and sipping coffee when I met you yesterday. You were much richer too!"

"How much money did you take?" Jay asked, signalling the waiter for a cup.

"One million, to be exact." Tanya licked her lips, "Channelled through various offshore accounts to me. All I had to do was walk around Tokyo withdrawing it from various ATMS."

"How did you do it?" Jay asked, taking the coffee the waiter brought.

"Did you think I was unprepared when I slept with you?" She laughed again. "I had a programme ready. You being a sound sleeper certainly helped."

"Who are you?"

"The answer to that question has a lot to do with why I did not leave."

"It would appear we have both not been completely honest with each other," Jay said reflectively.

"That's lucky for you," Tanya said. "It is the exact reason I did not run away with your money."

"Why?"

"I haven't heard your full story yet. I still don't know why you left the company you founded. I couldn't leave without knowing. So tell me."

Jay smiled. "We will need more coffee for that," he murmured.

###

As far as Jay was concerned, the new contract with the GPO was taking up far too much of time for him and his staff. They remained huddled in their premises in the Trident building for days and nights on end. Months passed speedily. Then the fateful day dawned that would shake his whole world and change everything.

It began when his lead engineer, a tubby Japanese named Shenzhou Lee, peeped into his cabin one evening. "You have a minute Cap?" he asked solemnly.

Jay looked up. Everyone at the office had begun calling him Cap, because of the frequent *we are a ship and we must not sink* speeches he had given in the boardroom during their fund crunch days.

"Sure, Lee." Jay waved for him to come in. "What's up?"

"We just completed uploading the entire postal database into our systems," Lee said, sitting down opposite Jay. "I am amazed by what we have accomplished and the magic we can do with this data."

Jay took off his glasses and smiled. "I'm glad I left it in your capable hands."

"We have gathered data that can be used in ways beyond our own imagination," Lee said excitedly. "Let me show you!"

Jay turned his computer terminal slightly and passed the keyboard to Lee. Lee began clicking and typing immediately, like a child who has just discovered the computer.

"I made an isolated application solely for accessing the data in a visual format." Lee said. "The guys at the Post are going to flip when we tell them all we can do with this."

"What can we do?" Jay asked, putting on his glasses again.

Lee opened up a screen which showed a search terminal. "While cataloguing the data," he said, "my team realized that the highest percentage of information in the database consists of addresses, all types, commercial, residential etc."

"So what did you do with the data?" Jay asked, hands on waist.

"Let me show you." Lee smiled, rubbing his palms together in glee. He typed his own name into the search box: Dr. Shinzkou Lee, then pressed search. The pointer turned into an hourglass. "What we basically did was correlate addresses with names."

"Amazing!"

By then the results were on the screen. Lee pointed. "Look! First, we have all the persons of my name in India." He showed the photos on the screen. "Their facebook profiles are pulled up based on the places their letters were addressed to."

"Not many would share your name here," Jay commented.

Lee nodded, clicking on his own profile. A whole list of items appeared on the screen. "Here, are all the letters addressed to me, sent through India Post. We can't see the contents of the letters obviously, but we have all the records here of when the letters were sent, when they were delivered, and who sent them. Isn't this amazing?"

"Mind blowing," Jay agreed.

"Think of all the things we could do for the Post with this. I'm thinking of customized addresses, automatically redirecting letters sent to old addresses, intelligent letters where addresses won't be needed one day, just a name or QR code would be enough."

"And what about historical records?" Jay asked, raising his eyebrows. India Post was established in 1774, almost three centuries ago "That would make for a shitload of data."

"I was surprised at the extensive and detailed records they had, even from the days of the British Raj," Lee said. "Much of it was offline. Data entry into our systems is what took the most time, and the most people."

"So you have all the records of India Post in your application, from the very beginning?" Jay asked, surprised.

"We have whatever they have conserved," Lee nodded.

"Bravo!" Jay patted him on the shoulder. "This is great work you and your team have done."

"But it is just the beginning," Lee said. "Now, we have to think what we can do with all this data. My team has some ideas."

"Let's schedule a board meeting to discuss your ideas," Jay replied patting him on the back.

"My team and I are going to work 24x7 on this. The potential is huge," he said, reaching out to close the dialogue box on the screen.

"Let it be," Jay said, stopping him.

"You understand this data is classified and for research only, don't you, Cap?" Lee said, suddenly serious.

"Relax, Lee. I just need to explore what you've created. Maybe I can come up with an idea or two of my own."

"Sure, Cap," Lee said. He got up and walked out with his characteristic waddling gait.

When Lee had gone, Jay pressed a button under his table to close the door to his cabin. He also clicked another button that darkened the glass windows around him. Taking a deep breath, he typed in his own name in the search box. Then he selected his own photo.

A thousand results came up and Jay scrolled through them. He found his childhood letters, exam results, letters from home, his own, written from his dorm address, and much more. But it was not what he was looking for. He rubbed his palms and typed in his father's name. In the next window, he selected his father's photo. Another list of results popped up. Jay did a micro search in the new window, under the keyword *sorry.*

Isolated results emerged, showing letters addressed to his father. But Jay still wasn't able to spot what he was looking for. Finally, he set the keyword as *Azaadi*. He clicked and waited as the results loaded for his biological mother.

What he found next made him curse. Only one result had popped up. The dialogue box showed the date and the address. For a moment Jay stared at the screen, his mouth wide open. Then he blinked and refreshed the page. No! His eyes hadn't deceived him. What he was seeing was crystal clear. Silently, Jay clicked the print button and picked up his jacket from the hanger in his cabin. It was late, but he had to go home.

###

Jay threw down the printout on the table. "You lied to me!" he said angrily.

"Will you keep your voice down!" his father whispered, worried his wife would wake up. "Speak softly. Your mother will hear!"

"I'll speak softly if you tell the truth this time," Jay retorted. "You said you were never contacted by my mother after she left, but the record proves otherwise."

His father stared at the printout Jay had thrown down on the table. "Show me," he said.

Jay tossed the paper to him. His father caught it and read silently. Then he sighed. "Where did you find this?" he asked.

"None of your concern," Jay replied harshly. "So you accept she wrote to you?"

"I do. And I have kept the letter. But I thought no good would come of showing it to you."

"You lied to me!" Jay yelled, pointing to the date in the record. "You said you didn't know where she went! But I think this letter was precisely written to tell you that."

"I never thought I'd have to bring it up," his father murmured.

"Well, you're going to have to bring it up now," Jay said, crossing his arms across his chest

His father walked to his desk and bent towards the side drawers where he kept all his documents. After twenty minutes of ruffling through the contents, he finally found a dusty old file and brought it out. Opening it, he showed it to Jay.

The first item was a black and white photograph. Jay recognized the young man as his father. There was a beautiful woman with him.

"That's the only picture I have of her," his father said.

The next item was the letter.

Dear Virag,

First, let me apologize for not writing to you all these days. But I am sure you will forgive me. You know how important this search for my parents is to me. And you know how passionately I have been searching for them all these years.

"You *knew* why she had gone away!" Jay said in disbelief. "She was looking for her parents. Yet you tarnished her memory saying she could have run off with someone else!"

"I'm sorry, son."

Jay stared at his father, his heart and mind in churn. Finally, his eyes fell to the letter and he read on:

I have finally learned that my parents, Major and Dr. Singh, were veterans of the INA, and disappeared in 1947. But they did not go alone. Some others disappeared with them – Harman Singh, Dinesh Khanna, and Irshad Akhtar. A letter reached me a few months ago, when you were away on your research trip. It was written to me by a person called Irshad Akhtar. He was a friend of my parents and the letter was dated 1949. The contents were so intriguing that I had to get up and leave. I hope you'll understand.

Furthermore, I have to go to Hong Kong to get the answers. I write this letter to ask you to come with me. We can leave our son with a friend.

Waiting to hear from you,

Your Azaadi.

"Why didn't you go?" Jay asked, slamming his hand on the table.

His father looked up to meet his gaze. "I did not go to her because I *could* not. I had you to take care of for one. And I had met your mother by then."

"I'm sorry," Jay said. "I should have thought about it from your point of view."

"I'm sorry I never tried to search for her," his father said. "But where would I have searched? No other communication came from her after this letter. I couldn't just book a flight and go to Hong Kong, could I? I never had that much money. I couldn't do anything."

Jay sat down, his hands clasped under his chin. "You couldn't," he said, finally, "but I can."

"What?"

"I can go to Hong Kong."

"But how will you know where to go in Hong Kong?"

"I'll go to the person who wrote to her."

"But how will you find her?"

"The same way I found this." Jay waved the printout.

"If you do find the person who sent the letter, promise me that you'll do what I could not. Promise me you will search for your mother."

Jay looked at his father's lined face. "I will," he promised.

###

Jay opened the laptop as soon as he was inside the cab on his way back to the office. He struggled with the net connection, to access the Internal GPO data on his servers on that rainy Mumbai night. When he was finally in, he didn't waste time. He knew what to type in now: *Azaadi Singh.*

The server displayed a clock on the screen as the search results began to be pulled. There was no photo as his mother had never had a Facebook profile. Jay filtered through the long list of results under the keywords *orphanage* and *Dehra Doon.* When he found the correct person, he clicked and a long list of letters appeared - college records, SSC certificate, tax returns. Finally, he found what he was looking for.

The date read 1989. Addressed to Ms. Azaadi Singh, IIT Bombay, Bombay.

Jay traced his finger across the screen. In the From column was the name of another woman: *Sasha Makijan, Yellow Quarters. Hong Kong.*

Jay scratched his head, confused. He opened the file he had taken from his father and read the lines his mother had written once again: *The letter was sent to me by a person called Irshad Akhtar.* But the postal records could not be wrong. It was certain that the person whose name was on the letter was not the one who had sent it.

So who was Irshad Akhtar? And who was Sasha Makijan? And what was their relation to each other and with his mother's parents? Jay sat in silence for a long time, pondering the puzzle. Finally, he gave up.

By then he had realized there was only one way to find out the truth.

###

Three hours later, Jay returned to his cabin with its glass walls looking out on the lights of the city. Every so often, his fingers would go to the phone on his desk. He would caress the cold steel before retreating to stare into the darkness again.

After much deliberation, he finally picked up the receiver and dialled a number.

"Well, hello Jay." The voice on the other end was British.

"Hello, John. I'm sorry for calling so late," Jay apologized.

"Oh bollocks! You know we fund-managers work all night."

John was Jay's financial manager, who managed his investments.

"I want you to find a buyer for my remaining 6% shares in Oranax Corp," Jay said bluntly.

The words took a moment to register in John's mind. When they did, he went ballistic. "What! Are you nuts?" he shouted. "Why do you want to sell your shares? You have enough funds. You just won a big Government contract."

"Calm down, John. I know it. I just need some money."

"Your valuation is going to rise tenfold once you execute this contract and win others like it. Why in seven hells would you want to put up your shares for sale now when they could be worth so much more later?"

"I need the money *now*." Jay said. "And I'm not asking for your advice. Just tell me are there interested buyers?"

"Interested buyers!" John laughed mirthlessly. "My dear friend, a hundred VCs call me every day for a piece of your company."

"Good. We'll get a good price then."

"You'll get 50 million for your 6% at the moment. And that estimate is on the higher end. I expect the final figure to be lower. It'll be 150 million in a year. Do you really want to do this?"

Jay opened his mouth to answer, but paused for a moment to stare beyond the glass into the dark again. He took a deep breath.

"Jay, you there?"

"Yeah, I'm here. And I'm sure. Get me the best deal possible *today*."

"I'm on it. Anything else you want from me?"

"No." Jay put down the receiver. He knew John would get him a good deal. He did not look out into the darkness anymore. Instead, he switched on his desk light, pulled forward his letterhead, grabbed the silver-nibbed pen on the stand, and began writing his resignation letter.

When he was done, he picked up his cell phone and switched it off. He knew it would be crammed with calls and messages the next morning.

Finally, he took off his jacket and flung it over the back of his chair. He loosened his tie and rolled his sleeves to the elbow. He took his personal cell phone, that only his parents knew about, from a drawer and dialled the first travel agency he found.

"Single ticket to Hong Kong, please," he told the girl at the other end.

As he reached the elevator doors to leave the building, his phone rang again. It was John.

"The highest offer I got was 42mil. After taxes, you should get 35."

"Process it," Jay said. "And channel the money to my international account."

"Wilco. But Jay, let me ask you again before I press the buttons. Do you really have to do this?"

"Two decades ago, another person had the same choice to make." Jay said. "And I say what he must have said, John: Yes!" He shut his phone and walked into the elevator. The doors closed behind him with a swish.

John, thousands of miles away, scratched his head, wondering who Jay had been referring to. 'The man had gone mad!' Shaking his head, he processed the deal.

PARIS, 2008

On that fateful night, Tanya was sitting in a café in Paris, sipping coffee with the WikiLeaks portal open on her laptop when a chat box popped up on her screen. It displayed that a user called bradass87 was trying to send her a message request.

The WikiLeaks portal was based on anonymity of sources. People had chat accounts on the backend of the website where they could indulge in discussions or one-on-one chats with the editors, with full anonymity. This time, a new user was trying to send her a message.

(1:41:12 PM) bradass87: hi

(1:44:04 PM) bradass87: how are you?

(1:47:01 PM) bradass87: I'm an army intelligence analyst, deployed to eastern Baghdad,

(1:58:31 PM) bradass87: if you had unprecedented access to classified networks 14 hours a day 7 days a week for 8+ months, what would you do?

Tanya took a deep breath. The user was implying that he was willing to share classified data of the US army. Either this was a big joke, or very serious.

(6:07:29 PM) info@adrianlamo.com: What's your MOS? Tanya typed

(3:16:24 AM) bradass87: re: "What's your MOS?" – Intelligence Analyst (35F)

(10:14:44 AM) bradass87: Location: Iraq

(10:14:50 AM) bradass87: I can't sleep with what I know. I gotta tell it to someone. I figured it could be you.

That much was enough for Tanya. She decided to take the case to Assange at once. She called and told him that an unknown man had contacted her with the intention of leaking classified data of the US army.

However, as would be later revealed, it wasn't actually a man.

###

In fact, bradass87 was a woman. It turned out that she was a US marine called Chelsea Manning. And she was sitting on a vast amount of data she had discovered with her access to classified army data. This data constituted vast logs of the Afghan wars, smuggled from military databases, and smuggled onto her private servers. She had first intended to send the materials to the Washington Herald. But when they did not show interest, she passed them on to WikiLeaks.

"Seems like hot stuff," Tanya told Assange. "We shouldn't touch it."

He laughed. "You think I'm stupid enough to create such a dangerous enemy?"

Tanya was relieved. But apparently he was not serious, because one month later, that was exactly what happened.

###

The fall of Julian Assange began with the release of the Manning material on WikiLeaks. A drone operation video with civilian casualties went viral almost immediately. With this action, Assange joined a group of men in history, from Hitler to Saddam, who made the same mistake - he messed with the USA.

After WikiLeaks released the Manning material, U.S. authorities began investigating WikiLeaks, and Assange personally, with a view to prosecuting both under the Espionage Act of 1917.

Assange was meanwhile trapped in a sexual harassment lawsuit in Sweden. The US government soon realized they couldn't damage WikiLeaks because it was based out of the continent, on ethical journalistic practices. However, there was a major entity under WikiLeaks, the entire operations of which were completely illegal, that they could target. So they gave the green light to the National Security Agency to proceed.

The NSA came down hard on the X Group. The CIA already had lengthy dossiers on all members of the hacking community. Those on US soil were arrested immediately. Those who were not, were placed on Interpol's Most Wanted list. Most were soon caught in Eastern European countries. The rest could do nothing but flee westwards.

Tanya Williams was one of them. She first took the euro rail to get from Paris to Greece. From there, she managed to get a seat on a shady shipping line to cross the Mediterranean. She holed up at an acquaintance's place in Crete for a while. Realizing that INTERPOL was after her, she wondered what to do next. Mustering her courage, she finally called Assange in Sweden, where he was detained, from a telephone booth.

"You need to get away as far as you can from this mess," he told her.

"But where would I go?" she asked, feeling vulnerable for the first time in many years.

"To the other end of the world if you can. First, get away. Take some time to breathe freely, then figure out what to do next."

After he hung up, Tanya considered what would be a perfect safe house for her, to calculate her next move. *An island*, she thought, *disconnected from the land, but still having modern amenities, and opportunities to disappear.* Where would she find such a place?

She found it two minutes later, going through Google Maps on her phone. Such a place did exist, though very far away. If she was careful, she could get to it in the next few weeks. It was across the expanse of Russia, in the Pacific Ocean, in the Far East. An island city exactly as she wanted.

It was called Hong Kong.

###

As Jay began his journey towards the momentous secret he would soon uncover, the wheels of the machinery that would work to stop him had begun to roll.

Far away, in Moscow, a middle-aged Russian was woken from his slumber by the irritating ringing of his cell phone. He struggled out of his comfortable bed and cursed as he groped to find his phone on the bed stand. But when he saw the contact name on the screen, his manner changed. The lines on his face became taught. This was a call he had hoping never to receive.

"Hello."

"Alexis!" The voice on the other end was computerized. "The target is on it."

Alexis paused for a moment before saying, "Are you sure? It has been more than two decades."

"I'm damn sure!" the mechanical voice said. "The target has booked a ticket to Hong Kong."

Alexis flicked on the light switch by his bed and the room flickered into light. "I guess the mission is a go then?"

"Yes. You know the stakes."

"I know."

"Do you know whom to use?"

"I do," Alexis said. "After all, we've planned it all before. Those two are a pair of sore assholes," Alexis sighed.

"But they have a history with this case."

"Okay, I'm on it."

"Don't fuck it up like last time!" the voice said.

Alexis cleared his throat. "Those were different times," he muttered, "different people. "

"Do not underestimate this one, Alexis," the voice warned. "He's an intelligent target."

"I won't."

"Then go, make the KGB proud, and save our souls."

Alexis sighed and put the phone back on his bed stand. He looked at his wristwatch. It was 1:00AM. The beginning of a series of sleepless nights... The first step was simple. He had to make some phone calls. It was time to call in that pair of sore, irritating heavyset Russians.

8
The Russians

2015

The room was old-fashioned in build but ultra-modern in its decor. The fact that it had no windows did not seem to bother the massive Russian who sat there, smoking and staring at the wall. His wide shoulders moved as he brought the cigar to his lips for each puff. The smoke travelled up to the ceiling and lingered there, giving the room a hazy look.

Another Russian entered and looked at the first man in amusement. "Hasn't that thing killed you yet Sergei?" he asked, waving his hands to clear the smoke.

The vast Sergei turned, a big smile on his face. "Good to see you, too, Char," he said. "What's it been? Two years?"

"One year and eight months," Charkov replied precisely, pulling a chair forward and sitting down. "What are you doing here?"

"I've been called for a job. Fancy running into you."

"I'm here for a job as well," Charkov muttered, knowing it was no coincidence that Sergei was there too.

"Bloody krauts and their secretive ways! Couldn't just tell us we were going to be working together, could they?"

"It's been a while, Serg. How are you keeping?"

"Retirement doesn't suit me," Sergei complained through pursed lips. "Took up a couple of jobs; tried my hands at being a Security Manager at a bank. Bloody idiots couldn't take my criticisms about the security system, so they fired me."

"You're just like me then," Charkov remarked, "sitting at home with nothing better to do."

"That's why I came when I got this call," Sergei said. "Wouldn't have bothered otherwise. What a coincidence you are here too!"

"I don't think it's a coincidence at all."

"What do you mean?"

"I think we have been chosen Serg, for something."

"For what?"

"I mean that our ex-paymasters were especially looking for us."

Sergei scratched his head. "You think so? What job could the KGB have for two retired operatives like us?"

"The kind of job the agency needs done but doesn't want to get involved in," Charkov said dryly.

"That sound like the kind of job I like," Sergei laughed. He finished his cigar and pushed the stub into an old ashtray that had seen better days.

"I worry, Serg," Charkov murmured. "I've got a bad feeling about what's to come."

"Relax, my friend. You always get a bad feeling about everything."

The two men waited in the room till their handler finally walked in and greeted them in Russian. "How are the two of you doing?" Alexis asked, holding a bunch of files.

"You know exactly how we're doing," Charkov said, ignoring the hand Alexis had extended.

"Yeah, we guess you have all that in those files you're holding," said Sergei.

"We know everything, gentlemen," Alexis agreed, "but it doesn't hurt to be polite does it?"

"But it hurts me to waste time," Charkov said shortly. "Can we move on now?"

"Yes. I forgot you're such busy individuals, aren't you?" Alexis responded sarcastically. He placed the files on the table and sat down.

"Fine, have it your way. So what do you want us to do?" Sergei asked.

"First of all, I want you to address me as The Boss, here onwards," Alexis said, his voice clipped and cold.

"Why?" Sergei laughed, glancing over at Charkov.

Alexis leaned forward and placed his elbow on Sergei's big palm and pressed down hard.

Sergei yelled in pain. "What's the matter with you?" he shouted.

Alexis' face did not change. He pressed harder. Sergei growled in pain, stomping his feet on the ground. "I get it, Boss Man!" he said.

"Good." Alexis smiled as he released the pressure.

Sergei caressed his aching palm as Charkov watched in amusement. "So what does the Agency want from us?" he asked Alexis.

"The Agency needs your help with a delicate mission,"

"I told you the Agency does not believe in retirement plans, Char," Sergei commented sourly.

"So what help does the Agency want?"

"To avoid scandal."

"What scandal?" Sergei asked.

"A scandal from the past." Alexis smiled. "Your past."

"I don't understand."

"You are both second generation enforcers of the KGB," Alexis said. "Let us say this is something that had to do with the first generation."

"So is it something our fathers did?" Sergei asked.

"Precisely." Alexis laid out a file. "Do you remember your families ever speaking of Operation Barbarossa?"

"Our families were diehard KGB," Charkov said. "You reckon they'd ever speak of missions outside those missions?"

Sergei glanced at the file lazily. "1945," he muttered. "It's a long way back, even before we were born."

"Yes, it was," said Alexis."That's exactly why we chose you."

"So where are we going?" Sergei asked, losing interest in the doings of his father.

Alexis smiled. "Hong Kong."

###

When Tanya landed in Hong Kong, she invariably burnt all her cash. But that wasn't a problem. She was a trained hacker. She could steal anybody's money. ATMs and electronic accounts were playthings for her.

But Tanya was no longer interested in small change. She was now tired of the chase and wanted to disappear; retire to the Cayman Islands maybe, or the exotic tropical locations of Indonesia or Thailand. For that she needed money...big money.

So she did the best thing possible. She checked into the Grand Hyatt, the largest hotel in Hong Kong. It was known to be frequented by billionaires and Saudi Princes, who had come to Hong Kong for business or pleasure. All she had to do after checking in was to hack into the hotel database. That was child's play, for there was a direct connection to the local server in the digital room service menu.

Once she was in, she quickly downloaded a list of all the hotel guests, quickly deleting executives staying at the hotel on company money. She was considering a media mogul when another interesting profile came up. She googled it. What she read in the search results made her mouth open wide.

In another hour, Tanya had made her choice.

Now all she needed was an action plan.

###

"I don't know why, but this feels like an Indiana Jones movie," Tanya said once they had finished explaining everything to each other.

"Is that because you are British?" Jay asked, finishing his coffee.

She stamped her heel on his foot. "I'm Australian!"

"Ouch!" Jay rubbed his foot with the other. "I could never have told."

"I have decided to give you your money back."

"That's most generous."

"And I'm going to stay and help you with your search!"

"That's too generous," Jay said.

"Your story interests me," Tanya said. "I have an inkling it is going to turn out to be more interesting than you had ever hoped."

"With you by my side the interest level is sure to be hundredfold."

"Plus you won't have to sleep alone." Tanya bit into a banana.

"What's your take?"

"Once we solve the mystery of your grandparents," Tanya said, "you help me to disappear. You give me some money and help me change my identity and move to...Indonesia perhaps."

"I can do that," Jay said.

"Then here's a high five." Tanya raised her palm.

Jay touched her palm with his own. "Seems reasonable," he said.

"More than reasonable," she drawled, "because I'm a brilliant lay."

9
The Team
File 4/14/Jan/XVII: Top Secret

1947

Major and Mrs. Singh kept no diaries or accounts of any part of their lives. But, as it happens, their partners, who went on this secret mission with them, did. And those diaries were what Jay managed to find after returning to India. The first one belonged to Harman Singh Soni, a fellow Punjabi from Dehra Doon. According to his diary, Harman was a truck driver in X Division. There were many references to Major Singh in his diary.

> *Singh Sir shortlisted me today to go on the expedition to Kohima. I am to drive a Jeep through the rocky mountain pass. An easy enough task if not for the fact that the bus is going to be filled with explosives.*
>
> *We hit the guard post at Kohima hard. Singh Sir is really happy with me.*
>
> *The war is over, but our beloved leader is dead in a plane crash. My tears cannot stop flowing.*
>
> *I stand trial today. Even if I'm sentenced to death, I shall face it like a man, for my motherland.*
>
> *Almost all of us have been acquitted. I have no family to go to. Wonder where I will go?*
>
> *Singh Sir asked me to come with him to Dehra Doon. He thinks that my skills with vehicles could be of use there. Rupali Ma'am was kind as well.*
>
> *We opened a garage in Dehra Doon. It has begun to work very well.*

According to these jottings, it would appear that there was regular communication between Harman and the Singh family. Apparently, Harman was also a regular invitee for dinner at the Singh house. So Harman felt no surprise when Singh went to meet him at the garage in October 1947.

According to the diary entry, it was exactly the day after Singh's meeting at the PMO in New Delhi. Harman was working under a truck when Singh arrived and tapped on the truck's upraised hood. Harman cursed as he retreated from below the vehicle but immediately apologized when he saw who it was.

Smiling, Singh said, "We need to talk."

Harman washed his greasy hands and came forward. "Would you like some tea?" he asked.

Singh politely declined; his mind on more important matters. They sat in the makeshift office Harman had put up. It served him well enough. A wall mounted fan blew cool air over them.

"You've made a nice place here," Singh said, looking around.

Harman nodded humbly. "Business has been good."

"What would you say if I told you to leave all this and come with me?" Singh asked.

He had expected Harman to fumble for the answer, but the Sardar was quick to say, "Of course, I'd come with you! I'd travel anywhere in this world with you. You made this garage possible after all."

"I must rephrase," Singh said solemnly. "What if I asked you to come with me on a mission where we have almost zero chance of returning alive?"

Harman gave a laugh. "You've asked me this before, during the war," he said, "You know what my answer was then. It is the same now."

Singh looked at his old comrade-in-arms. "You always had a tendency to say yes before you actually understood what you were saying yes to. Remember the Hanna canyon?"

"How can I forget?" Harman said, sitting back in his chair. "We gave the Brits hell that night! I drove the armored Jeep right through the canyon with a hundred of them on our tail."

"And you thought it was going to be just another drive, that mission," Singh reminded him.

Harman laughed again. "Yes, but did you see me complaining?"

"No, but none of those missions were as big as this one is." Singh let out a sigh. Of all the men in arms, they had been chosen for this death mission.

"Never thought we'd be going on another mission again," Harman said, eyes alight with excitement. "I thought, not a chance after they refused to have us in the army."

"Well, as it turns out," Singh said, "civilian life is not for us."

"Where are we going?"

"You'll know when we go." Singh grinned. It was what he had always said to the young Punjabi.

"What do I need to know?"

"It is a search and rescue mission; a covert operation."

"Things will get hot?"

"We will be landing right in the middle of a burning volcano."

Both men laughed at the image.

"That isn't a problem," Harman said. "I've already told you, I'd follow you to hell. You made all of this possible." He waved his hands around him.

Singh got up. "I'll contact you," he said.

Harman rose too. "Who is it we are going to rescue?"

Singh smiled. "The other man who made our lives possible." Turning, he walked away quickly.

###

The shooter the Singhs took with them was Dinesh Kumar. He had served under Singh since the start of his career in the British army. Actually, it was Dinesh, Singh was carrying in his arms when the Japanese captured them. Dinesh was with Singh when they became POWs of the Japanese, and he was with Singh when Singh was inducted into the INA. Dinesh was with Singh to the very end.

His military papers described him as of quiet bearing but exceptionally good with a pistol or rifle. One of his officers had added the subtext that he spoke with his gun, not his mouth.

After independence, Dinesh had settled in New Delhi, working as a janitor. But Singh kept in contact with him and knew his whereabouts.

The meeting we refer to, took place in October 1947, when both Singh and Harman, visited Dinesh. The ex-shooter had opened a shop selling groceries, in Agra. The meeting lasted an hour, after which the three men left together. Dinesh simply downed the shutters of his shop and followed Singh. He was never seen again.

###

There is reason to believe there was an argument between believe Major and Mrs. Singh over the inclusion of the last member of the team, at the end of October 1947. Who eventually won the argument was crystal clear when Rupali went alone to recruit the last member of the team.

Not much data is available in the archives about the elusive character who was the last to go on one of the most complicated missions in the history of covert operations. Irshad Akhtar – that is the name that appears in his military records. But after the war, he used a dozen different aliases. In 1947, his place of residence was shown as Old Delhi.

Notes about him, written by his comrades in the INA, show him to be a devout Moslem, one who would recite *namaz* every day at the appointed time, rain or shine. One of the donors at the Old Jama Masjid, in 1947, was one Irshad Akhtar. If it was the same man, then judging by the generous amount donated, he had become a wealthy man after the war.

Akhtar led Division Z in 1944-1945, the second Guerilla Division of the INA after Division X, which was led by Singh himself. Military records show Akhtar was a resolute commander and he was mentioned a dozen times in dispatches. The notations indicate he was a Sniper, one who would attack from afar, using a high-powered rifle with a scope.

Records of his pre-war life are as sparse as his post-war days, giving rise to the theory that Irshad Akhtar was not, in fact, his true name. The mystery surrounding Akhtar make one thing clear – he was a dangerous man, involved in illegal activites. This, coupled with the fact that Mrs. Singh went to see him alone, gives us reason to believe she knew him from before. And the fact that Singh was not involved in this meeting, suggests he did not want to see Akhtar, let alone include him in the mission.

Train records show Rupali went to Delhi on 30th October 1947. She took the early morning train from Dehra Doon and the 8pm train back the same evening. The quick trip indicates she knew where to find him.

She found him by his old habit of going to the mosque for *namaz*. When he spotted her standing outside the Jama Masjid that afternoon, he was more surprised than he had ever been in his life.

"Rupali!" he greeted her, a broad smile flashing across his usually taciturn face. "You're supposed to be married, aren't you?"

"And you're supposed to be hidden, aren't you?" she retorted, smiling.

"How did you find me?" he asked, pulling off his skull cap.

"Oh it wasn't hard," she told him. "The last letter you sent me was from Chandni Chowk post office. So I figured you were living in this area."

"And so all you had to do was stand outside the local masjid and catch me walking down the steps!" he chuckled. "Well, well, good thing the police aren't as sharp as you!"

"The police *are* as sharp, but you don't write them letters, do you?"

Akhtar laughed heartily. "Where are my manners? Let's find a place and catch up. It's been what, *three* years?"

They strolled to a nearby tea shop and sat down. Rupali saw that Akhtar's eyes were continuously fixed on her.

"Why haven't you answered my letters?" he asked her when they had sat down and ordered some tea and biscuits.

"I just did, didn't I?"

"Turning up like a bolt from the blue!"

"You always knew where I was. If you were missing me so much, you could have come to visit."

"With your husband in the house, or without him?" he asked slyly.

She did not smile. "I'm here to speak about an important matter," she told him seriously.

"You never did like foreplay much," he remarked, signalling to the tea shop owner for a cigarette.

Without warning, she slapped him hard, causing the people around them to turn to look at them.

Akhtar rubbed his cheek ruefully. "*I* used to like it though, remember?"

"You haven't changed one bit!" she muttered through clenched teeth.

"Nor have you. Beautiful as ever!" He stared at her shamelessly. His gaze stopped when he reached the *mangal sutra* around her neck.

"Are you still a practicing doctor?" he asked, handing her one of the tea glasses the serving boy had brought.

"I know what you are going to say next."

He laughed, "I'm a changed man now, Rupali."

"Doesn't seem that way!" she said curtly.

"Well, I haven't invited you up to my apartment, have I?"

"One more tasteless wisecrack and consider me gone," she told him.

"I've heard that from you countless times." He looked into her eyes. "Do you remember what happened the last time?"

She was the one who looked away. "I'm not here to talk about all that," she said, taking a sip of the steaming tea.

"Then you can begin by telling me why you haven't answered any of my damned letters."

"I'm married now." She looked at him, her gaze unflinching. "I love my husband. And he doesn't think that I should be writing to you."

"I still can't believe you married *him*!" Akhtar said tersely, "Sore Singh, we used to call him."

"I'm going." Rupali put the glass of tea down with a thud and got urgently to her feet.

Akhtar looked up at her with interest. "It was nice to see you too," he said, bringing the cigarette to his lips.

Rupali walked away into the crowd, her heart beating fast, silently cursing herself. This was not at all how she had expected this meeting to go. She had expected Akhtar to listen to her.

She hadn't walked more than halfway down the street when she heard him call out to her. She turned to find him standing there in the crowd.

"No more vile remarks," he said, raising his hands. "Do I also have to hold my ears?"

That brought a smile to her lips. They walked on to the park around the corner and sat down on a bench.

"So why are you here?" he asked her.

She told him. He was silent for quite some time. His face wore a grim expression as he stared at his chappals.

"So will you come?" she finally asked.

"I want to," he said, closing his eyes. "I really do. I want to come so much that I don't know how to say no to you."

"You don't have to say no."

"Really?" He gave her a disbelieving look. "You really want to put me and Singh in the same room after all that has happened in the past?"

"I am a Singh as well, now." she stated simply.

He did not have a comeback for that and sat there silently.

Rupali watched for some time. "It's for the greater cause," she finally said.

"I understand what it's for." He looked at her. "But I believe it will end badly."

"What are you doing with your life anyway?" she asked with a shrug. "That's going to end badly too."

"I'm doing fine," he responded, lighting another cigarette.

"You are a common criminal," she whispered angrily. "A murderer."

"Weren't we all?" he asked, taking a puff. "It the only thing we've ever known how to do. The only thing the war taught and left us with."

"That was for the independence of our country. Now you work as a gun on hire for the criminal scum of this city."

"You speak ill of my vocation," he observed with a smile. "I do the same thing I did in the INA - shoot people from afar with my sniper rifle." He sucked in the tobacco smoke. "But now it pays much more." He waved his wrist with its gold Rolex at her.

"I told you," she said, "that was for the independence of our country."

"Our country!" he sighed. "I'm no longer sure this is *my* country. Not after what happened six months ago," he said, referring to the partitions that had taken place as the British left. The country had been cut into two - India and Pakistan - one for Hindus, the other for Muslims. But life was never so clearly defined. Countless people on both sides had died as one of the greatest crossover migrations the world had ever known, took place.

"Netaji would not have let that happen," Akhtar said after a moment of painful pause. "You remember the INA don't you? It did not matter what was your religion or caste was, you were simply part of the Indian National Army." He flicked his cigarette away, his face sad.

"Then come on this mission for the sake of what could have been," she urged. "For what you owe the man we are going in search of."

He met her gaze. They looked at each other and time seemed to pause expectantly.

"I'm in," he finally said.

10
The Meeting
File 5/14/Jan/XVII: Top Secret

Hotel records show that the complete team was together for the first time on 14 November 1947, in New Delhi. It was the Prime Minister's birthday and as people thronged the streets to celebrate the day, Singh and the other four sat holed up in a conference room in the Ritz, the largest hotel in the city.

Pandit Nehru celebrated his birthday three floors below them in the grand Platinum Hall. The top leadership, including the Deputy Prime Minister and the Father of the Nation, were present. It is believed they used the opportunity to meet the whole team, though no proof exists of this.

Hotel entries show that Singh and the others remained at the hotel for a week, starting from that date. It was here that they set up the preliminary plan of action they later followed. Major and Mrs. Singh, accompanied by Harman, were the first to arrive. Dinesh Khanna joined them soon after. As was to be expected, Akhtar was the last to arrive.

Singh greeted him coldly with, "You're *late.*"

"I had stuff to take care of," Akhtar said, taking off his skull cap and sitting down. He folded his hands and leaned back, placing his legs on the table, pointing them squarely at Singh.

"Stuff more important than this?" Singh asked sarcastically.

Akhtar did not bother to answer. Instead, he scanned the others in the room. "Always nice to see you Rupali," he said, giving her a smile. which she did not return. "Harman Singh, the Punjabi Tank!" He rose to give the Sikh a playful punch on the shoulder. "How are you doing?"

"Just fine," Harman said, clearly uncomfortable with the tension in the room.

"Dinesh Khanna!" Akhtar formed a gun with his hands and pointed it at him. "You still as good as you used to be?"

"I believe so," Dinesh nodded solemnly.

"Why are you late?" Singh asked, leaning against a wall with arms folded.

"I told you, I had things to take care of." Akhtar waved a hand. "Now get a move on, will you?"

"I will," Singh replied calmly, "but first, some things to make clear."

Akhtar gave a yawn and closed his eyes.

Singh stepped away from the wall. "First of all, from this point on, this mission is the most important thing in our lives." He leaned over a chair and said, "You will wipe from your mind thoughts of everything else. All your mind space must be dedicated to this..."

"When are we leaving?" Akhtar asked, interrupting.

"We'll leave when it is time to leave," Singh snapped.

"Could you be a little more specific?" Akhtar spun an empty glass on the table before catching it. "Got a job to do before we leave."

"Didn't you hear what I just said?" Singh asked.

"No, my attention was elsewhere," Akhtar replied brashly, his gaze lingering on Rupali.

Singh banged his fist on the table angrily, looking at his wife. She shrugged helplessly. His angry gaze came back to Akhtar. "Let's get one thing clear here and now: I'm in charge on this one."

"Sure." Akhtar smiled in an offensive way. "You always loved to be in charge of everything. Now I...I hate being in charge of anything. So that's just fine by me."

"You'll do what I tell you to do," Singh said.

"As long as it is what I want," Akhtar replied, equally defiant.

"You're a sore bastard!" Singh said, folding his arms.

"I think I'd rather have a smoke than waste my time here." Akhtar got up and walked out of the room.

Singh looked at Rupali. "Not working."

She shrugged and said, "I'll go after him."

###

Akhtar stood leaning against the ornate railing of the staircase, one hand on the banister, the other holding a cigarette.

"You said you'd behave," Rupali said from behind him.

Akhtar turned. She was leaning against the opposite wall, her arms crossed.

"Did I?" he said bitterly. "I'm sorry then."

"He's behaving," she said, pointing to the closed door fot he room they had just left. "Why don't you?"

"He's behaving!" Akhtar scoffed. "Snapping at me isn't behaving."

"Well, you *were* late..."

"Going to take his side on this one?" Akhtar smoked furiously.

"Always...when he is right."

Akhtar did not reply.

"You aren't allowed to smoke in here," she pointed out.

"And you aren't supposed to infiltrate a foreign country and rescue an important POW either!"

"It's on account of these expensive carpets."

"Well, if we are to have a chance of succeeding in our mission," he said, "I have to do this." He dropped the glowing cigarette but onto the plush maroon carpet and stomped on it. It burnt a hole in the carpet.

That brought a smile to her lips, though it disappeared almost as soon as it had appeared. "Look at the bigger picture," she told him.

"Are you in that picture?" he asked slyly.

"No flirting, Irshad!"

"How can I resist when you call me Irshad like that!"

She was about to answer when the conference room doors opened and Singh strode into the hallway. He walked over to them.

"I thought you'd understand the seriousness of this," he said, looking Akhtar squarely in the eye.

"I do," Akhtar replied, "but the best way to counter seriousness is with humour."

"I thought you'd show some respect for the man we are going to search for."

"You know I have immense respect for him. It is why I am here. What I don't have is the same for you."

"You don't have to," Singh said. "All you have to do is not let your bitterness come in the way of our mission."

"I can do that."

"We've done it once before..." Singh reminded him.

Akhtar nodded. "That did not turn out too well."

"We have both learnt from our mistakes."

"Indeed we have."

"So will you behave?" Rupali asked.

Akhtar nodded, his eyes never leaving Singh.

"You must shake on it," Rupali said, looking from one to the other.

Singh stretched out his hand. Akhtar looked at it for a few seconds; then he nodded and shook it.

"Let's start the meeting then," Rupali said.

They walked back into the room, closing the doors behind them.

###

The Prime Minister and the Deputy Prime Minister stepped into the room at an opportune moment. Singh had laid out a large map of the Far East on the table and everyone was bent over it, inspecting it closely. So much so, that they failed to notice that the two most powerful men in the country were standing behind them.

Pandit Nehru and Sardar Patel watched their elite team for a few moments, before the Prime Minister cleared his throat to recall their attention. They all turned and Singh immediately sprang to attention and saluted.

"Happy Birthday, Sir!" they chorused.

Pandit Nehru smiled and sat down at the head of the table. "We don't have much time before the people at my party start to wonder where I've disappeared to," he chuckled. "But I daresay the time we do have is enough."

Sardar Patel leaned on Pandit Nehru's chair. "Your mission requires enormous courage and skill," he said quietly.

"Neither of which is of any use without commitment and dedication to the cause," Pandit Nehru added.

"We know you possess all three," Sardar Patel said.

"I'll be brief. You have the unofficial support of my Government, and all the money you need. But once you leave, you will be on your own."

"There will be dangers every step of the way," Sardar Patel said. "Your journey may take you to unexpected places. But you've been through all of it before. So all I want to say is: May you be victorious! And may you find our Netaji alive and well, and bring him home." With that, the Deputy Prime Minister stood up straight, preparing to leave.

Pandit Nehru rose from his seat. "God be with you on this journey," he said solemnly, turning to leave. At the door he turned and looked back. "I just wish... I could go too."

Both statesmen left the room and the door closed behind them.

11
RENKOJI
FILE 6/14/JAN/XVII: TOP SECRET

1948

The mission for the search and rescue of Netaji Subhash Chandra Bose began on 23rd November 1947. The team flew from New Delhi to the Far East in a cargo plane. It was one of the most secret operations to be ever pulled off in the history of the country. The flight records show they were bound for Singapore. What the flight plan did not show, however, was that after the refuelling stop at the British colony, they flew on north and did not stop till they landed in the Land of the Rising Sun – Japan.

###

Singh sat in the hold, cross-legged, as he pondered over the files the Prime Minister had handed over to him. 'You are one of the very few men in our country to see these files,' he had said. 'And I'd like to keep it that way.'

Singh turned the pages one by one, reading what he had read a dozen times before embarking on this journey.

Harman emerged from the door to the hold and bowed slightly. Singh returned the greeting with a quick wave. Harman walked up and sat down beside him as Singh closed the file with a sigh. He put it on top of the others beside him.

"Did the British botch the job of looking for our leader?" Harman asked, looking at the closed files.

"Quite the reverse," Singh said quietly. "I must say they did one hell of a good job."

"A good job without finding him at all?" Harman asked.

"They did find considerable anomalies in the way he is said to have met his end."

"Why did they stop looking then?" Harman wrapped his arms around his knees as he sat on the floor of the vibrating craft.

"The Brits didn't have much motivation for finding him," Singh said, tapping on the files. "All they were looking for was a missing war criminal. It is different for us. Besides, they had their own problems to deal with after leaving India. This wasn't exactly a priority."

"What did they manage to find?" Harman asked.

"They tracked him from Singapore, from the day he left."

"We were there," Harman coughed, "when he left."

"In his last speech, he told us he was going to Tokyo to negotiate a separate surrender of the Provincial Government of India. But the Brits believe he was going to do something entirely different."

"And what made them think that?"

"First of all, his flight plan." Singh pulled out a file. Opening it, he pointed to a page. "On leaving Singapore, he went to Bangkok. From there he went to Saigon, staying there for just one day."

"Then he went to Tokyo, right?"

"That's exactly what we all think," Singh said. "But the fact is that from Saigon, he went to Tourane."

"Isn't Tourane a little out of the way?" Harman said.

"There's more. The plane he flew in from Saigon to Tourane, was not the same one he took from Singapore."

"What...why?" Harman burst out.

"Some Jap officers confessed in their post-war interrogations that the US forces had put in place an order following the surrender that no private planes would fly in the Indo-China airspace. Netaji had flown with his associates, from Singapore, in a private plane."

"So what did they do?"

"The Japs put him and one other, in a Mitsubishi K21 Bomber."

"We called that beautiful bomber Sally," Harman remembered. "What a delicate piece of shit!"

"And guess who Netaji took with him in the bomber?" Singh asked, turning to look at Harman, his face giving nothing away.

"Who was it?"

"Habibur Rehman," Singh said.

"Doesn't make any sense." Harman rubbed his chin thoughtfully. "If he was going to negotiate a separate surrender, why would he take a two-bit gunner with him?"

"Especially when there were diplomats and ambassadors already with him," Singh agreed.

"What else did the Brits find out?"

"That Rehman survived the crash. The rest of the story is basically his testimony, which matches those of the Jap military men and doctors."

"If it all matches," Rehman said, eyes on the ground, "then why are we in this plane?"

"Because there are fallacies. No Death Certificate exists. The photographs of his body do not have his birthmarks. Habibur's testimony changes and he contradicts himself."

"Fucking Moslem!" Harman swore. "Did he sell Netaji out?"

"Did I just hear you say *Fucking Moslem*?" The sharp raspy voice could only belong to Akhtar. Singh and Harman turned to look. Akhtar stood leaning against the metal door leading into the main fuselage.

"Were you spying on us?" Singh asked.

"What difference does it make?" Akhtar walked up to them, "We're a team aren't we?"

"I don't like your shady ways," Singh said, closing the file.

"My shady ways are what I believe will keep us alive in the coming months," Akhtar said dryly. "You should learn the skill from me."

"I don't need to learn anything from you," Singh snapped.

"Why don't you continue the story?" Akhtar suggested. "We hate to be kept hanging, Harman and I," he said, patting the unresponsive Sikh on the back.

"Well, as it turns out," Singh said, "the Brits did discover where Netaji's ashes were taken after the plane crash."

"Where?" Harman asked, agog to know.

"To Renkoji Temple, in Tokyo."

"So are we going there?" Akhtar asked.

"I don't know where to start," Singh said, letting out a deep breath. "A part of me wants to go to Taiwan, where his plane crashed. But first we have to know where to look."

"Torn are you?" Akhtar said with a quick grin. "You should ask your wife how that feels."

"She was never torn!" Singh threw Akhtar a menacing look. "Are you here just to taunt or actually be of some help?"

"She had a hard choice," Akhtar reiterated cooly. "Frankly, I was surprised when she chose you."

Singh held up his hand, his eyes flashing dangerously. "Are you going to help or just keep blabbering about history that can't be changed?"

"I might be of great help," said Akhtar with a smirk, "since I know where we have to go."

"Where?" Singh asked, surprise replacing anger on his face.

"The place you just spoke of, that temple in Tokyo."

"Why?"

"Our whole mission is based on the premise that Netaji is alive," Akhtar said. "And if he is alive, then the ashes in that temple are not his."

"Perfect," Singh agreed. "And there we will pick up his scent."

"To Japan then!" Akhtar said.

Singh looked at him. "Look, we can be a good team," he said. "We can do it right - for Netaji."

"Yes, we *can* be a good team." Akhtar agreed, getting to his feet, "but we're *not*." He walked away whistling.

###

The supposed funeral of Netaji Subhash Chandra Bose was held on 18th September 1945 in the cold darkness of a wintry Japanese night. The place was a small courtyard in the vicinity of a Shinto temple in Tokyo. The temple, which the locals call Renkoji, has existed since 1594.

Almost two years after the day of the funeral, a group of Indians walked into its compound again. The visitor log records the names clearly enough.

Major Anish Singh was wearing a long jacket that came to his knees. His wife, wearing an equally long jacket, lined with fur, followed him. Then came a stern faced Akhtar, wearing a hat, and then the eager duo of Harman and Dinesh. The five of them stood in the courtyard of the temple admiring the Japanese architecture of the small but beautiful place. All except Akhtar, around whose neck was slung a fancy looking camera. He immediately held it up and began taking photographs.

"Taking our cover as tourists too seriously, are you?" Singh taunted.

"You can say that." Akhtar laughed dryly without taking his eyes off the peephole. "I like to think I'm gathering evidence for our investigation."

Singh shook his head and walked away to join Rupali and the others. Harman was looking distinctly distraught as he gazed at the temple in the centre of the courtyard.

"This place is too small!" he said. "Netaji should not be lying in a place like this."

Singh patted him on the back. "You forget that the ashes are not supposed to be his."

They were about to move away when a Japanese priest walked up to them, clutching his robes to prevent them from dragging in the dirt. He went straight to Akhtar and clapped his hands loudly to get his attention. When Akhtar did not respond, the priest went and stood directly in front of him, blocking his view. That got his attention.

The priest said something in Japanese and Akhtar removed the camera lazily.

"What?" he asked in English.

"You not supposed to photograph here!" the priest said in plain English this time.

"Well, sorry about that," Akhtar laughed as he put the lid back on the camera lens. "Won't happen again."

"Don't want your sorry," the priest stated firmly, hands on hips. "I need to take your camera to Priest Mochizuki right now!"

"What! Why?" Akhtar asked. "You know how much this thing costs?"

"I don't care," the priest said, extending his hand. "Give now!"

Ten paces away, Singh cursed softly under his breath. "Not five minutes after we get here, he's attracting attention," he whispered to Rupali.

"Well, do something then!" she retorted.

By now, the priest and Akhtar were tussling for the camera. Singh walked up to them and cleared his throat loudly to get their attention. "Surely, there's been a misunderstanding," he said, looking at the priest, palms folded respectfully. "You don't need to take my friend's camera."

Akthar grinned. "Friends are we now?"

Singh ignored him. "My friend will give you the photographs of the temple he took," he said to the priest. "That's why you want the camera, right? To remove the photographs."

The priest looked at him with confused eyes. "But photos can only be removed in dark room," he said.

Singh smiled. "Show him," he said to Akhtar.

Akhtar put his hand into his pocket and brought out square shaped glossy papers with photos printed on them. "Here," he said. "Look, here's the one of your temple." He handed it over to the priest. "And here's one of the courtyard." He handed that over as well.

The priest took them carefully, unsure what he was holding in his hands.

"That's all," Akhtar said. "You let me click just two."

"But you just clicked them!" the priest said, his eyes wide.

"And now I've given them to you. Now take them to your Reverend and leave my camera alone."

"Foreigner deceives me," the priest said. "If he just took these, how he can give them to me?"

Akhtar held up the camera and pointed it at the priest. He clicked a picture and a glossy paper rolled out of a slit in the camera. Akhtar pulled it out, waved it in the air for a moment, and then handed it over to the priest. On the glossy paper was the black and white image of the priest.

"Your camera is magic!" the priest exclaimed, looking up.

"So you see, he does not deceive you. Go now," Singh said.

"No! Now I must take you to Priest Mochizuki at all cost!"

###

Mochizuki looked at the camera with interest in his private chambers. He was an old man with long white hair done in a braid that fell down his back. He wore long robes like the junior priest, though richer in texture and colour. He moved his fingers over the camera, carefully examining it.

"I never expected anyone to walk into our humble temple with a Polaroid," he said in clear English.

"And I never expected an old Japanese priest to know its name," Akthar replied, smiling.

Singh stood in a corner, leaning against a wall, watching.

"I am certainly an old priest," Mochizuki laughed, "but I'm an old priest with an interest in cameras."

"This thing must be a beauty to your eyes then," Akthar said.

Mochizuki observed the dials and the slit on the camera intently. "This thing isn't even available in the market yet. When did you get it?"

"Few months ago."

"The Americans are assholes, but they sure know how to make good cameras," Mochizuki acknowledged. "How did you even get this? Must have cost a fortune!"

"I have friends in high places," Akthar said, looking at Singh. They had secured the camera with their investigation funds.

"I wish I could have one of these," Mochizuki looked at the camera, his eyes glowing. "May I try it?" he asked politely.

Akthar nodded. The old priest held up the camera and pointed it at them. His hands shook as he pressed the button. A photo slid out of the slit.

"Here, you shake it like this to dry," Akhtar explained, handing over the photograph to the old man.

Mochizuki smiled. "It's so clear!" he marvelled. "Just like magic! No wonder USA came up with the atom bomb."

Singh cleared his throat. "Now that we've met," he said, "perhaps we should tell you why we've come."

Mochizuki leaned back in his chair and put on his glasses. "Why are you here?" he asked.

"I'm an Indian businessman, in Tokyo on a business visit," Singh said. "These are my associates."

"And why have you graced our temple?" Mochizuki asked.

"We've come to pay our respects to the ashes of Netaji Subhash Chandra Bose," Singh said.

Mochizuki folded his arms. "Have you!" His tone changed drastically.

"So may we pay our respects?"

"He's a great national hero of yours, isn't he?" Mochizuki queried.

Singh nodded.

"Bullshit!" Mochizuki cursed in Japanese, slamming his fist on the table. "Why hasn't anyone from your country come for him then?" he asked, reverting to English.

"Well, *we* have," Singh said.

"You are tourists," Mochizuki said, making no effort to mask the disgust in his voice. "I meant, why hasn't anyone from your Government come to take his ashes back to India?"

"Well, India has just achieved independence from the British," Singh said. "There is much to be done. But someone will surely come."

"This is not a proper way to treat a national hero." Mochizuki said angrily, "to leave his ashes in a small temple in a foreign country. You want to see how we treat our national heroes, go visit Imperial Square in Kyoto."

"We will certainly relay your concerns when we go back," Akthar said.

"Do so!" Mochizuki said curtly. "I am a stranger to your Netaji, but I was asked to keep the ashes by people who were strangers as well, including some Indians from whom I have not heard since." He cleared his throat. 'I kept the ashes because I had heard what he did. You go back and tell your government that."

"Supposing the ashes were even his," Singh whispered to Rupali.

She gave him a disapproving look. "A little louder and that would have blown our cover," she murmured.

"Like your friend Akhtar isn't doing that already," Singh retorted.

The old reverend was still talking to Akhtar. "You better tell your government all this."

"So can we see him?" Akhtar asked.

"We don't let foreigners go into our crypts," Mochizuki said.

"But you let the ashes of a foreigner go in," Akhtar pointed out.

"He was no ordinary foreigner..."

"Nor are we," Singh said, coming forward. "If you show us the ashes, we will give you one of these." He pointed to the Polaroid on the table.

Mochizuki's eyes glowed with desire. "Maybe I can make an exception for you this one time," he said.

###

The chamber was dark with light coming from only one small window. Singh had expected the ashes to be in an urn, but they were kept in a rectangular box. He watched as Mochizuki lit one lamp at a time, filling the chamber with light.

"Here lies the greatest freedom fighter of your country," Mochizuki said, bowing.

Singh stood reverentially for a moment, then reminded himself that the ashes did not belong to Netaji.

"Can we see the ashes?" Akhtar asked.

"Our culture doesn't usually allow it," Mochizuki told him.

"But he was not of your culture," Akhtar reminded him.

The Reverend had no answer. He remained silent for a while and then said, "Alright, you have come a long way to see him."

He opened the lid of the rectangular box. What was inside made Singh swear softly. He had expected to see ashes, fine and black but what he saw were burnt bones. Akhtar looked amused.

"This is how he was brought to me," Mochizuki said.

After a few moments, the priest placed the lid back on the box and snuffed the lamps one by one as they left the chamber.

###

"I need a smoke," Akhtar said as they were walking to the car.

"I'll stay with you," Singh offered. Rupali threw him a warning look but he merely said, "We'll join you in five minutes."

The two men leaned against a tree as the others walked on. Singh lit his cigarette slowly. "Your lead has reached a dead end," he said to Akhtar.

"Oh really?" Akthar laughed. "Where have those sharp eyes and ears of yours gone, Singh? Has marriage dulled you? She does all the effort for you in your bed?"

"Stop these sexual jokes, man! Tell me what you mean, straight."

Akthar took a slow drag at his cigarette. "What I mean is we've stumbled on something incredibly ambiguous."

Singh looked at him. "Like what?"

"Like the looks the other priests gave us when we left the chamber. Rather, the looks they directed at their Head. Something like the look Rupali gave you just now."

"You think he is hiding something?" Singh asked.

"No, I'm not saying that." Akhtar took a last drag and tossed down the butt, grinding it into the ground so nothing remained; an old soldier's habit. "What I *am* saying is we should find out."

###

"It's cold," Rupali complained as they sat cross-legged on a large mat on the grass. "And the grass pinches." She was wearing two layers of clothing, but still shivering.

"I say it's rather romantic," Singh said. His eyes were glued to a binocular. "The moon is blue."

Rupali looked up, giving the moon a glance before looking back at the Renkoji temple ahead. "What if someone finds us here?"

"Then you just roll over and give me a kiss," Singh laughed. "Such sights are common in Japan, or so I've heard."

"Why are we here anyway?" Rupali said.

"Because Akhtar thinks something fishy will happen in the temple tonight."

"I know that," Rupali snapped, pulling her jacket closer. "What I mean is, if this is Akthar's idea, why he isn't he out here in the cold instead of us?"

"Because I don't trust him with something as important as this," Singh said without moving his eyes from the binoculars.

"If you don't trust him," Rupali yawned, "why did you bring him?"

"Because you insisted."

"Oh really!" she retorted, forgetting about the cold as she glared at him. "I insisted?"

"You kind of did."

"I put forward the argument that we needed him. And you agreed."

"Did I dare not to?"

"It was your decision, Major Singh!" she snapped.

"But based on your decision, Mrs. Singh, if you remember."

She pushed his binoculars away. "Is that what's making you so rough?" she asked.

Singh had expected a frown but she was smiling. He shrugged in answer.

Rupali put her hands over his ears, making them tingle with warmth. "I had a thing with Akthar ages ago..." she said, "long before I met you. It's ancient history."

Singh merely nodded.

"I love you," she said. "His presence does not change anything."

"I know." Singh brought the binoculars brought back to his eyes.

"Is that how you reply to *I love you!*" She smacked him on his head.

"Ow!" he winced, rubbing his head with one hand. "I love you too," he said.

Suddenly, his body tensed and he focused the binocular to get a better look.

"You see anything?" she asked.

"Yes...a man," Singh muttered.

"There were many priests in the temple," Rupali recalled.

"But this one's not a priest."

"Then who is he?" she asked.

"Looks like a military type," Singh remarked.

Rupali took the binoculars from him. "Isn't that Mochizuki's office?" she asked, throwing him a quick glance.

Singh nodded.

"Looks like they're arguing."

"Sure seems so."

She handed the binoculars back. "Who the hell *is* that guy?" she asked.

"Whoever he is," Singh replied, "he looks angry."

He watched through the binoculars as the man in military uniform came out of Mochizuki's chamber. The man was quite old, perhaps the same age as Mochizuki himself. He was shouting angrily. The sound travelled all the way to the hidden duo watching them.

"What's he saying?" she whispered.

"Hurling obscenities."

Singh watched Mochizuki walk up to the other old man and hold both of his hands, as if to apologize. That seemed to calm the man down for he nodded vigorously as Mochizuki spoke.

"I'm not being able to make any sense of this," Singh complained.

They watched the military man walk out of the temple, get into his car and drive off. Then they watched as Mochizuki was surrounded by the other priests, all talking and gesticulating, as if chastising him about something.

"This is getting more mysterious by the minute," Rupali remarked.

They heard footsteps approaching.

"Quick! Someone's coming," Singh whispered, hiding the binoculars.

Rupali fell into his embrace and they kissed, listened intently. After watching them for some time, the intruder finally cleared his throat. It was Akhtar.

"You two lovebirds better get your shit together," he laughed as Singh retreated from his wife.

"What are you doing here?"

"Did you see that mysterious scene at the temple?" Akhtar asked.

Singh nodded.

"I listened in from my position below," Akhtar told them. "I'll tell you what I heard; you tell me what you saw."

12
The Casino

2015

"What on earth made you come here with just one name, one lead, hoping you'll be set on the right track?" Tanya jabbed her finger angrily into the air as they lay huddled in his room, the air conditioner on high.

"I was just hoping to ask around," Jay said, caressing her hair.

"God, you're so lucky you ran into me! What were you going to do otherwise? Did you at least have a plan?"

"No. But now I have you, so I was right."

"Do you have anything more than James Bond lines?"

"Hey, I have money." He waved his wallet at her.

"Men always think money can buy anything." She cast her eyes at the ceiling, shook her head and began typing.

"What are you doing?"

"Lucky for you, you have me!" she said, without looking away from the screen. "And that Sasha Makijani lived in Hong Kong."

Five minutes later Tanya had finished explaining the process to him. "Hong Kong is a unique city. It was a British colony till 1994, and then it passed to China. It had always been pretty much self-sufficient."

"What's that got do with Makijan?" Jay asked.

"A rich self-sufficient city that has existed for hundreds of years," Tanya continued. "Self-governing. Where does that take you?"

Jay clapped his hands together. "An efficient administration."

"Hong Kong has always kept its records well," Tanya agreed. "And guess what, they..."

"...are now all online," Jay completed.

###

Five hours later they had managed to filter all Sasha Makijans from the Hong Kong address database. Tracking those present in the Yellow Quarters during the 1990s, they found just one match.

"We've found your girl!" Tanya exclaimed. "Now all we've got to do is track her movements."

As Tanya scrolled down, the articles started getting longer and more extensive. "Oh shit! She's a public figure." Tanya pointed to the screen.

Jay nodded as he read '...philanthropist, businesswoman, mother...'. "She's a star," he commented.

"I'm getting all the news clippings I can on her," Tanya said, typing furiously on her keyboard.

"This makes it easy. We've found her. Now all we've got to do is go and talk to her."

"No!" Tanya stopped clicking and turned her laptop towards him. "This makes it more complicated."

"Holy shit!" Jay whispered as he finished reading. "She's a gangster!"

"Mother of a gangster too. Her son is Masayoshi San," Tanya read. "Sensei of the Red Triad, who allegedly control over half the cocaine imports into Hong Kong."

"Well, we don't have to mess with them or anything like that," Jay said, trying to sound more confident than he felt. "We just have to set up a meeting."

"Did you read the full article?" Tanya asked. "Look what it says at the end. The Red Triad and the Blue Triad have been embroiled in a continuous turf war for months. Mrs. Makijan is said to be hiding on the topmost floor of the Blue Frog Casino, owing to a threat to her life... She hasn't appeared in public in six months." Tanya kept her finger on the screen. "She's been in that casino ever since."

"She must be bored then," Jay said reflectively.

"A casino isn't exactly a boring place, is it?" Tanya scoffed.

"So what are we going to do?"

Tanya picked up her duffel bag and tossed it at Jay, who caught it mid-air. "We're going to go case a joint," she said.

###

According to historical records, the Blue Frog was built in 2000, by Masayoshi San, as the first of his many real estate ventures. The exact role of his mother, Sasha Maikijan, was officially nil, but rumour said Sasha was close to many of the initial funders of the Blue Frog.

Over the years it was claimed that the casino was a front for the Blue Triad to launder the money earned from their drug operations. It was well known that Sasha had trashed such rumours by officially declaring it was she who owned the casino. She then went on a philanthropic spree that made her into one of the most beloved figures of the city and the guest of honour at every banquet that counted. She was also a regular contributor to many of the city's elite clubs.

Until 2014, when war began between the two Triads. Sasha immediately withdrew to her casino and stopped all public appearances. By then, the Red Triad had realized it was she who ran the show and death threats mushroomed. There had even been an IED explosion in the casino lobby that fortunately killed no one except a few of the lowly staff. If meeting Sasha had been difficult earlier, it was almost impossible now. She had isolated herself from the world as her son and his henchmen fought their enemies on the streets.

It was at this point in time that Jay and Tanya arrived in Hong Kong. Without contacting Sasha, Jay did not know how to proceed on his quest. It was essential he meet his only lead. The Triad security was hard to break, but Jay and Tanya were no fools. He had money and Tanya had specialist IT skills and enormous experience. The only question was whether Sasha still had something to tell them or would she turn out to be just a dead end?

###

"He's moving, Char." Sergei nudged awake his partner, who had been dozing with his head thrown back on the sofa. "Get up, you fool!"

It took a few moments for Charkov to open his eyes. He yawned and stretched his massive arms. "Bastard!" he said conversationally, "he couldn't have waited till I was awake?"

"It appears not," Sergei's eyes were on the lobby reception desk. "He's talking to the receptionist."

"Getting a cab, probably. Time to get up. Are we to bring him in?"

"No." Sergei shook his head, picking up his coat. "Boss said just to follow him."

Charkov coughed and got up. "Boss loves to keep us on our feet, doesn't he?"

"Looks like he's got a cab. He's heading out."

"Then let us head out too."

Charkov checked his pockets for the keys to the hired car and walked out. Sergei followed.

###

It had been less than twenty-four hours since they had reached Hong Kong, having flown in directly from Moscow. It was night when they arrived. They had got a room but remained in the lobby, owing to the job.

"Where do you think he'll be going?" Sergei asked.

"As long as it's not the airport," Charkov said, "I'm fine." He really hated flying.

The two men watched from their car as Jay stood at the hotel entrance, waiting for his cab.

"He doesn't look like a terrorist," Charkov remarked.

"And you look like a Sumo wrestler, not a spy," Sergei retorted. "So shut up."

Charkov cursed but said nothing more as he kept watch.

Their Boss, Alexis, was never communicative. All he had said was they were to follow this man.

"He doesn't even look dangerous," Charkov complained again.

"Neither do I." Sergei slammed his foot on Charkov's toe.

"Ouch!" Charkov yelled. "What did you do that for?"

"To keep you awake. Look, his car's here."

They watched as a sedan stopped in front of the hotel. Jay descended the steps, looked at his watch for a moment and then got into the car.

"He better have a long way to go," Charkov sighed as Sergei starting the ignition. "I plan on getting some sleep."

###

"HQ to Jay!" Tanya's voice was shrill in his ears; much too loud for comfort.

"God!" he protested. "Can't you speak softer?"

"Turn the volume down," she instructed. "The controls are in the app you just downloaded."

Before leaving the hotel, she had given him small ear pieces and a microphone, which she had stuck behind his ear. *Bluetooth controlled and operated...very discreet,* she had told him.

Jay opened the app that controlled the device on his phone and turned down the volume to reasonable levels.

"HQ to Jay," Tanya said again. "Do you copy?"

"HQ huh?" Jay chuckled. "You've been watching too many spy flicks."

She clucked disapprovingly. "It is the way we communicated for WikiLeaks," she said. "It's professional."

"It sounds like a cliche," Jay remarked.

"Will you shut up?"

"I can't with this microphone in my mouth, can I? If I as much as breathe, you hear."

"That was gross."

"More to the point, what exactly are we going to do in the casino?"

"I am just your contact from HQ," Tanya replied, grinning. "It is you who has to figure out what to do inside the casino."

###

"A casino!" Charkov said disbelievingly. "A sudden gambling bug bit our man, eh?"

"Shut up, Char! Let's find a spot to park." Sergei turned the car.

Charkov did not move his gaze from Jay, who had descended from his cab a hundred paces away. "Do you think he saw us?" he asked.

"How would he even know he's being followed?"

"We don't know who he is, Serg," Charkov reminded him. "Boss hasn't told us anything. He could be dangerous."

Sergei laughed. "Twenty minutes ago he didn't intimidate you at all."

"He's walking in."

The smirk faded from Sergei's face. Turning the ignition off, he opened the door. "Let's go after him," he said.

###

"So what do you see, Jay?" Tanya's voice filled his ears.

"I see a receptionist. She's wearing a red Goka."

"Is she hot?"

That brought a smile to Jay's lips. "Not as hot as you."

"Good. She won't distract you then."

The receptionist smiled and Jay nodded to her. "Are you staying at the hotel, Sir?" she asked.

Jay shook his head. "Just visiting."

"Welcome to the Blue Frog."

"Nice voice," Tanya said in his ear..

The receptionist handed him a card. "Please enjoy."

Jay nodded and walked into the large hall.

"Keep describing what you see," Tanya instructed.

"It's all normal," Jay said, strolling through the casino. "I see blackjack tables, roulette dealers, and wheels of fortune." He sat down at the bar.

"How many bouncers?"

Jay signalled for a drink and casually took in the lay of the land. "A dozen."

"Did you count the number of security cameras?"

"Relax, Tanya. We're not robbing the place, are we?"

"Could we?" The childlike expression made him smile. He took his drink from the bartender and sipped it slowly.

"Enough fun now." Tanya voice was stern. "Get down to business."

"What business?"

"I need a back door into the casino's surveillance system."

"Whoa...whoa...that is not what we talked about."

"We are talking about it now!" Tanya insisted. "So take a deep breath and do as I say. The first step is finding out which brand the system they are using is." Tanya was wearing a tight cotton shirt and no pants at all. She smiled thinking what Jay would say if he knew.

But Jay's voice was tense and worried. "What do I have to do?"

"You'll just have to create a ruckus."

###

Five minutes later, Jay was deeply regretting his decision to jump headlong into Tanya's advice. He was standing face to face with the floor's Pit Boss, who was almost twice his own size and wore a menacing smile on his shiny face. Jay didn't dare look down but was sure the man was carrying a gun.

"Say that again, will you?" The voice was deep and heavy with steroids.

"Uh, I lost my wallet," Jay stuttered.

"Was it important to you?" the Pit Boss asked lazily.

"Of course it was!"

"Was it really?"

"*Throw money at him,*" Tanya's voice whispered.

"Of course, it was important!" Jay insisted, raising his voice. "It contained my platinum gold card I needed to pay for your Alexander Suite."

The pit boss' attitude changed immediately. "I'm sorry, Sir. When did you lose it?"

"Some time after I entered."

"Please come with me, Sir. We'll talk to the bartender."

"*See how money changes everything?*" Tanya whispered as Jay followed.

"*You mean I don't just look rich?'* Jay murmured. He could almost see her smile.

"Alex here does not recall any suspicious person," the Pit Boss said after he was finished with the bartender.

Jay nodded. "I could have just dropped it, I suppose."

"We can go to the security room and watch the CCTV footage, Sir."

"*Bingo!*" Tanya whispered.

###

The security room was large, with flat LCD monitors everywhere. It resembled a war room from a 90s movie. Jay's mouth dropped in awe at the room's size and the number of people in it.

"This is Binny, our Surveillance-in-Charge." The Pit Boss took him to a short man who, to Jay's surprise, looked South Asian. "Mr. Jay here has lost his wallet."

"Jay or *Jaay*?" Binny asked, turning towards them.

"The latter."

"Wow! You're Indian! Good to meet a fellow countryman," he said.

Jay smiled, shaking hands. "Where are you from?"

"Mumbai."

"Well, that makes two of us then." Jay smiled again.

"So you lost your wallet huh?" Binny asked. "We don't get too many cases like that. People tend to hold onto their wallets in a casino, you know."

"I'm sorry to inconvenience you," Jay apologized, "but I think I must have dropped it after I entered the building."

Binny coughed, gesturing for them to sit down. "We'll track your movements after you entered and see where your wallet went."

"I'm not sure we'll be able to see that on camera," Jay said, sitting down.

"Are you nuts?" Binny laughed. "Don't you know about the power of casino surveillance?"

"Not really."

"Well then let me show you." He rewound the footage a few minutes.

"That's me, entering." Jay pointed at the screen, watching himself talk to the receptionist in the lobby.

Binny paused the screen and moved his mouse pointer. "Now, I'm going to zoom," he said.

Jay watched as the image of himself grew on the screen, focusing on his hands and blurring in the process.

"Now we adjust the focus," Binny said.

Jay almost swore as the zoomed image cleared and he could even read the digits of the credit cards in his hand. "This is high-tech stuff!" he exclaimed.

"Low tech, actually," Binny laughed. "I've been crying to the bosses to get facial recognition as soon as possible, but they don't listen."

"*That was important information,*" Tanya murmured in his ear. Jay merely nodded.

"We need this kind of zoom to monitor illicit activity in the casino." Binny zoomed out again. "Cheating, passed notes, verifying ID cards, that kind of stuff." He played the footage again, following Jay through the frames. He switched cameras as Jay entered the main casino, paused, and zoomed on his back pocket. "You still had your wallet at this time," he said.

Jay nodded. In his ear Tanya said, "*You need access to his terminal, Jay.*"

And how the fuck am I going to get that? he wondered, keeping an interested expression on his face.

"You need access just for a minute," she insisted.

"You are now at the bar," Binny said, zooming in on his drink. "That's a nice cocktail. You have good taste."

"Uh, thanks," Jay said, trying desperately to think of a way to access Binny's terminal.

"So let's fast forward a bit," Binny said, pressing a button. The video turned into hyper-lapse. "Ah-hah!" Binny said, pausing the video. It was the precise moment Jay's wallet had dropped to the floor.

"You have a good eye," Jay said. "I would never have caught it."

"Now let me call the Pit Boss to retrieve your wallet." Binny rose from his chair and walked off.

Jay couldn't believe his luck. As he watched Binny cross over to the corridor, he whispered to Tanya, "I have access. What do I do?"

"Open any browser," Tanya instructed quickly.

"Done!"

"Now type this," she said, reciting the IP address.

With one eye on the door, Jay typed it in with his left hand.

"Now press enter."

"I know that much! I have a degree in CSE."

"Just let the script run."

"How come you were so prepared?" Jay asked.

"I told you, I've done this before." Tanya replied. "I used the same script as last time. The surveillance system company is the same."

"Lucky you," Jay muttered as he watched the progress bar fill up slowly 70%...80%...

"They've found your wallet, Mr. Jay!" The overtly cheerful Binny was walking back to the desk. Jay looked at the progress bar. It was still filling.

"You have to go and check if the contents are all there," Binny said, very close to the terminal now.

Jay suddenly stood up to block his view and hugged him. Binny was surprised but returned the hug, patting his shoulder.

"Thank you, man," Jay said effusively.

"It's alright," Binny said.

Jay broke from the hug and glanced at the terminal. The dialogue box and window were gone. *Phew*! He quickly walked away from Binny's station.

"You can always thank me later," Tanya's voice said in his ear. "Now get your ass back here! I'm starting to miss it."

Jay smiled as he exited the busy surveillance room and walked back to the Pit Boss on the main casino floor.

###

"You'll kiss me when you see the work I've done while you were on your way back," Tanya said as he entered the hotel room.

"I'd kiss you anyway, you're so cute," Jay said with a wink. He took off his coat and hung it on the hangar.

"Our IP bug worked just as it was supposed to," Tanya told him.

"And how was it supposed to?"

"My IP bug created a backdoor directly into the system administrator's terminal and streamed data and past records directly here onto my laptop."

"Can't they catch external data movement?"

"They can, of course, but the scans happen hourly, and I plugged off the connection before the scans happened."

"So we are no longer connected to the casino?" Jay asked. "That's a shame. I was really looking forward to checking out those hot hostesses."

Tanya pinched him savagely. "Just a joke!" he protested.

"Well, I found what I needed in twenty minutes and spent the other forty ogling the hunks in the men's private room," Tanya laughed.

"So what did you find?"

Tanya turned the laptop screen towards him. It showed a couple making out behind the curtains on a sofa. The girl's dress was already over her waist and the man's hand was between her thighs.

"What is this?" Jay asked.

"Oops!" She flicked the screen. "This is what I wanted to show you."

The image showed a vast swimming pool with several people in it, wearing bikinis and shorts.

"Sure this isn't the wrong image?" Jay asked skeptically.

"Keep watching."

The footage moved on and the camera kept rotating slowly every five minutes. Suddenly Tanya paused the film and zoomed in on the balconies above the pool. Behind protective glass could be seen the face of an old lady, looking outwards contemplatively.

"The security guy at the casino told you they do not have face recognition, but I have," Tanya said, running another software. "I'll map this face and compare it with a picture we have of Mrs. Makijan." She ran the programme and waited.

"There we are!" Tanya clapped in childish delight when the screen showed an 80% match.

"So Mrs. Makijan is in the building for sure," Jay said, folding his arms. Tanya nodded. "So all we have to do now is get inside."

"I did some research on that too." Tanya opened another window. "I found the blueprints of the casino from the Hong Kong city survey database.

Oh don't worry, that's perfectly legal," she said coolly, seeing Jay's stern look. "Now most of these casinos run security the same way. The elevator goes up to the last floor of the hotel, but no further. The penthouses have different elevators which are guarded."

"So how do we get in?" Jay asked, throwing up his hands.

"Well, the other elevator ends on the seventh floor." Tanya showed him the floor on the blueprints. "The hotel ends on the sixth floor. So anyone who wants to get to the penthouse has to take the elevator to the sixth floor and then take the penthouse elevator."

"But access from the sixth to the seventh must be restricted," Jay observed, rubbing his chin.

"Exactly! But all the floors share one feature - fire exits."

"That's one way to get in."

"But we can be sure the fire exits will also be watched on CCTV."

Jay sighed. "What's the other way?"

"The other way would be to get to the seventh floor, escorted by the authorities themselves," Tanya said.

Jai looked at Tanya, shaking his head in wonder. "And how exactly would that be possible?" he asked.

"The security section is on the seventh floor," Tanya told him. "Any suspicious activity or persons would be taken to that floor for further investigation by the Pit Bosses."

"And if the investigation fails to reveal anything," Jay added, "the person is set free."

"Exactly!" Tanya turned her head to look at him. "And once he is free to go, he can simply take the elevator up to the penthouse."

"But in both cases," Jay pointed out, "we need a distraction."

"We don't need a distraction," Tanya smiled. "We need a Blackjack!"

###

"What did he even do at the casino?" Charkov wondered. "He left in less than three hours. Have you ever known someone to leave a casino in less than three hours?"

"Yeah," Sergei replied laconically. "Us!"

They had entered the casino after their quarry, and left before him, ready to follow him to his next destination. Surprisingly, he had returned to the hotel.

"I'm going to call the Boss," Charkov declared, watching the hotel doors. "This thing looks sinister to me."

"Are you sure the Boss wants to be disturbed by your small concerns?" Sergei asked, getting himself a fruit shake from the stand on the sidewalk.

"Yeah, he is called the Boss for a reason," Charkov replied, taking out his cell phone and tapping in a number. He put the speaker on and the ringing could be heard clear and loud.

"Hello!" Alexis' voice was cold and dry.

"Ugh...it's us, Boss," Charkov said, scratching his head.

"What's the status?"

"He just visited a casino for a few hours, Boss," Charkov said.

"Which casino?" asked Alexis.

Sergei gave him the name.

"Let me Google it." Alexis' voice was followed by the sound of keys being tapped.

"Sergei, Charkov!" It was Alexis. "This shit is getting serious. We need to bring him in."

"Anytime, Boss," Sergei said. "I'll bang on his room door if it comes to that."

"Slow down, big guy," Alexis warned. "Let me make some calls; get some clearances from above. You make sure you don't let him get away, even for a single moment, until I give you confirmation."

"Sure, Boss!" Charkov ended the call and dropped the phone into his coat pocket. "Let's go," he said to Sergei.

"Go where?" Sergei asked, folding his arms.

"Inside." Charkov nodded towards the hotel doors. "Didn't you hear the Boss? We have to keep an eye on this motherfucker."

###

Blackjacks, Tanya explained, was a slang term for blacklisted gamblers in casinos. The term was used for blackjack players with considerable expertise in the game and whose skill at counting cards placed the house at a considerable disadvantage. The thing about Blackjacks was that casinos then banned them from playing in the house. It was the perfect way to cut their losses – allow the bad players to play and ban the good ones.

If a player was caught counting cards in one casino, he was thereafter banned in all the casinos of the city. It was standard procedure with casinos to share information on such players. Once blacklisted, they got as much information on such a Blackjack as possible. Another standard procedure was to identify a Blackjack from his license plate number. Whenever his car pulled up, the casino security would know a Blackjack was on the property. He would be tailed and if he resorted to counting cards, he would immediately be thrown out.

"Priorities of casino surveillance change drastically when a Blackjack is on the floor," Tanya explained. "They concentrate on him rather than on other places, like fire exits."

"And that would clear our way."

"Not completely," Tanya drawled, tapping her front teeth with a gleaming red fingernail. "We will need a disguise, like a waiter."

"What about the other plan?" Jay asked, not enamoured by the thought of parading as a waiter under camera surveillance.

"That is more complicated, but a surer way in. But we will need to find and convince a Blackjack to take part."

"Well, I'll do the convincing if you can find one," Jay offered.

"Well, then you better put your convincing hat on," Tanya said, grinning, "'cause I've already found some."

She opened the CCTV footage again and went to the view of the Manager's chamber. The Manager was a bald guy, sitting on his chair discussing something with other persons, a list in his hand. Tanya zoomed in on the list. They could read the heading clearly: *Known Blackjacks in town.*

"So we have the names," Jay said. "Now are you going to do some cool hacker shit again and find them?"

"No need to do some hacker shit to find them," Tanya said with a wink as she opened another tab. "I can just use Facebook."

###

Abdul Rehman smoked compulsively as he sat on a corner stool at the bar at the Ritz. His hand shook as he brought the cigarette to his lips, but that was from withdrawal, not fear. In fact, he was more amused than afraid. Exactly four hours ago, a woman had called him on his cellphone. At first, Abdul had thought it was a telemarketer since women rarely called him. But she had soon made her intentions clear. The woman knew his full name and the hotel where he was staying. But more importantly, she knew what he did.

I know who you are, she had said. And that was no small deal. Abdul was a professional Blackjack. He changed identities daily. He had a dozen driving licenses and six fake passports in his bag right now. He instinctively clutched the bag closer and gestured for another drink.

The woman had been very clear. She wanted to meet him. When he refused outright, she threatened to leak his other identities to the casinos. That would have been disastrous. His real persona had been banned years ago in all the major casinos around the world. The only way he could play now was by using aliases. His aliases were worth more to him than his life.

Abdul sipped the pint the bartender pushed towards him. He fiddled with his cellphone, wondering who it was coming to meet him. The woman could have been anyone. CIA. The Triads. There were many people after him. He was ready for anything. But what he wasn't ready for was if the woman turned out to be a man.

###

Sergei and Charkov sat down at an empty table near the bar. "Who's this new guy he's meeting now?" Charkov wondered.

"Relax, Char." Sergei's eyes never left Jay, who was now shaking hands with a bearded man at the bar. "We're in perfect position. We will hear them clearly."

"Then we should probably order a bottle of vodka and shut up," Charkov said, "because if we can hear them, they can hear us."

"*Shush!*" Sergei brought his finger to his lips.

"I was to meet a Tanya Williams," Abdul said.

"Consider me her for this meeting," Jay said, sitting down on the empty bar stool beside Abdul.

"I don't understand. I spoke with her on the phone."

"And you can speak to her again now," Jay told him, handing over his phone and a pair of headphones. "Plug them in."

Abdul looked surprised for a moment, then he plugged the headphones in.

"Hi, Abdul."

The voice was the same he had heard earlier. "*Salam walekum*," he replied, holding the mouthpiece close to his face. "What do you want?"

"Nothing you won't be prepared to give," Tanya assured him.

"So you are not from the Triads?"

"No."

"Then how did you know about my disguises?"

"Because I am just like you, Abdul," Tanay said. "A woman with a dozen aliases. I know how these things work. And trust me, you are an amateur when it comes to identity changing."

"Alright, I'm listening. What do you want?"

"Something you don't hold close to your heart anyway." Tanya told him. "And don't worry, you will be properly compensated for your help."

"Something I don't hold close?" Abdul repeated. "What is that?"

Tanya paused for a moment. "The identity of Abdul Rehman."

###

"He's been talking on that phone for much too long," Sergei complained, pouring the last shot of vodka into his glass.

"Will you at least talk softly?" Charkov whispered. "He's done now."

"I'm tired of all this stalking," Sergei said loudly. "I think we should bring him in right now."

"Jesus! Volume, Serg," Charkov hissed. "You know Boss hasn't given us clearance yet."

"Clearances take too much time," Sergei grumbled. "You mark my words Char, we wait much longer and this snake will slip out of our hands."

"You mean the bird will fly away," Charkov said. "Now shut up! The Moslem's done talking on the phone."

Sergei leaned back in his chair to listen.

Jay took the phone and the earphones back from Abdul. "Do you understand what to do?" he asked.

"I do. But whatever you are trying to do man, I gotta warn you."

"We are not here for your advice." Jay put the phone back in his trouser pocket. "Just do what you've been told and you'll get paid. Besides, you are not exposing yourself to any risk."

"True," sighed Abdul. "But I gotta tell you, man, don't mess with the Blue Triad."

Jay stood up. "Make sure you take a cab home."

Abdul leaned forward. "That casino is impregnable," he murmured.

Jay merely nodded. "Just do what you were told," he said, walking away.

###

"We have a head start on him now, Boss," Charkov said on the phone as Sergei stood smoking a cigarette nearby.

"What kind of a head start?"

"Our guy is planning to do something at the casino he visited."

"I know what he plans to do," Alexis snapped. "The question is how exactly he is planning to do it?"

"That is exactly the information we have, Boss," Charkov said.

"Impressive." There was a pause, then Alexis asked, "So what do you know?"

"Our guy just spoke with a Moslem Blackjack," Charkov said. "After that I and Sergei had a little chat with him too." He smiled. "In our own style, of course."

"What did he tell you?"

"Oh much," Sergei said, throwing away his cigarette and walking up closer. "He told us our guy needs his identity cards and his car."

"Why?"

"Because our Moslem friend is a Blackjack," Charkov said. "His real identity is banned from all the casinos and our Indian friend requires exactly that identity."

"Interesting," Alexis mused, falling silent.

"Have you got the clearances yet?" Charkov asked.

"No, but I'll try to get them before this casino thing happens," Alexis said quickly. "It is imperative you bring him in before he does what he wants to do at the casino."

"Then we'll park ourselves at the casino," Sergei laughed. "Test our luck or something."

"You do that."

"Signing off then," said Charkov.

There was a pause. "Don't fuck up!" Alexis warned.

"We won't, Boss," the two men said together.

###

"Everything is set." Jay had found Tanya at the gymnasium beside the pool. She had already changed into a cotton skirt and tied her hair in a cute pony tail.

"Get ready to take your clothes off then," she said. "I was thinking of taking a dip in the pool."

Jay did not need to be told twice. The last few days had been strenuous and exhausting; the cool pool was immensely welcome.

When he emerged from the men's room, changed into blue shorts and flip flops, he found Tanya already wet from a dip in the pool, lounging on a chair on the sundeck. She looked incredibly cute in her three-piece flowery bikini and dark sunglasses. Jay smiled, momentarily forgetting the problems on hand.

"Well, someone's got a boner," Tanya said after a minute without opening her eyes.

"Well, someone gave it to me," Jay said, slyly.

"Maybe a dip in the pool will cure it," Tanya smiled.

She looked so damn cute! Jay turned to the pool and dived in. The cool water felt refreshing. He did six leisurely laps and then halted by the deck near Tanya, his racing heart returned to its normal rhythm.

"Tomorrow's going to be a big day, isn't it?" he said, looking up at her.

"Indeed." Tanya pushed up her sunglasses and leaned towards him.

"The Blackjack will meet us at 6 pm precisely."

"Then you will take his car and go to the casino. If all goes well, they'll think you are him. Then all you have to do is place a big bet on a table and play."

"And what will you be doing?" Jay asked, splashing some water onto her perfectly tanned legs.

"Oh I will get into a really sexy outfit, preferably of a waitress, and enter the parking lot of the casino," Tanya said.

"Walking up some stairs with a tray in your hand, wearing a fitted white waistcoat," Jay remarked dreamily.

"You watch too much porn," Tanya laughed. "I doubt I'll look glamorous and I'll try not to attract any attention at all as I climb up the stairs of the fire exit to the seventh floor."

"What if they catch you?" Jay asked, suddenly serious.

"I'll improvise." Tanya said, unconcerned by the daunting possibility. "I'll say I'm lost or something. You forget I've done such things before."

"It sounds dangerous."

"Jay, relax! It's you getting caught that I'm more worried about."

"Speaking of which," Jay said, "there's something I must tell you."

Tanya arched her brows in enquiry as she sipped the long drink the waiter had just brought.

"It's embarrassing," Jay said, rubbing his palms together.

“Did you pee in the pool?” Tanya asked.

Jay played with the water, then looked up. “Well, I really should tell you. It’s high time I did.”

“Then just say it!”

He told her.

13
The Ashes
File 7/14/Jan/XVII: Top Secret

1948

Back at their HQ in the hotel, they stitched the whole story together.

"The man doing the shouting thing was irritated with us," Akhtar told them.

"Why did you enter the temple without consulting with us first?" Singh asked, feeling anger rise within him like a flame.

"Why is your husband angry?" Akhtar retorted, turning to Rupali. "I've just brought important information."

"We are a team here. You are not acting like it," Rupali said curtly.

"That's right," agreed Singh. "You were lucky. But that will not always be so. I won't let you jeopardise our whole mission by your actions."

"Bullshit! You're angry because you can't control me."

Singh opened his mouth to speak but Harman interrupted him. "Guys," he said, "why don't we discuss what happened at the temple first?"

"The man was angry at the Reverend for letting us inside the ash chamber," Akhtar said.

"That is interesting." Singh folded his arms. "He seemed to have been quite angry for such a supposedly small thing."

"No." Akhtar shook his head. "One of the priests saw us opening the ash box. He must have told the others."

"Isn't the Reverend supposed to be boss at this temple?" Rupali asked. "Isn't his decision final?"

"The Reverend had no swagger while talking to this man," Akhtar recalled. "Every word that came from the Reverend's mouth was in apology."

"But who is this man?" Harman asked.

"He was dressed in military attire." Singh said. "Japanese. Quite old."

"It appears that the man thinks that our opening of the ash box defiled it," Akhtar said. "He mentioned some Japanese custom."

"What did the Reverend say?" Singh asked.

"The Reverend said that they could conduct a ceremony to make the ashes pure again. The man insisted it be done at once. But the Reverend said preparations needed to be made. They agreed on tomorrow night."

"Why does this man care so much about Netaji's ashes?" Harman wondered.

"Only the ashes are not Netaji's," Singh commented. "If the ceremony is tomorrow, then we can intercept him."

"Exactly what I was planning," said Akthar.

"Do we have the fake guns we brought from Delhi?" Singh asked.

"They're in that bag." Akthar pointed to the large canvas backpack.

"Are they the same ones that release a rubber bullet?" asked Rupali.

"The rubber bullets hit damn well too," Akthar told her.

"Not hard enough to injure though," said Singh.

Akhtar looked up. "Clearly you've never been hit by one."

"Have you?"

Akhtar shrugged. "I once had a girlfriend who liked guns. I gave her one of those to play with."

"You gave your girlfriend a gun to play with?" Singh asked in disbelief.

"It was a fake gun."

###

When the operation began the next night, Singh crouched alone on the small hill beside the temple. The moon shone brightly above his head. The cold wind ruffled his hair. He had donned black tights, covered from head to feet, as he had often done for urban covert operations during the war.

The car came from the east. Singh eyes never wavered as the target descended and slowly made his way to the temple doors. He was dressed in his full Japanese military uniform. Turning his head, Singh scanned the other side of the hill. There, another car waited. He caught sight of Harman's familiar turban at the wheel. It was where he would take the man.

Singh waited till the target reached the temple doors, then sprinted down the hill, appearing before the startled man like a phantom from the dark. He leaned in, pointing the gun at the man's chest. "Don't move!" he instructed in Japanese. "Don't speak!"

The man let out a soft curse and put up his hands. In that moment, Singh felt the barrel of a gun touch the back of his neck. Surprised, he turned his head. It was Akhtar.

"You!" he said, astonished.

"Yes, me."

Akhtar pressed the trigger and black night fell over Singh.

###

When he awoke, Singh felt intense pain in his head. He was in a moving car. He looked up to see Harman at the wheel. In the passenger seat sat Dinesh.

"What the hell happened?" he asked, rubbing his head.

"We heard a gunshot, Boss." Harman replied. "We ran to investigate."

Singh took a moment to recollect. "It was Akhtar," he said. "He shot me. Where am I wounded?"

"Akthar?" Dinesh looked surprise.

"You're not wounded, Boss," Harman told him. "There's blunt force trauma to your head. You lost consciousness for perhaps five minutes."

"Where did the target go?" Singh asked.

"We saw him get into his car and drive away."

"Did you see Akthar?"

"We did not see him at all," Dinesh observed.

"Damn!" Singh punched his fist on the car seat. Suddenly his eyes widened. "The hotel!" he ordered. "Rupali's alone. We must get to her."

###

"Are you really sure it was Akhtar you saw?" Rupali asked, handing him an ice pack.

"Damn sure!" Singh snapped, rubbing the back of his head with the cold ice.

"It doesn't make any sense!" Rupali sat down beside him and took the ice pack from him. "Why would he hit you?"

"I told you the bastard couldn't be trusted."

"Still, I don't see why he would hit you."

"Maybe I can explain," a voice said.

Everyone turned as Akhtar walked into the room. Instinctively, Dinesh raised his pistol, aiming at the heart. Akhtar raised both hands.

Singh shot to his feet angrily. "You betrayed us!" he said loudly.

"Now now..." Akthar replied, as if soothing a petulant child, as he walked into the room, hands raised. "There's no reason to be so dramatic."

"You shot me!" Singh accused him.

"With a fake gun," Akhtar observed, standing still. "I told you I have tried it; it doesn't even crack the skull. You must've been unconscious for five minutes at most."

"I woke up in the fucking car!"

"When I woke up, I was in handcuffs and my girlfriend was over me," Akhtar said. "But that's another story entirely."

"The target escaped!" Singh yelled in frustration.

"We don't need the target," Akhtar said cooly.

"Who are you to..."

"Listen to me." Akhtar raised his voice. "We don't need the target because he has already told us what we want to know."

"What?" Singh stared at Akhtar as if he had lost his mind.

"I spoke with him. The shooting was an act so he would trust me."

"You bastard!" Singh exclaimed disbelievingly. "You went behind my back."

"I did not go behind your back," Akhtar observed as he sat down on the sofa and put one leg over the other. "I went over your head."

"You pretentious bastard!"

"You can hurl obscenities at me all night long, but I'd prefer you to shut up and listen to me," Akhtar snapped, losing his cool, "because this shit just got serious."

"What do you mean?" Singh asked.

"I just found out a shitload of information from our target."

"Like what?" Rupali asked, folding her hands.

"That Netaji's plane didn't just crash," Akhtar said, looking at Singh. "It was made to crash!"

"What! By whom?"

"Our old friend," Akhtar said, looking straight into Singh's eyes. "Kobayashi."

14
Infiltration

2015

The alarm rang exactly at 4 pm and Charkov's big hairy hand groped for the phone and shut it off. A bunk away, Sergei opened his eyes and rubbed them furiously.

"Time to get up," Charkov said, rising and poking Sergei.

"I shouldn't have drank all that vodka last night," Sergei said, yawning and stretching his arms. "Did you get in touch with the Blackjack?"

"I did."

"So what's gonna be our modus operandi?"

"The Moslem is going to call us once he delivers his car and IDs to our target," Charkov said, lighting up. "We'll be waiting for him at the casino; waiting to hear the Boss has got us clearances. As soon as he okays us, we bring the target in, hopefully just as he enters the casino."

"What next?" Sergei asked, grabbing the cigarette and taking a puff.

"We take him to this safe house and wait."

"This place is too small already for the two of us," Sergei grumbled, closing his eyes and inhaling the smoke.

"Relax," Charkov said. "If we catch him, you won't be here. You'll be the one out there, securing our transport to Russia."

"Have you discussed the possible options with the Boss?" Sergei asked, handing over the cigarette reluctantly.

"We both think airlifting is best. The Boss has already found a single engine plane operator in the countryside who frequently smuggles small amounts of cocaine to Russia and hence won't deny us."

"Typical of the Boss," Sergei observed morosely. "I would have chosen to go by sea."

"You always liked slow things, Serg," Charkov commented.

"I don't like negotiating with tiny Chinese men," Sergei complained.

"And I enjoy holding a brown Indian prisoner?" Charkov laughed.

"So now that we know how fucked our next week is going to be," Sergei said, "it is time to go."

"Yeah, let's go," Sergei agreed, tossing the cigarette away and pulling his shoes on. "We got a target to catch."

###

"It's time," Tanya said looking at her wristwatch. She was wearing her sunglasses and had on a white shirt and a black skirt that came to her knees.

Jay stared at her as he came out of the washroom. "Damn, you look good!" he said.

"I have to." She flashed him an angry look as she turned the lipstick nozzle up to reveal the ruby red stick. "After the bombshell you dropped yesterday."

Jay bit his lip remembering last night at the pool. "I should have told you earlier," he agreed. "But it didn't cause any problems, did it?"

"Well, if it's going to, we'll soon know," Tanya said, putting on the black coat she had hung in the wardrobe.

"You look sexy when you are angry," Jay smiled.

Tanya opened her mouth to retort but closed it again. "Please don't get into trouble," she said.

"I won't!" Jay promised. He pulled her to him and holding her by the waist, leaned into her, planting a gentle kiss on her lips.

They stood like that for a long moment, then Tanya smiled and wiped her lipstick off his lips. "Did you put the hearing device into your ear?" she asked quietly.

"First thing I did; even before getting dressed," Jay laughed.

"Do you need another demo on using it?"

Jay picked up the small cell phone-sized case on the bed. He flipped it open to reveal a USB cable and VGA output. "No, I'm good," he said.

"I'm just worried about you!" Her feet moved towards him and her hands went to his coat lapels. "You've never done anything like this before."

"Don't worry," Jay winked. "I'll be fine. I'm an entrepreneur."

They walked out of the room together.

###

The seven stories of the Blue Frog Casino were glistening with light that evening as Sergei and Charkov drove their car past the archways and palm trees that lined the driveway. The hotel-casino was clearly inspired by Caesar's palace, Las Vegas, but Sergei and Charkov did not know that as they had never been to that part of the world.

Sergei watched the valets standing in line as their car moved along the curved sweep to the entrance. "This place looks entirely different at night," he noted.

"Who gives a fuck?" Charkov said as he moved forward slowly. "Get in, get drunk, gamble and get the job done. That's what we are here for."

"I've heard there are beautiful prostitutes in such places."

"You won't be able to afford them anyway so stop dreaming," said Charkov as he tossed the keys to one of the valets, who caught it and bowed.

"I hate this system," he told Sergei as the valet drove the car away. "I like to know where my car is if I need it on the spur of the moment."

"Relax. You're getting all worked up."

"I've got a bad feeling about this," Charkov mumbled. "This operation is running too smoothly. Remember what the General used to say at the Academy?"

"I remember," Sergei nodded. "If your target is too easy, it means you yourself are the target. But frankly, Char, we're chasing a normal guy here."

"The Boss hasn't said why he is so important. That makes me wonder."

"Has the Moslem called yet?"

"No."

"Then let's go in, relax, gamble a little," Sergei suggested.

"You're right," Charkov agreed. He took off his coat and the two walked into the plush interior.

###

Two miles away, Jay greeted Abdul Rehman with a smile. But the Moslem's face remained grim. "So you are totally in this madness are you?" he asked.

"Why do you care?" Jay asked. "You're getting paid, aren't you?"

"Just friendly concern, Brother," Abdul replied shortly, handing over the car keys.

Jay played with the keys. "Give me your IDs."

"I don't understand why you need so many of my IDs."

"You don't need to know. Just take the money and walk. It's not like you have anything to lose."

"If I get into trouble, I'll say I lost my wallet."

Jay smiled. *That's exactly what we want you to say.* "Goodbye then, Brother." Hugging a surprised Abdul, he got into the car and drove away, accelerating.

Abdul Rehman waited until his car was out of sight. Then he took out his cell phone and made the call

###

"It's on!" Charkov said.

"I'm losing anyway," Sergei replied dispiritedly.

Charkov looked at the slot machine in front of his partner. The bright screen showed two brinjals and a star.

"This thing is eating away my chips." Sergei slammed the machine.

"Didn't you hear me?" Charkov asked. "The Moslem just called. Our target has picked up the car and IDs from him."

"I heard you. It's nothing to get excited about."

"I'm not excited about that," Charkov laughed, flashing his phone at Sergei. "I'm excited about *this*."

The screen read under the contact name Boss: *Clearances received.*

"So it's really on," Sergei said, a small smile softening his rather harsh mouth. "Let's get to the front where we can see him coming in."

They moved away from the slot machines into the main hall, where Charkov found seats by the bar. "Two vodkas, plain," he told the bartender.

"I can't wait to finally get this son of a bitch," Sergei remarked.

"Well, all we have to do is wait!" Charkov said.

###

An hour later, Sergei tapped the bar counter again. "Which round is this?" he asked, pointing to his refilled glass.

The bartender raised five fingers. Sergei sighed and then pulled out his phone. His fingers struggled to punch in the numbers.

"Give it here!" Charkov growled, snatching the phone from him. He found Moslem's contact and called the number. "He should have been here, Serg," he said furiously, putting the phone to his ear.

"I know. And my eyes haven't left the entrance for a second." Sergei turned back to the bar.

"Neither have mine." Charkov called the number again and this time he got through. Sergei watched as Charkov spoke into the phone. "No, he isn't here yet. What do you mean he has to be here by now? ...No, we are not in the wrong casino...You get your tiny ass here as fast as you can and see if your car is in the parking. What is your license number? We'll look too." Charkov cut the call and looked at Sergei, his eyes glittering dangerously.

"I told you right at the start that I had a bad feeling about this one," Sergei remarked with a shrug.

"For fuck's sake, Serg! The Boss is going to kill us!" Charkov said, his voice shaking.

"Did he give you the registration number?" Sergei asked.

Charkov nodded, repeating it quickly.

"I'll go and check with the valets if such a car has come in while you keep watching the entrance."

"I thought you hated the valets," Charkov said morosely.

"I do. But now I hate Indians more." Sergei walked away.

###

Three floors above them, Jay climbed up the stairs of the fire exit slowly. He paused on the fourth floor as the door opening to the exit staircase was open. According to the building plans, this was the floor the restaurant was located on. Jay waited in the shadows, watching a silent figure in waiter's uniform standing some way away, smoking. Jay looked down at himself and smiled as he realized that the waiter's uniform matched his own almost perfectly. He hid in the shadows and waited for the waiter to finish.

Every moment of the last hour had seemed to last a lifetime. He wondered if Tanya was feeling the same. He recalled her horrified face when he had confessed, "I can't play poker."

"What!" she had yelled, loud enough to grab the attention of most others at the pool. "What do you mean you can't play poker?"

"I have never played poker in my life."

"How can you not have played poker?" Tanya hissed disbelievingly as she jumped into the pool beside him.

"I live in India. It's not a popular game there."

"Why didn't you tell me before?" she whispered angrily.

"Well, you've only just relayed the whole plan to me now. I thought I would be able to get away with my secret. But apparently not so."

"Well, this messes up my whole plan." Tanya stamped his foot underwater. "What are we going to do now?"

"It does not mess up everything."

"What are you talking about?"

"Well, I can't play poker," Jay agreed, "but you can."

###

"The valet says that a car with this number pulled up half an hour ago." Sergei had almost run to the bar with the dreadful news.

"What!" Charkov exclaimed. "Who was in it?"

"The valet said there was a couple." Sergei rubbed his palms together nervously. "The girl got down at the entrance and the man, cheap Indian he is, decided to drive the car himself to the parking."

"Goddamn it!" Charkov finished his shot in one gulp and got up. "Now which girl is this?"

"Blonde, Caucasian. The valet remembered her because she was hot."

"What are we going to do now?" Charkov asked, worry lines creasing his forehead.

"We are going to find this girl!" Sergei said. "I just paid the valet a hundred yuan for that."

###

Half a dozen tables away, completely oblivious to what was happening at the bar, Tanya sat at a high stakes poker game, concentrating on the deck in her dealer's hands. She had cursed Jay a hundred times but secretly worried about him even more. This last minute change had altered the metrics of their plan completely. She knew the fire exit went up to the seventh floor, but the seventh floor had many more security features such as key locks and laser walls. She had passed through such security countless times. It was child's play for her. But Jay! Could he do it? She had given him all the required devices, and would guide him with the earpiece, but would he make it?

"Raise," the man on her left declared, adding a fistful of chips to the pile on the table.

Tanya smiled. The man was a fool. She had already counted three jacks in the last round. There was no way he was going to get a full house. "I call." Tanya gently tapped the table and the game passed on. There was no need really to count the cards, but she wanted to seem suspicious.

When she won the last round, the Pit Boss in the corner had already taken note of her. She wondered how long they'd take to ID her. The car had definitely been scanned by the cameras at the entrance. It was standard casino practice and car registration numbers of all known Blackjacks was stored. The car would be spotted first.

As the next step, she had joined a high-stakes game – an area where the camera pointed continuously. Tanya was sure not much time would pass before a Pit Boss came over to try to ID her under the pretext of getting a form filled. Once she gave Abdul Rehman's fake ID, Security would immediately know that a Blackjack was in the house and call her in.

That part was easy. It was the next part that was harder, but she did not think about it then. Jay hadn't pinged the earphone either, which meant he had yet not reached the seventh floor. Her main concern was that Security should call her just as Jay entered the seventh floor, so most eyes in the security room would be on finding the Blackjack. She sighed. *I just hope they find me soon!*

###

A hundred paces away, Sergei and Charkov were wishing the same thing.

Sergei was negotiating with the receptionist, almost dragging in the valet he had spoken to. "This man is going to help us find a friend," he told her.

"But Bossman, we can't enter the casino floor!" the valet protested.

"Of course you can."

"Sir, it really isn't allowed. No external staff are allowed inside without security clearance," the receptionist explained, in vain.

"It'll just take a minute," Serge said and almost pulled the valet in. "You said she was hot," he said to the valet, "so now find her!"

"There are so many girls here, all hot..." the valet said, his voice trembling. He had never before set foot inside the casino. "How am I gonna find her?"

"Just use your imagination," Sergei whispered angrily. "Or I'll inform the management that you abused us."

"Please Sir, why are you doing this to me?" the valet pleaded. He was regretting having opened his mouth in the first place.

"Shut your mouth and concentrate!" Sergei's voice was stern, not to be denied. "What colour jacket was she wearing?"

The valet closed his eyes. "Black."

"What else do you remember?"

"A very short black skirt." The valet's ears burned, turning red.

"So go and look!" Sergei said, pushing him. "And look fast!"

###

"I'm on the seventh," Jay said into his earpiece. It had been so easy. But now there was no reply. Probably Tanya was busy. He touched the door and pushed it. It opened to reveal a long corridor. Jay stepped inside and walked down the corridor, his heart thudding in his chest. *Just let Tanya get to me quickly!* he prayed.

###

Tanya tried not to notice when the Pit Boss walked up to her and bent to say, "Miss, would you like to fill in a form for a complementary stay at our hotel?"

Tanya looked at him. "Do I have to?"

"It won't take a minute," the Pit Boss assured her. "I just need an ID, that's all. We'll fill everything else."

Just what I wanted! Tanya opened her purse and extracted Abdul's ID. Holding it between two slim fingers, she handed it over.

"I'll be right back," the man in the tuxedo said and walked away.

###

"It's gotta be her!" the valet said, pointing at a blonde at the bar.

"Did she have long hair?" Sergei asked.

"Umm, no, rather short." The valet coughed and looked at the floor. Sergei raised his voice. "Then look again!"

The valet took a deep breath and turned his head to scan the hall. His gaze stopped at the poker tables.

"That's her!" He was breathless in his excitement.

"You sure?" Sergei asked.

"A hundred percent. That's definitely her."

Charkov walked up to them and looked at the quarry. She was a blonde woman in a black suit and skirt.

"Are you really sure that it's her?" Sergei asked again.

The valet nodded vigorously.

"Fine. I'll go get her," Charkov said.

"How will you get her?" Sergei asked.

"I'll just go and tell her there's a problem with her car. I'll point to you. Maybe she'll recognize the valet."

"Ask her to find her partner, to attend to the car," Sergei suggested "Meanwhile I'll stand here."

Charkov nodded and slowly walked towards the blonde. When he was halfway, he paused as the Pit Boss came and bent by the blonde's side. The Pit Boss urged her to rise and go with him and she began arguing with him. Charkov trotted over as fast as he could without appearing to be running, but the Pit Boss took her hand and led her away from the table. She picked up her purse as she went. They went to an elevator and disappeared inside it, the doors closing behind them.

Damn! Charkov cursed. The Boss was going to be very angry indeed.

###

Jay was stuck. The corridor he had entered had curved along the seventh floor and ended at a wooden door requiring a passcode. Fortunately, there were no cameras. Tanya had guessed that correctly. 'I don't think they'll be cameras on the seventh,' she had said, 'because it's Sasha's residence."

Jay gazed at the lock code solemnly for some time before getting to his knees and whisking out his phone from his jacket pocket.

Tanya's device had a protruding USB cable. 'All key codes have a USB port,' she had told him. 'It is a gateway in case the owners forget the code.' Jay searched and found the port. He inserted the cable and waited for the device to come to life. The screen glowed after a few moments. They had practiced with their hotel room keycode last night. Silently, Jay began to work.

###

"I think there's been a mistake," the Security Manager on the sixth floor said, looking at the ID card and then at Tanya. The lines on his face were contracted in confusion. "This ID belongs to a different person."

"Does it?" Tanya took the ID from him, opened her purse and sighed. "It must have been exchanged at the car rental," she said.

"You rented your car, ma'am?" the security guy asked, his eyes never moving from her face.

"I did," Tanya told him. "I rented it from a gentleman named Abdul Rehman and this ID is his. We must have exchanged our IDs by mistake."

"Did Mr. Abdul come with you?" the Manager asked, still holding the ID card.

"No." She shook her head. "I just rented his car. I guess I'll have to go back and get my ID now. How bothersome when I was having such a winning streak."

"We are sorry for the inconvenience, ma'am." The Manager handed the card back after glancing at it one last time. "Drinks are on the house."

"That's lovely of you." Tanya gave him a big smile and began walking away. She glanced back to make sure the Manager was back at his station.

She found the elevator to the seventh floor just across the hall. Ignoring the bystanders on calls at the large glass panels, she pressed the button. If anyone caught her, all she had to say was she was on the wrong elevator.

The doors opened with a ding. Tanya took a deep breath and walked in.

###

Jay pondered over the digits. The process had seemed much simpler last night. Here, under pressure, he could not think clearly. It took some time, but he finally managed to crack the key code.

The door opened with a click and Jay walked inside. Now, all he had to do was find Mrs. Makijan and hope that she was not some crazy old lady who walked around with an SMG and grenades.

###

"I'm on the seventh," Tanya said into her mouthpiece once the elevator doors opened to let her out. To her great relief, there was no one there as she stepped out.

"I'm here too," Jay's voice came over the crackle. "I just broke the key code."

Tanya smiled. "Wow! I'm proud of you. Have you found her yet?"

"No," Jay said, falling silent.

"What happened, Jay?"

There was no reply.

###

"Speak, Jay!" Tanya said nervously. "What happened?"

There was silence for a few moments. Then Jay's voice whispered through her earpiece, "I hear something, wait!" He had heard low, gruff sounds from the end of the corridor.

"What is it?" Tanya asked again.

"Will you stop talking so I can hear?" Jay said. The sounds seemed familiar. "Fuck! A dog!" Jay cursed under his breath.

"Are you sure?"

Jay grunted in irritation. The growling was coming from behind the door.

"Well, toss it some meat or something," Tanya said.

"That doesn't work," Jay whispered back. He recalled reading in an article that trained dogs did not accept food from anyone but their trainers.

"We must distract him." Tanya said. "Where are you exactly?"

"The corridor leading to the fire exit."

In his head, he remembered the building plans they had studied the night before. Tanya had come in from the elevator, that meant she had entered the floor in the middle, while he was on the east side.

"I'll come towards you," she said. "We'll deal with the dog together."

"Be careful!" Jay warned.

"I will be," she replied confidently.

In the earpiece he could hear footsteps and then a door being unlocked. He heard a female voice call to the dog. The dog barked happily in answer.

Tanya's really good, Jay thought as he opened the door. He froze, the door only half open. The woman next to the dog was not Tanya. And she was looking at him.

###

Tanya trod along the hallway slowly, careful not to trip on the rugs that lined the floor. She had one more room to pass to get to where Jay was. *Hope the dog hasn't smelt him yet,* she thought as she heard a soft bark from the room. She took hold of the doorknob and carefully turned it, expecting to see the dog Jay was so nervous about.

She did not see the dog.

Jay recovered first. When the elderly Asian lady before him began shouting in Chinese, Jay quickly said, "Please allow me to explain, Mrs. Makijan."

The woman did not seem to understand and kept shouting. Behind her, Jay saw Tanya at the other door. She shrugged as if to say, 'What should we do?' At the woman's feet the Pomerian jumped about, confused whether to growl at Jay or Tanya.

"Mrs. Makijan, please hear what I have to say!" Jay said, stepping into the room.

The old woman, visibly terrified at his advance, raised her voice.

"Mrs. Makijan, please stop screaming," Jay said.

The old woman suddenly stopped shouting.

"Thank god!" Jay said, relieved. "My name is Jay Rasbihari, and I want to..." He stopped as he realized the woman was not looking at him. She was looking behind him. Jay's heart skipped a beat.

"She is not Ms. Makijan," another voice said from behind him.

Jay turned slowly. Behind him, another elderly Asian woman, dressed in a gown and speaking impeccable English, stood with her arms folded across her chest.

"I am Ms. Makijan," she said.

15
MANCHURIA
FILE 8/JAN/XVII/14: TOP SECRET

1949

According to what Akhtar told the four of them in the hotel that night, and what he later wrote in his diary, he had pulled off what is called in tactical terms, a *Cress de Laure*, widely accepted as one of the most difficult maneuvers a spy can execute to fool his quarry. And Akhtar had done just that.

In this classic French move, made popular by Napoleon in his battles, there are two participants. One is the *spy* who plans and puts the plan into motion. The other is the *victim* whom it befalls on. The spy ambushes the victim at a time and place the victim least expects. Before the victim is alarmed, the spy declares himself as friendly. The spy then creates a fictional character, the villain, and makes the victim believe the villain is out to get him by inventing a story. Furthermore, the spy tells the victim that he can save himself from the villain if he does exactly what the spy says.

The spy then leads the victim to a controlled situation in which the villain appears. In reality, the villain is an accomplice of the spy and is controlled by him. Believing that the villain is out to get him, the victim flees. The spy appears as pre-decided and rids the victim of the villain, apparently saving him. Believing he owes the spy his life, he gives the spy whatever information he asks for, never realizing the whole thing was an act to extract that information.

In the present scenario, the victim was the mysterious man whose name was later revealed to be Mr. Okura. The spy who thought up of the deception was Akhtar. The only difference here from the conventional *Cress de Laure* was the role of the villain, played by an unwilling Singh.

According to Akhtar, the man they were after was Okura San, a long serving Colonel in the Imperial Japanese Army. He had fought in the

Great War of 1914-1918, but was now retired. His son, Ichiro Okura, had also served in the Imperial Japanese army, continuing the family tradition of soldiering, but had been killed in action. The man, Akhtar said, was interested in the ashes for one reason only – the ashes did not belong to Bose, but to his son.

Akhtar explained how he had made the man confess the truth, having rightly deduced that the ashes must belong to someone he was related to. This clearly implied that the man had knowledge of what actually happened in the Bose mystery crash. Judging by the man's military manner and advanced age, Akhtar had been sure the man would not speak under the interrogation Singh and the rest of the team planned to subject him to on capture. Being part of the Delhi underworld, where everything was ruled by men like this, Akhtar had a very good idea of their tenacity. However, he had an inkling the man would open up if they approached him as friends. The only way to make this possible was a *Cress de Laure*.

Akhtar rightly assumed that if the ceremony that was to be conducted at the temple that night was so important to the man, he would turn up before that to see how the preparations were coming along. So while the others were busy planning the kidnap at the hotel, Akhtar lurked about the temple, waiting for his quarry to arrive.

His assumption turned out to be right. Okura arrived at the temple that afternoon. He did not stay long and left the temple compound within an hour of his arrival. Akhtar tailed him, paying the nearest cabbie to follow Okura's car.

It turned out that Okura lived in a comfortable mansion in the countryside outside Tokyo. Akhtar realized it was time to put his plan into motion. He clutched the fake gun he had lifted from their supplies and slipped inside the compound. The guard at the entrance, long used to inaction, was asleep. It was easy as pie to climb over the wall and go over to Okura's car. It was a Toyota and Akhtar was a past master at picking locks. He had done it a hundred times in Japanese-occupied Indo-China. Opening the back door, he hid between the back and front seats, covering himself with a blanket he found in the car. He waited patiently, something every spy learns to do, hoping Okura would not spot him when he came.

When Okura got into the car, dressed in full military uniform, darkness had fallen. With the shadows around him and his own weakening eyesight, he did not notice anything amiss. He carried with him a photo frame, which he placed on the backseat. As Okura drove, Akhtar took a good look at the frame. He hunched back under the blanket in shock. The young boy in the frame looked very much like Netaji, though the face had clear Mongoloid features.

By the time car entered Tokyo, Akhtar had begun to piece the whole thing together. The age of the boy in the photograph strongly suggested he was Okura's slain son. The ashes lying in Renkoji Temple were his. This was then the reason why, when the four Indians had disturbed the sanctity of the ashes chamber, the priests of the temple had relayed the information to Okura-San, who had then arrived to vent his fury on the Reverend. This was why the Reverend had been so hesitant about letting them see the ashes at all. It had taken the costly bribe of the camera to get him to agree.

Next, things happened very quickly. Akhtar was counting on the speed of events to disorient Okura. As the car drove up to the temple, Akhtar put the fake gun to Okura's head. Okura made no effort to resist, simply asking what Akhtar wanted. Akhtar quickly explained that he was a friend, that he would help Okura. Taking a big gamble, he told Okura some Indians were after his life; that they knew about Bose and Okura's son.

Okura's reaction confirmed Akhtar's deduction had been right. Okura said he had always known this day would come. The secret could not be kept forever. Akhtar told him he worked for the Indian Government and would save him. He told Okura that, as soon as he stepped out of the car, a man would come to shoot him. However, they would deceive this man and kill him instead. Akhtar asked Okura to step out and walk towards the temple doors slowly.

From the corner of his eye, he watched Singh slowly descending the hill. Akhtar waited till Okura was halfway between the car and the door and then ran to the other side, flanking Singh. That way, when Singh descended the hill, he was between Akhtar and Okura. As Singh pointed his fake gun at Okura, Akthar pointed his at Singh's head. He felt a devilish satisfaction as he shot Singh in the head.

Singh had been merely knocked out, but Okura could not tell that in the dark. Akhtar rushed Okura back to the car. Though shocked, Okura took the wheel and they drove away. In the rear view mirror Akhtar caught sight of Dinesh and Harman's car hurrying towards the temple. He hid a smile as they drove away from the temple. The *Cress de Laure* had been a success.

Akhtar said he covertly interrogated Okura as they drove towards his home in the countryside. Perhaps the shock of events made him less guarded in his answers. He confirmed that the ashes did not belong to Netaji, but his son, Ichiro Okura, a spy in the Japanese army. Ichiro had been recruited as Bose's body double by the Japanese army due to the likeness. But Ichiro had been killed in Indo-China during the last American offensive of 1945. But when Okura went to get his son's ashes, he discovered that the Military had nor had a military burial for him, nor would they hand over his son's ashes. Even the records of his son's service had been erased. It was as if Ichiro had never existed.

But Okura was no common man. Following his retirement from the military, he had been running a successful securities business. With this money and his old military connections, he managed to find out that Ichiro's ashes were involved in a highly covert operation. He learned that Ichiro was working for a Japanese mercenary called Kobayashi when he died. Okura searched for Kobayashi.

The trail led to Taiwan, where he found that his son's body had been preserved in an ice box. Upon heated interrogation, higher Japanese officials contacted him and told him his son's body was required for a national cause; that he would be serving his Emperor by remaining silent. By 1945 it was already clear that Japan would eventually lose the war. Okura had indeed remained silent, till now.

It was clear Kobayashi was involved in some big way. Akhtar parted ways with Okura outside his house, telling him to lay low for a while. Then he rushed back to the hotel, to find himself greeted by three pistols pointed at his heart.

"Your plan could have failed at so many places," Singh said disapprovingly, once he had heard the whole story. "You have been reckless!"

"But it did *not* fail, and here we are," Akhtar pointed out, getting some coffee for himself from the thermos.

"I never thought we'd run into Kobayashi again," Singh murmured, sitting down. He had completely forgotten about his aching head.

"Wait..." Rupali said, sitting down too, "you *know* this Kobayashi?"

"Do we know him!" Akhtar laughed mirthlessly.

"He is the greatest guerilla mercenary to ever exist," Singh said quietly, reaching into his jacket and taking out a pack of cigarettes. He offered it to Akhtar, who took a cigarette with a brief nod.

"We tutored under him," Akhtar said, lighting up.

"What!" Rupali gasped.

"He's the most dangerous person I've ever met," Singh mused, taking a drag on his own cigarette.

"I know you guys consider me something of an asshole," Akhtar said, gently blowing out smoke rings, "but this Kobayashi guy makes me look like a sweet teddy bear."

"You never told me about this part of your life," Rupali said, looking at Singh.

"Believe me, it was not worth telling. After we were recruited into the INA, they sent us to Manchuria, to be trained under Kobayashi. We served under him for a year and then returned to take up positions as officers of the INA."

"We did horrible things for him," Akhtar said. "If you thought Burma was hell, it was nothing compared to Manchuria."

"He works only for money." Singh observed. "Kobayashi has no loyalty to anyone."

"If Kobayashi downed Netaji's plane," Harman said, "we must find him, no matter how dangerous he is! We must find him and bring him to justice."

"Knowing Kobayashi," Akhtar said, "he couldn't have done this on his own. He must've done it for money."

"Then someone else must have asked him to do it!" Rupali said.

"Who?" Harman wondered.

"There's only one way to find out." Singh said, tossing his cigarette into the ashtray. "We'll find him and ask him ourselves."

###

Kobayashi San, also called Vakhoma Tajiki, 'The Dragon' in Japanese, was believed to be one of the few who profited enormously from World War II. He was thought to have been born in Tokyo, but few people were privy to the details of Kobayashi's birth and parentage. Due to the lack of information, many stories grew up around the man. Some said he was the bastard son of Emperor Hirohito. Others said he was a Shinto priest who had managed to raise the Old Gods, who granted him great powers. Some even said he was an American double agent. There was no credible proof to support any of these suppositions.

Not many knew what Kobayashi had done before he became Head of his mercenary company, Green Dragons. Some said that he had been an opium distributor in Korea, others said he had run a shipping company from Hiroshima. And some said he undertook CIA training in America. But every account of Kobayashi's life converged on one fact - that sometime around 1935, he became involved with Hazuka, the previous Head of Green Dragons. He seemed to have impressed Hazuka because Kobayashi was the one Hazuka left the leadership of the Green Dragons to on his deathbed.

Thus Kobayashi ended up with the leadership of Green Dragons sometime around 1937. His first client was the Government of Nationalist China, then fighting a civil war against the Communist China of Mao Tse Tung. Kobayashi distinguished himself as a guerilla mercenary. His offensive against Communist China was deadly and fateful. It ended in 1939, when Japan invaded China. Some said he betrayed his Chinese masters and crossed to the Japanese because of his affiliation to his birth country, but most people believed it was because the Japanese government had offered him more money.

As part of the Japanese vanguard in China, Kobayashi penetrated deep behind enemy lines, conducting raids of all kinds. His earlier operations in the same land had made him something of an expert in local warfare.

Kobayashi remained in Japanese employ during 1939-1945, during the entire span of WWII. It is almost certain that he took over the training of the INA recruits such as Singh and Akhtar, during this period. Under Kobayashi, the INA recruits fought Chinese troops in mainland China. There is a strong consensus that Kobayashi personally knew both Akhtar and Singh due to the bravery and grit the two displayed in operations. It was said that the rivalry between Singh and Akhtar, went back to those days under Kobayashi.

But Kobayashi's current location was unknown. The team took quite some time to find anything more about him. They dug for information at the Indian as well as Japanese Embassies. They remained in Tokyo for almost six months during this period. Then they found a nugget that told them Kobayashi was in the employ of his older masters again, the Government of Nationalist China. The Green Dragons were camped in Manchuria, waiting to launch an offensive against Communist China.

So that was where the team flew to.

###

Singh and the others landed in Manchuria in July 1948. They discovered the rough location of Kobayashi and his mercenary troupe but had still to zero in on their target. Kobayashi's exact location was a state military secret due to the civil war in the mainland.

After a day spent asking around the local taverns and gambling houses, the team gathered at their inn. Fluttering Chinese lamps hung from the ceiling, casting a pale yellow light as the team discussed what they had found.

"I did locate a few sheep herders who knew of his location, but would not speak of it," Dinesh said.

"It is obvious they are afraid to disclose his location," Rupali said. "He is clearly a terror in this area. Even the local doctors will not speak of him."

"It's also obvious none of you have found anything," Akhtar said lounging back in his chair, "because you went about it in the wrong way."

"It's true," Singh agreed. "The two of us found out much more."

"Because we were aware of his modus operandi, we knew exactly what to look for," Akhtar smiled.

"It's good to see you two working together without bickering for once," Rupali observed.

"We bonded over smoke," Singh said.

"While the rest of you were roaming about trying to find information," Akhtar said, "Singh and I were lounging in the VIP section of the biggest opium den in town."

"It was quite a high for me, being the first time I had ever ingested the substance," Singh remarked. "But Akhtar seemed quite in the habit."

Akhtar shrugged. "A man's got to unwind sometimes. The important point is that we discovered the exact location of Kobayashi's camp and a possible way to infiltrate into it."

"Are we to sneak in under cover of night?" Harman asked.

"I would never try something of that sort with Kobayashi," Akhtar said, his voice hard. "If we are to go in that way, I'm certain we will never come out alive."

"So what exactly did you find out?" Dinesh asked.

"Well, first we smoked opium and hallucinated," Akhtar laughed.

"Isn't opium illegal?" Rupali asked, not sure she approved of this.

"Not here." Singh shook his head. "Everyone smokes the stuff in these small Chinese towns."

"However, what is rare, even in the heartland of China, is this." Akhtar showed them a small glass bottle.

"Heroin," Singh clarified. "It delivers a more potent dose of opium than opium itself. Following the 1924 ban on heroin in the US, black markets for the substance mushroomed in China towns across America."

"They get their supply from China," Akhtar added. "A supply guaranteed and maintained by numerous men like Kobayashi."

"And if someone wants heroin in this region," Singh told the others, "they must get it from men like him."

"The opium den owner pointed us in the right direction as soon as we told him we wanted a good stock," Akhtar said cynically. "Kobayashi must be the only supplier in the region."

"And it must be most profitable for them both," Singh agreed.

"Chatting up the opium den owner gave us even more information," Akhtar added. "It seems that Kobayashi gets his supply of heroin from Shan, down south. A motorcade arrives at his camp from the fields every week."

"And one motorcade arrived yesterday," Singh added. "So we have a week to plan our way in."

"Are we going to ambush the motorcade?" Harman Singh asked.

"I wouldn't dare do that," Akhtar laughed. "The motorcade carries enough firepower to flatten an army. It is said to have ten tanks and five dozen men with rifles."

"Then how are we going to get to Kobayashi?" Rupali asked.

"We both learned one thing from our time with Kobayashi," Singh said. "The reason he is not dead is because he trusts no one."

"He sees no one and is surrounded by bodyguards," Akhtar said.

"Even the women he sleeps with are stripped and searched before they are brought to him," Singh told them.

"And I'm sure he still has the habit of wearing important keys around his neck at all times, like that of the truck carrying the shipment."

"The only people who meet Kobayashi are those who bring him something of importance."

"Money or information," Akhtar observed curtly.

"So that is our way in," Singh said. "We will take him information that is important to him."

"What information could we possibly have that would be of interest to him?" Dinesh asked sceptically.

"At this moment, nothing." Akhtar rubbed his hands together. "But Singh here has learned something from that act I pulled off in Renkoji and has come up with a plan."

"Heroin is expensive," Singh said, ignoring the jibe. "And it is an important part of Kobayashi's income."

"So are we going to steal his opium convoy?" Harman asked.

"No. We are going to make it seem that his heroin shipment has been stolen."

"And then?" Dinesh asked.

"And then we are going to bring it back to him."

"But how are we going to steal it in the first place?" Rupali wanted to know, hoping there were no lingering opium fumes befuddling her husband's brain.

"Here's the fun part," Singh said. "We are not going to steal it."

"Who is?" asked Rupali, not sure what was next.

"I have just the person in mind," Akhtar said, smiling.

###

Enough evidence exists to indicate that Akhtar had known Sasha Makijan even before the team ventured on this mission to Japan. Analyzing Sasha's known history, they could have met in Singapore, where there were many Japanese military men in the occupied British colony. Coupled with the rich traders who called Singapore home, the services of an attractive young lady like Sasha would have been in great demand. Akhtar perhaps knew her as a regular client or from having used her in his operations, as he planned to use her again. Whatever the circumstances of their acquaintance, Sasha flew from Tokyo to Manchuria on 15th August 1948, the first anniversary of independent India. And she flew in exclusively for Akhtar.

Sasha never met most of the team, interacting only with Akhtar. The other one from the team who got to see her was Singh, when he went with Akhtar to deliver her to her target on the fateful day of 21st August 1948.

It was afternoon and the opium den was crowded as usual. The owner ran over to welcome the two foreign gentlemen, remembering them from their generous tip the last time. He ushered them into the biggest lounge in his establishment.

"Have you got what we asked for, San?"

Though Akhtar's Mandarin was broken at best, the den owner nodded. "The heroin is packed and loaded," he said. "In the basement; paid by you in full."

"It is a great honor to do business with Kobayashi San," Akhtar said. "We would like to offer him a gift." He pointed to Sasha, dressed in a traditional kimono.

The den owner nodded. "Kobayashi San will like your gift."

Akhtar took him aside. "The girl is for Kobayashi San exclusively," he whispered. "Anyone who dares touch her..." he moved a finger across his throat.

"I understand. I will take the girl to Kobayashi San."

"Maybe we could take her ourselves?" Akhtar said.

The man shook his head furiously. "Not a chance. I already told you. Kobayashi San does not do business himself, only through proxies."

Akhtar nodded. "So be it."

###

Sasha Makjan was taken to the Kobayashi compound that night. Apparently, Kobayashi did not like to keep beautiful young women waiting. Either that or he could not wait to disport himself in the company of beautiful young women. Sasha certainly went through all the routine checks for Kobayashi's women. She was stripped and inspected for weapons; made to kiss a woman slave to ensure she was carrying no poison in her mouth. Finally, her nails were cut short. She was also bathed and dabbed with fragrances before being taken to a bedroom where Kobayashi would grace her with his presence.

How Kobayashi San graced Sasha we do not know, but it must have been an exhausting session for he soon fell asleep. In the dark of night, Sasha took the keys to the truck from around his neck and crept downstairs, as silent as a shadow. She slipped behind the wheel of the truck and drove away, probably the only prostitute in the Far East who could fuck and drive a truck equally well. She did her job perfectly and drove out of the Kobayashi compound, watching each door opening automatically before her because the guards thought that it was Kobayashi-San himself driving the truck.

The next day word spread that Kobayashi's heroin shipment had been stolen. Soldiers visited towns nearby and afar, trying to get information. The opium den owner who had brought the girl to Kobayashi was flogged. Weeping in fear, he blurted out the news about the two foreigners who had gifted her to him. Kobayashi began searching vigorously for the two foreigners who had outsmarted him but they were nowhere to be found.

He received word that a couple living a few miles away had news about his shipment. The word grew stronger when a photograph of Sasha arrived, retrieved from the couple by his minions. Kobayashi decided to have the couple brought to the compound for a personal audience.

###

That morning, Singh rose early, just as the alarm on his wristwatch rang at 6:00am. Seeing that his wife was still fast asleep under the white blankets, he gently rolled away. After the truck and heroin shipment had been stolen from the Kobayashi compound, Akhtar and he had met Sasha in the outskirts of the town, as decided. They had taken over the truck and sped away in another direction, picking the rest of the team up on the way.

Sasha flew back to Tokyo immediately, where she was safe from Kobayashi's clutches. She went back to her business as a geisha. How much she was paid for this daring act we cannot know, but it must have been a worthwhile amount, giving her a headstart in her criminal career.

Some distance on, Singh and Rupali had got down from the truck. They then succeeded in renting a small house in a local small town, as per plan. Akhtar drove the others, along with the heroin, to a safe house.

Singh and Rupali waited for a few days, watching Kobayashi's men search the countryside. Then they leaked word that they had news of the thieves. Singh told Kobayashi's minions just enough to make them believe the thieves had stopped at his house that night, in passing. Singh insisted he would only tell everything to the Big Boss. So, the next day, Singh and Rupali were driven to the Kobayashi compound where they were thoroughly frisked. Then they were taken to Kobayashi's study in his sprawling mansion.

The legendary Japanese mercenary, once lean as a whip, was now obese with indulgence. He sat at his table, smoking. His traditional Japanese beard was longer than Singh remembered, but the glittering eyes had lost none of their sharpness.

"I recognize you," Kobayashi said instantly, chewing on his big cigar which smelled of hash. "Is this a joke?"

Singh bowed formally. "It is not a joke," he said. "Allow me to introduce you to my wife, Kobayashi San."

Kobayashi rose. Taking Rupali's hand, he kissed with gallant grace. "Your hand does not smell like that of the whore who stole my shipment," he said. "Besides, she was Japanese."

"We had your shipment stolen," Singh told him. "It is safe, with Akhtar."

"Akhtar is here too?" Kobayashi laughed. "Are we having a student-teacher reunion?"

"No. We are looking for Bose. Netaji."

Kobayashi's faced turned grim. "What would I know about that?" he said. 'I am a simple Japanese mercenary."

"We know about Ichiro Okura," Singh said. "We know you downed Netaji's plane."

"And why would I tell you anything?"

"Because you want your shipment," Singh said softly. "And if Akhtar does not hear from us today, he will set fire to the entire consignment."

"Working together now are you?" Kobayashi mocked. "In those days you could never see eye to eye."

"All we need is the name of the person who ordered you to down Netaji's plane and cover up the whole business."

Kobayashi laughed in genuine amusement. "You went to all this trouble just for that?" he asked, his belly shaking with mirth.

Singh nodded in silence.

"You could have just asked me. I always liked you, Singh."

"You're not exactly an easy man to meet."

"Easier than your Netaji."

"You mean Netaji is alive?" Singh asked, astonished.

"If he wasn't," Kobayashi replied lazily, "why would I have to take such pains to present Okura's ashes as his?"

"That's what we wanted to ask you. Why did you do it?"

"Because Netaji himself asked me to," Kobayashi said.

"What...and you did it? why?"

"For one good reason," Kobayashi said. "Because he paid me."

###

According to Kobayashi's statement to Singh, witnessed by Rupali, Netaji Subhash Chandra Bose himself hired the mercenary to down his plane. Privy to the plan were a few Japanese military officials and some close associates of Bose from the INA. Kobayashi said Bose met him at the end of 1944, in Indo-China, to discuss the plan. It was clear at the time that Japan would lose the war. The American offensive in the Pacific had begun. Bose knew the allies would go after him.

The plan was that Kobayashi would engineer the plane crash, only that it would not be an actual crash and the plane would be brought down from air very slowly. Nobody would be hurt. A charred body would be shown as Bose's.

"The apparatus for this project was being built in Formosa," Kobayashi said. "We were expecting Japanese surrender around the end of 1945, but Bose contacted me in June 1945, asking me to put our plan into motion."

"So Bose knew the Japanese would surrender soon?" Singh asked.

"I wouldn't know. I merely do what I'm paid for."

"What did Bose tell you in June 1945?" Rupali asked, speaking for the first time. It all seemed incredible to her. "That was precisely a month before his death."

"Not his death. But yes, one month before our operation."

"What did you tell him?" Singh asked.

"That I could not transport the equipment to Singapore in the short time span he was asking for."

"And so he said he would come to Formosa?" Singh's eyes narrowed into slits as he put the story together.

"Precisely." Kobayashi agreed.

"Why didn't you do it in June then?" Rupali asked.

Kobayashi shrugged. "Perhaps Bose wanted a good enough reason to leave Singapore and come to Taiwan."

"And the surrender provided that," Singh said.

"What happened after the crash?" Rupali wanted to know.

"After the crash, I sent Bose to Manchuria," Kobayashi said. "Near the Russian border."

"Why would Netaji go to Manchuria?" Singh wondered. He dredged his memory for some clue from their last days with Netaji.

"I didn't give a damn where he went," Kobayashi retorted, annoyed by the questioning. "I did my job."

"You just said you admired the man," Rupali reminded him. "If he is alive, he needs to be found."

"I also admire Vivian Leigh and her thighs," Kobayashi smirked. "If I was to find everything on my admiration list, I'd go after her first."

Singh slammed his fist into his palm. He had remembered something. "The last speech!" he exclaimed.

"What?" Rupali and Kobayashi said in unison, both looking confused.

"In his last speech, Netaji said he'd go to any lengths to win freedom for our country."

Rupali shrugged. "That doesn't add anything new."

"No," Singh agreed, "but his next words do."

Closing her eyes, Rupali tried to remember. Finally she said, "I would go to any lengths to win freedom for my country. I'd even go to the Russians."

"Do you think he went to Russia?" Singh asked.

Kobayashi rubbed his chin. "It is possible. The border was easily crossed in those days. Not anymore."

"Did he speak to you about going to Russia?" Singh asked again.

"He did not. And why would he go to Russia? They were part of the Allies. They would have handed him over to the British."

"They aren't part of the Allies now," Singh said.

"Bose would never have gone to the Russians," Kobayashi insisted. "The Russians could not have helped him."

"He went to the *Japanese*," Singh argued.

"That was different," Kobayashi said. "The Japanese were occupying Indian territory."

Singh sighed, running a hand over his hair. "There is only one way to find out," he finally said. "We'll follow his footsteps. We'll go into Russia."

"The border is tough these days," Kobayashi warned him. "Only my men can go in and out."

Singh looked at the ageing mercenary, a mischievous gleam in his eyes. "Exactly. So you are going to take us across the border."

"And why would I do that?" Kobayashi mocked.

"So you get your opium shipment back," Singh said.

"I gave you *this* information for the shipment. I'll do nothing more."

"You will."

Kobayashi looked at the Indian, his eyes hard as agates. "And why would I do that?"

"Because we are going in to find out what happened after you left him in Manchuria," Singh said, unperturbed by the latent hostility. "I believe you want that information as much as we do."

Kobayashi folded his arms across his chest. "Do I? I think you have misunderstood. I admired Bose, but I will not put my men in danger to find out what happened to him. About that part, I don't give a shite about him."

"I know," Singh said, "you only give a shite about money."

"You know me well," Kobayashi smiled.

"And that is exactly why you will take us across the border." Singh folded his arms too.

"You lost me there," Kobayashi said.

"Can I ask how much Netaji paid you for the operation?" Singh asked.

"Five pounds of solid gold," Kobayashi said without hesitation.

"That was generous," Singh said, nodding. "Did you ever think how he had so much money to give?"

"It was not my concern."

"It should have been," Singh told him. "It is our good fortune you did not care, else you would have killed Netaji and seized what he was carrying."

Kobayashi leaned forward, chin on hand. "What was he carrying?"

"One hundred pounds of gold. Remnants of the INA treasury he raised in Singapore.

Kobayashi whistled softly. "That much?"

"Bose was carrying a vast treasure into Russia," Singh told him. "He was alone. He erased his tracks using your fake crash. And the fact that he used you to cover his tracks shows how desperate he was."

"Maybe he ran away with the money," Kobayashi laughed.

"He wasn't a man like you," Singh said softly. "He was a true patriot."

"You have raised a very curious point." Kobayashi gazed at the ceiling.

"Netaji was carrying a hundred pounds of gold into Russia," Singh said. "And if we find him, we'll know where that gold is as well."

Kobayashi's gaze fell from the ceiling and fixed itself on Singh's face. "And if you find him," he said, "you know where to find me. I will take you across the border."

15
The Geisha

2015

On the eighth floor of the Blue Frog Casino, Jay and Tanya were embroiled in a Mexican standoff with the real Sasha Makijan. The elderly, perfectly coiffed woman waved a small switch at them menacingly, as Jay and Tanya stood rooted at either door to the room.

"Jay, she has an alarm in her hand," Tanya cautioned.

Sasha was indeed holding a switch in her hand. The small Pomeranian loitered at her feet, growling at them incessantly. The other Chinese woman bowed and moved to her mistress' side, facing the two intruders. Jay felt his heart thudding in his chest. They were so close!

"So what was it that you wanted to tell me?" Sasha asked, holding the switch up in her right hand. "I give you three tries before I press the button."

"We want to speak with you, Ma'am," Jay said.

"Wrong," she said, lifting her thumb.

"We want to speak to you about your past."

"Wrong," she said again.

"We believe you have something we want."

"It's done." She pressed the alarm. A siren started ululating overhead.

Jay looked at Tanya who had turned pale. "We just wanted to speak to you about Irshad Akhtar," Jay shouted above the shrill sound of the alarm.

"You want to speak to me about what?" the old lady asked, lowering the switch.

"Irshad Akhtar," Jay repeated. "We believe you knew each other."

"Akhtar," she said. Her face was no longer blank. The lines on her forehead told Jay the name had struck a chord. She pressed a button and the siren fell instantly silent. "Who are you to him?" she asked.

Outside, they could hear footsteps approaching. *Fuck!* cursed Jay as the door opened and a dozen Chinese carrying UZIs stormed into the room. They were certainly not from the Security they had seen downstairs in the casino but tattooed necks and had wore black leather jackets. It appeared that an entirely different kind of security protected Sasha Makijan. The Chinese Commander who led the group quickly scanned the room from corner to corner. His gaze stopped when it reached Jay. From the corner of his eye Jay noticed the UZIs had their safety catches off.

"Is there a problem, Mrs. Makijan?" the Commander asked.

"The problem is with this damn alarm." Sasha showed him the control. "It goes off when it shouldn't, especially when I have guests."

The Chinese looked at Jay and slowly turned his gaze towards Tanya. His eyes were confused. "These are your guests?" he asked.

"Indeed," Sasha said. The Chinese took in Jay's waiter's garb. "What about him?" he asked.

"He came with the drinks," Sasha said. "Now please take this faulty alarm and make sure I get a new one, will you?"

"Yes, ma'am." The Chinese took it from her and handed it over to one of his men.

"And make sure no one disturbs us," she called after them as they filed out of the room.

Sasha sat down on the sofa and indicated her guests should be seated as well. Her maid brought them green tea. The white Pomeranian, now silent, sat at her feet like a harmless ball of fur.

"You two took a great risk in trying to reach me."

"Frankly, we had no other choice," Jay said, taking the beaker of fragrant tea the maid offered him. "You were our only lead."

"Only lead for what?" Sasha's eyes never left his face.

"To find my mother."

Sasha's gaze did not waver and there was no sign of surprise on her lined but still beautiful face. "I will repeat the question I asked you before," she said. "Who are you to Irshad Akhtar? And what do you know about us?"

"Years ago, you sent a letter to my mother, Azaadi Singh," Jay explained. "The letter was addressed to my mother by Irshad Akhtar, yet you were the one who actually sent it."

Sasha rubbed her chin with one finger. "How did you find out it was I who sent that letter?"

"I have my ways," Jay said calmly.

"So you are the grandson of Major and Dr. Singh." Sasha remarked thoughtfully. "You look like your grandfather, though I saw him only once."

"So you accept it was you who sent the letter?" Jay asked, leaning forward intently.

"I did indeed send it, about two decades ago." Sasha sipped her tea. "I did it because Irshad Akhtar asked me to."

"And my mother decided to follow the source of the letter – to you?"

Sasha Makijan sighed. "Yes."

"So did you meet my mother?"

"Yes."

"So where's my mother now?"

For the first time that evening, Sasha's gaze fell. "Your mother is dead."

Jay jerked back but the shock did not linger for more than a few moments. Tanya, who sat beside him, immediately put a hand over his. When Sasha looked up, her eyes held sympathy.

Something about the old lady gave him comfort. And he had expected something like this. "How did she go?" Jay asked.

Sasha sighed. "She was already half-dead by the time she met me, the poor little thing. She had taken a ship to Hong Kong, all the way from India. It was 1990 and the journey was rough even for the toughest of men. When she reached Hong Kong, she had high-grade yellow fever."

"So how did she reach you?" Jay asked.

"She didn't." Sasha put down her cup of tea. "I found her. A dock head told me one evening that a South Asian woman had been admitted to a local hospital; the woman kept saying my name. I was a famous personality in the dock area then, you see. There was only one Sasha Makijan."

"What did she say to you?" Jay asked.

"Nothing. She was gone by the time I reached her. In her belongings they found the letter I had sent her. That was how I realized who she was."

Jay said nothing. He sat in silence, looking down at the priceless Persian carpet at his feet.

"I'm sorry, young man." Sasha's voice was gentle. "But the world is a cruel place."

Jay looked up at her. "What was in the letter? Who was Irshad Akhtar and what was in this letter?"

"Irshad Akhtar was my lover." Sasha gave a quick toothless smile as she spoke the name. "One of many but perhaps the best. He had fire. It was a long time ago."

"But why did he ask you to send a letter to my mother, Mrs. Makijan?" Jay asked, puzzled by the fluttering threads of the story.

"Please call me Sasha," she said, patting her hair. "Irshad asked me to send the letter because he believed that your mother, the Singhs' daughter, deserved to know the truth about her parents."

"If he cared so much about my mother," Jay said, "why didn't he send that letter himself?"

"Because, my dear boy, he could not. He was on a secret mission. He could not compromise his identity by sending a letter back home."

"A secret mission?"

"Yes. So were your grandparents. And two others...what were their names...ah yes...Harman and Dinesh."

"Where was this?" Jay asked, bewildered by what he was hearing.

"I saw them for the last time in China, in 1949."

"What were they doing there?" Why had five ex-INA soldiers ended up in China two years after Independence, Jay wondered. It didn't make any sense.

"I told you, they were on a mission."

"What was the mission?"

Sasha paused for a moment, trying to remember the details. It had all happened so long ago. "To find and rescue Netaji Subhash Chandra Bose. The case of

Bose's plane crash remains one of the most intriguing unsolved mysteries of modern India, does it not?" she said, looking out of the windows at the night sky. "Indeed, Mr. Bose did phenomenal work raising the INA in Singapore. He was truly a pillar for India's independence. I know. I was there."

Jay felt dizzy as he quickly explained the history to Tanya, realizing how unpredictable this puzzle had become. "Historical records say he died in a plane crash in 1945. But there have been conspiracy theories from as early as the 1950s."

"Are you saying he survived?" Tanya asked Sasha. "And Jay's grandparents were trying to find him in Russia?"

"No." Sasha shook her head. "I'm not saying they were trying to find him. I am saying they *found* him."

Jay sat back feeling winded. The yellow lilies on the red wallpaper seemed to have a life of their own, moving gently in some unseen breeze.

A mahogany table stood before a tall window that gave a panoramic view of Hong Kong. Along one wall, carved cupboards stretched to the ceiling, towering over the space like sentinels.

Sasha rose and went to the farthest cupboard, unlocking it with a silver key from the bunch she carried at her waist. She opened the panels to reveal drawers, and began going through the contents.

"When Akhtar wrote to me for the last time," she said, "the letter came from a Siberian city called Yakutsk."

"Were all of them alive then?" Jay wondered.

"They were." Sasha extracted an unmarked file from the drawer and brought it back to the sofa. "Akhtar says so clearly, though he worries things are about to change." She carefully opened the file to reveal a tattered letter, placed in a plastic case to protect it. She showed it to them.

Jay looked at it uneasily. The ink had faded but the writing was still visible.

Dear Sasha,

I write to you from the main post office in Yakutsk. I fear this will be my last letter to you and the end of our voyage.

The last time we met, I told you the end we were working for. Now I want to tell you that our goal is right in front of us.

But my dear friend Singh has botched all our chances with a single foolish decision. He has collaborated with an English General he met here in the city and leaked our plan to him. We have been exposed.

It pains me to realize that we came so close and yet so far, due to Singh's foolishness. But I do not blame him. The time for blame is over. I write to ensure that our findings are not destroyed if we are compromised.

I enclose another letter here addressed to Singh's young daughter Azaadi, who is holed up in an orphanage in Dehra Doon. Please find out where she is and deliver my letter to her.

If I am captured, I shall remain loyal to our cause to the very end. I will take our secret to the grave.

Always Yours,

Irshad Akhtar.

"It took me quite some time to discover the exact orphanage your mother was kept in," Sasha sighed. "Those were different times, not like now, when we can learn everything about everyone at the click of a button. When I finally found her, she had already been moved. I kept looking, though. When I finally found her, she was living in Bombay. I did my part and sent her Akhtar's letter."

Sasha rummaged through the file and drew out another laminated scrap. "This was the letter that he asked me to send your mother, which I took from her after her death."

Jay and Tanya took it and read in silence.

Dear Azaadi,

You may not know me, and by the time this letter reaches you, all possibility of you ever knowing me will have ended. But know this much, you could have called me Irshad Uncle if all had gone well.

I don't know when this letter will reach you, but when it does, please know that you are not an orphan. Your parents, Maj Anish Singh and Dr. Rupali Singh, were my dear friends, and great human beings. Though I never saw eye to eye with your father, I respected him immensely.

I accompanied your parents on a secret mission in late 1947, after our country became independent. I fear we have now come to the end of our tale. We are at such a juncture that either we will return as heroes, and all will be well, or we will never come back at all.

I want you to know that if the worst happens, and you know nothing about your parents, seek out a woman called Sasha Makijan in Hong Kong. She will have all the answers you seek.

As for me, I swear I will never compromise your parents and shall take our secret to my grave.

Lovingly yours,

Irshad Akhtar.

"The last two lines of both letters are almost identical," Jay said, looking up, a strange, unfamiliar sense of sadness filling him.

"Yes. I believe that all of them, including your grandparents, perished in Russia, on their mission."

Jay shook his head; he looked like a man in a fog. "My mother is dead. My grandparents were trying to solve one of the greatest unsolved mysteries of the century. What do I do now!"

Sasha sighed. "I'm sorry it turned out this way. But you can always do what your mother wanted to do – to try and find what exactly happened to your grandparents. It was the question your mother wanted an answer to."

"Looks like it has become a long chain now," Jay said. "I am looking for my mother, who was looking for her parents, who in turn were looking for Netaji Subhash Chandra Bose."

"Maybe," Sasha said, "finding what happened to one of them will give you the answers to the rest."

Jay looked at her bleakly. "You're right. If I cannot find my mother, I should start looking for what she was trying to unearth."

"You have more than you need to go ahead," Sasha reminded him.

"Thank you, Mrs. Makijan," Jay said, getting to his feet.

"You're welcome, child," Sasha replied. "Don't forget to call me after you have got to the root of all this."

###

"So have we lost them, motherfucker?" Sergei stood smoking in the parking lot below the casino. He was angry.

"Mind your tongue!" Charkov snapped. Their position gave them a clear view of the elevator doors. "They came by car and they'll leave by car. When they do, we'll see them."

"Oh really?" Sergei said bitterly. They had been so close to catching the woman who had supposedly arrived with Jay, but she had escaped and walked away with one of the floor managers of the casino. As for their target, Jay himself, there was no sign of him. "What if they do not leave by car?" he asked. "What if they deceive us?"

"Why wouldn't they leave by car, Serg?" Charkov said, annoyed. "They don't have any reason to suspect they are being followed."

Sergei tossed the butt down and ground it out. "I feel exposed here," he said.

"This is the perfect spot," Charkov assured him. "We see them; we follow them; we catch them."

"What if they see us first?" Sergei drew out another cigarette from the pack in his pocket.

"We'll just seem like two Russians."

"Still," Sergei said, lighting up, "we can be spotted."

"But we have no idea which car it is, do we?" Charkov mocked. "Even the god damn valet couldn't point it out. It is better to be here, from where we can see the whole lot."

"But we'll lose precious time getting to our car. We might lose them."

"But we don't have to get to them immediately." A smile crept across Charkov's face. "We just need to get to them."

###

"This thing has just blown out of proportion," Jay said as he and Tanya exited the elevator to enter the parking lot.

Tanya nodded as she kept pace beside him. "What are we going to do?"

"Dig for more information. Deduce if what Mrs. Makijan told us is in fact true."

"So you don't trust her testimony?"

"I don't know," Jay murmured. "But what I have learned in my life, running my business is, when in doubt get a second opinion."

"And how exactly are we going to do that?"

"I have some ideas," Jay said. "Let's get into the car first."

###

"There he is!" Sergei pointed to the level below. "And the blonde bitch is with him. Let's get down before they hit the road."

"Not before we do this." Charkov whipped out what looked like a small pistol from his jacket pocket and pointed it towards their targets.

"What the fuck, Char! What are you doing?"

"Just giving him what he deserves." Charkov stabilized his elbow, pointing the gun squarely at the couple who had emerged from the elevator.

"Don't shoot him, Char. The Boss said to take him alive."

"Yeah," Charkov smiled, "but he didn't say anything about her. It'll only take a minute."

Sergei saw the gun swing towards the unsuspecting blonde. "No Char!" he whispered harshly, lunging for his partner. But he was too late.

Charkov had already pressed the trigger.

###

"Ouch!" Tanya said, putting her hand up to the back of her neck. "The mosquitoes in these tropical countries are such a nuisance!"

"I hope that wasn't addressed to me," Jay said with a grin, trying to locate their car in the parking lot. "Where do these damn valets put them?"

Tanya stopped scratching and shrugged. "What now!"

"What we learned today is overwhelming," Jay said. "But I believe we are in luck. I think this isn't a dead end."

Tanya looked at him, surprised. "What are you saying?"

"Come, I'll tell you in the car." Jay said, walking over to where he had just spotted their Mercedes.

###

"Why the hell did you shove me?" Charkov asked angrily, flat out on the ground.

Sergei stood over him, inspecting the small gun he had wrested from his partner's hand. To his surprise, it was made of plastic and had the words Track Gun moulded on it. "I guess I should apologize," he said. "I thought it was a real gun."

"And that I was going to shoot them?" Charkov mocked, getting up and dusting himself off. "When the Boss had specifically told us not to?"

"I didn't know you had one of these," Sergei said somewhat sheepishly, still inspecting the gun. "This is high-tech stuff."

"You really are behind the times," Charkov scoffed, still angry. "I bought this on E-bay." He opened his cell phone and tapped vigorously. "Let's see if I hit the target."

A few taps later, he smiled. "They are driving out now," he said, just as they heard a car accelerate out of the parking lot. "Let's get our car and follow them," he said, still peering at the screen which showed a blinking blip on the GPS.

###

"The plane crash that killed Subhash Chandra Bose happened in 1945," Tanya said, reading from her laptop. "Your grandparents disappeared in 1947. Well, the timing matches, if nothing else. And they left your mother at the orphanage when they went."

"Other things match too, not just the timing," Jay said. "I visited the Dehra Doon Orphanage before I came here. The records show my mother was taken there in 1947."

"So is it really possible that your grandparents left on a mission to find Netaji Subhash Chandra Bose?" Tanya asked.

"It seems so unbelievable!"

"You can't believe they went to find Netaji?"

"No, I can't believe that it never occurred to me till now that they did." The coincidences were so pointed. The dates matched perfectly. Mrs. Makijan's account fits the mould exactly. All of it, Akhtar's letters included, were part of the same chain of events.

"But Mrs. Makijan said they did find him," Tanya reminded Jay. "If that is so, why does Netaji's disappearance remain an unsolved mystery?"

Jay shook his head. "No...not according to the Government. They've always supported the plane crash theory and quashed other conjectures."

"But there have been discrepancies, haven't there?'

"I did some research," Jay told her. "The last Commission to investigate this matter was instituted in India less than five years ago – the Mukherjee Commission of 2007."

"Well, what did they find?"

"I'm not sure. Nor do I know where to go next. That is why I think we should get a second opinion."

"And how are we going to do that?" Tanya asked.

"By following standard procedure," Jay said. "By talking to an expert."

###

Among journalists, when the topic of Netaji Subhash Chandra Bose was under discussion, there was just one name that towered authoritatively above the others – Anu Dhār.

Anu was born in Kolkata in 1968. She was an alumnus of the prestigious Indian School of Journalism, New Delhi, and had worked with several international dailies before turning into an RTI activist. She had published several books on the death of Subhash Chandra Bose and was a strong supporter of the theory that he did not die in the plane crash of 1945. She was also the founder of a non-profit organization that worked to increase awareness about Netaji's life and his supposed death, among the student community of the country. Luckily for Jay, she was in Hong Kong.

###

Tanya glanced at her open laptop as they circled around an overpass. "Luck favours the brave," she said. "Anu Dhār is in Hong Kong. Her social media update says she checked into Hotel Trident six hours ago." Scrolling down, she saw Anu had posted a picture of a pamphlet titled, 'International Journalists Conference 15, Hong Kong'.

"Wow! So she's here," Jay said. Did such things happen unless they were destined to be? "We need only figure out now how to talk to her."

"Oh that's simple; by going to meet her."

"No, it isn't that simple. She's a celebrity journo in India," Jay explained. "She won't talk to just anyone."

"Then we'll not go as anyone. You are forgetting that she's a journalist and you're a great candidate for an interview after your disappearance from the business scene."

"Better yet," Jay smiled. "The thing journalists love to do, apart from conducting interviews, is giving one."

"Well, if that's how we're going to do it, there's a slight hiccup I should point out," Tanya said, looking through the rear windscreen.

"What is it?" Jay asked, his eyes on the road.

"I think we're being followed."

###

"I've seen them before," Jay said, looking into the rearview mirror. "I think they're Russians."

"Russians!" Tanya gasped. "This could be serious; I'm a felon!"

"I think it *is* serious," Jay agreed, "but not for you. I think they have been following me since the day I cased the casino." He had noticed the two bulky Russians in their hotel lobby, and again at the Blue Frog.

"Why are they after you?" Tanya asked, surprised.

"I don't know. Look ahead. Don't let them know we're onto them."

Tanya tied her hair and turned back to the road ahead. "How do we get to Anu and get rid of them at the same time?"

"Well, you figure out the latter part because I've already thought of the first bit."

"You know how to get to Anu?"

"I do." Jay smiled. "We need just one thing."

"And that is?"

"A million dollars of my money."

###

"Yes, thank you, please keep it ready, I'll be there in an hour," Jay said into his phone as Tanya kept an eye on the car behind them.

"Just look at what can be booked online and on the phone, if you have that kind of money," Jay said, disconnecting the call. "The booking is done." Then he explained his plan to Tanya.

"It's a bold plan," she said, once Jay had finished. "Even dangerous, I would say. And there's still the hiccup. They're still following us." Tanya pointed behind them discreetly. "We can't seem to shake off that car."

"Well, if we can't lose them, we really have a problem," Jay said. "My plan won't work with two Russians on our tail."

"I wonder how they are following us so efficiently," Tanya said. "Maybe that's the key to shaking them off."

"And you have a plan for that?" Jay asked, hopefully.

"I think I may be able to do that," Tanya replied thoughtfully. "But for that I'll need one thing."

"What's that?"

"Another million dollars of your money."

###

"Could I have a moment, Ma'am?"

Anu Dhar's attention was caught by the handsome young man dressed in jacket and denims. She wondered briefly if she had seen him somewhere before, but couldn't quite remember.

"Sure," she said, putting her cell phone away.

They were on the eighteenth floor of the Grand Hyatt building. It was the third day of the International Journalists Conference and Anu was frankly bored of the pop extravaganza attached to the event.

"Now that I have a moment," the young man said with an engaging smile, "I wanted to ask if I could have twenty minutes to interview you?"

"Interview me!" Anu bit back the smile that came to her lips at this unexpected request. This was a global conference, with many journalistic luminaries. She had seen many of them speaking to reporters and magazine representatives, but she hadn't expected to be approached herself.

"Just twenty minutes," Jay coaxed.

Anu managed a smile and nodded.

"It's too crowded here," Jay said, looking around. "Can we go a floor up and talk?"

"Certainly. The conference lectures were boring anyway."

Jay bowed, allowing her to lead the way.

"So which organization do you work for?" Anu asked as they walked to the elevator.

"I work for the outfit called Mission Netaji," Jay replied. It was a large organisation with members in high places.

"Interesting," Anu said, throwing him a quick glance. "I've met your Chairmen on multiple occasions but they have never wanted to interview me. Rather, they have always wanted to be interviewed by me."

"Times change," Jay shrugged, waiting for the elevator doors to open.

"Your organization is doing a nice job," Anu commended him casually. "We are going to need more people behind us if we ever hope to force the Government to uncover the truth."

"True. But I don't think that day is too far now."

The elevator doors opened and they walked in. Jay pressed a button and felt the sudden rush as the elevator took them to the next floor and the doors opened again to reveal a silent foyer; the entire floor was empty.

"Are we at the wrong level?" Anu asked, gazing around.

Jay shook his head, stepping out of the elevator. He pointed to a door ahead of them saying, "We have a camera set up inside that room."

She followed him doubtfully, pulling her phone from her purse.

"Come, I'll show you." Jay opened the door.

Inside, there was a chair and a fixed camera. The background was covered with a green screen. The familiar setup seemed to relax Anu.

"Please have a seat." Jay pointed to the chair and then went to the camera. In his ear he heard Tanya say, 'Turn it a little'. He turned the camera. 'It's perfect now,' she said. Jay looked up to find Anu had indeed taken her place. He walked to the door and shut it.

"I must first apologise to you, ma'am," he said as he walked back to the camera. "This is not precisely an interview."

Anu sighed, disappointed. "What is this then?" she asked.

Jay pressed the recording button. "Well, I needed to speak with you, but I couldn't do it out in the open because some men are following me."

Anu's eyebrows rose. "Why are they following you?"

"Perhaps because I know something they don't want me to spread."

"And what do you know?" Anu asked, unsure where this was leading.

"I'm not sure that what I know is truth or illusion," Jay replied. "That is why I had to speak with you – to confirm if my deductions are correct."

"So what happens now?"

"I shall ask you some questions, and you will answer them to the best of your knowledge. An interview, like I said."

"And what will the questions be about?" Anu asked.

Jay smiled at her reassuringly. "About a cause you've been devoted to all your life – the mystery of Netaji's plane crash."

"So all you need are answers?" Anu asked. "This is not a kidnapping?"

"It isn't." Jay assured her. "Unless you refuse to tell me what I want." He was sure Tanya was smiling at that menacing statement.

"Then there will be no need to be hostile," she said. "You know I love to publicly and privately share my findings on this subject."

Jay glanced at his watch. "We don't have much time," he said, "so I'd prefer it if you kept it brief."

"I'm a journalist," she retorted. "I know how to keep it brief. Tell me what you want to know."

"Do you think the plane crash story involving Netaji Subash Chandra Bose is false?"

Anu laughed, throwing back her head. "And you expect me to be brief about this?" she asked.

"I just need to know your take on the matter," Jay told her. "Whether you believe it to be true or a fabrication?"

Anu sat looking at him. "Young man, I have spent my whole career pursuing answers to that question. I'm afraid it is not a straightforward yes or no."

"Then what is it?" Jay asked, pacing behind the camera.

"I think you're going to have to sit down," she said with a quick smile. "I promise to be brief."

Jay glanced at the camera, which blinked slightly and then moved up and down, as if nodding. *Damn you, Tanya!* Jay thought, sitting down.

###

"There have been three Commissions appointed by the Government of India to investigate Netaji's plane crash," Anu said, holding up three fingers. "Whenever I applied for any documents on the Bose case, I was always asked what I hoped to accomplish that the committees could not."

"And what was your answer?" Jay asked.

"My answer was always that I wished to uncover the *truth*."

"So these committees did not uncover the truth?"

"They were mere publicity gimmicks!" Anu angrily slapped the armrest of her chair. "The only job of the committees was to make it appear to the public that some investigation was taking place."

"Are you certain? The Government has a great deal of power."

"Power my foot!" Anu exclaimed scornfully. "Tell me how did the Shah Nawaz Committee of 1952 investigate the plane crash without physically stepping foot out of India?"

"Is that what happened?"

Anu nodded solemnly. "The only committee to do some real research and actually visit the relevant places was the recent one – the Mukherjee Commission. They found that Bose did not die in the plane crash. But their findings were rubbished."

"What about the testimonies of those who were on the plane with Bose?" Jay asked.

"You are right. The only persons who can say what actually happened in the crash are those that survived it. Habibur Rehman, the only INA man

Netaji took on that fateful flight, did."

"And what did he tell the Committees?"

"Nothing! Because the committees could never get to him."

"But why, if he survived?"

Anu sighed wearily. "Because he went to Pakistan."

"But there must have been someone who interrogated Habibur."

"The British did. And his testimony points clearly to the fact that he was in on the plan."

"What plan?"

"To make it seem that Bose died in the plane crash."

"Why would he do that?"

"I don't know. That question has not yet been answered."

Jay nodded. "Why do you think Habibur was in on it?"

"First, he did not allow the body to be photographed in full," Anu said. "The last photograph of Netaji shows his upper torso only."

"That can't be the only thing."

"It is not. Habibur's conduct after the incident was most unusual. He should have immediately contacted the INA top brass in Singapore. But he remained silent about what had happened and made no attempt to contact anyone. Apparently, he wanted the news to be delayed as much as possible."

"So the question you are trying to answer is whether Netaji's really died in the plane crash all those years ago?" Jay asked.

"No, that's not the question at all." Anu shook her head. "I know for a fact that he did *not* die in the plane crash."

"So what are you trying to unearth?" Jay asked, his heart hammering.

"Whether Bose was murdered," Anu said, "or whether he escaped."

###

"Damn these tall buildings," Sergei said, punching the elevator button again. The doors remained stubbornly closed. "Maybe we should take the stairs," he suggested.

"You are right," Charkov said, retreating from the elevators. "Look for the fire exit sign."

"How are we going to find them anyway?" Sergei asked, searching for the sign. "The GPS signal has given us the location, but not the floor."

Charkov showed him the device in his hands. "We'll find them by using indoor tracking."

"What's that?" Sergei hissed.

Charkov pointed to a blinking blue light on the screen. "As we near them, the light blinks faster."

"That's smooth," Sergei said, nodding appreciatively before pointing and running ahead. "I've found the staircase."

Charkov did not hesitate. He entered the dark stairwell and slammed the door shut behind them. He checked the device in his hand. "They're above us somewhere," he said. "The blinking is getting quicker."

As they moved up the staircase, the blinking light frantically increased in frequency. Then suddenly, it slowed down again.

"We have passed them," Charkov said.

Sergei checked the floor. "Thirty-first. Let's descend slowly."

The blinking got quicker and then slowed as they reached the twenty-eighth.

"They're on the thirtieth," Charkov said. "I'm certain."

"Then pray we get the bastard this time," Sergei said.

As they climbed to the twenty-ninth, Charkov brought out his pistol.

###

"So the plane crash story is in doubt," Jay said. "That's what I wanted to know."

"It is in certain doubt," Anu confirmed, her voice firm. "There are theories, of course, about what happened. One of the most famous is of Gumnami Baba, that Netaji returned to India secretly and lived his final days in Bengal as a godman, without ever disclosing his identity."

"Do you think it could be true?" Jay asked.

"Many people believe it but I don't!" Anu stated emphatically. "Those who do believe, point to the remarkable similarity between Netaji and Gumnami Baba. It is also said that their handwriting was similar, and that the Baba knew intimate details about Netaji's life which no one except Netaji could have known."

"So why does the theory lose your interest?" Jay asked.

"From my certain knowledge that Netaji used body doubles," Anu said. "As the INA Chief, his life was always in danger. There is no doubt he had made many enemies and there was always a bounty on his head. It is only logical that he found people similar in appearance to himself, whom he used as body doubles."

"So you think Gumnami Baba was one of his body doubles?"

"I do," Anu nodded. "Body doubles are not merely used as decoys physically. They are required to be able to impersonate the person, if captured. It is thus reasonable to suppose doubles were made to memorize details of Netaji's personal life and taught to emulate his handwriting."

"So Gumnami Baba could have been one of his body doubles, who later returned to India," Jay said thoughtfully.

"Yes, though it's too late to confront him now. He died years ago."

"So which theory do you believe? What do *you* think happened to the real Netaji after the Taipei crash?"

Anu took a deep breath. "I believe he went to Russia. There is, of course, the big question why? I have not been able to find an answer to that. But yes, I think he went to Russia and that the Russians caught and jailed him in one of their many gulags."

"What reinforces this chain of thought for you?"

"Have you ever heard of Dr. Satyanarayan Sinha?"

"I have not." Jay's study of Indian history had never moved beyond the Independence struggle.

"He was a Member of Parliament MP as well as a Russian language expert. He was also a witness for the Khosla Commission."

"And he initiated this chain of thought?"

"He did. He said under oath before the Khosla Commission that a Russian agent called Kozlov had told him Netaji was doing time in Russia."

"And who was this Kozlov?"

"A double agent, working for the British," Anu told him. "Dr. Sinha knew him from his days in Calcutta. Kozlov was caught by the KGB and served time in Yakutsk, the biggest gulag in Siberia, until he was rescued through British diplomacy."

"So Kozlov saw Netaji in Yakutsk?"

"He did."

"So why did this theory fail to gain ground?"

"Because the English General who went to Yakutsk to secure Kozlov's release in 1949, disputed his testimony." Anu browsed on her cell phone for the details. "He said he had been given access to the internal files of the Yakutsk Gulag and that Netaji was not there; that Kozlov was mistaken." She held out her phone and showed Jay a newspaper article.

As Jay scanned the headline *English General says Netaji not in Siberia*, static crackled in his ear, followed by Tanya's voice: 'Jay, the Russians have come. We should be going now.'

"Thank you for the information," Jay said, handing back the phone.

"You have asked all the questions so far, now I will ask you one," Anu said. "Why are you interested in all this?"

Jay paused for a moment before saying, "I believe I may be able to provide the answers to your unanswered questions."

Anu's brows lifted in surprise. "Well, if you are going to solve this, give it your everything."

"I've given it my everything," Jay told her.

###

"An empty floor," Charkov whispered, circling the large hall like a panther. "A perfect spot."

"For what they are doing or what we are about to do?" Sergei whispered back.

Charkov held up the device; it pointed to one door. "It's time to go get him," Charkov said.

They moved slowly towards the door, Charkov's revolver pointing straight at it. They positioned themselves on either side, their backs to the wall.

"Check the knob," Sergei said.

Charkov extended his hands and tried turning it. "It's locked."

"We're gonna have to kick it in. Wanna do the honours?"

"Gladly." Charkov turned and handed over the gun to Sergei and faced the door. He took a deep breath.

"Don't break your leg for god's sake!"

"I've done this before remember," Charkov said, throwing his partner a scornful glance.

"That was long ago," Sergei reminded him.

Ignoring him, Charkov stretched out his leg. "On the count of three. One...two..."

"Three!" they said together.

Charkov felt the impact on his leg as the door opened with a bang. He rushed in, gun at the ready.

It was empty.

"Fuck!" Charkov looked at the device. The light was blinking continuously. "They have to be here, unless..." He looked around and then bent and picked up a small tracker lying on the ground "Bastards!" he growled.

###

Three floors below, Tanya closed the door behind her and almost ran into Jay. He steadied her with both hands and asked, "Where are they?"

"They took the bait," she said. "But we need to go *now*."

Jay nodded. "Let's go then."

Taking Tanya's hand, Jay ran out of the corridor, emerging into the crowded lobby. Tanya pointed to the elevator they had blocked. They reached it and Tanya typed in the code and the doors opened. They walked in and the doors closed with a woosh.

As the elevator began its downward journey, Tanya fell into Jay's arms gasping, "I died a thousand deaths there."

Jay patted her back reassuringly. "Don't worry, we've lost them now."

"But we're lost too!" she snapped. "Where do we go from here?"

The doors opened at the ground floor. Jay took her hand and they made their way through the crowd in the lobby.

"Where are we going?" she asked.

"Didn't you hear the last part of the conversation with Anu?"

"No. I was too busy tracking the Russians."

"Then you don't know," Jay said, smiling.

"Don't know what?"

"Anu gave us our next lead."

They crossed the glass doors of the building and reached the street. Jay raised his hand and hailed a taxi.

"A lead to what?" Tanya asked impatiently.

"Somewhere far away."

"So where are we going?"

"To the airport. After you ma'am," Jay replied, opening the cab door for her with a flourish.

###

"You two fucked up!" Alexis' voice was cold and angry on the phone.

"I swear we did not see him, Boss!" Sergei's voice trembled as he spoke into the mouthpiece. "It was as if he walked into the casino completely invisible."

"There was a woman working with him, Boss," Charkov added. "That is how they were able to fool us. We were looking for him and she walked right by us."

"I know who the woman is now," Alexis said. "And it makes me angry because you two morons should have known before me."

"We are sorry, Boss," Sergei said in abject apology.

"Are you?" Alexis shouted. "The presence of this woman just doubled the stakes of this assignment. Now it is imperative that you bring both in."

"We did everything we could, Boss," Sergei told him. "We chased them to another building following the GPS we had tagged him with."

"And?"

"He deceived us, Boss," Sergei told him. "We found the tracker on an abandoned floor."

"And where was he?" Alexis asked shortly.

"On another abandoned floor below us," Charkov sighed. "The manager told us that a mysterious Indian had booked two complete floors for a day, online, a few hours previously."

"Which hotel?" Alexis' voice had risen.

"The Plaza," Sergei replied.

"It's where the International Journalists Conference is being held," Alexis said.

"Yeah, we saw the boards," Charkov muttered.

"You two have no idea how high the stakes have risen now," Alexis snapped. "Bring them in *now*!"

"But we have lost them, Boss." Sergei said. "What can we do now?"

"You are going to drag your sorry asses to the airport," Alexis told them, his voice as cold as ice.

"Why?" Charkov wanted to know.

"Because," Alexis told him, "our two friends just booked tickets out of Hong Kong."

###

"London?" Tanya said anxiously. "What are we going to find in London?"

"Not what but whom. Do you remember Makijan mentioning an English General?" Jay asked. "Akhtar's letter mentioned that my grandfather collaborated with an English General."

"Yes, I remember," Tanya replied with a quick nod.

"Well," Jay said, looking at her, "Anu gave me the General's name. Open your laptop. Looks like you've got some googling to do."

17
Yakutsk
File 9/14/Jan/XVII: Top Secret

1948

They crossed over into Soviet territory in the chilling cold of night with a thunderstorm raging and lightning strikes lighting up the sky. The makeshift roof of the truck provided poor cover from the chilling drizzle. Rupali sat in a corner, huddled in a shawl, almost asleep. Singh looked at her sadly. *I had no business bringing her here*, he thought. The others were used to the perils of covert ops. They had moved into enemy territory before, saved and killed men. She, on the other hand, was a doctor. Though she had seen a lot of blood, she had never shed any.

Harman stood at the back of the truck, looking out at the rain. Dinesh stood beside him but they did not speak. Akhtar sat by the canvas window, his body curled like a snake, a cigarette between his lips.

"I've never stepped into so much danger just for transporting men," Hachiko, Kobayashi's lieutenant complained as he entered the covered area of the truck. "Mostly, it's just drugs."

Singh offered the short Japanese in military uniform a towel. "Have we crossed yet?" he asked as Hachiko wiped his wet hair

"Yes, we have. The danger is four-fold now. I wonder how much you are paying the old man for this."

"That is not for your ears." Having worked for Kobayashi before, Singh knew exactly which words would soften his soldiers.

"True. I am just a soldier." Hachiko threw the towel away. "You, on the other hand, must be quite important to him to warrant a transfer like this."

"You've been doing this long?" Singh asked, catching the towel mid-air.

"Almost two years now." Hachiko sat down beside Singh. "The border was easy before. Any novice could pass through."

"How much farther are you going to take us?"

"To the first shanty town. I deal with the Headman of that village. See a lot of cash each visit, selling him heroin. But not this time it seems."

"Know the Headman well?" Singh asked, passing him a cigarette.

"Well enough."

"You going to help us interrogate him," Singh said calmly.

"Not part of my job." Hachiko smoked vigorously. "I just drop you off and leave."

"Your presence could make the Headman speak sooner."

"Not my concern." Hachiko tossed the cigarette out.

Singh held onto his hand. "You listen to me," he said. "We are not some regular civilians. You have seen how your Boss specially arranged this transport for us. You'll do as I ask."

Hachiko gazed into Singh's eyes. For a moment Singh was not sure if it was fear or wrath he saw. Then Hachiko softened. "I'll do as you say, Sir."

Singh loosened his grip and Hachiko rose and walked away. Akhtar came to sit in his place. "Scaring young soldiers are you?"

"Securing the help we need." Singh looked at him. Akhtar was staring intently at Rupali in the corner. "I'd prefer you not staring at my wife."

"You wouldn't say so if you knew my thoughts." Akhtar said, his gaze remaining fixed on the unmoving form in the corner.

"And what *are* your thoughts?" Singh asked.

"She shouldn't be here."

"I know," Singh sighed.

"So what are you going to do about it?"

"Nothing."

Akhtar hit the tarpaulin cover with his fist. "I thought you loved her."

"I do," Singh said quietly. "With all my heart."

"Then send her back. Ask Kobayashi to send her back to India."

"She won't go." Singh took out a cigarette and lit it.

"Then *make* her go, goddamnit!" Akhtar said raising his voice.

Singh shushed him, raising a finger to his lips. “She chose to be here. I cannot disrespect her judgment by questioning her resolve.”

“Oh look at you, you selfish son of a bitch!’ Akhtar sighed. “You don’t love her; you just want her to be around so you can fuck her.”

Singh looked up, his eyes hard and stern. “Do not say such things, ever.”

“Then send her back!”

“I would if she would go, but she doesn’t want that.”

“She doesn’t know what she wants!” Akhtar said. “She never has! That is why she married you.”

“You go beyond acceptable bounds, Irshad.” Singh smoked lazily. “But I won’t fight you tonight. It is time to be united, to act mature.”

“If you loved her,” Akhtar said, “you’d forcibly send her back.”

“And that is what you’ve never understood about love.” Singh finished his smoke and got up. “You don’t force a loved one to do what you want.”

He walked away, leaving Akhtar behind, smoking alone.

###

“How long have you been Headman?” Singh asked the old Russian with the long white beard and vodka glass in his hand.

The Russian drank up before answering, “Long enough.”

Singh looked at him. He seemed old. Singh turned to Hachiko.

“Thirty, maybe forty years,” Hachiko shrugged.

“Then you’ll know what I’m asking about,” Singh said.

“Maybe.” The Headman poured himself another glassful.

“Tell him to be straight with me,” Singh said.

Hachiko translated into the local dialect. The Russian said something in reply. Hachiko turned to Singh. “He says he knows what you speak of.”

“A foreigner,” Singh said. “Eastern. About as short as Hachiko here.”

The Russian nodded. He raised his hand and showed four fingers.

“The man you describe came here four years ago,” Hachiko said.

“That was 1945. Does he recall the month?”

The Russian showed his yellow teeth and nodded. "Winter. Cold!" he said.

"Must have been after September," Hachiko surmised.

"What happened to the man?"

"He lived here for some days," Hachiko translated, "then they took him away."

"Who took him?" Singh asked.

"Those who take everyone," the man said.

"Do you mean he died?" Singh asked. "Do you mean the Gods took him?"

The old Russian laughed. "What God?" he asked. "Whose God?"

"They don't worship gods here, Sir," Hachiko said. "It's not allowed in Soviet Russia."

"Then who took him?"

"The Soviets," Hachiko said. "They are the ones who take everyone. They even took his son," he pointed at the Headman.

"Why did they take your son?" Singh asked.

"Capitalist affiliations and drugs," the old man sighed.

"The Soviets, where did they take the man we are looking for?"

"Where everyone is taken," the old man replied, shaking his head.

"And where is everyone taken?"

"Doesn't he know?" the old man asked Hachiko in amazement.

Hachiko merely shook his head.

"Where is everyone taken?" Singh repeated, looking at Hachiko and then the old man.

"Just one place," Hachiko said, pouring out some vodka. "The Road of Bones."

###

R504 Kolyma Highway, also known as the Road of Bones, was not the stuff of legend but a cruel reality. It was and is, a symbol of how low men can stoop to torture their fellow human beings. The highway is part of the M56 route that runs through the Russian Far East, along the Lena River. The road is so named because it was literally built on dead men's bones. The construction of the road began in 1932, using gulag labour. Prisoners from the local Siberian gulags were forced to work their life out in the harsh climate. The bones of the men who died while building it were buried along the road.

The Lena River, where the road ends, was home to the largest gulag in Siberia. Yakutsk had a reputation as a harsh and ruthless place. Singh and the team arrived in Yakutsk in 1949, knowing their target had been taken there. Yakutsk was then known as the coldest town in the world.

Between 1940–1950, 80,000 to 1,20,000 prisoners were deployed in Siberia. Of these, most lived in the gulags on the banks of the Lena River. The most important ones were lodged in Yakutsk prison. The prison complex was intimidating, with high walls and watchtowers with big spotlights atop them.

Singh and Akhtar surveyed the prison complex from an elevation, in the dead of night. The others were holed up at an inn in Yakutsk.

"Impregnable," Akhtar commented briefly.

"Sure looks like it," Singh agreed. The spotlights wandered around the prison walls in all directions.

"We must take photographs in the morning."

"For what?"

"To take back to India; to show those who sent us here." With every word, vapour poured from Akhtar's mouth like some primeval dragon.

"We need to get inside," Singh said, looking through his binoculars.

"Are you freaking mad?" Akhtar gasped. "Getting into that thing is impossible."

"What do you propose we do then?"

"It's simple," Akhtar said. "We go back to India and tell the Government all we know. They'll do the rest."

Singh gave a harsh laugh. "They'll do nothing, my friend, if we do not bring them enough evidence."

"We have enough evidence. We have Kobayashi's statement."

"As if Kobayashi is going to take the stand for us."

"There's nothing more we can do," Akhtar said emphatically. "We are done here."

"There is one more thing." Singh pointed towards the prison complex. "We can get inside and find evidence. And if we are lucky, we may even find Netaji."

Akhtar looked at him in disbelief. "I already told you, getting in is impossible."

"Didn't Netaji tell us that nothing is impossible?" Singh said. "Ten years ago, independence too, seemed out of reach, yet look at us today."

Akhtar shook his head. "Too much security, too hard."

"There's nothing we can't do with you on this hill with a sniper gun in your hands and me out there in camouflage," Singh said. "We've done this before."

"Don't you dare!" Akhtar warned, his eyes flashing dangerously. "Don't you dare remind me of that!"

"We can do it, Akhtar," Singh said, shaking him by the shoulders.

"Don't you remember what happened the last time? Innocents were killed and I ended up hating you forever."

"But this time we'll do it for Netaji. Believe me, we can."

"We can," Akhtar agreed. "We very well can, but we are not doing it." He walked away without looking back.

###

"The walls are impregnable," Singh told the others back at the inn. "Too straight and smooth for climbing."

"And there are too many watchtowers with spotlights," Akhtar added. "Too many guards."

"But the spotlights have a certain movement pattern," Singh said, "And the guards have pre-decided patrol routes."

"We're not doing it, Singh!" Akhtar said tersely.

"Doing what?" Rupali and Harman asked together.

"Singh wants to infiltrate the compound," Akhtar told them. "I consider it a suicide mission."

"Yes, it's impossible to get over the wall, but if we look around we could find some way in."

"There is no way," Akhtar said.

"There is always a way," Singh reminded him.

"We've done our best," Akhtar stated. "I say we go back."

"It is not your decision to make," Singh told him.

"Nor is it yours," Akhtar retorted, eyeing him angrily. Why was the man so stubborn, so darn adamant?

"Then let's ask everyone." Singh turned to the others. "Harman, what do you think?"

"We came here to rescue Netaji," Harman said without preamble. "I say we're not done till we have done that."

"Of course you'd say that, pet dog!" Akhtar sat down in disgust.

"Dinesh?" Singh asked, looking over at him.

"We'll have to find some clever ruse," Dinesh said. "A normal covert infiltration won't work here. We need to find some good cover."

"And we'll find it," Singh said, looking at his wife for her vote.

Rupali shrugged. "I left my baby daughter to come here, so you know I'm in this till the very end." She looked across at Akhtar and said, "And I expected better from you, Irshad."

"Am I the only realist in this room?" Akhtar got up angrily. "Do all of you really think that infiltrating the prison will be a success?" He spun towards Rupali. "You get me wrong!" he said. "I am dedicated to Netaji. But this infiltration will end in disaster for everyone. And if all of us die, there will be no one left to take the information back home."

"I'm not proposing that we should dive headlong into the prison," Singh said. "All I'm asking is that we not lose hope and turn back. I think we can figure out a way to get inside."

"How?" Akhtar asked.

"Destiny favours the bold," Singh reminded him.

"Fine," said Akhtar, turning away. "We'll stay."

###

The night was cold and dark. Singh lay on the bed watching Rupali brush her hair before the mirror. She looked beautiful. He stretched out a hand to touch her bare back. "Come here," he said softly.

"Let me tie my hair first," she replied.

"It's going to get messed up anyway," Singh told her with a grin.

She smiled and came to him, her bosom pressing against his chest. Their lovemaking was intense and passionate, touched with mortal danger. Afterward, they both lay, gazing up at the ceiling.

"We shouldn't have brought him," Singh said. "Akhtar is going to bolt on us."

"He will not run away," Rupali said. "I know him. He'll stay."

"He wants you to go back, you know," Singh told her, still staring at the ceiling.

Rupali rose on one elbow and turned his face to look at her. "I'm in this with you," she said. "We are husband and wife. Our paths are one to the very end."

Singh pulled her into a hug. "Do you think we'll find a way in?"

"We will," she replied. "We've come this far haven't we? We have luck on our side."

"Luck!" Singh laughed. "I hope we have that for we are going to need every bit of it."

###

Luck was indeed on their side, or call it God's will, for coincidences like the one that occurred in Yakutsk in 1949, were one in a billion.

The team had a regular routine. Each night, predecided pairs would scout the Yakutsk prison compound, looking for ways to get in. During the day, the others would ferret the town for any piece of news of Netaji. It was when Singh and Akhtar were scouting in town that they saw a car approach flying, the flag they had once hated to their core – the Union Jack.

"What are the Brits doing here?" Akhtar wondered.

"Maybe we should find out," Singh said. "Could be useful."

They followed the car through the town. It stopped at a few places and then drove out of the town.

"It's going to the prison," Akhtar said as the car turned east.

"Let's go to the hill," said Singh.

From their elevated observation point, they observed the car through binoculars. They watched as big iron gates opened for the car with the Union Jack.

"Perhaps we serve a country with the wrong flag," Akhtar joked, handing over the binoculars to Singh.

"The car indeed opens doors," Singh agreed, handing them back.

Akhtar kept his eyes glued. "Some *firangi* military man and his assistants," he said, watching the car doors open and the passengers get down.

"What are they doing?" Singh asked.

"The prison officials have come to welcome them," Akhtar said. "The prison officer is shaking hands with the military man."

"Let me see." Singh took the binoculars and stared through them, adjusting the focus. Then he cursed.

"What?' Akhtar asked.

"That face. I've seen it before."

"We saw a lot of *firangi* faces in the war." Akhtar said, "It could be one of them."

Singh shook his head. "No...this face I saw after the war."

"So who is he?" Akhtar asked.

"I just can't place him," Singh said, trying hard to remember. "We should try to get a closer look."

They waited for the car to leave the compound, an hour later, and returned to the town. They followed it till it halted at the biggest hotel in town and the British military man and his assistants walked in. Singh and Akhtar waited for a while before following them.

Singh walked up to the reception and cleared his throat. "I require your Presidential Suite for tonight," he declared in Russian.

"I'm sorry Sir, but the Presidential Suite is taken for a week," the receptionist said, looking up.

"The next best room then," Singh said curtly.

"Certainly, Sir." The girl offered him the register to sign.

As he signed, Singh's heart began thudding in his chest. Against Presidential Suite was a carelessly scribbled signature, yet legible enough.

General Thomas Hardy, 7Th Hussars.

18
England

2015

General Hardy of the 7th Hussars had lived an immensely successful life. He was a decorated war hero, hailing from a family of lifelong military men. He saw promotions from a young age and served the British Army all his life. He was a key factor in British victory in the Falklands. And he was Jay's next lead. Anu had confirmed that the British General was the only one to visit Yakutsk and had claimed Netaji was not there.

The only problem was that he was dead.

"The General died five days ago," Tanya said, handing Jay The Times, folded to the obituaries. "There is a memorial service next week. This is a dead end."

"It is not." Jay tapped the third paragraph. "It says here that the General wrote an autobiography."

"So what! It was half a decade ago."

"Chances are that if he wrote a book," Jay mused, "he had a diary."

"And he wrote about your grandparents in his diary?"

"Well, he wrote about them in his book. I downloaded the kindle version before boarding the plane," Jay told her smugly. "He mentioned them twice, on pages 89 and 90. So I am guessing his diary includes them too, perhaps things omitted from the book. Perhaps, even the truth."

"How in the world are we even going to find that diary?" Tanya asked, exasperated.

"If it exists, it will be in his home. And this is our way into his home," Jay said, tapping the word *funeral.* "The service is certain to be followed by a gathering with food and drinks, at home."

London's Heathrow airport was as busy as ever, serving hundreds of thousands of passengers a day. The artificial lighting inside the terminal made it impossible to know whether it was day or night outside.

"First, we need to get a guest list for those attending the service," Tanya said as they waited at the luggage belt.

"Then we'll need to ambush one of the guests and get in," Jay added coolly, as if it was the most natural thing in the world.

"And we'll need the plans of the General's estate, where the after service gathering is taking place," Tanya said. "That should be easy."

"We're getting really good at this," Jay laughed.

###

Getting the guest list was the easiest part. It was available online as the funeral had a dedicated website.

"The best way to break a chain is to find the weakest link," Jay said. "Let's find a guest whom we can exploit to get in."

Tanya scrolled down the list. "Quite a crowd," she murmured, clicking on various names.

"Plan to read all of it tonight?" Jay asked hanging his jacket carefully in the closet.

Her tongue slid over her lips. "No, I plan to ride you like a wild cat tonight."

"Who is going to do all the reading then?"

"Don't you know anything about python scripts?" she asked, glaring.

"I should have hired you years ago," Jay laughed, taking off his shirt.

###

Later, as he lay soaking in the pleasure of their lovemaking, Tanya rolled over onto her stomach and propped herself up on her elbows to check her laptop screen. "We have three matches," she said.

"What criteria did you search for?" Jay asked, eyes still closed, loth to break the bubble.

"Sexy young singles looking for men," Tanya typed away.

"So which of the three beautiful ladies is our target?" Reluctantly, Jay opened his eyes.

"Let's look at their profiles and find out." Tanya showed him the first: 23, journalist, The Sun. "No!" Tanya declared emphatically, clicking out.

"But she's sexy!" Jay protested.

"And she's also a journalist. You need someone dumb."

"Well, journalists can be dumb," Jay offered from the bed. "You for one slept with me."

"I am *not* a journalist. I am a hacker," Tanya said succinctly as she brought up the second match on the screen. "This one's interesting," she murmured.

"Dumb interesting or sexy interesting?" Jay asked.

"A fashion model." Tanya told him. "This could work!" She clicked open the third match and turned to Jay with a big smile on her face.

Warily Jay looked to see read what she was smiling about. "No way!" he said a moment later. "No way am I doing this!"

###

Why the fuck am I doing this? Jay cursed, twelve hours later, as he sat dressed in tight jeans and a v-neck T-shirt at the only pub in Smallwood. Tanya had also placed a glittering stud in his ear. Every time he leaned forward, he was sure his boxers showed. *I don't even look gay!* he thought morosely. How in the world was he going to attract his quarry?

But Tanya had not been at all nervous. "It'll all go smoothly," she had told him. "It's not like you have to sleep with him!"

The date had been set up. Tanya had been most creative, downloading an app called Tinder on his phone and building his profile. She had made him dress in inappropriate clothing and pose for photographs.

"This is embarrassing!" he had said.

"So now you know how models feel," she told him.

"Well, I know how homosexuals feel."

She had entered his preference as 'male'. "Congratulations!" she smiled. "You are now officially gay."

The third match Tanya had found on the guest list was a trust fund child kid called Gaby German. Rich, single and officially homosexual. They quickly found him on Tinder and swiped on him. Gaby appeared to be a horny SOB for he swiped back on Jay in less than an hour. The chat was on! Tanya snatched Jay's phone and messaged away with their quarry.

Two hours later, when she finally gave him back his phone, Jay found the chat had gone from 'It's so hard to find Tommy's in Smallwood' to 'Let's grab a beer'.

"You've got a date buddy," Tanya laughed.

"Let me go and vomit in the sink."

"Stop fidgeting and see what a great opportunity this is," she said. "Being gay will make people keep their distance. The cover will be great."

"What if he finds me so great that he wants to skip the funeral and make love?"

"Then you'll have to find a way to lead him there," Tanya responded cooly. "And I think I know how."

"You know how?" Jay looked at her, shocked. "You have broad experience with gays, do you?"

"No," Tanya smiled, "but I have extensive experience in men."

###

Gaby arrived at the pub in a Hummer. Jay recognized him immediately as he parked for Tanya had made him stalk all his social media profiles. "You must have topics to talk about," she had insisted.

Jay rose to meet him with a smile. He tried not to twitch when Gaby hugged him. He could even feel his boner. They sat down and ordered beers. As the glasses kept being refilled, Jay was surprised at how quickly the conversation turned to sex.

"I've done it on the beach, on an airplane. But my fantasy is to do it on a train," Gaby said, dropping his left eyelid in a half wink.

"Well, one of my weirdest fantasies is doing it at someone's funeral," Jay said, remembering Tanya's line.

"Well, well," Gaby smiled. "It just so happens that I'm attending a memorial service tomorrow."

"Are you?" Jay was surprised at how easily he had managed to lean in and rub his leg against Gaby's.

"I am. But I was thinking of skipping the service...so depressing those sermons...and just go to the gathering afterwards in the house grounds."

"So...can I...?" Jay's lazy smile did the trick.

"I'll find you a way in, never fear," Gaby said, raising one hand.

"And then you'll find a way in here," Jay said, taking Gaby's hand and rubbing it on his pants, suppressing his nausea.

###

On Saturday afternoon, Jay dressed in a black suit and bow tie. Tanya helped him tie the knot and then tucked a silk handkerchief into his coat pocket. "You look wow!" she told him.

"A bi-wow or a gay-wow?"

"You look just fine," Tanya laughed. "Now go."

"Aren't you going to give me a goodbye kiss?"

"On the cheek you mean?"

"Jeez, Tanya!" Jay fixed his cufflinks. "What's our strategy?"

"Get inside the grounds, then look for the diary."

"How will I dump Gaby?"

"That's totally up to you. Just knock him out, I say."

"I've never hit anybody in my life!" Jay protested.

"Really?" Tanya looked at him in awe.

"I'm an engineer, not a policeman."

"Didn't you ever get into fights?"

"We Indians are a rather peaceful lot."

"Oh my god!" Tanya laughed. "You're telling me that you have never hit a single person in your entire life!"

"That's nothing to laugh about," Jay said piously. "I'm a peace-loving person. Gandhian."

"Well, you better hit him tonight," Tanya said, handing him his coat, "else you'll become a man-loving person."

###

Gaby called at 4pm precisely. "Babe, I'm waiting for you downstairs," he said

"I'm coming for you then," Jay said cheesily, with a disgusted look on his face, picking up his coat.

Tanya laughed out loud at his expression. "Your dedication to the cause is unquestionable."

Jay looked at her, his eyes wary. "You're the one who put me up to this! You better make it up to me."

"Well this is better than knowing you are out there with a girl, doing god knows what," she smirked. "Do you have the device?"

Jay nodded. "And the earpiece too."

"Best of luck!" Tanya said, placing her hands on his shoulders. "Don't get defiled."

Jay pinched her cheek. "Ouch!" she protested. Holding him by the cheeks, she planted a deep kiss on his lips.

"What if we find the diary, Tanya?" he asked, opening the door. "What if it has something we don't want to see?"

"Then we make sure the whole world sees it," she said.

Jay sighed and walked out of the room.

###

"It's some old military hotshot's funeral," Gabby told Jay as they drove along the narrow country lanes. "A family friend. My father went to school with his son."

Jay nodded, lost in his own thoughts.

"Care to give me some on the way?" Gaby asked slyly.

"Let's wait till we get there," Jay said, feeling the bile rise to his throat.

The large estate appeared on their left. "Sometimes I wish I had enlisted," Gaby said enviously.

"So do I, buddy, so do I," Jay said.

The tall gates opened smoothly to let them in. The Hummer came to a halt in the parking lot arranged for the funeral. As he got out, under cover of the large vehicle, Jay whispered into his device, "We're here." There was no reply. He quickly opened the app on his phone and checked if the earphones were working. They were.

A valet caught the keys Gaby flung to him. "Not a scratch, mind you mate," Gaby warned.

They walked down the avenue to the house. Jay felt awkward walking along with a man holding his hand, but said nothing.

"It's a nice night," Gaby said. "I get to kill two birds with one stone, pardon the expression!"

"What do you mean?" Jay asked.

"I get to do you as well as square it with the owner of this fine establishment."

"Colonel Hardy?"

"Colonel Hardy Jr." Gaby said with unnecessary emphasis.

"You know the son well?"

"Speak of the devil." Gaby pointed ahead to where a man in full military uniform stood speaking to a group of guests at the entrance to the grounds. When he caught sight of them, he broke away and stared at them. He did not look pleased.

"What are you doing here, Gaby?" Col Hardy Jr. asked, a sullen look on his face as he stood blocking their way to the grounds.

Jay casually walked away a few steps, as if to give them privacy. "You there Tanya?" he whispered into the mouthpiece. No answer.

"What do you mean what am I doing here?" Gabby waved the gilt edged card. "I received an invitation from...let me see...oh yes, you!"

"You've got some balls!" Col Hardy Jr. stood ramrod straight. "The invitation was a formality. I never expected you to set foot on my lands."

"Nor would I have come if my date here wasn't interested in witnessing a British military funeral. So, do we have an open bar tonight?"

"Pay your respects and leave quickly, you poof!" the Colonel hissed angrily. "Else I'll remind you there is a shotgun in my study, loaded." Turning sharply, he walked away.

"Phew! That was close," Gaby said, pulling Jay along.

"You didn't tell me the Colonel hates you," Jay remarked as they walked to where the crowd had gathered.

"Yeah, the Colonel hates gays. As did his old man. And guess what? I was the most famous gay in town. No doubt they were jealous."

"So you'd like to irritate the Colonel tonight," Jay said.

"Let's get a drink," Gaby said. "The Colonel never fails to get on my nerves and there's an open bar." He pointed to the crowded counter. People surrounded it in huddled groups.

Jay followed blindly. Tanya was still not speaking. Had she abandoned him at this critical moment? Gaby made his way through the crowd hurriedly, focused on getting to the bar. Feeling somewhat forlorn, Jay decided he needed a drink too and made his way around the bar counter. Gaby was already leaning on it, having asked for a whiskey on the rocks. Jay stopped behind a woman in black who was blocking his way, her back to him. Her hair smelled strangely familiar.

"Excuse me," Jay said, hoping she would move. When she did, Jay swore. "Tanya!"

She looked entirely different. She was wearing a black dress that came to her knees. Drop diamonds shone in her ears. She was holding a wine glass and her face wore the look of a cat who had got the cream.

"Oh Jay," she said sweetly, "so nice to see you here. Such a loss to the country don't you think?"

"You know each other?" The man with Tanya gave Jay a long measured look.

"Oh yes," Tanya smiled, giving Jay a hug. "In fact, Jay here was the first homosexual I ever befriended."

"Homo?" The man instinctively stepped back a pace.

In reply, Tanya put her glass to her lips and drank the remaining wine. "Would you be kind enough to refill this for me, dear?" she asked, smiling sweetly at her escort.

"Certainly." With another look at Jay, he took her glass and walked away to get her another drink.

"What the fuck, Tanya!" Jay whispered harshly as soon as he was out of earshot.

She simply shrugged. "I know how to use Tinder too. And it seems we girls get dates much quicker than you gays."

"What in the world are you doing here?" Jay asked, pointing to the earphone in his ear. "I was worried something had happened to you."

"I reckoned you would need some help inside," Tanya said with a wink. "So I found myself a suitable escort and walked in."

"Interesting. So what are we going to do now?"

"I've had a look at the house. I say we dump our dates and meet at the kitchen entrance around the back."

"Hi!" It was Gaby. He walked up to them, drink in hand. "Looks like you've found a friend."

Tanya flashed him a smile. "And looks like my old buddy here has found a new friend."

"Sure looks like it." Jay felt Gaby's arm come round his waist. He looked at Tanya, embarrassed.

"Well, I'll leave you to it then," she said, and walked away.

"So shall we get to it?" Gaby asked, keeping his arm about Jay's waist, "or would you like to get tipsy first? Might loosen the knots."

Jay was still looking at Tanya, who now was chatting with her escort. "No drinks," he said firmly. "Let's go."

"There's a wonderful place just round there." Gaby gestured towards the back of the house. The pathways around the large house were empty. "Behind there is the garage. I was always interested in the General's cars."

"Sounds good," Jay agreed.

They left the crowd and set upon the trail to the garage.

"I hope nobody is watching us," Jay said nervously.

"Even if somebody is," Gaby said, "they'll probably think we're two buddies going for a quick smoke."

Jay did not respond. He glanced back at Tanya, but she seemed busy with her date. He shrugged.

"Why so nervous, partner?" Gaby asked. "Your wish is about to be fulfilled."

They found the garage unlocked. Inside, it was dark except for the late afternoon light filtering in through two windows. Gaby entered first. "Don't bump into anything other than me," he chuckled.

Jay entered and immediately found Gaby's hands groping him. "Stop," he said. But Gaby's moist lips were already on his neck. A shiver of revulsion went down Jay's spine.

"Come on, kiss me," Gaby urged.

Thwack! Jay never knew afterwards whether the action had been voluntary or a reflex reaction. Bending his elbow, he punched Gaby hard in the stomach. The force of the hit rammed Gaby against the wall. Jay did not waste a moment. He reached for him again and banged his head against the wall. Gaby slid down to the ground.

Jay ran over to the window and looked out. Tanya had broken away from her escort and was walking towards the garage. He went to the door and beckoned.

"Whoa!" Tanya said when she saw Gaby lying on the ground. "You finally got your cherry busted. Congratulations."

"This is no time for jokes, Tanya," Jay said, anything but amused. He undid his bow tie and one of his collar buttons. He desperately needed air.

"Relax," Tanya said, putting a hand on his shoulder. "Let's leave your friend here and find our way to the Late General's study."

"How do you know the diary will be in the study?"

"My father was British." Tanya said, watching him, "I just know."

Jay bent and dragged Gaby's unconscious form next to a car, out of sight.

###

They entered the house together, walking around the house till they found some French doors and walked into what appeared to be a morning room.

"The study is on this side according to the plans," Tanya said softly, pointing to her right.

They walked along the corridor to the right and came to a door. It was closed. Jay put his hand out and gingerly turned the door knob. The wooden door opened with a slight creak. They entered together. The room was in darkness.

Tanya whisked out her phone and put on the flashlight. "Let's check the desk," she said.

The Late General's desk was crowded with papers and memorabilia. As Jay nervously ruffled through the papers, Tanya managed to save an Egyptian glass ink bottle from tumbling to the floor. "Careful!" she whispered.

Jay nodded and slowed down.

"Quickly!" Tanya urged. "We don't have much time."

Jay threw her a harassed look. "I can't be fast and careful at the same time."

"Then at least be lucky!" she hissed.

And they were indeed lucky, for lying on the desk, by the side of the computer, was a large leather bound journal. When Jay opened it, he saw the Colonel's name handwritten on the inside cover.

"Bingo!" Tanya said.

"Let's get out of here," Jay said, picking up the journal.

"You're going nowhere!" a deep voice said from behind them as the room was suddenly bathed in light. Jay instinctively put the journal back on the desk. His heart missed a beat as he felt the metallic muzzle of a gun pushed into the small of his back.

"Don't move!" the voice ordered.

Jay clutched Tanya's hand.

"You lovebirds make me wonder whether to laugh or to cry. Turn around now."

Jay looked at Tanya, not letting go of her hand. They turned around together. The barrel of the shotgun was pointed right at their faces. And the man holding the gun was Colonel Hardy Jr.

"I followed you as soon as I saw that slimy bastard take you by the hand and walk off." Hardy said, not moving an inch. "I expected to catch myself a pair of fags. What I never expected was to find one of them lying unconscious on my garage floor."

"Looks like I did your work for you then," Jay said.

Hardy rammed the barrel hard under Jay's ribs, making him stagger.

"No wisecracks boy," Hardy warned. "What are you doing here?"

"Please lower the gun," Tanya begged. "We're not here to cause you any harm."

"I'll decide that," Hardy snapped.

"How about we do it the other way round," Jay said.

"What are you talking about, fool?" Hardy said angrily.

Jay grabbed the diary on the desk and held it between the gun and his face. "The reverse way. You tell us what we want, and we give you this diary."

"Put it away!" Hardy shouted. "Or I'll shoot."

"You can, of course, shoot me, but you'll have to do it through this." Jay opened the diary, holding it between them.

"It's my father's legacy," Hardy said. "The last thing I have in his own hand. Put it away and face me like a man."

"I'm sorry, but tonight I'm disguised as a poof," Jay said.

Hardy swung his shotgun to point squarely at Tanya. Jay took a deep breath to slow his heartbeat. He had anticipated the Colonel's move before he made it. Jay tossed the diary at Tanya. She was alert and caught it squarely, placing it between her and the barrel. Jay turned to place his arms around her. They were now one target with only the diary as a shield.

"Dammit!" Hardy shouted, his voice rising to the high beams above them. "Give me the diary for god's sake."

Jay nodded. The first step had been accomplished. Hardy had stopped making threats. The next step was to make him dance to their tune. "Tanya, give me the lighter from your purse," he said.

Hardy understood what Jay was doing and rushed forward to snatch the lighter from Tanya. Jay stopped him by holding up the open diary in one hand and flicking on the lighter with the other. "You move and I burn it," he said quietly.

Hardy halted and a moment later, tossed the shotgun on the sofa. "You win," he said, raising his arms, his voice bitter and hard. "Why do you want the diary anyway?"

When Jay told him, he let out a long sigh and sank down into a stuffed chair with embroidered birds in flight.

"I know what you speak of," he admitted. "I will tell you, but you will never be able to prove it."

"We don't need to prove anything," Jay said. "We just need to know."

"So you don't plan to use what you hear to malign my father?" Hardy asked, a sense of relief rushing through him.

"No," Jay said, leaning on the desk where the diary lay, his arms folded across his chest.

Tanya walked over to sit down in another chair, beside Hardy. "We need it for an entirely different reason," she said.

"What reason?" Hardy asked, unconvinced.

Jay took a deep breath. This was going to take a while.

###

"I will tell you what you want." Hardy said after Jay had finished his story. "You put your lighter away and I will not raise my shotgun. Your cause seems noble."

Jay looked at Tanya, who nodded and popped the unlit lighter she had been holding, back into her purse. "Tell us," Jay said.

Hardy pointed to the journal. "Open it to page 266."

Jay picked up the diary once more and carefully flipped the pages to the one mentioned. "It says 22 December 1949."

"I know what it says." Hardy closed his eyes. "I know what it says by heart. My father made me swear an oath of secrecy when he told me. I suppose I was the only person in the world he told. He would often wake at night, sweating profusely, cursing himself. It was only towards the end, when he had cancer and knew he would not live long, that he told me. Perhaps it gave him some relief to tell someone."

"So did he meet a man called Irshad Akhtar in Yakutsk?" Jay asked.

"No, he did not. However, the man you speak of sent him a letter."

"And what did it say?"

"Why don't you read it yourself?"

The Colonel rose and came over to where Jay stood, still holding the diary. Without taking it from him, Hardy turned a few pages. Stapled to the yellowing page was a letter on equally brittle paper, browning at the edges. A touch would have turned it into dust. Carefully, Jay read the writing on the yellowed surface without touching it.

"I repeatedly told my father to destroy this," Hardy said. "But he loved to keep souvenirs."

Jay handed the diary to Tanya to read. She had risen with Hardy and was now standing beside Jay.

Dear General Hardy

When you read this, I may be dead. But if I am alive, know that I will be coming for you next. I know you ratted on my friends. I followed the Russians who came to talk to you after the incident.

You British like to call yourselves gentlemen, but what nobility have you shown by turning back on your own word? You demonstrated cowardice of the worst kind. Why did you agree to help my friends in the first place if you only wished to snitch on them afterwards?

I take no names so that you do not get into trouble in case this letter is discovered. But if you have any shame, you will preserve this letter and give it to the proper persons who will see to it that the work my friends started does not go to waste.

As for me, I won't betray my friends like you did. I will take our secret to my grave.

Irshad Akhtar.

"So what exactly happened?" Jay asked.

"It would appear that my father double-crossed your grandfather," Hardy replied. "Akhtar found out and sent him this letter, in Yakutsk. My father must have felt guilty, for he preserved the letter."

"Jay, the last line is still the same," Tanya said, pointing.

Jay nodded. "Maybe that was how Akhtar signed all his letters."

"So now that you know my father's story," Hardy said, "what are you going to do?"

Jay stared into nothing for a while. "I thank you for your help, Colonel," he said finally. "I promise I will not malign your father's name. We'll be going now. And yes, don't forget to take the poof to the hospital, no matter how much you hate him."

The Colonel laughed. "I don't seem to have a choice in the matter," he said.

###

As they walked out and called a cab, Tanya looked at Jay. "What are we going to do now, Jay? This is another dead end."

"We're going to get ourselves air tickets," Jay said.

"Where to?"

"Home."

###

"You two give Russians a bad name," Alexis shouted over the phone.

"You are being too harsh, Boss," Sergei said. "There was no way we could have found them. London's a big city."

"So you just loitered at the airport?"

"We reckoned they'd be back when they wanted to leave the city," Charkov said, scratching his head.

"And which terminal were you planning to watch, 1, 2, 3 or 4? Unlike you, they had the sense not to use the same airport they came in through." Alexis snapped.

"Shit, Boss!" Sergei said. "What are we going to do now?"

"It is fortunate that I don't just depend on you," Alexis said. "They are at the Edinburgh airport at this moment."

"So should we get tickets for Edinburgh, Boss?"

"No, you idiot! Get tickets for India; our targets just did the same."

"Will do, Boss," Charkov said. "We won't fuck up this time."

"No you won't," said Alexis coldly, "because I am coming to handle things myself."

19
THE PLAN
FILE 10/14/JAN/XVII: TOP SECRET

1949

"This is bullshit!" Akhtar paced the room irritably, having heard what Singh had to say. "This is the stupidest idea I ever heard."

"You consider everything I say stupid," Singh snapped. "I don't want your opinion. I want to hear what Rupali has to say." He turned to his wife, who had thus far stood in silence.

"It can be done," she said. "The Colonel was kind. Perhaps we could convince him."

"He is a Brit!" Akhtar grasped Singh by the collar. "Don't you know that? They declared Netaji a war criminal."

"So were we when the INA trials took place," Singh reminded him. "But the Colonel was decent to us during the trials. He even saw to it that Rupali and I got to see each other."

"He called us brave souls," Rupali remembered.

"I think I can convince him to help us," Singh said.

Akhtar clenched his fists. "You are a fool, Singh!"

"Is she a fool too?"

"All he saw was a heroic couple. He probably felt a sense of satisfaction in helping you meet. The war was over. This is different."

"Not too different," Rupali said, looking Akhtar in the eye.

"You too, Rupali?" Akhtar stared at her in disbelief.

"All I'm saying is that we should speak to the Colonel," Singh said. "Bump into him at the hotel maybe. Find out why he's here. This isn't Singapore or some British enclave. It's Siberia! You saw how his car entered the prison. It may be our way in."

"Will he even recognize you, Singh?" Akhtar asked. "You're just some *desi* he saw once."

"I'm not just *some desi!*" Singh retorted angrily. "And I think this method will work."

"Let's speak with the Colonel and then decide what to do next," Rupali suggested calmly.

"Fine," Akhtar said, looking at her. "But I don't like this one bit."

"Trust her if not me," Singh said. "You can at least trust her."

Akhtar looked down at Rupali. "Alright, do it," he said, walking away.

###

"I can't believe my eyes!" Colonel Hardy looked in astonishment at the couple in front of him. "Major and Dr. Singh."

"And you are the good Colonel who was so kind to us in the trials." Singh shook hands. "We never had the opportunity to thank you, Sir."

"You don't need to thank me," Hardy said. "I was merely doing my duty as a human being."

"I never thought we'd run into you here of all places." Rupali stretched out her hand. The Colonel took it in his and kissed it gallantly.

"Nor did I think to see an Indian here," he said. "Please, have a seat."

The three of them sat in the hotel lobby.

"They don't drink proper tea in this godforsaken place," Hardy complained. "Three days without tea and I'm almost about to go mad."

"Perhaps you could visit our inn," Singh offered. "Rupali will make a nice brew for you."

"You know what, let's do that." The Colonel rose and led the way out.

###

Hardy took the steaming cup and curled his fingers around it. "The only warm thing in this damn cold town," he said.

"The tea or me?" Rupali smiled as she added some sugar to his cup.

"Both, my dear," the Colonel laughed. "I'd heard great things about Indian hospitality but never seen it. But you're independent now."

"Yes, everything changed after independence," Singh said.

"You've changed too," Hardy observed. "Fur business, huh? At the trial I took you for a lifelong soldier."

"You British put in a strict condition before leaving our country," Singh told him. "We veterans of the INA could not be in the Indian army, so here we are, scratching our way through life."

"Your business any good?"

"I get good yak furs from here that I sell to the spinning mills in India. We make it through."

"Sure looks like it." The Colonel sipped his tea happily.

"So what are *you* doing here Colonel?" Rupali asked, sitting down.

"Official business."

"Top secret?" Singh asked, smiling.

"Nothing that exciting," the Colonel sighed. "Ever since the war ended, life has been dull. I've been promoted but the excitement of wartime has been reduced to mere paperwork now."

"So what paperwork brings you to Yakutsk of all places?"

"Prisoner transfer," Hardy said briefly. "Apparently, a man from the 9th Hussar's has been lodged in this gulag since the war. Her Majesty's Government has been negotiating with the Soviets for his rescue. Finally, Stalin has agreed."

"So you are here to ensure he gets out?" Singh asked.

"Yes. The 9th Hussars fall in my Division, so it fell to me to handle the matter. I've been all over, from Turkey to here, to rescue British soldiers from prisons."

"It's a noble cause," said Rupali.

"Just paperwork," Hardy sighed. "I'm bored of it. And the more experience I gather doing this, the more assignments the Government sends me on."

"Do the Russians just give a prisoner away?" Singh wondered.

"The negotiations are done at the Ambassador level. It takes time, but they get it done."

"So how much longer are you here in this cold?" Rupali asked.

"Perhaps a week," Hardy told her. "Once the paperwork is done, the release will be approved from Moscow."

"And then what?" Singh asked. "Do you head home with him?"

"They give the prisoner into my custody and we leave," Hardy said, finishing his tea.

"Sounds tedious," said Rupali sympathetically.

"It is. Well, time to go." Hardy rose. "Thank you for the delicious tea. I've been craving it. And it was wonderful catching up with you."

"I'm sure we'll meet again," Singh bowed.

###

"This is our way in," Singh said to the team, gathered in their room at the inn. Rupali stood beside her husband, hands folded over each other.

"It rather sounds like our way up," Akhtar said tersely.

"You spit on every suggestion he makes," Dinesh remarked.

"Why do you even listen to him?" Akhtar asked. "All he has done till now is give shit suggestions, while I'm the one who has been doing all the good work."

"Oh really!" Harman mocked. "Like what?"

"I discovered the truth about the ashes at Renkoji," Akhtar reminded them. "And I found a way to get to Kobayashi."

"That's where you're wrong, Irshad." It was Rupali who spoke. "It was not just you who did it all. *We* did it. All of us. The concept of a team is something you can't seem to grasp."

"This place is too cold for concepts," Akhtar murmured.

"This isn't your decision to make," Singh said.

"Nor is it yours," Akhtar retorted. "You can't decide what to do unless all of us agree to it."

"Try to understand," Singh pleaded, "this may be our only way in. We don't know what is happening to Netaji with every day that passes. We don't have any concrete evidence to take back to our Government. This is our chance to maybe rescue him."

"What do you propose?" Dinesh asked.

"The British prisoner is to be moved from his cell to a waiting room the night before his release," Singh said. "The paperwork is completed and the British official verifies the prisoner that night. The next morning, he is released. We will enter the prison and find out which cell contains Netaji, and then move him to the waiting room."

"The Colonel will have to know for this to work," Akhtar said.

"Then we will tell him," Singh said.

Akhtar slammed his fist down angrily on the table again and again. "You will tell a *Brit*?" he shouted. "What is wrong with you, Singh? Why won't you listen to me?"

"I need to take a walk," Singh said and left the room.

###

The cold wind ruffled his hair. Singh pulled his overcoat closer as he watched Yakutsk prison from atop the hill. His boots felt damp from the snow that had got into them. He wiggled his toes to keep them warm.

Within, he felt equally cold and disheartened. If Netaji was inside the prison, this was the chance to rescue him. It was his duty as a veteran of the INA and a citizen of his newly independent country. How he performed in this situation would be an ode to what his country was capable of. He was not merely here to save Netaji. He was here for his country.

Feeling the weight of the mission on his shoulders, Singh returned to the town, his boots sinking knee deep into the snow as he walked. His tracks stopped when he halted before the hotel where the Colonel was staying. Involuntarily, he walked in. The receptionist looked up at his snow-laden overcoat.

"Can you please tell Major Hardy in the Presidential Suite," he said, "that Major Anish Singh is here to see him?"

###

"What you ask me to condone is treason," Hardy said, frowning.

"It is not treason but patriotism for us," Singh said.

"I understand your loyalties," Hardy said, "but he is a listed war criminal by Her Majesty's Government."

"You know as well as I do that he is not a war criminal," Singh stated.

"It is nevertheless my duty to my country to capture him if I know where he is."

"You never would have known if not for me."

"But I know now."

"And I'm asking you to forget what you know," Singh said, his eyes steady on the Colonel's face. "That is not treason."

"It is my honour that is at stake," Hardy said.

"Yes, your honour as a human being."

"I may be regarded as a fool," Hardy said.

"No. It will appear that the Russians made a mistake. They have already signed a deal with your Government. They are bound to release the prisoner, whatever happens."

"You speak well." Hardy rubbed his chin. "But what you want to do is highly dangerous."

"The danger is balanced by the reward," Singh told him.

"Alright, I'll help you," Hardy said finally. "Tell me how."

"You've seen the prisons from the inside," Singh said, hiding his elation. "Describe it to me."

Hardy pulled a paper napkin towards him and bent over the table, pulling a pen from his pocket. He quickly drew a rough map.

Singh nodded when he had finished. "Now, about the rest of the plan."

"Tell me," Hardy said.

Singh told him.

###

Akhtar slammed his fist against the wall. "You fool!" he said to Singh, who stood with his arms folded in one corner. "You've condemned us all!"

"It is done," Singh said. "You can't change it now."

"You have doomed us!"

"That is not how I look at it."

"How do you look at it?" Rupali asked.

"Before this," Singh replied, "we didn't have the hell of a chance of getting inside the prison. Now we do."

"It's not a chance," Akhtar laughed sarcastically, "it's a massacre."

"You listen to me." Singh raised his voice. "We do have a chance. It may not be the best or safest plan in the world, but it offers a chance of success. It is the only one we have."

Akhtar opened his mouth to speak but Singh silenced him with an uplifted hand. "When Netaji went to Japan from Berlin, he didn't have a plan. But he had a vision. He believed he could create an army with Indian war conscripts. It wasn't the easiest task in the world, but he managed to do it. He jumped into the fray using the first opportunity he got. Netaji was a wise man. He knew that opportunities don't lurk around every corner." He looked at Akhtar. "Sometimes we have to do the best with the least, because that is all we have. Sometimes our best is not good enough. But it is what must be done. It is what Netaji did, and it is what I will do to rescue him. Are you with me?"

"I am Boss," Harman said.

Rupali placed a hand on his shoulder and nodded. Across the room, Dinesh nodded.

Akhtar stood by the door, the lines on his face deep and prominent. "You talk too much," he said. "These people follow you blindly because they trust your inspirational speech. But here's the thing. I don't trust you."

"You have your reasons," Singh said. "But this one is for Netaji."

"It's not who or what it is for. You have committed the cardinal sin in covert ops, you have put your trust in a foreigner. You're a fool."

"I'm only a fool if I'm wrong," Singh said, "which time will tell."

"The stakes are too high to let time decide," Akhtar retorted harshly. "I know you are all going to perish in this attempt. But I won't be a part of a wasted effort."

Rupali glared at Akhtar. "I never thought you were a coward."

Akhtar sighed and shook his head sadly. "It's not cowardice," he said.

Rupali was about to retort but Singh placed a hand on her shoulder to silence her. "If he wants to opt out, let him go. I don't want a man who does not believe in me to be part of this."

Akhtar looked at the others. "And all of you, you believe him?"

He was greeted with stony silence.

He gave a bitter laugh. "Good for you then, but I know better. I'm leaving. I won't be part of this damn fool operation."

"Have you no shame, no loyalty?" Rupali asked, unable to remain silent a moment longer.

Akhtar spun round to face her. "Don't you teach me about shame!" he said. "You are coming with me."

"What!" Rupali took an instinctive step backwards.

Akhtar looked at Singh. "It's the only sane thing, Singh. You know it, I know it; everyone in the room knows it."

"It's her decision," Singh said.

"You have involved outsiders in the plan. This will not end well. Let her go with me; she will be safe."

"It's her decision," Singh insisted.

"You are walking into the devil's mouth," Akhtar said. "She's a doctor; she's not made for this."

"It's her decision." Singh's face showed no emotion.

"It *is* my decision," Rupali said. "And I refuse to be a coward."

Singh smiled, curling his palm around hers.

"Well if you won't come this way," Akhtar said, his face set, "perhaps it is time to tell him."

"Irshad, no! You promised you would never speak!" Rupali pleaded.

Breaking the clasp on his wife's hand, Sing came forward. "Tell me what?"

"Will you come or do I tell him?" Akhtar asked, his eyes never moving from Rupali's face.

"Not like this, Irshad," she begged, visibly shaken. "Not in front of everyone. I'll do it, later."

"It's too late for that. Last warning. Are you coming with me or should I tell him?"

"Tell me what?" Singh grabbed Akhtar by the collar. He didn't like the sound of this.

"We slept together," Akhtar said, pushing Singh's hands away.

Silence filled the room.

"When?" Singh's voice was barely audible.

"Multiple times, but just once after you were married."

Singh grabbed Akhtar again and pushed him against the wall. "When?" he demanded.

"Please Anish, it was in Singapore, a long time ago." Rupali tried to pull Singh away but he ignored her, glaring at Akhtar.

"Who initiated it?" he asked.

"Would I be telling you this if I had initiated it?" Akhtar asked.

Singh's hands fell away. He turned to look at Rupali in disbelief, cold rage etched in the veins of his face. He grabbed her cheek, hurting her. "Is it true?" he asked.

"Please, Anish..." she pleaded. "You were missing in Burma. We all thought you were dead."

"Did you initiate it?" Singh asked, tightening his hold. She writhed in pain. "Did you?"

"Yes," she sighed.

Singh pushed her to the ground and turned to look at Akhtar. "Go!" he said, his voice trembling with anger. "Never show me your face again!"

Akhtar spat on the floor. "Never fear, you won't see it again, because you are going to die in this foolhardy attempt."

"I go with my husband. I will die with him," Rupali said, reaching out to Singh, but he turned away from her touch.

Rupali lifted her chin in the characteristic gesture she had had since childhood. Looking into Akhtar's eyes, she said, "He is my husband and I will stay with him to my last day."

"You had better reconsider," Singh said, "because from this day on, you are no longer my wife."

Turning away, he walked over to the window and stared out at the bleak landscape. Behind him he could hear Rupali's quiet sobbing and the murmurs of the others. A door slammed; probably Akhtar leaving. Closing his eyes, he prayed to a God he had long forsaken: 'If you are indeed just, give us Netaji. Only his rescue will outweigh the mess I've made.'

20
The Heist

2015

It was raining in torrents when they landed at Chhatrapati Shivaji International Airport, Mumbai. The rain fell rhythmically over the plane, sounding like muted forest drums.

"It feels good to be home," Jay said once they had exited the terminal.

"What exactly about this feels good?" Tanya asked. She had already started sweating in the high humidity. Besides, the rain didn't seem to stop as they got a cab to the hotel.

"Oh, just being back on home territory," Jay told her. "I feel safe here. I feel I can outplay anyone on our trail."

"Well, I haven't seen the two Russians since Hong Kong," Tanya said, "so I guess we have outplayed them."

"With Russians you never know," Jay cautioned. "Remember Stalingrad!"

Their cab remained stalled in the flooded streets of Mumbai as the driver honked and cursed. Jay smiled; he was home.

"So what are we going to do here?" Tanya asked.

"We are going to get us a new hacker," Jay said.

Tanya looked at him in surprise. "Why do we need a new hacker?"

"To break into the NAI," Jay told her.

"What the hell is NAI?"

###

Eight hours later, Sergei and Charkov landed in Mumbai, to find Alexis waiting for them in the VIP lobby, talking on his cellphone. He signalled for them to wait, still on the phone.

"Still the same old sloppy bastard," Charkov said to Sergei softly, watching Alexis finish his call and walk towards them.

"Welcome to India," Alexis said sarcastically. "Looks like I made it here quicker than you bozos."

"In our defense, you were closer," Sergei said. "What's the status?"

"Our targets landed before me and have disappeared after leaving the airport." Alexis said. "Much to my displeasure, I had to get our local teams involved in this highly covert operation; something I was trying to avoid. But your incompetence left me with no choice."

"What are the locals going to do?" Charkov asked.

"I am having the target's parents, business associates and subordinates watched, in case he contacts them."

"Good move," Sergei agreed. "What do you think he's doing here?"

"I was wondering the same thing until I managed to hack into his Gmail account," Alexis replied. "It was a fluke. I have been sending him proxy emails, one each day, hoping he might click on at least one. And he did, yesterday."

"So doesn't that give us his location?" Sergei asked.

"Unfortunately, he had switched off the location services on his phone. But guess what I did find?"

"His porn collection?" Sergei chuckled.

"Better. His search history. And guess what the bastard is searching for desperately ever since he left England?" Alexis held up his phone.

"Mother of God!" they said in unison.

###

"The NAI is the National Archives of India." Jay told Tanya.

"Isn't robbing the national archives rather extreme?" she asked.

"We have no choice," Jay shrugged. "Akhtar's letters are a dead end. It does seem that he took his secret to the grave."

"So what are you hoping to find in the NAI?"

"I don't know. Anything. Something. We must have a lead."

"The NAI is a premier government institute," Tanya said, stressing each word. "We can't just walk in and look for classified information."

"You're not hearing me. We have no choice. We have to do this."

Tanya sat back and gave a long sigh. "If we are going to do this, we will need more people," she said finally.

"That is exactly why we are getting another hacker," Jay said.

"Who?" Tanya asked sceptically.

"An old friend of mine," Jay replied, whisking out his phone.

###

Dr. Lee cursed as he stood outside the Oranax Head Office on the topmost floor of the Bandra-Kurla Business Center. The elevator doors refused to open despite his repeated jabbing at the switch. Sighing, he wondered if he would have to walk all the way to the other end of the floor, where the stairs led down. He looked around to see if anyone was in the office to help with the elevator problem. But the work stations were empty. Even the receptionists had left. Lee cursed again, looking at his wristwatch. It was almost midnight. He had been testing the new software and had simply lost track of time.

He pressed the elevator button again. Suddenly, he saw the lights go dim all around him. In the blink of an eye, the lights went out, leaving him standing in complete darkness. Lee took a deep breath. This part of the city was not prone to power shutdowns. And there was a generator back-up in the building. He pulled out his cell phone, but there was no connectivity. That was strange, Lee thought. He had had connectivity less than five minutes ago when he had called his wife to let her know he was coming. He fiddled with the buttons, trying to shut off the OS and reboot it. As the phone shut down. The darkness felt overwhelming.

Lee felt his heart start hammering. There was definitely someone there. He could hear footsteps.

"Joy, is that you?" he called out to his lead engineer, who could have been working late. There was no reply. Lee pressed the start-up button on his cellphone, but the phone took its own sweet time.

The footsteps stopped and then moved again, coming closer. "Is that you Priya?" Lee called, retreating to the wall. He had seen Priya, his tech associate, head to the loos twenty minutes ago. There was no reply. The footsteps were very close now, barely two meters away. Then they stopped.

Lee's phone finally came to life and he raised the lit screen in the direction of the footsteps. His anxious face broke into a smile. "Oh, it's you, Cap!" he said, relieved.

Jay smiled in the light of the cellphone. "I wondered if you were pulling one of your late-nighters; otherwise I'd have had to abandon my plan."

"Did you cause the blackout?" Lee asked, holding his phone up to give themselves more light.

"I did," Jay said. "And also I messed with the elevator. I'm also holding in my hand a phone network jammer."

"Well, you were ever the discreet boss," Lee said. "Now tell me why you went to all this trouble? Could have just emailed me that you're back and we'd have met up for coffee."

"I wanted to talk to you about something important and I couldn't have contacted you in broad daylight because someone is trying to find me."

"Well, there's no one here, Cap. So why don't you speak up?"

"I will," Jay replied, "but not here. Let me take you to my associate."

"You got an associate now?" Lee asked, raising his eyebrows.

"Yeah, you'll like her," Jay said.

"A her?" Lee smiled.

"Also a hacker." Jay winked.

###

Two hours later, the three of them sat in a huddle in Jay's hotel room, pondering over what Lee had just told them.

"I don't think I can help you, Jay," Lee said when they had explained everything.

"And why is that?" Jay asked.

"What you propose to do carries too much risk, with almost zero chance of survival. I can't let you do this, nor do it myself."

"Actually, you can," Tanya said, leaning forward.

Lee merely shook his head and poured another round of whiskey for them.

"The Grime Hypothesis," Jay said, raising his glass to his lips.

Lee nervously drummed his fingers on the table. "What's he talking about?" he asked Tanya.

"It's rather simple," she said. "It's gotta do with probability."

"What's the hypothesis?"

"A conspiracy cannot remain a conspiracy forever." Jay put down his glass. "Secrets cannot be kept forever."

"And who is this Grime?" Lee mocked. "Some internet Guru?"

Jay shook his head. "Actually, he was a physicist at Oxford."

"An expert in radiation physics," Tanya added.

"And what is his hypothesis based on?" Lee asked.

"His equations," Jay said. "While studying subatomic particles, he realized that their behaviours are very similar to humans, rather too similar."

"And how do conspiracies come into this?"

"What Grime discovered was fantastic," Tanya told him. "He found that his equations predicting the behaviours of particles, could predict the behaviours of humans too."

"And just like the probability of collisions depends on the number of particles," Jay added, "the strength of conspiracies depends on the number of persons involved."

"So Grime says no one can hold onto a secret forever?" asked Lee

"Exactly," Jay said, nodding. "And the number of years required for a conspiracy to blow depends also on number of conspirators."

"If we assume that all 10,000 of the INA soldiers knew about Netaji's conspiracy," Tanya said, "then Grime's equation predicts the secret would have blown in 3.7 years."

"But over 60 years have passed, bringing down the number of conspirators to 237, which makes sense," Jay remarked.

"And Grime's equations change dramatically when catalysts are involved," Tanya explained. "Just as a catalyst speeds up a reaction, Grime's catalysts are persons who have seen through the conspiracy and are trying to break it."

"The presence of a catalyst lifts the probability dramatically," Jay said.

"And as the catalysts increase," Tanya said, "the rate of solution increases in exponential powers."

"We are asking you to be that catalyst," Jay said. "To join us and bring the probability to one."

Lee took a deep breath. "Fuck it!" he finally said. "I'm in."

###

The National Archives of India Repository or the NAI, is located at the famous intersection of Janpath and Rajpath. It is an impressive building, built during the British era, and it housed records from as early as the 18th century. Open to the public as a museum, the Archive were usually crowded on Sunday afternoons. The only non-Indians that day were the three Russians standing beside their hired car in the parking lot.

Sergei and Charkov were visibly sweaty and uncomfortable in the hot and humid Delhi weather. Alexis was continuously on his phone, cursing at the other two to be more vigilant in the intervals between calls.

"News!" he finally said, after his twentieth call. "The targets booked into the Plaza Hotel using pseudonyms. My men managed to track them because Jay used his credit card to make the payment."

"So where are they?" Sergei asked, checking the holster on his belt.

"I called the hotel and it seems that our friends rented a black van after checking out and left."

"So let's keep an eye for a dark van," Sergei said.

"We'll take them as soon as they get here," Alexsis said. "This has been going on for much too long. I'd prefer to finish it today."

"Yes, Boss," Sergei and Charkov said together.

The three Russians lit cigarettes and waited for their quarry to arrive.

###

"Are you nervous, Tanya?" Jay asked as their van drove along Delhi's wide roads. They sat in the enclosed back section that had no windows. Lee was in the driver's seat.

"A little," Tanya admitted. "I once saw a Hindi movie called *Rang de Basanti*. I wonder if that's what's going to happen to us."

"If you compare our situation with the movie," Jay said, "Then I'll say what Amir Khan said in the movie, 'What happens to us won't matter because we are together'."

"Indeed we are." Tanya snuggled into his side. Jay reciprocated by putting his arms around her.

They sat like that, not talking anymore, until the tires of the van screeched to a harsh halt. Lee opened the doors a few moments later and handed them two small black covered books. "Your new passports," he said. "Bon voyage."

"Why do we need passports for the NAI?" Tanya asked, bewildered.

"We are not going to rob the NAI," Jay said, stepping out of the van.

"Then where are we going?"

Jay smiled. "Why don't you step down and find out?"

###

"They never planned to rob this place," Alexis said, getting off yet another phone call.

"Then where did they go?" Sergei asked.

"I've been a fool!" Alexis cursed as he yanked open the door of the car. "It was a diversion to deceive us." He rammed his fist onto the hot metal of the car. It gave a protesting twang. "Give me the Sat phone," he said.

Sergei whipped out the satellite phone from his coat pocket and unlocked it, his hands shaking.

"Give it here!" Alexis snatched it away and dialled a number. After a brief conversation in Hindi, he slammed his open palm onto the car again and cursed.

"What's happened, Boss?" Charkov asked.

Alexis frowned. "They hoodwinked us into following them here, to India."

"So where are they headed now?" Sergei asked.

Alexis turned off the Sat phone. "To Russia," he said.

###

As their plane took off, Jay explained to Tanya what he had been doing. "Akhtar's letters were not useless," he said.

"They weren't?"

"No. They told us exactly where to go. They lead to a place in Russia." Jay took the cups of coffee the air hostess was offering them on a tray and handed one cup to Tanya.

"Holy shit!" Tanya sat back in her chair. The revelation was shocking.

Jay put his free hand over her's comfortingly. "I realized by the time we left the General's house that the Russians had been following us. We couldn't go into their country with them hot on our trail. So I brought them to mine."

"So what Lee planned was not an infiltration into the NAI?"

"No," Jay laughed. "What Lee did was get us tickets to Russia under false identities. No one would dream of breaking into the NAI. Not even me. I just played that part to mislead the Russians."

Tanya punched him lightly on the shoulder. "Why didn't you tell me?"

"Wanted to get you, for once." Jay winked. "You have been getting me since we met. In Hong Kong, then that homosexual shit in London... Well, this is revenge."

"Touché," acknowledged Tanya. "So what makes you think Akhtar's letters lead us to Russia?"

"To a barren hill in Yakutsk, to be precise," Jay said. "If my deduction is correct, Akhtar hid his diary there."

"Why would he do that?" Tanya asked.

"Remember the letters? The last lines were always the same. At first I thought it was just the way he signed off his letters. But then I realized there was a reason why he put that in each time."

"I wondered about it too," Tanya said.

"*I shall take my secret to the grave*," Jay recalled. "I didn't realize till recently that he meant it literally."

"Literally?"

"That there really would be a gravestone with his name, in Yakutsk. That was the clue he was leaving in all his letters; that he would leave his secret buried in his gave. But I wasn't sure. So I did an experiment."

"What experiment?"

"I put up a gig on Fiverr.com. For 5 dollars I got an adventurous Russian teen to go to the old graveyard in Yakutsk and confirm that one of the gravestones indeed bore marks that looked like 'Irshad Akhtar'."

"That is so thrilling!" Tanya said, her eyes shining.

"So now we are off to Russia," Jay said. "Let's hope it's the final stop of our journey."

"I wonder what we'll find?" Tanya mused.

Jay shook his head. "I don't know. But I have a feeling it's the final piece of the puzzle."

"Do you think we'll find Akhtar's diary? So many years have passed."

Jay shrugged. "We've come too far to stop now."

As the plane soared into the clouds, Tanya placed her head on Jay's shoulder. "I feel like I need to get all the sleep I can get," she said.

Jay pulled her closer. "Me too," he sighed.

They drifted into slumber, holding each other, somewhere over Tibet.

###

“Our flight has been delayed by six hours,” Sergei said, returning to the smoking lounge at the New Delhi international airport. The other two had already filled the narrow room with a smoky haze.

Charkov cursed and Alexis got up and began pacing along the glass walls like a caged animal. *Plain bad luck,* he thought.

“They’ve got a head start on us,” he said, after a while.

“Can’t we ask the Siberian Chief to step in?” Sergei asked.

Alexis shook his head. “This operation is classified. *We* have to handle this.”

“We’ll catch them in Yakutsk then,” said Charkov.

“You’ve been saying that since Hong Kong.” Alexis’s voice was sharp and angry. “We wouldn’t be in this mess if you had just caught them there.”

Sergei looked up. “We didn’t even know they were a *they* in Hong Kong.”

Alexis put his cigarette to his lips and took a long drag. “That’s true,” he finally admitted. “My intelligence has been not been as efficient as it usually is, in this operation. I underestimated our target. It won’t happen again.”

“We’ll catch him, Boss,” Charkov said. “He won’t escape this time.”

Alexis took a deep breath. “No, he won’t. But catching him is just the beginning.”

###

Yakutsk, located in Russian Siberia, had the reputation of being the coldest city in the world. Winters there were colder and longer than in Alaska. Jay felt the increasing chill as their rented an SUV neared the city. Tanya was visibly frozen, her cheeks rosy. Both felt dog tired. After a direct flight to Verkoyansk, they had driven along the infamous Kolyma Highway to reach Yakutsk in less than a day.

They found a three-storied hotel in the outskirts of the town and wearily checked in. When they finally got to their room, it was almost midnight.

“It says the old graveyard is five miles from here,” Tanya said, looking at her phone.

“On a barren hilltop in an abandoned state probably,” Jay sighed.

“You’ll need a shovel,” Tanya said, looking out at the darkness beyond the windows. “What if the Russians catch us, Jay?” Tanya finally asked the question uppermost in her mind.

“We probably should have a back-up for that,” he said. “A plan B.”

"I still have my journalist sources from my days in WikiLeaks. I could prepare a list, hunt for their email ids and write a code to send them our files at the push of a button."

"We have quite a lot," Jay reminded her. They had collected a lot of data - pictures, audio logs, recordings of their talks with Anu and Mrs. Makijan... It ran into gigabytes. "It could do a great deal of damage if it falls into the wrong hands."

"I'll send them only if we have no other option," Tanya said. "Let's hope it doesn't come to that."

"Pray rather than hope," Jay said. "Come, let's get some sleep."

"I still have the code to write," Tanya said.

Jay leaned forward and kissed her on the forehead. "Thank you for everything, Tanya." He fell onto the bed and was asleep immediately.

###

When Jay awoke, he found Tanya sitting by the window.

"I'll ring for coffee," she said, seeing him stir.

"Didn't you sleep?" Jay asked as he stretched and got up.

"I couldn't. Every five minutes I thought I heard vehicles pulling up to the hotel entrance."

Jay caressed her face. "You're anxious. I'll go the graveyard today, find whatever there is to be found, and it will soon be all over."

"I hope it goes smoothly."

"Did you create the plan B?" Jay asked, brushing his teeth.

"I did," she nodded. "If anything goes wrong, one click and our information will be all over the web."

"Good. Let's get some breakfast."

Jay turned on the shower. The water was hot and he reveled in the moist heat, knowing he would soon be out in the sub-zero cold. When he walked out, towel wrapped around his waist, Tanya pointed to a package on the bed.

"Your cold suit just arrived." The package contained thermal clothing. "Your shovel arrived too." She pointed to the long, sturdy implement propped in one corner.

"Well if everything is ready, let's eat and then I'll be on my way." Jay began systematically donning layer upon layer of clothing.

"I'll rent a car for you," Tanya said, crossing to the bedside phone.

"An SUV will arrive soon," she said when she had made the call.

They sat down at the table, the breakfast tray they had ordered from room service between them. They ate in silence.

An hour later, the SUV had arrived. Jay and Tanya were in the lobby waiting and the driver handed over the keys to Jay. They signed the paperwork and then Tanya helped Jay put the equipment into the back.

"I love you Jay," Tanya said suddenly as he prepared to get in.

Jay stopped. It was the first time she had said it. He turned to face her. Tanya's face was visibly distraught though she was determined to hold back her tears. Jay put an arm around her shoulders. "I love you too," he said quietly.

"What if they catch you?"

"Then you know what to do."

They had come to the end of their campaign, but things could still go wrong. They had decided that if the KGB found them, Tanya would release the information they had gathered, online. The report she had created as they travelled, would cause a sensation.

"I must go now," Jay told her.

"Get back soon."

"I will, with proof!"

Jay climbed into the SUV and turned on the ignition. In another moment he was gone, rear lights glowing in the misty morning.

21
The Escape
File 11/14/Jan/XVII: Top Secret

1949

The wild winds howled, causing the large trees and waist high bushes to sway from side to side. The crimson blossoms moved with equal vigour. It was a poppy farm and plants covered his approach. Singh held his subatomic MG32 in his right hand, strapped to the belt across his back. He kept his head down as he walked through the fields towards the small hamlet that lay beyond. It was little more than a few wooden houses, a barn and a yard. To one side, he could see two trucks, waiting. The strong fragrance from the poppies tickled his nose but he kept moving. Strapped to his helmet was an earpiece and speaker, the wires attached to a radio on his back.

Static crackled through his earphones and then Akhtar's raspy voice said, "Are you there yet?"

"Nearly," Singh whispered. "Can't you see me?"

"Not at all." Singh heard metallic noises as Akhtar changed position.

"I thought you were a great sniper."

"If a great sniper could see in the dark," Akhtar's voice said, "he wouldn't need you, would he?"

Singh stopped where the fields ended and gazed back at the hill from where he had come. He tried to locate Akhtar's position, but could not. "Aren't you a little too far away?" he asked. He knew that the greater the distance between the target and the shooter, external factors like wind speed became critical considerations.

"Well, you just said I'm a great sniper," Akhtar chuckled.

Singh watched the vehicles. He could see two figures standing next to the wooden two-storied building. One was a guard with a long bayonet fixed to his rifle. He stood leaning against the building, his head drooping on his chest, asleep. The other man was on one knee beside the jeep, working on a tyre.

"The action begins," Singh whispered.

"Kobayashi better pay us potfulls for this," Akhtar said and then the earpiece went silent.

Singh crouched down at the edge of the fields. The poppy blossoms waved over his shoulder as he raised his MG39, pointing it at the dozing guard. With his other hand, he scratched the ground, clutching a fistful of pebbles and earth. Raising his hand, he threw it over his head.

The mud ball hit the sleeping man in the face. His eyes flew open. Cursing in Mandarin, he started towards the man beside the jeep, deducing it was he who had played the prank. Singh placed his finger on the trigger.

###

Over from the hill, Akhtar peered through the scope on his sniper rifle. It was so dark he could see almost nothing. With his other hand, he pushed the earpiece tighter in case Singh whispered something.

It was the settlement they were after. Kobayashi wanted it to burnt down. Just the settlement, not the fields. The owner had been selling his poppy yield to the Chinese. Kobayashi wanted it for himself. When the owner refused to negotiate, Kobayashi decided it was time to change the owner.

Waiting for Singh's signal, Akhtar adjusted the position of his rifle. In his mind he calculated the angle of inclination for a clean shot. Singh had relayed the information to him. Ninety-five steps. A man of Singh's height covered almost a meter in a single stride. So 50 meters. The wind meter on his right glowed at 2m/s radium. Akhtar adjusted the inclination to roughly a few degrees above the lights he could see. Now, all he had to do was wait.

They had recived information that there were two petrol tankers in the settlement. The plan was to blast them with sniper fire. But the tankers could not be seen in the dark so it was Singh's job to get inside and mark their location.

Lying prone on the ground, Akhtar casually lit a cigarette. The warm wisps slowly rose up into the air as a sense of calm filled him. He waited.

###

Singh moved quietly, keeping to the shadows, his back to the barn doors. He had noticed two more guards at the entrance, sharing a smoke. Shooting the first two near the jeep had been easy. This was more tricky.

He leaned around the corner of the barn searching for a back entrance. There didn't seem to be one. Glancing up, he saw a square window, a little above his head. Singh slung his rifle onto his back and jumped, grabbing the sill with both hands and hauling himself up till his head was on a level. Peering in, he could see no one. Cautiously, he pushed himself through the opening, landing with a soft thud on the other side.

Inside, the light was dim, coming from the single lantern at the entrance. But he could make out two tankers immediately. The soldiers still stood at the doors, smoking. Singh knew the keys to the tankers would be with them. He had not noticed any other soldiers in the compound. For a moment Singh wondered how best to tackle them. The two were chatting, wide awake. He could not shoot them both at once. If he shot one, the other would immediately take cover behind the doors and it would turn into a shooting match.

Slowly, he made his way to one of the trucks. One hand on the tanker, he leaned out to scout the guards. The cold metal froze his palm. Stealthily he moved towards the front. Suddenly he felt his jacket snag on a protrusion. Singh looked down and smiled. The fools had left the keys in the door.

Holding his breath, he gently turned the key. There was a soft click as the lock disengaged. Singh dropped to the ground in a crouch but the two soldiers remained engrossed in their discussion. 'Complacent,' Singh thought disapprovingly. 'A bad trait in a soldier.' Carefully, he opened the tanker door with one hand, the other on his rifle. He expected the soldiers to look up as the door gave a creak. But no one turned. Extracting the keys from the door, Singh climbed in, pulling the door inwards but not clicking it shut. He flicked through the keys and found the one for the ignition. Inserting it, he turned it, knowing the roar would instantly alert the guards. Quickly he turned on the head lights.

The engine whirred loudly and the soldiers turned, startled, but were blinded by the lights. Singh wasted no time in throwing the truck into gear and ramming his foot down on the accelerator. The heavy vehicle moved towards the doors like a juggernaut. Singh heard a cry as he passed the doors, sure he had hit at least one soldier. When the tanker was out in the road, Singh turned and looked back.

The second soldier had raised his rifle but hesitated to shoot at the petrol tanker. He was shouting and calling to the other guards, unaware they were already dead. Singh got him in two shots from his MG 39.

Leaving the engine running, he descended from the tanker. Running across to the guard, lying on the ground, he checked his pockets. He found the keys to the second tanker. Before entering the barn, he quickly glanced behind. He could see lights being switched on in the other buildings. The others had heard the disturbance and would soon appear on the scene to investigate. Singh hastened into the barn.

###

Akhtar watched the lights though the scope, eyes wide. It was the headlights of a tanker. He tossed away his cigarette and waited for Singh's voice in his earpiece.

Another pair of lights emerged from the darkness – the second truck. Singh would give the signal any moment now. Akhtar saw the lights move and stop beside the first tanker. Then static crackled his earpiece.

"Do you see me?" Singh asked, breathing heavily.

"Clear as day." Akthar's finger moved to the trigger. He sucked in his breath.

"I'm getting down from the tanker." Singh said.

"What is that?" Akhtar asked suddenly. "Do I hear a baby crying?"

There was silence for a moment, then Singh said, "No baby. Just cats yowling."

"Are you sure? It does sound like a baby crying."

"Yeah yeah...sure...just cats."

"But I can hear a woman yelling..."

"No women here, Irshad."

"Are you sure?"

"I'm right here, aren't I?" Singh voice was raised. "Do you see the tankers?"

"I see them," Akhtar said.

"Then shoot. I'm clear."

"You sure?"

"I'm in the field now," Singh told him.

The ambient noise died away as Singh ran through the poppy fields. Akhtar took a deep breath. "Inshallah!" he whispered, as he always did before firing a shot. He held his breath and moved the rife so the truck lights sat a little to the left of the crosshairs. The wind was blowing from the right. He compensated for the distance and pressed the trigger.

One second...two seconds...then the trucks burst into a ball of light and flame. Angry flames leapt up at the dark sky and a deafening blast shook the ground, echoing over the poppy fields. Akhtar watched the flames envelop the entire settlement as night turned to day.

"It's done," Singh said into the earpiece.

"Then let's get out of here." Akhtar got to his knees and then rose to his feet, slinging his rifle over his shoulder.

"See you back at base," Singh said.

###

"Wake up, Singh!" The voice was loud and angry.

Singh opened his eyes lazily. It was Akhtar, shaking him by the collar. "What the fuck are you doing?" Singh asked.

"You're a mean bastard!" Akhtar yelled at him. "Heartless and evil."

"What are you talking about?"

"You know what I'm talking about!" Akhtar snapped.

Singh sighed. He knew. "How did you find out?" he asked.

Akhtar retreated and lit a cigarette. "There were families in the settlement. Innocent people. So many times I asked you!"

"I didn't see anyone," Singh said.

"You fucking didn't see?" Akhtar yelled. "I fucking heard a baby cry on the radio, damn you! You did see. But you did not tell me."

There was a moment of silence as the two men stared at each other.

"I did see," Singh admitted, finally. "What was I to do? It's war."

"Right on all counts except one." Akhtar flicked the cigarette butt in Singh's face. "Last night wasn't Our War. It was Kobayashi's war."

"Would you have shot the trucks had I told you there were families there?" Singh asked.

"No...never!"

"That's why I didn't tell you. Because you wouldn't have done your part and the mission would have failed. Kobayashi would have sent us away to Singapore and we would not have been trained by him, which is what we came here to do."

"You could have got the innocents out and then told me to shoot!"

Singh took Akhtar by the shoulders and shook him. "There wasn't time! Who knew how many more guards there were?"

Akhtar angrily thrust Singh's hands away. "You're a sore man, Singh," he said, and walked away.

###

Singh's eyes flew open, his heart still thudding in his chest. He remembered it as clearly as if it had happened yesterday. He took a deep breath and got up. The feeble rays of the Yakutsk sun peeped into the room, reflecting on the wood panels. It was time to go.

Singh walked into the shower. The lukewarm water brought him some relief. He dried himself and dressed quickly. Opening his backpack, he checked his weapons. The Uzis were fitted with silencers and there was extra ammunition. Singh closed the backpack and put on his black skull cap. He was ready.

At the cafeteria, Harman greeted him with a can of hot coffee.

Singh held the steaming cup in both hands, feeling its warmth travel from his fingers to the rest of his body. "Have you procured the trucks?"

Harman nodded. "I have. And Dinesh is out at this moment finding a good ambush spot."

"Then all that remains is for me to go and do the job," Singh said, drinking his coffee.

"I'll drive you," Harman said.

At the door he saw Rupali, her eyes still red from weeping. She reached out to hug him but Singh stepped aside. Dropping her arms, she said quietly, "Please be safe."

Singh nodded in silence. Putting on his backpack, he walked out the door with Harman.

###

When Singh returned to the safe house, everyone was in the living room, with a fire burning. All eyes turned to him as he walked in. Singh brushed the snowflakes off his clothes and took off his jacket, going towards the fire, and reaching for its warmth.

"How did it go?" Dinesh asked, unable to bear the suspence a moment longer.

"It's done," Singh said, sitting down.

"Did you find Netaji?" Harman asked, suppressed excitement evident in his face.

Singh did not speak for a minute. Finally he looked up and said, "Almost."

Dinesh jumped up. "Almost?"

"I infiltrated the compound without incident," Singh told them. "The guards were slack enough."

"Did you reach the record room?" Rupali's voice shook.

"Entering the record room was the tricky part," Singh said. "The Warden was there. When he finally took a pee break, I sneaked in."

"Did you find the records?" Harman asked. "Was Netaji's name there?"

"There were no Indian names," Singh said. "They would have used aliases for the prisoners anyway."

"So what did you look for?" Dinesh asked.

"Arrest records," Singh said. "Fortunately, they were arranged alphabetically, according to where the arrest was made. I found what I was looking for."

"Arrests made in the shanty town in 1945," Rupali said. "How many were they?"

"Three. I got their cell numbers. Turns out one man died in 1946."

"So did you visit the other two?" Dinesh asked.

Singh nodded. "I sneaked outside their cells and called, 'Netaji!'."

"What happened?" asked Dinesh.

"The first man did not respond. The second one did."

"Was he Netaji?" Harman asked, forgetting to breathe.

"Like I said," Singh said, letting out a long sigh, "almost..."

The second prisoner Singh found in the Yakutsk prison in that daring infiltration that night was someone who was familiar with the name Netaji.

"He responded when I said the name Netaji," Singh told them.

"But he wasn't Netaji?" Harman asked, disappointment feeling as heavy as led in his chest.

"No, he wasn't."

"Are you sure?" Harman asked.

"Of course, I'm sure!" Singh said angrily. "You think I wouldn't recognize Netaji if I saw him? Besides, this man was Caucasian."

"Netaji disguised himself as a Caucasian before," Harman reminded him, "when he escaped from Calcutta."

"This man was not Netaji," Singh said decisively.

"So who was he?" Dinesh asked.

"That's the catch. He refused to say who he was unless..." Singh let out another sigh.

As soon as the prisoner learned Singh was here to rescue Netaji, he refused to open his mouth.

"That crafty devil wants us to bail him out of prison first," Singh said, drinking from the hot cup of coffee Dinesh handed him. "Till then, he won't tell us what he knows."

"So what did you do?" Rupali asked.

Singh replied without looking at her. "I didn't have a choice. I had to find something and get out of the prison fast, and that is exactly what I did."

"So are we really going to bail this prisoner out?" It was Rupali again.

"What choice do we have, Rupali?" Singh said angrily, suddenly rising from his chair. "If we do not get him out, we face a dead end."

"Maybe you could enter the prison again, look for signs of Netaji again," Harman suggested.

"No. The prisoner transfer happens this morning. This is our only chance."

"So are we really busting a complete stranger out?" Rupali asked.

Singh stood up and faced her. "What do you want to say?" he asked. "That Akhtar was right all along?"

Rupali folded her arms. "No," she said. "You're the one saying that."

"You can go if you want," Singh told her. "I want nothing to do with you anyway."

"I am staying," she insisted.

"Have you scouted a hideout?" Singh asked, looking at Dinesh.

Dinesh nodded. "An abandoned warehouse out of town, in the middle of nowhere; snow to cover our tracks."

"How about the vehicle?"

"I've secured a Marshall truck," Harman said. "It'll be perfect."

Singh nodded. "Good. The weapons are already with us."

"This is on," Dinesh said.

"Let's decide on the ambush spot." Singh leaned over the table with Harman, drawing forward the rough map they had been able to secure.

Rupali looked at them for some time. No one turned to include her. Finally, she walked into the bedroom to get some sleep, an unwitting tear sliding down her cheek.

###

The whole crux of Singh's plan was based on a major flaw in the way shifts changed at Yakutsk. The prison ran on two twelve-hour shifts. The entire staff was rotated in the morning and at night. So, when the actual prisoner transfer began the next morning, the official who handled it was not the person who had moved the prisoner to the holding cell the night before. And so he did not notice that Singh had switched prisoners.

The flag was hoisted early that morning at Yakutsk prison. As the soldiers sang the communist anthem, the Warden kept looking at his wristwatch. There was a lot to do that morning.

The English General arrived at 8am, having consumed a hearty breakfast. The paperwork for the transfer was still incomplete but his arrival made the clerks work faster. In their haste, no one even checked the prisoner when he was moved from the holding cell to the courtyard for the General's inspection. The General gave the man a cursory glance and waved his hand to get on with it. The prisoner was moved to the rescue jeep and his shackles loosened. The General shook hands with the Warden and whistling an old English tune, climbed into the jeep behind the one with the prisoner.

The British convoy consisting of three jeeps left the prison complex at 10 am. The gates closed behind them. On the way, the General asked the cars to stop at a certain point, close to a rocky outcrop, and got down for a quick smoke. It was part of the plan.

Singh and Dinesh were waiting. As soon as the General had finished his cigarette, they stormed onto the scene, flashing their weapons. None of the General's men were carrying guns given the rules at the prison. They surrendered almost immediately.

The General kept hurling obscenities as Singh unloaded the prisoner from the jeep and hauled him to where Harman was waiting with his truck. He glanced back at the General one last time and then climbed into the truck with Dinesh and the prisoner. The truck immediately sped away through the snow towards their hideout in the outskirts of the town, where Rupali was waiting for them.

As the General and his men disappeared behind the cliff, Singh breathed a sigh of relief.

###

When they reached the hideout, an abandoned warehouse, they quickly drove the truck in and shut the doors. There were two glass windows embedded in the wall, one to either side of the door. Some rickety stairs led to the loft. The cavernous space was empty except for the small stove on one side, an empty bunk and a couple of chairs.

Singh sprang down from the truck and the others followed. "Put the kettle on," he said, addressing Rupali, standing silently beside the stove. "We could all use some coffee."

Rupali did not move, her eyes remained fixed on the Caucasian man Harman and Dinesh had bought in. "So who is he?" she asked.

"Get the coffee," Singh said, "and we'll find out."

Harman pushed the man into a chair. Singh lit a cigarette and offered it to him, but the man shook his head. Singh put it to his own lips and stood looking down at the man.

"We've got you out," he said. "Now it's your turn to speak."

The man's gaunt frame was wracked by coughing. Finally he nodded. "It is only fair that I tell you my complete story."

"We just want to know about Netaji," Harman said.

"Patience, lad," the man said. "You'll find my story interesting. And it will answer many of your questions."

Singh watched as Rupali poured the coffee into cups and handed them out. She offered a cup to the prisoner as well. He took it from her with a flashing look of thanks and sat holding it in his hands, relished the warmth.

"Let's begin with your name," Singh said. "What's your name?"

The man took a sip of the hot liquid and then looked up. "Bormann," he said. "Martin Bormann."

###

It should be no surprise that it was Martin Bormann who finally turned out to be the prisoner of Yakutsk. After all, his case had many things in common with the Netaji mystery. He had been an important political figure in Germany. He was Personal Secretary to Adolf Hitler, and was present in the bunker when the Red Army converged on Berlin. Bormann left Berlin on Hitler's explicit orders. The Russians never admitted to finding him or his body, which started the mystery of Bormann's location.

Over the next couple of years, Bormann sightings were reported across the globe. Though most were false, they contributed to the theory that Bormann was still alive. It was thus no surprise when he reappeared in Russia. But what was he doing there? And what was his connection to Netaji?

###

"How did you get here?" Singh asked curiously. The others listened with bated breath.

"On orders from Das Fuhrer."

"Did the Fuhrer order you to meet Netaji?" Singh asked.

"That was the plan in 1945. By then it was evident we were going to lose the war."

"What was this plan?" Singh asked with deep interest.

"Our scientists had developed new technologies and sophisticated machinery," Bormann said. "Knowing Germany would be crushed by the Allies, Fuhrer wished to hand over this legacy to those who would continue the fight. Hitler chose Bose. They had met before and the Fuhrer always said the Aryans of India would one day rise up. It was Das Fuhrer who gave him the name Netaji."

"What was this technology you speak of?" Singh asked.

"The one that ended the war," said Bormann. "The nuclear bomb."

###

Comparisons between the American Manhattan project and the German Uranverein nuclear project have consistently been drawn since the 1940s. It was unclear what level the German nuclear programme had reached. David Irving's 1967 book, *The Virus House*, claimed that some of Diebner's researchers had unsuccessfully attempted to produce fusion using conventional explosives and heavy paraffin as a deuterium carrier. Irving also describes an experiment in 1943, carried out by Trinks and Sachs, using a hollow sphere of silver filled with deuterium and imploded by conventional explosives. Again it was unsuccessful, no radioactivity being produced.

Karlsch alleged that Diebner's team conducted the first successful nuclear weapon test in Ohrdruf, Thuringia, on 4 March 1945. He quoted a purported eyewitness named Clare Werner, who claimed to have been standing on a hillside in Thuringia at the time of the test: *Not too far away was the military training base near the town of Ohrdruf. Unexpectedly there was a flash of light. I suddenly saw something, it was as bright as hundreds of bolts of lightning, red on the inside and yellow on the outside, so bright you could've read the newspaper. It all happened so quickly, and then we couldn't see anything at all. We just noticed there was a powerful wind...*

Two months later, Germany surrendered. Hitler never to ceased to believe in the Aryan dream. He knew the German scientists were close to handing him the tools of world domination. But time had run out. In secrecy, he arranged for the equipment to be sent to a man who shared his Aryan bloodline, a man with power and personality, and the funds, to make use of it. Bormann was the courier.

###

"A hundred pounds in gold," Bormann said. "That was the agreed price to deliver the goods."

"By the gods!" Harman whispered, aghast. "What did Netaji walk into!"

"He had just one goal – to help his people." Bormann told them what each knew to their very soul. "At first he was not interested, not at all. He couldn't understand what we were trying to sell him."

"What changed his mind?" asked Singh.

"He saw it for himself," Bormann said.

###

Irshad Akhtar pressed his binoculars to his eyes as he sat crouched in the Yakutsk snow. There was snow in his boots as well. He wriggled his toes, trying to get circulation back into them. The fur lining of his jacket was wet as well. Akhtar ignored it all and kept his eyes glued to the sights.

Two miles away, the jeeps he was tracking had slowed down and were now moving at a snail's pace. Akhtar swung his binoculars in an arc, taking in the landscape further along the road. There was nothing to be seen but snow and leafless trees. He wondered where the jeeps were going.

Three hours before, he had begun following them from the outskirts of Yakutsk prison. The prison siren had begun to ululate some time before that, telling Akhtar the prison authorities had discovered that a prisoner had escaped, or rather, been rescued. Akhtar had previously decided the best thing he could do was keep an eye on the Brit whom Singh and Rupali had so carelessly included in their plan.

The first thing he had done on leaving the hideout was to seek out the nearest tavern. He had found a table and ordered the best whiskey he could find on the shelves. His faith did not permit him to drink, but he didn't care. There was no God out there, just snow and freezing cold!

As Akhtar sat there drinking, he had time to ponder the events that had taken place. He couldn't remember when he had last felt so intoxicated. Singh was a fool! He had always been a fool. It was a mistake to have come on this mission at all! Trusting a *firangi* General! But that wasn't Singh's first mistake. Each of his moves had been faulty. If not for himself, Akhtar, they would not have reached even this far.

And Rupali was walking blindly to her doom with her foolhardy husband! The others Akhtar did not care about - Harman the bootlicker and Dinesh the silent snake - but he should have taken Rupali out of there. He wondered if he could still go back and convince her. She wouldn't budge he knew. Bitch! Slut! He needed a slut.

A sign to the bartender revealed the way to the local brothel. They spoke a different language but the signs were universal. Akhtar walked along the wet roads in a drunken stupor to where the bartender had pointed. He didn't even feel the cold. Inside the cathouse, he put his money on the table and asked for the best girl.

The memory was a blur. Akhtar didn't remember how much he paid for that encounter. The Madame had certainly duped him, taking advantage of his state. But Akhtar didn't care. The girl was nice, fair with golden hair. Like a fairy. In her arms, inside her, Akhtar had forgotten his troubles. He had forgotten his country, forgotten about that bastard Singh, and the others. But he shouted Rupali's name as he came, falling asleep after the momentary pleasure.

When he awoke, he was lying on the bed in the cathouse, naked, smelling of vomit. Water, he craved water! His head aching, he rose and put on his clothes. Picking up his backpack he went downstairs and asked for a jug of water. After emptying the jug, he left the place.

For the first time he wondered what to do. He had abandoned the others in a fit of rage last night, but leaving was not an option. Now, in the clear and sober light of day, as he ate breakfast at a small wayside eatery, Akhtar knew he was in this to the very end. There was no going back. But he was not going to take emotional decisions like Singh, he told himself. He considered every aspect carefully. If the mission ended in failure, then in all probability they would all be dead. They had no link to the outside world. The data they had gathered would be buried here with them, in a frozen wilderness.

Sitting there, coffee in hand to dispel his hangover, Akhtar pondered who could be entrusted with the data they had gathered. Entrusting the data to some outside person now seemed the immediate task. But he could not just hand it over to anyone, as Singh had done, compromising their plan by taking a foreign General into confidence. But who could he trust? He regretted not having developed any deep relationships back home. He regretted that all the girls he had fucked were either dead or whores. Whores! Then it hit him. He knew the perfect person.

All he needed was a ride to the nearest general store in town. He found it less than two blocks from their hideout. There, he bought a stainless steel container and a jar of dry silica gel, which was in ample supply from having been used in gas masks in the war. Next, he hurried to a workshop round the corner. Fortunately, the welder there knew a smattering of English. Between that and Akhtar's broken Russian, Akhtar managed to get him to agree to weld something, in return for more money than the man had seen in a month.

To anyone who had served in an army, it would have been crystal clear that Akhtar was trying to make a time capsule – a standard method of leaving messages during covert operations. Akhtar was well-versed in the process, having made hundreds of such capsules while working for Kobayashi behind enemy lines. He would leave messages buried in the ground, to be picked up later. The method worked perfectly for short-term messages, but with some tweaks, he was sure it could be used to store messages for a longer period.

Akhtar opened his backpack and found the photographs from his Polaroid, and the mission reports he had written ever since Tokyo. Rolling them up, he placed them in the steel thermos he had bought, filling the remaining space with sand from the workshop. The sand would act to further insulate the papers. The final step was to weld the thermos cover to the flask.

The welder, watching Akhtar's actions with interest, put on a welding mask and moved his flaming point in a circle round over the circumference of the flask. The capsule was ready. He placed it carefully in his backpack. Turning back to the welder, he asked the man to stamp a metal plate with certain letters. It was an easy task, done regularly at the workshop. The man heated a metal plate, stamped in the letters and then tossed it into a basin to cool.

Akhtar paid the welder and asked if he could borrow a shovel. The welder merely nodded. He had made good money today. Akhtar walked out carrying the backpack and the long shovel. He had to rent a car.

###

Akhtar drove out of the town with the prison to his left, looking for a good spot to bury the capsule. Finally, he caught sight gravestones along a small hill to his right. He stopped and got out. The bag felt heavy as he made his way uphill in the face of the freezing wind. Looking around, he found an empty spot by a grave and began to dig. The work was laborious and the ground frozen, but he managed to dig a hole. He placed the thermos in the hole and quickly filled the hole, burying the capsule. Taking out the stamped metal plate, he stood it on top of the spot and hammered it into the rock hard ground using the handle of the shovel. Now only the plate remained in view. Akhtar wiped the sweat off his brow. He walked back to the car, leaving one more grave at the cemetery, marked by a metal plate which clearly read: *Irshad Akhtar 1920-1949*

###

There were no international couriers in Yakutsk. With the heater in the car at full blast, Akhtar drove to the next large town. Much time was wasted in standing in lines and mailing a letter to Japan. By the time his task was over, it was dark and his stomach was growling. It would have been foolhardy to drive through the snow in the dark, so Akhtar found a small hotel and spent the night.

He drove back to Yakutsk early the next morning. By the time he reached the hideout, it was locked and bolted, with no one there, not even their vehicles. He still had his key so he let himself in. He found his things exactly where he had left them. After packing his high-powered sniper rifle in the briefcase, Akhtar grabbed some more ammunition, changed his clothes and headed out again.

He had absolutely no idea where the others were. He enquired casually at the tavern if anything interesting had happened. When the bartender replied that the greatest thrill in his life was taking his dog for a walk, Akhtar realized nothing untoward had occurred. He decided to go watch the prison. It was there that he heard the alarm sound after the British Colonel had left. Akhtar decided to watch the Colonel. He still had his doubts about the white man. He took up position on the roof of an abandoned building opposite the General's hotel. Military personnel as well as plain clothes men arrived at the hotel in less than half an hour. Akhtar guessed they were KGB. The prison authorities must have called in the Russian Gestapo.

Akhtar decided to follow the KGB guys when they left the General's hotel. He hastily scribbled a letter, shoved it into the stamped envelope he was carrying in his inner coat pocket, and dropped it in the first letterbox he saw. Then he set out on foot for the hill behind the prison. Soon he saw the vans, slowing down.

Akhtar knew the KGB had soldiers in the vans. The only question was, where they were going? He moved his binoculars in an arc, looking for any habitation. Apart from a seemingly abandoned warehouse covered with snow, there were no buildings in the vicinity. So why were the vans slowing? Akhtar swung his binoculars back to the vans and cursed. Why hadn't he seen it before? There were tracks in the snow, clearly visible, leading to the abandoned warehouse. The vans were following the tracks.

Akhtar's heart skipped a beat. Putting his binoculars down in the snow, he opened his briefcase and slowly began assembling his high-powered scoped sniper rifle.

###

Singh sat down on the bunk, his eyes dreamy, like a man high on cocaine. "It all makes sense now," he said.

"Of course it does," Bormann retorted, "because it's what happened."

"And that is why Netaji hurried Kobayashi to fake the crash."

"And that is why he was carrying the gold," Rupali added.

Avoiding her gaze, Singh looked back at Bormann. "Where did you meet?"

"A shanty town just beyond the border into Russia. Everything was supposed to go smoothly from there. I was to hand over to him the papers and prototype equipment in my truck. He was to give me the gold. I was going to use the gold to fly away and never return. I remember clearly that fateful night when we met in a small hut in that decrepit little place."

"What went wrong?" Singh asked.

"We got fucked!" Bormann yelled angrily.

"By whom?"

"By those who fuck everyone in Russia," Bormann said, clenching his teeth. "The KGB."

###

Back in the 1940s, all the major powers of the world were after just one thing – nuclear technology. The Germans wanted it, the USA wanted it, and so did the Communists in the Soviet Union. However, the Soviets soon realized that their oppressive policies were not creating an atmosphere conducive to serious research. So Stalin decided that if he could not research the technology, he could simply steal it.

That was how the KGB first instituted their band of atomic spies. They were just like double agents, playing both sides, doling out information. Some of KGB's atomic spies were even located in the heart of the action, at Los Alamos, in the Manhattan project. They were wherever nuclear research was being conducted - in England, in Japan, and in this case, in Germany.

It is unclear when the KGB learned of Bormann's presence in Russia. Bormann himself imagined he had fooled the Soviets by hiding in their own country, thinking they would never look for him there. But he was wrong. The Russians knew exactly where he was. Moreover, they knew why.

What Bormann had with him was a lottery for the Russians. He was carrying all the fruit bearing results of the German nuclear program, including papers, data, and prototypes design sheets. It constituted a decade of German nuclear research. It was every Soviet scientist's wet dream come true. But the Russians were not like a desperate virgin trying to find his first lay. Rather, they were silent stalkers, about to commit an act of rape before slipping away into the darkness.

They inferred that if Bormann had the merchandise, there had to be a buyer. So they hid and waited, like sly cops who wait till a prostitute meets her customer and then apprehends both. The Russians were not in a hurry. But Bormann was. Rather than crossing over to Japanese territory and risk capture, he invited Netaji to Russia, to exchange the technology for gold.

Netaji did not understand the gravity of the research Bormann was carrying and stalled him for a month, until the news of Hiroshima and Nagasaki shook the world. It was at that point that he realized the potential of what Bormann had. And he understood what a treasure it would be in the hands of Indian freedom fighters. He agreed to cross over to Russia to take the goods from Bormann at a shanty town near the Manchurian-Soviet border. While he pressured Kobayashi to launch the plane-crash plan, Bormann arrived and found himself a home in the shanty town.

Netaji planned to cross the border, make the exchange and double back to the safety of Kobayashi's base in Manchuria. From there, whether he planned to return to India or Japan, is not known. Bormann planned to take the gold and disappear to some distant land, possibly South America. However, both men failed to consider one small factor - the KGB presence nearby, who were waiting for the perfect opportunity.

And so fortune smiled on the Russians when Netaji Bose landed inside their borders with enough gold to buy the nuclear research. Their patience had paid off. They swooped down and captured both men and the gold.

###

Akhtar attached the scope and tightened it. He peered through the glass, the magnification double now. He watched the vans stop beside the road. He took aim on the vans doors. He watched them open and men wearing SMGS military outfits walk out. He watched their black-hatted leader descend from the front of the van, holding a radio transmitter in his hand.

Akhtar held his aim and waited. He watched more soldiers descend from the other van. They were going to the warehouse to check who had created the tracks. Softly, Akhtar whispered his *dua* in Urdu. He waited for the precise moment to strike as the soldiers walked towards the warehouse.

###

Bormann said the fateful KGB attack happened the moment Netaji stepped foot in the Russian shanty town.

"We were in the same room for less than a minute when they fell upon us," Bormann recalled. "Bose evidently thought I had double-crossed him." He gave a weary sigh. "Their timing was perfect. As we shook hands, the KGB Jeeps stopped outside the hut."

"What happened to Netaji?" Singh asked, hand to chin. This was worse than anything he had imagined.

"I don't know." Bormann coughed harshly. "They took both of us to Yakutsk. In different trucks."

"Was Netaji in the prison with you?" Singh asked.

"I saw him sometimes, at a distance, or in the yard," Bormann said. "Not recently though."

Singh walked up to Bormann and looked him in the eye. "You *must* remember! This is important."

"I've told you all I know. I don't know what happened to Bose. He was in Yakutsk, but I don't know where they took him after that."

Singh shook him vigorously. "You lie! I saw the prison records. There were no other prisoners apprehended in the shanty town raid other than you."

"Perhaps they deliberately did not keep a record of him," Bormann suggested. "Or they took him somewhere else."

Singh turned away and punched the wall angrily. After a minute he turned to look at Harman and Dinesh, standing in silence with their arms folded.

"It's done then," Singh said. "We go back now. And we take him with us. We have enough evidence now."

"And what then, Boss?" Harman asked.

"Then he tells his story to the Prime Minister. We need more resources to find Netaji. We have to tell the whole world that he is here."

"Let's go!" was all Harman said.

In that instant the window beside them shattered. Singh, Dinesh and Harman immediately dropped to the floor. Bormann looked up fearfully from his chair.

###

Akhtar watched the steam seep out from the rifle nozzle. Through the scope he saw the window shatter and then Singh's face appear briefly to take stock. His warning shot had worked. Singh and the others were indeed in there. He moved his rifle towards the startled KGB commandos who were now looking in his direction to see where the shot had come from. Akhtar aimed for one of the soldiers and pulled the trigger. The bullet missed and hit the snow. Immediately, the soldiers dispersed, diving to the ground and crawling to cover wherever they could find it.

Moving his lips in silent prayer, Akhtar squeezed the trigger again.

###

"They are onto us!" Singh said, ducking under the shattered window.

Dinesh and Harman ran across the room to get the guns. Bormann tried to rise but Rupali pushed him down into the chair again.

"Get down, Rupali!" Singh instructed, saying her name for the first time since the incident with Akhtar. She immediately complied, crouching near the bunk.

Dinesh slid a rifle across the floor to Singh. Suddenly there was another loud crack. They could hear Russians yelling outside.

"What the fuck is happening?" Harman yelled as he took his place beside Singh.

Holding the rifle, Singh raised his head to see out of the shattered window. For a moment he could see nothing but snow, then he caught sight of soldiers, dressed in white, scurrying for cover.

Singh crouched down again. Glancing at Rupali, he said, "Stay here." He signalled to Dinesh and Harman to follow him.

The three men moved from the front to the back of the warehouse. There was more gunfire, shattering the glass on the other side of the warehouse.

"They've surrounded us!" Dinesh said, his heart racing. He clutched his SMG tighter.

Singh looked around the warehouse. A rickety staircase rose to the attic above. "Escort them up there and return," he ordered Harman.

The Sikh raised his rifle and gestured to Rupali to follow him. She helped Bormann to rise and they followed where he led.

There was another loud crack and blood spattered on one of the warehouse walls.

"What the fuck!" Singh exclaimed "What's happening outside?"

###

What the fuck is happening inside? Akhtar wondered as he fired another shot, killing another Russian soldier. There were no others visible through his scope. They had all moved to the other side of the warehouse, away from his line of sight. He kept his rifle up, firing a few more shots.

Why had the others not moved out of the warehouse? He had seen Singh, so they were definitely inside. Why had they not run? Had the soldiers got them?

Cursing, Akhtar rose and slung his carbine across his chest. He ran down the hill with the gun in his hands.

###

Singh waited till Rupali and Bormann were safely above, in the loft. Taking a deep breath, he retreated towards the door and kicked it open. Dinesh who was by his side, leaned out, rifle at the ready. They stood waiting, backs to the wall. They heard more gunfire.

"Shit! We're surrounded," Harman said, joining them.

Singh nodded, waiting for the barrage to end. "See if we have some grenades in the truck!"

Harman disappeared. Singh and Dinesh took turns in doling out suppressing fire.

"They are too many of them," Dinesh said just as Harman returned with the grenades.

"Give them here," Singh said. Taking two, he pulled the pins one by one and flicked them in the direction of the gunfire. There were loud explosions, causing snow to fly in all directions, creating chaos.

"Let's go!" Singh shouted.

The three men ran out of the warehouse, desperately searching for cover.

###

Akhtar stopped for a moment to slow his racing heart. He had run all the way down, and now it felt like it would explode out of his chest. He took short breaths till a deep one was possible.

He looked up as the sound of two quick explosions filled the air. *Fuck!* he cursed to himself. *Did they have grenades?* He began to run again, his gun pointed forward.

He saw a Russian emerge from the side of the warehouse. Akhtar fell to the ground and fired. The Russian went down from the direct hits. Akhtar waited to see if any others would appear. When none did, he got up and started moving again.

###

Singh was crouched in the snow, by the side of a rock he had found. Harman and Dinesh were behind a wooden fence to the right of him. By then, Singh had spotted almost a dozen soldiers, in the tree line on the other side of the warehouse. Their gunfire was keeping them pinned down but they progressed, slowly.

"Fuck!" Harman cursed. "What are we going to do?"

"Try to flank them," Singh shouted back, though he wasn't sure how in the world were they going to do it.

"We are pinned down!" Dinesh shouted back, "We can't do anything without a window!"

A small window of opportunity, Singh thought. *Who in the world was going to provide it to them in this godforsaken place?*

Little did he know that the window he prayed for was about to open.

###

Akhtar leaned out from behind the warehouse and took stock of the situation. He had been relieved to see Singh and the other two alive and behind cover. He prayed Rupali was safe, that Singh had decided not to include her in the operation. He caught sight of Russian soldiers in the trees and wondered what to do. His gaze fell on a trench dug from the warehouse to the treeline. He descended into it and moved towards the trees.

###

"The gunfire has changed direction," Singh said. He noticed the Russians were now firing to the left.

Beside him, he saw Harman and Dinesh rise and fire towards the trees.

"What the fuck are they shooting at?" Harman wondered.

Singh looked at the tree line, and then he saw.

###

Akhtar stayed behind a tree. He took deep breaths as bullets flew around him, cutting into the wood. With one hand he pressed his shoulder, where a bullet had grazed him. His sudden appearance had distracted the Russians from Singh and the others, but now their bullets were concentrated at him. He hoped Singh, Dinesh and Harman would make good use of the diversion.

And they did.

As Akhtar noticed the bullets coming at him decrease and then stop, he heard a familiar voice say, "What in the *fuck* are you doing here?"

It was Singh.

"We don't have time," Akhtar said as Dinesh and Harman scanned the area for soldiers. "They must have called for back-up. We must leave."

"You're right," Singh agreed. "Let's get back to the truck."

"Fuck the truck!" Akhtar hissed. "Their vans are there at 9 o'clock. Let's take those." He looked at Singh. "Did you find Netaji?"

Singh shook his head. "No. But we found a man who confirmed Netaji came here."

"A man?" Akhtar asked. "Where is he?"

"In the warehouse, with Rupali."

"You brought Rupali here?" Akhtar shouted.

The three men ran towards the warehouse.

###

"Something's wrong," Singh said, rattling the doors. They would not open. "I did not tell them to lock it from inside."

"Rupali!" Akhtar shouted. "Open the door!"

There was no response. Harman kicked at the door but it did not give. "I'll break it down," he said.

"Wait!" Akhtar held up a hand. "Let's check the other side."

They ran to the other side of the building, guns in hand. There they saw it - a trail of blood in the snow, leading to the warehouse door.

"It must be one of the soldiers I shot," Akhtar said.

"We have to get in." Singh said, fear clutching his heart.

"We can get in through one of the windows," Akhtar said, clutching his gun. "I'll go first."

They raced to a window and smashed in the protruding glass shards so Akhtar could climb in. Suddenly bullets hit the wooden frame. Akhtar quickly ducked down.

"What did you see? "Singh asked, clutching his shoulder.

"There is no one downstairs. They must be held in the loft," Akhtar said, trying to speak calmly.

"Rupali!" Singh shouted. "Scream if you can hear us."

They heard Rupali scream, then someone shouting in Russian. Silence.

"What did he say?" Singh asked.

"That he has a grenade," Harman said grimly.

Once again they heard the wounded soldier shouting in Russian.

"He is threatening to blow up the truck if we don't give him a radio," Harman translated.

Singh looked at Akhtar. "What are we going to do?"

"What else can we do? We have to give him a radio."

Singh began to protest but stopped when he saw the knife in Akhtar's hand. "Get me a radio," he said.

Harman and Dinesh jumped into action, racing out to search the bodies of the Russians that lay strewn around in the snow.

"We don't have much time," Akhtar said to Singh. "The keys must be in the vans. Bring the vans here."

"We'll do that," Singh said, looking up as Harman ran back with the radio he had found. "Meanwhile, you bring him down."

Akhtar nodded, taking the radio. He slid the knife into his boot and took hold of his sniper rifle.

"The vans," Singh called to Harman and Dinesh, and took off at a run towards the road.

###

Akhtar watched the three men sprint towards the vans. Taking a deep breath, he extended his hand with the radio into the window embrasure. He expected bullets to blow his hand off, but the Russian inside merely shouted a few words. Akhtar waved the radio.

"Put it on the ground," the Russian instructed. That much Akhtar understood.

Taking a deep breath, Akhtar put his head inside to take in the lay of the land. The Russian was in the loft, holding Rupali by the throat. Akhtar shook his head vigorously. "Take it," he said in faltering Russian.

The man moved and as he did, Akhtar realized he was limping. He must have been hit in the leg. He held a grenade in his left hand.

"Take it," Akhtar said again, "then let them go."

The Russian shook his head, pointing the grenade at Rupali.

Akhtar had to take a judgment call. He retreated from the window, placing the radio on the sill. He glanced behind him. Singh and the others had almost reached the vans. The Russian pulled Rupali in front of him as a human shield and pushed her down the stairs. As the man limped to the window, Akhtar's eyes met his.

Akhtar's hand went for the blade in his boot. His mouth opened in a primeval yell as he raised the knife behind his head and threw it in a flashing arc through the window. Time seemed to move in slow motion as he saw the blade move in deadly flight and the grenade fall from the soldier's hand onto the floor. His whole life seemed to flash before his eyes in that moment. He was happy that the last face he saw was Rupali's.

###

The blast erupted in a huge ball of fire as the fuel in the truck lit up as well, blowing metal, splinters and snow everywhere. Singh froze in his tracks and turned. The roar of the explosion was deafening. For a moment he went completely deaf as understanding registered in his brain. Yelling like a mad man, he began running towards the exploding building. But strong arms caught and held him back.

"We must leave!" Dinesh shouted. "The explosion will have attracted attention."

"Rupali!" Singh shouted, struggling to escape their grip. For a moment he managed to break free but the next instant Harman's powerful arm was across his throat.

"We need to go Boss," he said. "We need to go now."

It was true. Once the initial shock had passed, Singh's military instincts slowly took over. He stopped struggling but Harman still held onto him.

"I'm alright," Singh finally muttered, coughing from the smoke. "You are right, we need to go."

As Harman loosened his grip, he saw the unshed tears in Singh's eyes.

###

Kobayashi's men moved them expertly across the border on a moonless night. They had to wait for an opportune moment as a manhunt had been launched in Yakutsk following the prison incident.

Singh spent most of the journey in silence, huddled in a corner, chain smoking. Harman and Dinesh were worried about him but decided to let him heal himself. The journey was uneventful and they encountered no guards. Once they had crossed the border, Kobayashi's men stopped to drink and celebrate.

Singh did not join them, preferring to remain in the truck. Harman carried a whiskey bottle to him but Singh shook his head.

"You have to keep warm, Boss," Harman told him.

"It feels like I will never be warm again," Singh murmured.

"Let it out," Harman advised. "Do not punish yourself like this."

"My life has no purpose now, Harman. I would get down and lie in this godforsaken place if I could. But I can't. Our work is not finished."

"What are we going to do?"

"What did you do when you were sent on a recon mission and found the target, but could not rescue him alone?" Singh asked.

"I called for back-up."

"We now know for certain that Netaji was here," Singh said. "We have traced his path. Now we must go back and call for back-up.

###

The mission debriefing took place in 1949, in the Prime Minister's Office. Singh was the only one allowed in, while Harman and Dinesh waited outside. Bored of just sitting there, they rose and strolled into the grounds. Finally, they caught sight of Singh walking out, his face set like granite.

"They did not believe me!" he said when they rushed up to him. Seeing their flabbergasted faces, he explained exactly what had happened behind the closed doors of the PMO.

###

The investigating committee believed there were several reasons why the claims of Singh and his team were summarily rejected by the Founding Fathers. First and foremost, they did not bring back enough proof from Russia to support their claims. Secondly, the persons they claimed as witnesses, were all intractable. One was a vigilante mercenary, somewhere in China; another was a Russian agent, protected by Moscow; and the third was a Nazi war criminal whom they had left behind, dead. No governmental action was possible against the USSR based on information from a group of ex-INA men who had no convincing evidence. Furthermore, the Indian leadership was looking to Russia as a strategic partner after independence.

The Founding Fathers thus decided to ignore the report presented by Singh and his team, and support the plane crash theory instead. That, as they were soon to learn, was one of the worst mistakes of their illustrious lives.

22
Yakutsk

2015

"There's a chopper ready at the airfield," Alexis told Sergei and Charkov as their Gulfstream prepared to land at Yakutsk. "Use it to get to the spot immediately."

"Wilco," Sergei nodded, pulling on his boots.

Charkov put on his fur-lined gloves. "And what will you do?" he asked.

"I have a team in the town, looking for our targets," Alexis said. "I will join them."

"We'll get them this time, positively," Charkov muttered.

"Yes, we will," Alexis nodded.

###

From his SUV Alexis watched the chopper take off and then looked at the four other SUVS parked in a huddle in the airfield.

"We have positive confirmation on our targets," one of the men informed him, "a South Asian male and a Caucasian female. They were holed up at the Riverfront Hotel."

"What do you mean *were*?" Alexis asked.

"The Asian took a Land Rover and left the town this morning. The woman must still be at the hotel."

"Then let's go get her," Alexis said, putting on his seatbelt.

###

Jay kept one eye on the GPS on his dashboard, and the other on the road as he drove along the Kolyma Highway. Snow covered both sides and there was no sign of life anywhere. Google Maps was his only guide. Finally, he pulled up to one side and shut off the ignition. Taking a deep breath, he pressed the earphone in his ear to check that it was working.

Tanya responded after a few taps. "I was about to fall asleep," she said. "I think I'll make some coffee."

"Ah coffee...seems the most desirable thing in the world right now. I'm freezing here," Jay responded.

"Have you reached the spot?" she asked.

"I'm going to have to walk from here. Can you direct me?"

"Yes, I see you onscreen."

"Good." Jay got his backpack from the SUV and hit the snow.

###

Alexis drove his Range Rover at quickly as the snowbound conditions would allow, slowing down at the turns to avoid skidding. Behind him, the three other SUVs did the same, following his tail lights.

"Did you call the hotel?" he asked the hired man travelling with him.

"Yes, Senor." The man nodded, gripping the door handle as the SUV lurched round a bend. "They have confirmed that she is still in her room."

A grim smile curled his lips as Alexis pressed down on the accelerator on the now straight road. "Any word from Sergei and Char?" he asked.

"Not yet, Senor! They chose a nice place as their hideout."

Alexis nodded. The hotel they were heading to was, in fact, located in the outskirts of the town and part of a well-known chain. They had finally caught up with those two! *The KGB always did,* Alexis thought. It was impossible for anyone to hoodwink the KGB, CIA or MOSSAD for any length of time. This simple truth had been proved again and again, countless times in the course of the history of the modern world. A single man could not defeat or deceive an organization. *But these two came very close to it,* Alexis admitted silently to himself. *Just as Bose did all those years ago.*

The five-storied hotel building appeared on the horizon, a dark silhouette against the light blue sky and the harsh snow glare. It was time. The SUVs braked in unison, their tires screeching on the asphalt. The vehicles skid a little, then stopped at the hotel gates. Turning the engine off, Alexis jumped nimbly to the ground.

"Have you got the jammer?" he asked the man with him, who had followed him out of the vehicle. When he nodded, Alexis merely nodded and said, "Get on it." Turning to the others, he called out, "You three, go with him. You others, follow me."

The hotel Manager, dressed in a pristine white shirt and dark trousers and tie, hurried to greet them as they walked into the hotel lobby. "She's here, in her room," he assured Alexis.

"You and you, guard the lobby," Alexis ordered two of the men with him. "Make sure she does not escape through here."

The men nodded and broke away from the group. Alexis moved on. "Take us to her room...quickly!" he said to the Manager.

The Manager hurried over to the reception and picked up a master card. "Follow me," he said, moving to the elevator doors.

"Did you personally check that she was in the room?" Alexis asked."Because she can deceive the cameras."

"I personally checked as you asked," the Manager responded. "She ordered coffee and I went to deliver it to her not ten minutes ago."

"Perfect."

The elevator doors closed and Alexis felt the pressure build in his ears as it moved up. It stopped at the third floor and the doors opened. The Manager walked out first, followed by Alexsis and his five men.

"Down the corridor to the right," the Manager said, leading them along the carpeted hallway. "There," he said, pointing "at the end, 310."

Alexis moved forward, signalling for two of the men to follow. They reached the door that said 310. Alexis held out his hand for the card. The Manager handed it over without a word.

Alexis looked at his men. "On my count," he whispered, inserting the card. "One...Two..."

The door opened and they stormed in, in pairs. Alexis entered last. The room was empty, the curtains open. Alexis cursed as he flung open the bathroom door. There was no one.

"Check the cupboards," he ordered the men as he went to check the window. It was shut tight. Opening it, he looked out. He could clearly see their SUVs parked below. "The bitch is not here," he said curtly, turning away from the window.

"I swear she was here!" the Manager stuttered in fear. "I saw her..."

"Shut up!" Alexis snapped. "She's not here but she's somewhere close." The room lights were on. Alexis noticed the butt marks on the bedsheet. The bed was still warm. He looked at the bags tucked into one corner and noticed a laptop charger still attached to one of the sockets.

"She's hiding," he finally said. "She must have seen us. You! Go check the bar downstairs." The man indicated left immediately. "Is there a fire exit?" he asked the Manager.

"Yes, it leads to the terrace."

Alexis closed the window. "Let's check the terrace then."

They followed the Manager out of the room. He pointed to the other end of the corridor. "That's the fire exit."

The men moved towards the fire exit and flung open the door. A short flight of stairs led to the terrace.

She couldn't have outsmarted me this time! Alexis thought nervously. *I was so thorough.*

"Senor!" one of his men called from above. "The bitch has blocked the terrace door."

Alexis raced up the stairs to where his men were straining to get the terrace door open. They stopped as he reached them. "Open the damn door!" he yelled furiously.

There was no response from the other side.

"It's over, Tanya Williams!" he shouted again, using her name. *That ought to shock her,* he thought grimly.

There was still no response.

"Open the door!" he yelled, his voice ringing in the stairwell.

There were sounds of movements on the other side.

"We've got a jammer, Tanya, watch it!" Alexis called, rapping the door. "It's over!"

Suddenly he heard the movements cease and the bolt being drawn. The door opened.

It was indeed over.

###

Jay felt the cold blast hit his face as the chopper that had been hovering above him, made its slow descent. Sergei still stood in the hold with the loudspeaker in one hand, the other hand caressing the MG42.

Is he going to kill me? Jay wondered. A frisson of fear ran down his spine. He knew that trying to run would be pointless. It would merely incite the Russians to shoot.

The chopper made its way down. "Don't you dare move!" Sergei shouted in accented English.

Jay did not move. He did not even peel the Mylar foil off himself. He just lay there in the snow, unmoving, though it was too cold for comfort. He heard the Russian laugh and say something to his partner. Jay fidgeted uneasily in the snow. Were they talking about killing him? The Russian had said *It's over*. Did that mean they were going to kill him?

How in the world had they found him, he wondered? Was Tanya compromised? *Let her be safe!* he prayed. She was the last link with the world. They had prepared for a situation like this. If he was caught, she was to release their database to a cloud server. She still had her old contacts in the papers. The data would be emailed to all of them. It would not matter if the Russians killed them both for their data would move on.

"Look at him, cornered like his English bitch," Sergei laughed.

Shit! So they had got Tanya. Had she had enough time to upload the data?

The chopper was now hovering inches above the snow.

"Get up slowly and put your hands over your head," Sergei instructed through the loudspeaker.

Jay complied, digging his elbows into the snow to rise. He realized his feet were frozen and tried to wiggle his toes to bring back circulation into them. He brushed the snow off his back and hair.

"Now walk slowly towards us."

Jay put one foot forward, slowly. He observed the two Russians and their chopper. The MG42 was attached to the hold. That meant it could not rotate more than one eighty degrees. But they could have pistols. Was that a chance he was willing to take?

"Easy...no sudden movements," Sergei said as Jay turned to one side, wondering if he could run around the chopper.

"There is no way out," came the voice over the loudspeaker.

It dawned on Jay that he should try speaking to them and stall for time. "I think I've broken my leg," he said, collapsing onto the ground again.

"You'll break far more than a leg if you don't get up and walk!" the Russian said angrily.

They had seen through his ploy. *I have money*, Jay suddenly thought. *All men have a price.* "Do you know who I am?" he asked, rising and taking a slow step forward. “I can give you 500,000 dollars now, and ten times more if you give me one more day.”

The Russian laughed in genuine amusement. “We know your net worth, Mr. Rasbihari,” he said. “But it appears you don’t know our code.”

Jay felt his heart sink. *Didn’t work,* he thought, taking another step.

The Russian held out a gloved hand and pulled Jay into the chopper. Then, putting a hand on his shoulder, forced him to sit down. The pilot pulled on the stick and they immediately lifted into the air.

“Who are you?” Jay asked.

“Relax, Mr. Rasbihari.” The pilot said softly. “My name is Charkov, and my friend here is Sergei.”

“Where are you taking me?”

“Why were you here in the first place?” Charkov asked.

“To find answers!” Jay muttered, his teeth chattering in the cold.

“That is exactly where we are taking you,” Charkov said grimly, “to find answers.”

###

When the chopper finally stopped moving forward and began to hover, the skies were tinted with orange hues and the sun had disappeared behind the far horizon.

Jay watched Sergei, who had sat beside him silently, get to his feet. “Time to get down, Mr. Rasbihari,” he said in heavily accented English.

As the Charkov slowly brought the chopper down, Jay caught sight of the surroundings. They were landing in the courtyard of a small farm. There was a two-storied house with lights on inside. “Where are we?” he asked Sergei, who now stood beside the MG42 fixed to the rear of the chopper.

“This is what we like to call the Barnyard,” he smiled. “Think of it as one of many KGB safe houses scattered through the dry wastes of Siberia.”

“A concentration camp?” Jay asked. ‘KGB’ and ‘Siberia’ spoken together had only one connotation in his mind.

Sergei laughed. “Oh no no...we are no longer ruled by the Soviets, Mr. Rasbihari.”

The snow rose up in a white vortex of flakes as their chopper neared the ground. To one side of the house, Jay noticed a couple of black Range Rovers, parked one behind the other.

"No snow on the roof," Charkov noted from the pilot's seat, "so it appears the Boss is already here."

"The Boss?" Jay asked. "Is he the person you are taking me to?"

Sergei grinned. "Yes, indeed."

"Is he going to torture me?" Suddenly Jay recalled scenes from the spy movies he had watched religiously in colleges.

The Russian smiled. "But not with weapons, Mr. Jay."

"Then with what?" Jay asked, wondering what on earth he was in for.

"With words, Mr. Jay, with words."

The Russian turned away as the chopper landed in the courtyard.

###

Tanya had spotted Jay in the chopper from the second-floor window of the farmhouse. She watched helplessly as the chopper descended and a heavyset Russian helped Jay out, gripping him firmly by one arm.

"Looks like your partner has finally arrived." The slim, well-dressed Russian called Alexis, who sat opposite her, said. "About time I'd say. Supper was about to get cold."

"What do you want with us?" Tanya snapped angrily.

After they had cornered her on the roof of the hotel and jammed her attempts to release the files to the web, she had had no choice but to surrender. There had been no buildings nearby she could have jumped to. Nor were there any trees she could have used to get down to ground level.

As she had stood helplessly, her laptop discarded on the snowy roof, the Russian on the other side of the terrace door had introduced himself saying, "My name is Alexis. I don't wish to hurt you. I just want to talk."

'That's what they all say,' Tanya had thought. They were the same words her rapist Alberto had used the first time he had abused her. Long repressed memories suddenly flooded her mind and she gave felt weak and vulnerable.

"Open the door!" Alexis had yelled.

Tanya had unbolted the door. Now, three hours later, she looked up and noticed a strange smile on the Russian's lips. "What do you want from us?" she asked, looking him in the eye.

"As I have said before, have patience. I shall tell you everything when Mr. Rasbihari gets here."

Indeed, he had said the same thing when they escorted her to the Range Rovers, parked below. Tanya had expected to be bound and gagged, but to her surprise, this had not happened. They had indicated that she get into the front of one of the vehicles and sit beside the driver.

Alexis had politely requested her not to disturb the driver, saying, "You are safe. We just need to talk."

Tanya did not believe a single word. *Had they been following Jay and her across three continents just to talk?* When they reached the farmhouse in the snow, they had given her hot chocolate to drink and breakfast to eat. She had then been taken to the room on the top floor. Her captor had refused to speak till Jay arrived.

Somehow, in the deep confines of her mind, Tanya had hoped Jay would escape, that he would fool his pursuers in the snow and mist of the Siberian countryside. But the practical side of her mind knew Jay was no match for a team of trained KGB agents. And now he was finally here, Tanya thought as she watched the huddled figures disappear into the house.

"Bring him up and serve him food in this room," Alexis ordered the man who stood guard at the door. "Ms. Williams is too desperate for answers to let him eat in peace first."

###

"Tanya!" Jay called as the door to the large room on the second floor opened. His eyes lingered on hers before slowly trailing to the Russian sitting opposite her. "Are you all right?" he asked her, one eye on the man.

Tanya sprang to her feet. "I'm all right. Are you?"

Jay nodded, rubbing his shoulders. "Are you the one they call Boss?" he asked the dapper Russian.

"Do they?" Alexis smiled but his voice was cold. It sent a shiver down Jay's spine. "Please have a seat, Mr. Rasbihari. Would you like some warm soup? Or would you prefer our local delicacy, *Poison-shop*?"

"You want to poison us?" Jay asked, folding his arms across his chest.

"*Poison-shop* is just noodles," Alexis said. "But they do call it the poison of the east for its bitter flavor."

"Now that Jay is here," Tanya said, glaring at the Russian, "will you tell us what this is all about or are you just going to sit there making small talk?"

Alexis threw her a hooded glance and smiled briefly. There was no trace of warmth in either the look or the smile. "Would you both care to sit down?" he asked.

"I prefer to stand," Jay replied briefly while Tanya sank back on the chair she had been sitting on earlier.

Alexis rose and stood with his hands on the back of his chair. "I know it's but natural for you to distrust me after all that has happened."

"Your men have been following us since Hong Kong," Jay reminded him shortly.

"But in their defense," Alexis said, "they never tried to hurt you. Their orders were to capture you and bring you in for a discussion. But you never gave them a chance to get close enough."

"'Capture' rings rather like 'arrest'," Tanya said.

"It's just official lingo," Alexis replied casually.

"So if you weren't after us to kill us," Jay said, "who exactly are you and what do you want?"

Alexis smiled. "I am Alexis Ivanovich, one of the Directors of the KGB. I oversee the Far East sector. If you would care to sit down, I'll tell you what you have come so far to find."

"And what would that be?" Jay asked.

"The truth about your grandparents," Alexis said.

###

"You surprise me, Mr. Rasbihari." Alexis paced across the room. "You of all people thought a half century-old time capsule would survive after all these years?"

"I don't know what you're talking about," Jay said, sitting down.

"There's no need to hide," Alexis said. "We already know everything there is to know about this case, and we know it better than you."

"If you say so." Jay's manner was terse.

"Also, you had the spot wrong by half a kilometer," Alexis told him.

Jay stared straight into Alexis' cold blue eyes. "Why should I cooperate? You represent the people who killed my grandparents."

"Did we really?" Alexis looked back at Jay, his gaze unwavering.

"They came to Yakutsk and never returned," Jay said. "The KGB killed them."

Alexis extended his hand and picked up an old box file from the table behind him. "I think you should dig into your dinner, Mr. Rasbihari," he said, "because what I have to tell you will take some time."

"And what do you want to tell me?"

"That the KGB did not kill your grandparents."

###

"When people hear the words *Operation Barbarossa*," Alexis said when he had narrated the events that took place at the end of 1949, in Yakutsk, "they remember Hitler's attack on the Soviet Union during World War II. But, for these two gentlemen, *Operation Barbarossa* means something else entirely. Their parents were involved in it." He indicated Sergei and Charkov, who stood beside the door, their arms folded. Alexis opened the file on the table.

"What was *Operation Barbarossa*?" asked Jay.

"It was a highly classified KGB operation, conducted in the first half of 1950," Alexis told him, turning a page. "And the important part of this story is that it was conducted in your country – in India."

"What did the KGB hope to find in India?" Jay asked, taken aback.

"As I have already told you, both your grandparents did not die here in Yakutsk. Your grandfather and his two companions survived. As for those who did not, it was not the KGB but General Hardy, who was responsible for their deaths."

"So did General Hardy rat out their plan to you?" Jay asked.

Alexis nodded. "He did. These papers say the General was not as brave as he appeared to be. His empathy for the Singhs made him collaborate with them, but as soon as the actual escape happened, he lost his nerve and he summoned the Prison Warden to his hotel to explain. By then, the matter had already been handed over to the KGB and was being led by Mr. Zavarotko, the father of these two gentlemen."

"So the General told them what had happened," Jay mused. "And the KGB began a search operation."

Alexis nodded. "They did. But as you now know, the entire team who found them in an abandoned warehouse on the eastern outskirts, perished. So did two of your father's team, along with the prisoner. Their bodies were found in the warehouse."

"So my grandmother and Irshad Akhtar died here," Jay said, looking down at the floor.

"They did. But the important point was that your grandfather escaped. He had hit the KGB like a bolt from the blue and we needed to find him again, or rather, find who had sent him."

"So your people followed him back to India?" The truth suddenly dawned on Jay.

"Yes, Zavarotko did. And he did not merely follow them; he did some phenomenal work. He found their trail. He discovered their purpose. And he wove together the entire story that we had not known until then. And the records he sent back to Russia are the ones present in this file."

Alexis passed the box file to Jay, who looked down at it with wonder. Tanya rose and came over to look over his shoulder.

"It contains copies of the records from the Dehra Doon orphanage where your mother was lodged, the diaries kept by Harman and Dinesh, who accompanied your grandparents, along with some sensitive documents from your Prime Minister's Office. But all of that is not the important part."

"What is the important part?" Jay asked.

"That Zavarotko managed to find your grandfather and follow him to the very end, and report back to us."

"So what happened after Yakutsk?" Jay wanted to know.

"Turn to the last pages of these records, Mr. Jay," Alexis said, "and pay close attention, because what you are about to learn will change your entire perception of this long, dark story."

23
Hara-Kiri
File 12/14/Jan/XVII: Top Secret

1949

Major Anish Singh of the INA visited the Dehra Doon orphanage for the first and last time in December 1949. He signed in the visitor's register using a pseudonym, but his two companions, Harman and Dinesh, signed their true names. They left blank the column for the reason of their visit. But it was a simple assumption they were there to visit Singh's infant daughter, whom he was seeing after two years.

Did she smile at her father? Did Singh take her in his arms? Did she know her mother was dead? Or did Singh and the others just watch her play happily in the grounds of the orphanage, watching from afar? We do not know. But it must certainly have been like a knife to the heart for Singh. Afterwards, the three men stood outside, watching the setting sun and smoking in silence.

"We failed." It was Harman who finally broke the silence, his voice heavy as lead. "We miserably failed everyone who put their trust in us."

"Those we put our trust in failed us too, Harman," Singh said. "General Hardy, the Prime Minister..."

Dinesh placed a hand on Singh's shoulder. "It's much worse for you. The two of us came back unscathed. You lost everything."

Harman nodded. "But Netaji is still out there," he reminded them.

"And that is why our work is not finished," Singh said, gazing at the setting sun.

Harman looked up. "The Prime Minister debriefed us. What more can we do? It's over."

"The Prime Minister debriefed us because they did not believe us," Singh said. "We can start by making them believe. It is not over."

"And how exactly are we going to do that?" Dinesh asked.

Singh rubbed his chin thoughtfully. In that moment he missed Akhtar and his strategies, but he brushed away the thought. "The Prime Minister believes in the plane crash theory," he said. "That is why he did not believe the part that came after it." Singh turned to Harman. "Did you learn how Kobayashi caused the plane to crash?" he asked.

"I discussed it with Kobayashi's Lieutenant," Harman replied.

Singh smiled briefly. "So now discuss it with me."

###

In terms of psychological analysis, *seppuku*, more commonly known as *hara-kiri*, was always based on a feeling of hopelessness. This Japanese tradition stemmed from the 10th century AD. The first recorded act is from the year 1180. From then on, it represented the code of the Samurai warriors, who killed themselves to avoid the shame of capture. It soon became part of Japanese culture as an act of preserving honour. However, under this noble garb, it remained what it always was – an act of suicide.

There is no doubt that Singh was exposed to it during his time with the Japanese army. There is every possibility that he had seen his Japanese counterparts commit the act after the failed invasion of Burma. It is not known what effect these experiences had on Singh, but that it was part of his psyche is certain.

###

The mission had had the worst possible outcome. It had begun in the perfect way, with the lofty goal of searching for and rescuing a leader they loved. They had had initial successes in Renkoji and Manchuria, only to have fate catch up with them in Yakutsk.

They had failed to accomplish their task. They had neither found nor rescued Netaji. They had lost two members of their team, one of whom was Singh's own wife. Given their estrangement and her sudden death, the couple had never had the opportunity to bid each other farewell. Unable to find closure, Singh carried the trauma within him like a silent festering wound.

On their return, to request back-up, the very people who had sent them on the mission abandoned them, erasing any hope that eventual good would come of all the disasters they had faced. Singh and the others had gambled their lives for a greater cause, and they had lost. They had lost everything dear to them, except the cause that had led them on – Netaji! The three survivors became men desperate to accomplish their goal by any means.

And as it is truly said there is nothing more dangerous than a man with nothing to lose.

As they stood outside the orphanage that evening, in the backdrop of this emotional churn, Singh came up with the final deadly plan which they were to embark on,

"This will take money," Harman finally said, when Singh finished giving them instructions.

"We have money," Singh said.

They did indeed. He had purposely set aside enough funds during the mission debriefing in Delhi, knowing that something like this would come.

"Then let's do it for Netaji," Harman said.

Dinesh nodded, committed to the plan as he been from the start of the mission. There was no turning back.

"For Netaji," Singh agreed. Then, drawn from the deepest recesses of his mind and heart came the cry, "For Rupali and Akhtar!"

###

The office of the Prime Minister of free India was located in South Block of the Secretariat, in the heart of New Delhi. Before Independence, the building had housed the administrative offices of the government of British India. Beyond the Secretariat rose the imposing dome of the Viceroy's mansion, now the official residence of the President of India.

Pandit Nehru was writing in his journal when the usher announced a visitor. He looked up, rather annoyed, for he had been drafting an important speech he was to give. He glanced at the old clock on the wall; it was precisely 8pm. He looked out of the window and saw that darkness had fallen. Sighing, he gestured for the visitor to be brought in.

The visitor was a tall man in a blue turban. Pandit Nehru recognized him immediately. "Capt Dalbir Singh of the RAF," he said. "And what can I do for you?"

The Captain saluted and then looked at the Prime Minister, noting how he had aged since taking office. "There is a problem, Sir," he said.

"What kind of problem?"

"You should get in touch with V.P. Menon immediately, Sir." The Captain's gaze did not waver from Panditji's face.

"But Menon is in Jaipur," Nehru said, "for the inauguration."

"The problem is in Jaipur."

Nehru's heart skipped a beat. It was the inauguration of the new state of Rajasthan, in Jaipur. The Deputy Prime Minister, Sardar Vallabbhai Patel, had worked tirelessly to bring the state into existence. "What is the problem?" he asked.

"It's the Deputy Prime Minister, Sir."

Pandit Nehru sat still. *What had happened to Sardar?* "Details please, Captain," he said curtly.

The Captain's gaze fell. "I don't know how to say this, Sir."

"Loud and clear, Captain, loud and clear."

The Captain looked up. "His plane is missing, Sir."

###

Sardar Patel, the first Deputy Prime Minister of India, had planned to sleep on that fateful flight from Tashkent. He had had a busy day and had boarded the small four-seater RAF Devon with relief. Accompanying him were his daughter Maniben, and his friend, the Maharaja of Patiala.

"Fly slowly, Bhimrao," he had said to the pilot as the plane moved from the hangar to the strip. "I plan to catch up on some sleep."

The pilot had nodded and Sardar Patel had closed his eyes. He felt the usual backward pull as the plane gathered speed and the familiar blocking sensation in his ears as it took off, losing contact with the runway. Patel had taken hundreds of airplane rides and they were no longer a novelty for him. But, what happened next was something he had never experienced before.

A minute after takeoff, when the plane was still climbing, rumbling sounds came from one of the engines. Then the body of the plane began to vibrate as if caught in a storm. Mani and the Maharaja began shouting at the pilot, asking what was wrong. A blinking red light came on in the cockpit.

It all happened quickly. The plane began to nosedive. Patel felt his head ram into the back of the seat in front before the seatbelt pulled back his torso. He grabbed the armrest as the plane fell through the air. Patel wondered if these were his last moments. He tried to turn his head backwards to see his daughter, Maniben, whose screams were ringing in his ears, but the backward surge of the freefall made it impossible. Sardar Patel closed his eyes and began to pray.

Magically, as if his prayers had been answered, the fall began to decelerate. Patel heard a huge bang, followed by a violent vibration, as if some external object had attached itself to the plane's body. The descent suddenly stopped and the plane began to oscillate.

Patel turned to look at his daughter, who was visibly shaken but unharmed. "Are you all right?" he asked. She nodded, as did the Maharaja in the seat beside her.

Patel felt dizzy as the plane began to lower slowly, as if by some magical external force. He looked towards the cockpit. "Bhimrao!" he called to the pilot. "What's happening?"

There was no reply. Patel reached for his seatbelt, clipped off the buckle and got to his feet. The plane was still being lowered slowly by an invisible force.

"Where are you going, Papa?" Maniben asked from behind him.

"To find out what's going on," Patel replied, clutching the seats near him in order to stay upright.

He moved slowly forward. The door of the cockpit had slammed shut. Clinging to the seats he reached the door and pushed as hard as he could. The pilot was lying with his head on the wheel, motionless. One hand lay on the ALARM button to his side. Looking through the windshield, Patel saw they were now close to the ground, still being lowered slowly. He pulled the pilot back into his seat to check his pulse. To his horror, there was a gaping circular hole in the pilot's forehead. There was no doubt he had been shot.

At the same moment, with a loud thud, Patel felt the body of the plane finally touch the ground. "Mani!" he called to his daughter from the cockpit. "Find me my Sat phone!"

Someone was banging on the plane door. Patel let the pilot's body fall back in the seat and turned. His daughter was desperately searching for the Sat phone in their hand luggage. "Mani hurry!" Patel called.

All of a sudden, the plane door burst open and a man jumped in. It did not take Sardar Patel more than a moment to recognize the face he had seen less than three months ago. It was Major Anish Singh of the INA. Only, this time, he was holding a gun.

###

The Deputy Prime Minister's plane went missing on 29 March 1950. He was scheduled to land in Jaipur that evening, flying in from Tashkent. His pilot sent a message to the Jaipur traffic control to say they had been delayed by 45 minutes. The message was relayed to the various political figures like V.P. Menon and the Maharajah of Jaipur, who were waiting at the landing strip to receive him. However, the plane did not appear at all. Panic struck everyone at the Jaipur aerodrome. Messages flew around the country. From Delhi, three RAF squadrons were deployed to search for the plane. Menon left Jaipur for Delhi and hurried to the Prime Minister's residence.

The news was kept classified to avoid panic setting in amongst the people. The Deputy Prime Minister was affectionately known as the Iron Man of India. But the ordinary populace did not know that the Deputy Prime Minister had in his jacket a homing beacon that send a signal every hour to pinpoint his location. It had been designed for a situation exactly like this.

The RAF waited for the first signal to arrive. When it did, they noted that it was a few kilometers away from Jaipur. Captain Dalbir Singh immediately commissioned the best possible equipment for the search and rescue operation - helicopters.

The concept of the helicopter had been invented way back in ancient China, where a helicopter toy was made for kids. But it was not until the drawings of Leonardo Da Vinci in the 1480s, that the idea took concrete form. The practical conversion of the idea took a long time, though. In 1906, two French brothers, Jacques and Louis Breguet, managed to build a miniature flying machine which was probably the first gyrocopter. But it was not until the First World War that helicopters were commercially produced. The pioneer in this was a Russian-born engineer, Igor Sikorsky, who managed to build the world's first military helicopter.

In 1950, helicopters were a novel concept. They could take off from anywhere, land anywhere, occupied much less space than a plane and could hover effectively. This made them perfect for search operations, which was precisely why the RAF deployed every last chopper in its fleet to find Patel.

###

Singh had absolutely no idea what a helicopter was when he stopped his truck on the dusty road for a quick smoke. Nor had he any knowledge of the homing beacon stitched into the Deputy Prime Minister's jacket. Neither had Harman, waiting impatiently in the driver's seat for Singh to finish his cigarette, nor Dinesh, sitting in the truck's hold with his rifle pointed at the illustrious hostage they had taken. The Deputy Prime Minister was neither impatient nor uncooperative. He had let himself be taken without offering the slightest resistance. They had left the others on the plane, bound to their chairs with rope.

Singh breathed deeply as he tossed the butt to the ground and climbed back into the truck's hold. He tapped the metal separator to signal to Harman to drive on. As the truck began to move, Singh stood at the opening, holding the beams for support. As he watched the dry wastes of the Thar Desert roll by, little did he know that he had just smoked his last cigarette.

###

Captain Dalbir Singh and his team of four commandos spotted the truck in the wilderness around 6.30 pm, with the sky turning orange and cloudy.

"They are moving continuously," one of the commandos said.

"That's good for us," Dalbir replied.

"We won't get a shot this way," the commando pointed out.

"But if they keep moving him long enough," Dalbir told him, "they'll have to stop to refuel."

###

They stopped to refuel when the last rays of the sun had completely disappeared beyond the horizon and it was dark and cold. They stopped in the middle of a dusty desert road. The only signs of life were some dim lights from a distant hamlet. The only sound a rumbling from somewhere far away.

Harman stopped the truck and turned the ignition off and opened the door. He made the mistake of leaving the headlights of the truck on.

"Make it quick," Singh said to Dinesh, who had lifted one of the fuel cans and was about to get down. Dinesh nodded and Singh gave him a hand with the can.

Singh turned back to the Deputy Prime Minister. He drew a pack of cigarettes from his pocket and cracked a flame on his lighter.

"May I have one?" Sardar Patel asked from where he was seated.

Singh looked down, his brows lifted, then crouched and placed the cigarette between Patel's lips and held the lighter for him.

"You look surprised," Sardar Patel said taking a deep drag and then sighing as the smoke filtered out.

"I never imagined you smoked," Singh said.

"Leaders too, are human," Patel said. "Though we carry the cares of a million people."

"So it would appear."

"Why did you kidnap me, Singh?" Patel asked. "How did you bring the plane down? That was quite remarkable."

"We bought it down in the same way that the Japanese mercenary brought Netaji's plane down," Singh said. "You and the Prime Minister did not believe that such a thing was possible. Well, here's your proof."

"Did you do this as proof?" Patel asked. "This is no proof, Singh. All you have done is give rise to reasonable doubt about the plane crash."

"I no longer care whether I have convinced you are not," Singh said bitterly. "What matters is that I have you."

"What do you plan to do with me?" Sardar Patel asked, looking up.

"I plan to send an ultimatum to the Prime Minister; to tell him that unless he takes real action to find and rescue Netaji, we will kill you."

"So your plan is to resort to terrorism and death threats," Patel said calmly. "Is that what you have been reduced to?"

"You left us with no choice," Singh retorted, his brow furrowed.

"But what if the Prime Minister sends you an ultimatum?" Patel asked. "What would you do then?"

Singh laughed. "I've kidnapped people before."

"Those were different times. It was war. Now it is time for peace, a time for nation-building."

The buzzing sound they had heard was getting closer and louder.

"What would you have me do, huh?" Singh asked angrily, slamming his fist into the side of the truck.

"You should let me go, Singh," Sardar Patel advised. "Let me talk to the Prime Minister. Perhaps we can start a new commission to investigate the air crash. We can do something in a proper legal way."

"No!" Singh said firmly. "The time for that is long gone. I no longer trust you, Sir."

"Violence only breeds violence, Singh."

The buzzing sound was now too loud to ignore. "Harman!" Singh shouted from the back of the truck. "Check what that noise is."

Suddenly there was the distinct swooshing sound of a bullet traversing through air. He had heard it countless times before yet goosebumps rose on his skin every time, as they did now. There was a muffled cry from Harman.

Singh jumped down from the back of the truck, whipping out a pistol from his belt as Patel watched.

There was another stream of bullets, followed by loud gunfire from Dinesh's rifle. "You bastards!" he yelled as his gun emptied its bullets at their unknown assailants. "Bastards!"

Singh's heart missed a beat as Dinesh's crackling gun stopped abruptly. He quickly got back into the truck and returned to Patel. In the low light of the moon, Patel saw that his face was lined and gaunt.

"Get up!" Singh ordered. There was no compassion in his voice. "Now!"

Sardar Patel tried to rise but his weak knees shook. Impatiently, Singh pulled him up and wrapped an arm across Patel's neck. "Walk!" he ordered.

Using him as a human shield, Singh moved to the opening of the truck. "Harman!" he shouted. "You there?" When there was no response, he yelled, "Dinesh! You there?" Again there was no response.

"We have to get down," Singh told his captive. Patel nodded his understanding. Together they jumped from the back of the truck, hitting the ground with a thud. The Deputy Prime Minister moaned as his feet hit the ground but Singh kept his balance and held him upright. Singh looked to his left. A body lay in the desert sand, strangled. It was too dark to see more but Singh's grip on Patel's neck tightened.

The buzzing sound was now above them. Suddenly, a light from the heavens fell upon them, followed by a man's voice, amplified through a loudspeaker, "Get down on your knees!"

Singh lifted his pistol hand to shade his eyes from the blinding light. He dragged Patel to the side of the truck. "What is that thing?" he shouted, his voice barely audible in the roar of the flying object above them.

Patel did not utter a word. Another body lay in the sand, face down. It was Harman. His red turban had melted and seeped into the sand. Or was it blood?

"Get down on your knees!" the voice boomed again.

"I am a veteran of the Indian National Army," Singh shouted at the top of his voice.

Under the helicopter rotor, Dalbir and his commandos looked at each other. "What's he trying to say?" Dalbir asked.

"I can't hear him, Sir," one of his men answered.

"Is he threatening to kill the Deputy Prime Minister?" asked another.

Dalbir cursed under his breath. "Keep the crosshairs on him," he instructed.

Below them, Singh, still holding Patel as a shield, sidled along the side of the truck slowly. "Dammit!" he cursed, "they can't hear me."

"It's the noise of the helicopter," Patel said, trying to keep his balance.

"Fuck the noise!" Holding the Deputy Prime Minister firmly with one hand, Singh groped for the driver's door handle. They had reached the front of the truck.

"He's trying to get into the truck," Dalbir said. "Fire warning shots. Get the tires."

There were loud cracks as two of the commandos fired into the air and two others at the truck wheels. Singh felt the vehicle sink into the sand as the pressurized air escaped from the tires. He knew in that moment that time had run out.

"You should surrender," Patel said to his captor calmly. "They will not kill you, I'll make sure of that."

Singh thought of Harman and Dinesh's bodies, lying in the sand. "And what about them?" he said bitterly. "What will you do about them?"

"I'm sorry, Singh," Patel said. "But those soldiers are just doing their job. You did kidnap me after all."

Singh looked down at his captive, the Iron Man of India. "I too, am doing my job," he said.

Above them, Dalbir watched, his eyes never moving from the huddled figures beside the truck. "Is he threatening the DPM?" he asked.

"Sure looks like it," one of the commandos said.

"No window yet?" Dalbir asked.

The commando shook his head. "He has the DPM as a human shield."

As Dalbir stood up from his crouched position, the commando asked without turning his eyes from his target, "What are you doing, Sir?"

"I am going to talk to that fucker. Meanwhile, make sure you don't miss any window you get. Take the chopper down!" he yelled to the pilot.

###

Singh tightened his grip on Patel's shoulder, keeping the nozzle of his gun firmly placed on his temple. "It's no use," he said. "They can't hear me."

"Let me go to them," Patel said. "They will not kill you, Singh. I give you my word."

Singh smiled grimly. "That's not how the military works, Sir," Singh said. "I know." His eyes turned from the chopper on the sand to the officer walking towards them. There was nowhere to run, nowhere to hide.

"Look, he is coming to talk. Let me speak to him," Patel urged.

Singh stood as still as a statue, his hand firmly across the Deputy Prime Minister's neck.

"You can trust me, son." Patel said. "The entire country does."

Suddenly, Singh's grip loosened. "Go!" he said.

Sardar Patel did not waste any time. He moved as quickly as he could towards Dalbir, shouting, "Do not shoot him!"

Behind him, Singh calmly stuck his revolver back into his belt and reached for a cigarette. He flicked on the lighter. It was enough. The commando on the chopper had his window. *Crack!*

Patel stood still, hearing the sudden burst of gunfire.

Dalbir ran towards him shouting, "You are secured, Sir!"

Patel looked up at him. "You were not supposed to shoot him." He turned and hurried back to where Singh lay on the ground. The bullet had entered his chest. Patel felt warm blood on his hand as he touched him.

Gasping in pain, Singh grabbed Patel's hand. "I am dying. Rupali is dead. Akhtar is dead. Harman and Dinesh are dead! Soon you too, will be dead. But Netaji is still alive!"

He fell back into the dust, his eyes still on the Deputy Prime Minister. Major Anish Singh of the INA had reached the end of his tortuous journey.

###

Sardar Patel was given a rousing welcome in Delhi. The official word was that his plane had crash landed near Jaipur. The true story was known only to the Prime Minister, the Defence Minister, and those involved in the operation. There was general rejoicing that Patel had been saved from mortal danger.

When Patel finally shook the last outstretched hand and entered the PMO, he breathed a deep sigh of relief.

"What in God's name happened?" Nehru asked, meeting him at the door and showing him to a chair.

When Patel had finished his narration, Nehru sat silently for a long time, his mood sombre. Finally he asked, "Are they all dead?"

"Yes, every last one," Patel said. "The IAF men did what they had to."

"I don't blame anyone, just myself," Nehru said. "I did not take them seriously. I should have. They were men of honour."

"Nor did I," said Patel.

"What happened shows just how serious they were."

Patel gave a weary sigh. "They were deadly serious but they did not have the proof we needed to act."

"That is true...that is true..."

"We did the best we could," Patel said.

"For India," Nehru nodded.

"We are no longer revolutionaries, doing what our hearts tell us to do," Patel reminded him. "We are now the face of this nation."

"Are we dishonourable men?" Nehru asked sadly.

"I would accept dishonor if it would take our country forward," Patel replied quietly.

The Prime Minister leaned back in his chair, his face lined with weariness. "So what now?"

"We must see to it that the story of the crash is what is accepted and established. There must be no further media coverage."

"Indeed. But someday, someone will come forward to ask questions. Perhaps, India will be a strong country then and he will get the answers he seeks and the truth will finally prevail."

24
The End

2015

Jay opened his eyes as the Russian ended his narrative. The account he had related had been chilling. Jay gazed blankly at the wooden wall for some time before finally looking up. "And you have proof of all this?" he asked.

Alexis pointed to the heap of papers on the desk. "We have our own classified reports," he said. "But I'm sure you will find similar material in your own country. I suggest checking the records of the Dehra Doon orphanage for starters."

"It would appear that my grandfather did not die in Russia." Jay let out a sigh and looked across at Tanya.

She sat rigid and unmoving, staring at the Russian. "The world needs to know," she said.

"The world? Bah! Not so much." Alexis played with the ashtray on the desk. "The world doesn't care about some long lost hero from the Indian freedom struggle." He looked up. "And I don't mean any disrespect. But that's just how it is."

"Then India deserves to know!" Tanya retorted angrily. She looked towards Jay, who was still staring into nothingness.

"Do you really think so?" said Alexis, his tone neutral. "According to your passport, you never visited India before this. Your boyfriend can tell you about the conditions in his country."

Jay stopped studying the woodwork. "It's true," he said. "People in India have stopped caring what really happened to Netaji, accepting the Taipei air crash theory."

"You people accepted the theory years ago, in 1945. That is why the file has remained closed...until now."

Tanya put her hand on Jay's shoulders. "You can't leave it like this. Your country needs to know!"

"It does not." Alexis stated, leaning back in his chair. "The only person who needed to know was him, because his family was involved."

"He is right," Jay finally said. "I am honestly confused about what I should do."

"You can always leak it," Alexis suggested. "This is the 21st century. We can't stop you. But leaking it won't change things." He stood up and walked to the window, standing there with his back to them. "We always blame the Soviets for things like this. It is an easy reprieve. We brought down their statues and we'll hide behind their mistakes once again if the story surfaces. But you need to consider the situation in your own country."

"Netaji's death has remained a closed chapter for decades," Jay said. "Commissions have been instituted and they have repeatedly supported the air crash theory. The issue of Netaji has been raised only by politicians and journalists seeking media coverage." He paused and then added quietly, "But never by the people."

"You Indians are a wise lot," Alexis said, turning around. "You know what is done is done. That is why your country has survived and moved forward. You know it is pointless to cry over spilt milk. Your people are wise but your politicians are not."

"True...true..." Jay murmured. "If details of these events are revealed, it would just serve as fodder for our politicians. And what would happen after that no one can tell."

"I can," Alexis said. "It will cause chaos. Quite unnecessary chaos, I may add. And all for no advantage. There is no sane reason to reveal what you now know."

"Perhaps it would end in poetic justice," Tanya said.

Alexis gave her a flickering smile. "Poetic justice doesn't always end well," he said. "Your own Shakespeare wrote that, didn't he?"

"I'm Australian!" she snapped and then turned to look at Jay. "You can't really be taking him seriously!" she said.

"He would be wise to do so," Alexis said, returning to his chair. "And so would you."

Tanya did not deign to acknowledge his words, merely saying, "I'd like to leave now so I can release this data."

Alexis pressed a buzzer on the desk. Sergei and Charkov came in. "Come in, gentlemen. Please take Ms. Williams to the other room and explain the charges pending against her."

"What!" Tanya exclaimed. "You promised to let us go!"

"I promised to cause you no harm," Alexis reminded her coldly. "I will let Mr. Jay go. But you already have warrants out in your name. INTERPOL loves you, it seems."

Throwing Alexis a look of loathing, Tanya pushed away Charkov's hand as he and Sergei guided her out of the room. She continued to call down curses on their heads until her voice finally trailed away behind closed doors.

"She'll be alright, won't she?" Jay asked once she was gone.

"She will," Alexis said. "We will merely remind her of the jail time she is looking at if INTERPOL gets their hands on her. We were planning to broker a deal for the data chip, in return for immunity and Russian citizenship. Without the data she has nothing. But I don't think she will accept the deal."

"She will," Jay said. "I know her."

"So is this a satisfying conclusion?" Alexis asked him.

Jay shook his head. "Not satisfying enough. There is one more thing."

"And that is?"

"Show me Netaji's last resting place. The real one."

###

Their car drove slowly along the snowy road, the heater on at full blast.

"It's true that he died on the Road of Bones," Alexis said, peering out at the white landscape. "He was amongst the men taken from the Yakutsk Gulag to work as laborers for the construction of the road. It was a way of torture. His remains were kept in the Gulag's graveyard for many years. Soon after the Soviet disarmament, the KGB brought his remains here, to the war memorial, knowing of his legacy."

Their car stopped at what looked like a large graveyard, with a small chapel. "We buried our soldiers from the world wars and the Korean wars here." Alexis told Jay. "Perhaps they thought his soul would be in good company here, as you Hindus say."

Jay gazed in silent awe at the unending lines of headstones. Alexis led him along one of the snow-covered walkways. They stopped in front of a headstone that read:

ICHIRO OKURA
SOLDIER. LEADER. VISIONARY.
1950

"Do you see it?" Alexis asked.

Jay nodded. Just as Ichiro's ashes lay in Netaji's name, Netaji's bones lay in Ichiro's. It had come full circle.

"It was generous of you to bury him with military honours," Jay said.

"Military honours yes, but we cremated him in the Hindu way. His ashes are kept in the chapel crypt, along with the Japanese soldiers who followed the same method of cremation."

They walked down the dilapidated steps of the chapel to the damp darkness beneath. Sergei and Charkov put on the powerful torches they carried.

Alexis showed Jay the urn. "Valuables and personal effects are kept in the War Memorial Museum. A golden tooth is all that remains if I am correct."

As Jay stood in reverence before the urn, time seemed to stand still. He knew that nothing in his life would ever mark him as that moment did. Finally, he nodded and they climbed back to the ground level.

Alexis led him back to the car, saying, "We'll go to the War Memorial Museum now. There are several things there that you may find interesting."

As they drove on, Alexis pointed to the vast Yakutsk complex on the horizon. "Fifteen million prisoners were held and killed inside the gulags," he said. "Even the road we drive on has thousands of bodies beneath it."

"A tragic past..." Jay sighed.

"Tragic, but not our's," Alexis said seriously. "We have disowned it. All of it."

"What do you mean?' Jay asked.

"After the perestroika," Alexis said, "we brought down the statues of Stalin. All this was his doing. We have acknowledged it internationally."

"I think I understand the point you are making," Jay said. The information about Netaji, if it was to see the light of day, would cause a great flurry in India. But the Russians would merely do what they always did - blame it on the commies! *Their commies* to be precise. It would cause no international impact or internal complications for Russia.

"Your friend is misguided," Alexis said.

"I will convince her," Jay told him.

"You must, for it is your country she will hurt."

They pulled up in front of the War Memorial Museum and they got down.

"This building was built after the Reformation," Alexis explained. "It was our way of cleaning up the atrocities committed by those who came before us."

Jay watched the usual tourists walking around the building and wondered if they had any idea what secrets lay buried there.

"The KGB of fifty years ago would just have killed you and ended it," Alexis said dryly as he led Jay to the stairs. He showed his ID card at the entrance and they were allowed in.

"So why didn't you?" Jay asked once they were inside.

"What...kill you?" Alexis smiled briefly. "It's no longer the way we do things, Mr. Rasbihari. There is the Media and the Internet. And there is a free India now, unlike sixty years ago. And we can do something so much better than kill you."

"And that would be?"

"Convince you," Alexis said, leading him to a corridor with glass boxes. "This is where we keep soldiers' mementos...souvenirs."

"So you think you have convinced me?" Jay asked.

"I think you will convince yourself," Alexis said, leading him to a certain box. "In this case, the truth is strongly on our side."

Jay looked through the glass at the lone golden tooth gently placed on a red cushion. Then he looked at the name plate: *Ichiro Okura*

"It would appear that the truth is hidden in plain sight," Jay said.

"In a nation where everyone is blind to it."

"Does the Indian government know about this?" Jay asked.

"No...there is no proof. All we have is legend and heresay...told from generation to generation. Your Netaji's story has spread like that of Christ."

"So I have a decision to make," Jay said, his eyes still on the tooth.

"Indeed." Alexis folded his arms.

"I have one more thing to ask before I do."

"And what is that?"

"Can I have that tooth?"

###

Tanya ran to the door when she saw Jay's face appear at the window. "Oh my god!" she yelled. "Where have you been?"

"Alexis has been taking me around town, showing me some interesting sights," Jay told her.

Tanya put her hands on her hips. "So Alexis is your friend now?"

"He is your friend too," Jay reminded her. "He didn't hand you over to the Interpol did he?"

"But he did manage to stop our investigation," Tanya said bitterly. "Now we'll never know the truth about what happened to Netaji."

Jay shook his head. "No Tanya... Alexis told me exactly what happened. He even showed me Netaji's final resting place."

"And you believed him?" Tanya asked incredulously. "What proof did he give? How do you know he isn't selling you some fabricated bullshit?"

"No proof at all," Jay agreed. "But what proof did we have to start with, apart from a long lost diary and some letters?"

"So now you believe him?"

"No," Jay said, "but he has convinced me about one thing."

"Convinced you of what?"

"That we must stop here. Alexis is right. Digging up old dirt isn't always good. Not when there is nothing to be gained and many problems that can be created."

"But we need to know the truth!"

"Do we? My parents never told me the truth till they thought I was old enough to understand. It didn't matter to me. My life was driven by greater truths. It didn't matter that my mother was my real mother or not. The fact remains she has always loved me like she was. And ever since I learned the truth, I have been miserable. I left everything that was valuable to me - my company, my calling - and went off on a wild goose chase I had no business going on. The only good thing to have come of it is you."

"Oh Jay..." Tanya felt suddenly overcome and vulnerable as her anger dissolved.

"It's true." Jay ran a fingertip along the ridge of her nose. "I love you. You know that. So, Ms. Williams, will you marry me?"

Tanya smiled. "This isn't exactly a great moment for a proposal, is it?"

"So what's your answer?"

"Yes! Yes, of course!"

"So you will come with me?"

Tanya stared at him for some moments in silence. Had there ever been any doubt in her heart that where this man led she would follow, till death ended their journey? She nodded, her face breaking into a smile. "Are we going to India?" she asked.

Jay looked at her, a smile tugging at his lips. "Yes, but we have a short stop to make on the way," he replied.

Epilogue

2016

The pagoda in Renkoji Temple was small and dark. The only light that trickled in came through the circular holes high in the wall, near the ceiling. Enclosed for hundreds of years, it smelt of moisture and burnt wood.

"This is the place," the priest said, opening the doors.

They walked into the small square space. At its centre, stood a wooden box, atop a circular table made of stone.

"May I pray here for some time?" Jay asked the priest. "Alone."

The priest bowed and walked out. Jay turned to look at the box containing the ashes of Ichiro Okura, disguised as the ashes of Netaji, which lay in a country far from the land of his birth. But, perhaps it was as it should have been. Netaji had fought alongside the Japanese, and it was but natural that he should lie in a place they considered holy.

Jay opened the box and looked in. The charred fragments of bone lay as they had for 60 years. A deep sense of reverence filled him as he stood there. He could feel the powerful presence of Netaji, leader of men, man of destiny. *It does not matter if this symbol is true*, Jay thought. *What matters is that the symbol is present.*

He knelt before the ashes and prayed. He prayed for his country, for the souls of the men and women who had laid down their lives for freedom; he prayed for the future of the land of his birth. Finally, he rose, closed the box and left.

Behind him, in the box of ashes, now lay the golden tooth of Netaji. Nestled amidst the bones and ashes of Ichiro Okura it lay, a symbol of the enduring power of men who are destined to live forever in the hearts of future generations.

Conclusion

File 13/Jan/XVII: Top Secret

The 21st century is often called the Information Age. It is a time when the clicking of a button connects you to the expanse of the World Wide Web. We have stepped into an era of unparalleled connectivity. Even a casual video shot in your backyard has the potential to go viral. New trends rise and fall every year. The monopoly of studios and publishers on news has disappeared. Every person today has the power to record, create and present news to the world.

Such is the way our words and our world have been transformed in the last six decades. The era in which the Singhs, Dinesh, Harman and Akhtar lived, was strikingly different. To call attention to the truth, Singh felt compelled to resort to kidnapping and terror. He and his team fell to the last man.

Jay Rashbehari, Singh's grandson, however, belongs to a different century. He is far more empowered than the team sent to search for Netaji could ever have been. All he had to do was release the information on the internet. With an expert like Tanya Williams at his side, he could have gained global attention. In a world where people crave spice, mystery and inspiration in equal measure, their story would have made headlines around the world. However, they have not done so.

We have kept Jay Rashbehari under surveillance for the better part of a year. He has returned to running Oranax Inc, the company he founded, and has been doing sterling work in managing the enormous data load of some of our organizations. This Committee takes pleasure in applauding his efforts. Jay Rasbihari is known today as a brilliant Indian technocrat rather than yet another conspiracy theorist contributing to the Netaji mystery.

There have been recent demands for DNA testing of the Renkoji ashes, along with the golden tooth found in the ashes. It is true that Netaji had a golden tooth. However, whether the tooth in question belonged to him or how it came to be part of the ashes at the Renkoji Temple, lie beyond this Committee's brief. This Committee believes that DNA testing will provide answers to some of the queries being raised. It is thus this Committee's considered advisement that such testing be conducted.

The woman Tanya Williams now uses her Russian passport, issued in the name of Natasha Yakanova. She has resided in Mumbai with Jay, since their return from Japan. They plan to marry later in the year. Her earlier name remains on Interpol's wanted list. This Committee considers there is no existing threat in allowing her to remain in the country, and that there is nothing to be gained by disclosing her real identity, considering the sensitive factors involved.

It is the unanimous opinion of this Committee that Jay Rasbihari and Tanya Williams no longer constitute threats to national security and it is recommended that surveillance be discontinued.

In conclusion, this Committee advises that the truth about Netaji Subhash Chandra Bose be left in the annals of history. That he be remembered by the people of India for his service to the nation, rather than for his mysterious death.

Jai Hind!

Cc: Prime Minister's Office (PMO), New Delhi

ACKNOWLEDGEMENTS

Good books are rarely the end result of the efforts of a single person. Nothing could be truer, and it is with deep gratitude and appreciation that I highlight the contribution of those without whom this book could not have been.

I thank my parents, Rajeev and Swati, without whose continued support I could not have been a writer.

I thank fellow writers Ashwin Sanghi and Anuj Dhar, for being the inspiration behind this book. Ashwin for the 'fiction presented as fact' approach and Anuj Dhar's 'India's biggest cover-up', for the concept.

As this book deals with a controversial topic, I did not send it out to many beta-readers, but the few who did read it before it became a book, helped me with important inputs. Special mention must be made of my sister Abha Bhuskute, and dear friend Salil Rana, and my friend from Bengal, Ashrujit Basu, who is involved with Mission Netaji. I also thank Mukund Sanghi of Pirates Publishing, for his inputs about the book.

I thank my Publisher, Leadstart Publishing, for having faith in my work. I thank Malini Nair, for bringing me into the Leadstart fold, and I am indebted to my Commissioning Editor, Chandralekha Maitra, who believes in me and inspires me to write stories that I hope will be worthy of her. I thank her with all my heart for waving her magic wand over my story, totally transforming it into from what it was to what it deserved to be. I also thank Swarup Nanda for being a great Publisher.

My thanks also to the Leadstart team for the cover and their efforts in having my work take its place on the bookshelf.

Finally, I have to thank Netaji Subhash Chandra Bose, for his immense contribution to the history of our country. This book was written because of my immense respect for the man he was, and I have tried to create a satisfying conclusion to his story.

If you have enjoyed the book, please rate it on Amazon & Goodreads and share the word about it on your Social Media. If you hated it, please let me know the parts you didn't like, so I can work on them and improve as a writer. Email me at shre14uses@gmail.com for any questions regarding the book or visit my website: www.authorshreyas.wordpress.com

I hope, with your support, I will come up with many more books that speak of our country and the people who shaped it.

Printed in Great Britain
by Amazon